AUTHOR	CLASS
PHILLIPS, M.	F G

TITLE

Point of darkness

Point of Darkness

Point of Darkness

MIKE PHILLIPS

MICHAEL JOSEPH · LONDON

MICHAEL JOSEPH LTD
Published by the Penguin Group
27 Wrights Lane, London W8 5TZ
Viking Penguin Inc., 375 Hudson Street, New York, New York 10014, USA
Penguin Books Australia Ltd, Ringwood, Victoria, Australia
Penguin Books Canada Ltd, 10 Alcorn Avenue, Toronto, Ontario, Canada M4V 3B2
Penguin Books (NZ) Ltd, 182–190 Wairau Road, Auckland 10, New Zealand

Penguin Books Ltd, Registered Offices: Harmondsworth, Middlesex, England

First published 1994

The quotation on page 14 is an extract from the Authorized Version of the
Bible (The King James Bible), the rights in which are vested in the Crown, and is
reproduced by permission of the Crown's Patentee, Cambridge University Press.

Typeset by Datix International Limited, Bungay, Suffolk
Set in Monophoto Palatino 11½/13 pt
Printed in England by Clays Ltd, St Ives plc

ISBN 0 7181 3598 9

For Carl

Grateful thanks to Jenny, Kwesi, and Ivor
for their help and ideas; and to Richenda and
Ant for their patience and encouragement.

Thanks also to Officer Anthony Spencer and
his colleagues at the 75th Precinct, Brooklyn.

CPL
0675174

Chapter 1

'*Là bas, là bas,*' I said loudly. I pointed vigorously. 'Down there. *Ici.*'

I wasn't sure the Haitian driver understood my French, but I knew that my English confused him even more, and I'd reverted to type, using the old English strategy of articulating a few words loudly and clearly, then hoping for the best.

The driver nodded without answering and the car wheezed and rattled as it crept round the corner. He braked suddenly, throwing me sideways over the cracked leather seat and for a moment I thought he was stopping but he'd only slowed down to avoid a huge pothole. He looked over his shoulder. A big grin as if something funny had happened. The engine coughed and heaved, then we took off again with a jerk. I looked moodily at the back of his head. I was sure we were lost, but I was too dispirited to get into another round of explanations.

The worst of it was that I'd brought all this on myself. Back at Kennedy I could have got into one of the shiny new cabs lined up just outside the terminal under the watchful eye of the black dispatcher, but just as I moved to the kerbside a dilapidated old car had wheezed up and stopped opposite me. A card in the window said 'TAXI'. The name under it was Alphonse Césaire. I guessed that he was a freelance operator who'd dropped someone off at the Department building, and was now on the lookout for a fare back into the city.

'Move, move, asshole,' the dispatcher shouted behind me. 'I said move. Learn the language, why don't you? Get outta here.'

I took another look. The driver was black too. A sharp profile under a peaked hat: Haitian. On an impulse I ran across and jerked the door open. 'Go,' I told him.

He gave me a wide grin. I gave him the address, then sat back, my mind racing ahead to the end of the trip. I was going to stay at my brother's flat, but he'd be away, in Florida, and the keys would be where he usually left them, at Alvin Persaud's store in Jamaica Avenue, locked in a safe in the back room. At that precise moment the driver turned round and told me he was Haitian, and asked me where I wanted to go. A moment of incomprehension before I realized what had happened.

'When I said Jamaica,' I told him, 'I didn't mean I was from Jamaica. That is where I want to go. Jamaica, Queens. Jamaica Avenue.'

He nodded energetically, then turned on to the Belt Parkway towards Howard Beach. It was too late to get out; instead I shouted at him: 'Non, Non. Ce n'est pas la direction. Prenez la prochaine exit, Là. Là bas.'

That was how it went for close on the next hour. My own memory of the place had faded a little, so that sometimes I gave him the wrong direction or gave it to him too late. Sometimes the combination of my accent and the unfamiliar words I was using defeated him. In any case, every time I relaxed Alphonse inevitably took the wrong turning. Eventually we hit Roosevelt Avenue and began wandering towards Flushing. By now I'd begun to get my bearings, and when I realized where we were I had to clench my fists and grit my teeth to stop myself shouting at him. We'd made a long detour round Jamaica and come out in Corona.

'Oh bugger,' I said loudly.

Alphonse turned round, still smiling. 'What?'

'Here's the problem, Alphonse,' I told him. 'Instead of dropping me in bleeding Jamaica half an hour ago you've brought me up to Corona where my brother lives and where I'm going to stay. But I was supposed to collect the keys in Jamaica Avenue, and even if I get out of the cab I still can't get in without going back down to Jamaica. See what I mean?'

He grinned and shrugged, amiable to the last.

I looked at him moodily. I could try directing him over to Flushing Main Street and down into Jamaica, but I didn't trust either of us to get it right. On the other hand, my brother's upstairs neighbour, Melda, was a nurse who worked odd hours and she could well be at home. She'd let me in, or at least allow me to leave my bag in her flat.

'Stop,' I said. 'Let me out. Stop.'

He pulled over to the kerb. I got out and paid him. He gave me his card with a flourish.

'You call. I come.'

I nodded and he grinned at me, settled his peaked hat more firmly on his head, and pulled away into the traffic. I looked around. It was one of those bright, sunny spring days, the air heavy with hope and moisture. The last time I'd seen this street thick snowflakes were pelting down, but the difference in the weather hadn't changed much about the scene in front of me. It still looked like any other main street in a poor-to-middling district in the outer boroughs. Liquor store, bars, diners and bodegas. But nowadays, I thought, the place was more of a mixture than it used to be. Back in the days when Louis Armstrong lived here, and Harlem was the showbiz and crime capital of the black world, Corona had been a staging post in the migration of the black middle classes into Queens. Now the Caribbean immigrants — Haitians, Jamaicans, Puerto Ricans — were following along the same escape route, and wherever you saw a soul-food diner you could find two or three bodegas nearby offering *comidas criollas*.

I was standing opposite the Muslim school, which meant that the flat would be off the next block.

I picked up my bag and started across the road, but the

3

sound of screeching brakes and the grinding crash of metal on metal stopped me as I was about to step off the pavement. On the other side of the road a beat-up Honda driven by an Indian had pulled out immediately in front of a Chinese man driving a new Ford. The Chinese had swerved, but all he'd got for his efforts was a long scar in the side of the Ford, and now he was spectacularly angry.

He threw open the door of his car and climbed out, a stick in his hand, his long hair flying, shouting a stream of abuse at the other driver.

The echo of the crash had barely died away but a line of spectators, mostly black, had already gathered, and beside me there was a chorus of scattered cheers. 'Kick ass,' one voice suggested. 'Asian champion, round one,' screeched another.

But the Indian driver wasn't playing. As the Chinese approached the Honda began moving, and in a moment it was leaving the scene, weaving fast into the traffic. The Chinese ran alongside, passionately whacking the battered paintwork and screaming at the top of his voice.

At the same time a young black man pushed past me and walked casually across the road. He was carrying a plastic shopping bag and he had the light-skinned frizzy-haired look of a Dominican. But his manner was so relaxed and self-assured that, when he threw the shopping bag into the back of the Ford, got in, and slammed the door shut, it took me a few seconds to register what was happening. The signal lights flashed and the car took off, moving smoothly past the Chinese man, who had abandoned his pursuit and was walking back, muttering angrily to himself. In a moment, though, the frenzied chorus of yells from the kerbside alerted him. 'Your car's gone.' 'Go get your car.'

He did a quick double take and realized that his car was receding into the distance. Silence for a moment. The street seemed to be holding its breath. Two pulse beats before he threw up his arms and howled, shrieking his disbelief to the sky. In the next instant he was running, legs pumping so fast that it seemed he'd catch up with the Ford, but then it turned the next corner, picking up speed, and both of them disappeared from view.

In a few seconds the crowd had dispersed and the street was back to normal. I crossed the road and walked down the block. As I went past the bodega on the corner a young black woman came out and bumped into me. I hadn't seen her because I'd been looking around the way I always did in an unfamiliar place, taking in details, trying to get the feel. She glared at me angrily. On her it looked good.

She was tall, only a couple of inches shorter than my six feet, and she was wearing jeans and a cream-coloured sweater and her hair was cut short and tight to the shape of her skull. Big bright brown eyes and a smooth chocolate skin.

'Sorry,' I said.

Her eyes flashed at me and she walked away in the direction I was going. I followed. This was the first woman that I'd been close to in a couple of days, and as I walked behind her I began trying to work out who she was and what she did. She walked with a version of the athletic strut on which black North Americans have a patent, sneakers planted firmly, thrusting away on the toes, buttocks pumping like piston drivers. She had the look of a student but she was certainly in her late twenties, so she was probably more likely to be a teacher. Something like that. Teacher. I'd bring her an apple any day.

We'd come round the corner and walked halfway down the block before she looked around. The houses here were reached by a flight of about six steps, separated from the road by a short strip of yard bordered by a low brick wall, and to my surprise she walked through the gap in the wall which fronted my brother's house.

She was halfway up the crazy paving which led to the bottom of the front steps before she realized that I was following her.

She halted, turned right round and faced me. 'Stop right there, creep,' she said. 'I don't know what you want but this is not the place. Just take off before I get pissed.'

Her face was set and angry, and she was holding herself in an open fighting stance, legs well apart as if she was getting ready to throw a punch.

I smiled at her, guessing that she'd either taken over Melda's apartment or was visiting her. Nurse. 'Sorry,' I said. 'You don't understand. I'm coming to see my brother. He lives here.'

Uncertainty replaced anger. 'What's your brother's name?'

I told her.

'You're from England. Right?'

'That's right.'

She grinned. 'Oh shit. We're family. I'm Hadida. Grace is my mother.'

My turn to look puzzled, but then I twigged. Hadida wasn't the name Grace had christened her, but she was family, as we recognized it in the country where I was born. Her mother's brother had married one of my aunts. Her family had moved to the States in the early sixties and she'd been born in New York. But even though most of my own relatives had gone there from England a few years later and I had visited them regularly, I'd never met Hadida.

I dug into my memory for what I knew about her. So far she'd lived a life which was the stuff of fantasy for black people in various parts of the world. A brilliant student, she'd been to an Ivy League college on a scholarship, then won a fellowship to another prestigious university. The last time I'd heard about her, she'd been lecturing in Boston. For an African-American all this was unusual but not extraordinary. For the people who remained in the village from which our families had come it was part of the myth of African America, like millionaire basketball players, Eddie Murphy and Cadillacs. America was wealth and privilege and opportunity and these things were the proof. The irony was, I thought, that white people's notions about African America were bounded by images of jazz, blues, and rap music; tap dancing; riots and heavyweight boxing; street violence, guns and poverty. But then, as all the world knows, black people have different dreams.

'Come on in,' Hadida said. 'Your damn brother didn't tell me you were coming, or I'd have met you or something.'

'No big thing,' I told her.

On the way into the flat I began telling her about the incident I'd just seen and I was halfway through when I realized she was laughing at me. 'Tief de car,' she said, and I realized I'd been talking to her in our dialect, which of course was the way I usually spoke to family.

'I just love that accent,' she said.

'What accent?' I asked her, poker faced.

She laughed again. 'I can do it,' she said, 'when I'm at home and I practise. But I don't think I can do it here in the States. I love it, but it's so funny hearing you switching from the English accent to that tief de car shit.'

'Don't talk to me about funny,' I said. 'You can't speak the dialect and you've only been there on holiday and you're calling it home. That's funny.'

She looked at me soberly. 'You're right,' she said, 'but it's the way we always talk about it in the family. I've thought about it once or twice, but it's nice. I don't care if it's irrational.'

We sat in the kitchen at the back of the house, and she told me how she came to be there in my brother's place.

She was writing a book about immigrant health workers. Sociology was her subject, and she was researching case studies in a hospital nearby. She lived in Boston, though, and when she heard my brother was going to be away on holiday she'd rung up and asked him whether she could stay in his apartment for a while. He'd said yes without bothering to tell her about me. But, we agreed, this was just like him. He would have forgotten, or not thought it very important.

It was odd sitting in his home, talking about him, with his things around us. The paintings he did in his spare time lined the walls. All of them were about the same sort of subject. A tropical landscape, beautifully drawn in realistic colour and detail. Red, green, purple; the hallucinatory pinks and whites of Regina lilies and Antirrhinums. The walls were white, so that the effect along the corridor which led to the kitchen at the back was like a small and eccentric art gallery. For an engineer it was strange. On the other hand, it was the sort of contradiction – secrecy and revelation – which was typical of us, and typical of every immigrant family I knew.

I was just about to say something about this to Hadida when she looked at her watch and got up.

'Got to go. I've got a meeting.'

I asked her about the keys and when we'd worked out that there wasn't another set in the house I rang Alvin. When his voice came on the line it sounded the same, his accent hardly touched by the years he'd spent in America. Yes. My brother had left some keys. Come any time.

I put the phone down and made another couple of calls. One of them was to Sophie, the woman I lived with on and off. She had given me a number in her letter, but now there was no answer.

'I'll give you a ride,' Hadida said.

On the way down I remembered her original name. Bonny. I guessed that, like a lot of young African-Americans, she'd thought of her English name as the badge of slavery.

'Some people still call me Bonny,' she said, 'but I prefer Hadida.'

She dropped me off in Jamaica Avenue in front of Alvin's shop. I felt an odd tingle of excitement. This was the place. Some people, I knew, when they pictured New York, got the image of the Statue of Liberty or Bloomingdales or the Empire State Building. The image I got was Jamaica Avenue. When I first saw it at the end of the sixties, the crowds were a mixture, more than half of them white. Ten years later the great department stores were closed and boarded up, all the other shops cheapo crap except Modells and Woolworth; the crowds were all black; and the district had begun to take on the desolate air of a place where women and children would soon begin to flee from the creeping incursion of crack houses and attack dogs. In another ten years it had changed again. CUNY opened up another new college round the corner and they'd built a beautiful new subway station nearby at Parsons Boulevard, and the energy was back. But this time the dynamism was Caribbean, the groceries and bodegas spilling over with yams and roti, saltfish and Brazilian hassa. Standing on the kerbside I felt as surrounded and buoyed up by the familiar as I would have in a Caribbean city.

It was about four in the afternoon and the pavement was jammed with knots of black schoolkids going home. All the girls seemed to be wearing round gold earrings, and they moved with an erratic grace, the groups forming and reforming as the kids got in line at the bus stops or dashed across the road or rushed towards their friends, their voices screeching and swooping like exotic birdcalls.

I found myself staring, thinking that I'd have to tell my son what they were wearing and how they spoke. Then I stopped. It wasn't necessary. I knew now from experience that teenagers had a mysterious process by which they determined these things, and he'd already know.

Alvin's shop had a series of stalls hung with cut-price articles: jeans, T-shirts, sneakers. Since the last time I'd been there, Alvin had tried to give it the look of a real American store, with everything arranged in separate racks and neatly labelled with the prices. But his customers were mostly Caribbean women, who could stand in the shop for hours chatting and fingering the merchandise. By this time of day the order of the displays had more or less disappeared, and the front of the place had begun to look like a market back home, with piles of shoes blocking the aisles and a litter of clothes carelessly dumped over the racks.

I weaved my way past the racks through to the back of the shop where the huge bolts of cloth were lined up against the wall like dumb soldiers. Alvin, small and dapper in shirtsleeves, tape measure round his neck, was fiddling with a swathe of curtain material and chatting with a couple of elderly women, Jamaican by the looks of them. As he talked he waved the scissors in his hand and the gold trimmings in his teeth flashed. 'Too much bribe,' he was saying. 'Too much. Last time I went back I even had to bribe the taxi driver.'

9

They'd be talking about going home. Or just talking about the place, because I would have bet anything that, having got out, none of them would be going back. Not for long anyway. But for a moment, listening to the familiar accent, it would have been easy to imagine that there was a dusty South American street outside.

Watching Alvin I had the weird sensation that I was seeing his father, Mr Persaud. He had developed into the same kind of short, thin, bespectacled adulthood, and it was just about this time that we used to get home from school. Alvin would put his books down in a corner and immediately take over behind the counter of his father's shop in the market square, while his dad worked the customers. When the rest of us kids were worrying about cricket scores, Alvin was already a man of business, and somehow, across this impossible reach of time and space, he'd reproduced almost exactly the same kind of shop as his father used to run back in our village.

He turned and saw me coming. His mouth opened and stretched to show me the row of bright gold fillings. 'Sammy. The old Sammy.'

He introduced me to the old ladies, who turned out to have known my mother.

'He's my old schoolmate,' he said. 'But now he live in England.' Alvin made it sound as if I'd deliberately chosen a dodgy career move. I made the correct noises of Caribbean politeness, and then drew him away into the overhang created by some of the bolts. Behind the counter a teenage boy with Alvin's features watched us impassively.

'It's Hector,' I told him, and his expression turned serious.

Hector and Alvin used to walk home from school with me every day of my early life. We had been born in the same street in the same village, within a few days of each other; and the bond had held, even when our families emigrated to different countries.

'Hector's dying,' I said. 'That's partly why I'm here.'

Alvin looked a little puzzled when I said that, but he held in his curiosity for the moment. Instead of speaking he looked up, snapped his fingers, and signalled. Almost immediately his son was beside us carrying a couple of chairs, and we sat down in a huddle at the back of the shop to begin talking about Hector. In a while the son brought us a tray with two small glasses and a bottle of Barbados rum, Mount Gay. We drank and talked some more. Everything I said was news to Alvin. He hadn't heard anything about Hector for a very long time, so he knew nothing about the first wife, Sarah, or the second wife, Dot, or about the fact that Hector had a daughter; and he listened to what I was saying with rapt attention, something like excitement flickering across his face, as if I was describing an exotic adventure. When I mentioned Gloucester he interrupted.

'I have a cousin living somewhere around there. Wolverhampton. The son play cricket. One day I'm going to go over and take a look.'

'That's nowhere near it, man.'

He shrugged and grinned. 'All right. What do I know? It's somewhere out of London.'

I nodded agreement. Alvin flew home every year to look after his father's business. His sister lived in Toronto and one of her boys was studying in Germany. His view of the world was now more dashing, less parochial than mine. A distance of a hundred miles or so was nothing. On the other hand I too had relatives scattered all over the world, all of them driven by that same lust. *Go and take a look.*

I told him about how Dot had given me a letter for Hector's daughter, and he frowned. He shook his head firmly.

'No, it don't sound good, boy.'

By now we'd gone back to the way we used to speak all those years ago, the same phrases flowing naturally.

'When they start with that out-of-touch business is trouble. This ain't London. You don't know what can happen to these children. Look, you see that one?' He indicated his son with a jerk of his chin. 'I have to know where he is every minute of the day. I don't trust nothing here. Nothing. OK. Do what you told the woman. Deliver the letter. Thank you very much and leave. Don't involve yourself. You don't know where it will end.'

A good rule of thumb for the sort of people we came from. In our country any of us could be crushed as casually as an insect if we got in the way of the powerful. But in three generations Alvin's family had moved from cutting cane on a sugar estate to urban wealth, without causing a ripple. It was a trick that living in the USA and Britain taught our children to forget. An image of my own son flashed through my mind, and I felt the irrational impulse to rush back to the airport.

'I have another letter for the girl. Is Hector's only daughter, man.'

He frowned and he poured himself another shot before he spoke. 'I know. But Hector always made his own problems. Look at it this way. Either she'll come back or she won't. If she does, well and good. If not, nothing you can do. Don't go looking for trouble, Sammy.'

Chapter 2

It was too dark to see anything but the dimmest outlines. The explosion had woken me up, but that was immediately followed by the sort of small, stealthy noises someone makes when they're trying to move without sound. I reached out slowly for the bedside lamp but when I pressed the switch nothing happened. I pulled my arm back but when I tried to move it again it wouldn't do what I wanted. I tried moving my legs with the same degree of caution, and when they also refused to react I began to panic, throwing myself from side to side and moaning so loudly that I could hear myself, my panic growing as the thought struck me that the intruder could probably hear me too and would now know that I was awake. Suddenly someone called my name in a stern and peremptory tone: 'Sam, Sam,' and I woke up sweating and moaning.

It was still dark, but now I knew I was awake I began trying to work out where I was. I raised my body off the sofa and peeped through the curtains at the street. I was in the room at the front of the apartment. There was only one bedroom and Hadida was sleeping in there. I hadn't seen her since I'd come back, but I guessed she was already tucked up in bed. Two o'clock. At home in London it would be about seven. As I regained my equilibrium I began wondering about the voice that I'd heard calling my name. Perhaps someone in the street outside had spoken and I'd registered it halfway between sleeping and waking. I hoped that was how it was, because the alternative was that I was hearing voices. The thought was too depressing and frightening for me to go back to sleep again, and I rolled over and gazed at the grey outlines of the paintings on the wall.

I'd been drawn here because of Hector, my brother, and Sophie, who'd already been here for a couple of weeks, but now I felt alone and isolated, sunk in confusion. I'd bought a ticket then rung my brother, the way I usually did, to give him a surprise, instead of which he'd told me he would be away for a while; and when I'd rung Sophie there was no answer. But I was already committed. Hector's fault. Thinking about Hector, an image of him flashed into my mind, the way I'd seen him only a few days before, and, for a moment, although I wished it away immediately, it wouldn't go.

'"And darkness was upon the face of the deep,"' Hector had said.

His voice used to be low and resonant, but now it had a feeble muttering sound and I'd been obliged to strain in order to hear it. That shouldn't have been difficult, but the fact was that I didn't want to get any closer, because the state to which his illness had reduced him was both sad and painful, and what I'd really felt like was getting out of that room and away from him as fast as I could.

He'd been a decent-sized man, not much smaller than I was, but now, curled up in the white hospital bed, he looked like a grotesquely hairless and oversized monkey. Nowadays, they said, he hardly moved. Only his eyes, glowing huge and brilliant, retained any trace of the vitality he used to possess. The light from the monitor in the corner gave them a peculiar greenish shine, and even though I knew what was causing it, I still had the strange feeling that there was an alien being looking at me from inside Hector's wasted body.

14

I'd looked round, maybe for reassurance.

There were a few other beds in the room but only two of them were occupied and they were on the far side and well away from us. The patients in them were no help either. Two old white men, they lay straight and motionless, no sign of life.

I faced Hector again, trying to decide whether or not what he was saying was supposed to make sense. 'What's that?' I asked him.

The phosphorescent eyes pleaded with me for understanding. Somehow I knew that what he was trying to tell me was important. '"This too,"' he said, '"has been one of the dark places of the earth."'

'Don't worry,' Dot's voice said behind me, 'sometimes it doesn't make sense. He doesn't know what he's saying.'

She pushed past me, sat on the bed and stroked his cheek. She was a big brassy-haired woman, her body growing soft and doughy in middle age, but the bright colours of her presence, pink face, red nails and lipstick, gave her a flamelike vibrancy next to Hector.

'It's a bad day,' she said. 'I don't think he knows who we are.'

He hadn't taken his eyes off me. 'Who is that man?'

Dot gave me a meaningful look. 'It's Sammy, love. Sammy. You asked him to come.'

'Not Sammy,' Hector said, his voice suddenly gathering a surprising strength. 'I know Sammy. The other one I mean. The one who walks always beside you?'

I looked round, but there was no one there. When I turned back to the bed Hector's eyes were closed.

Dot got up, picked up her bag, and began stuffing things into it. 'He's asleep,' she said. 'You won't get anything out of him for a while.'

And I'd come all the way from London.

'When you rang you said he wanted to speak to me. I thought he'd be able to.'

'Don't aggravate me,' Dot said angrily. She straightened up

and looked around the quiet room as if she'd given something away. There were no signs of life but she moved away from Hector's bed cautiously, almost on tiptoe. 'Let's talk outside,' she said.

Out in the corridor Dot tugged at her skirt and her blouse, took out her compact and patted her hair, then found her lipstick and began touching up her lips.

A couple of nurses went by and one of them waved. Dot lowered the mirror a little, smiled, waggled her lipstick in the air like a conductor's baton, then started working on her pout again. One of the nurses looked at me curiously, as if trying to work out who I was, and suddenly I saw myself through her eyes, a stranger in the middle of their well-worn and private rituals. Through the glass wall of the corridor I could see the rush-hour traffic in the distance, the big orange-and-white buses giving the scene an unfamiliar, foreign feel, as if I were somewhere abroad, instead of only a couple of hundred miles away from London.

Dot snapped the mirror shut and looked at me. 'It's his daughter Mary.'

I struggled to work out how old Mary would be. I remembered her as a bright little poppet who used to climb on me and demand sweeties. But that had been more than ten years ago, when Hector worked at the Town Hall in Manchester. Not much later Mary's mother had died in the passenger seat of a Rover driven by a salesman of bathroom appliances when it ploughed into the back of a container lorry.

The tabloids had some sly fun with the fact that the salesman had no trousers on at the time, but Hector took the whole thing badly. After that his drinking began to interfere with his work and they sacked him out of the Town Hall. Then he decided to move to Gloucester, where, he said, the child stood a chance of growing up decent. At that time Hector had been living in a council house off Moss Lane, and the primary school Mary was due to attend faced a row of clubs and pubs where the local prostitutes hung out, and where one black kid stabbing another was a regular event.

'Where is she?'

'I don't know,' Dot said irritably. She heaved a long breath, looked away down the corridor, then faced me again. 'She's supposed to be in New York with his brother.'

That was the younger son, Rupert. In the old days, back home, he used to trail around behind Hector. Memory brought me the picture of a snot-nosed toddler wearing a pair of red wellies. Someone had brought them back for him from England and he wore them all the time. In that place of palm trees and unrelenting sunshine few people had seen a pair of wellingtons, much less red ones, and up and down our street the neighbours used to come out and stand around laughing at the sight of Rupert wading along in them. 'Little boots', they used to call him, and sometimes 'Caligula' after the mad emperor in *The Robe*. It got worse after our local cinema showed a remake of *The Prisoner of Zenda*. The villain in it was called Rupert and every time our Rupert walked through the market place clutching his ma's hand, someone would shout, 'Rupert, you got the boots. Where the sword?' which was about as subtle as our village wit ever got.

'Poor Rupert,' the adults used to say, laughing. It had got so bad that even his mother started calling him Bootsy. I smiled at the memory and Dot misinterpreted my expression.

'That's what I thought,' she said. 'Joke. Hector's brother didn't have much time for him and I don't suppose he was that bothered about Mary. I rang up anyway, three or four times. He said she was living somewhere in the city and he'd try to contact her but nothing's happened.'

'Doesn't she write?'

'In the beginning. She wrote a few times. Then it stopped. I don't know. Every time he's conscious he asks for her. A couple of weeks ago he said you'd be going to America soon. He made out he wanted you to take her a present. But you know what he really wants, don't you? He wants you to bring her back or talk her into coming to see him. I tried to change his mind, but he wouldn't be told. He went on and on. Sammy this, Sammy that. So I rang you.'

17

'What am I supposed to do?' I said.

'Do?' She'd lowered her voice but it took on the force of suppressed resentment. 'You go over there often enough, don't you? I'd do what he was asking if I was a friend of his. That's what I would do.'

I'd looked away down the corridor, wondering what to tell her. Hector had been part of my childhood, then after we came to England our paths had diverged. At first we'd clung together. We'd lived in different areas – his parents went to South London, mine went north of the river – but at weekends and evenings we'd visit each other and hang out together, talking about the new things that were happening to us. That's how it was when we first came. But in less than a year we had begun to drift apart, initially because of the geography, then because we'd both changed in ways I could only understand later. On the surface it began to seem that Hector had a crazy boldness about him, a lack of fear that made me wary. In those days we saw the city as a threatening and dangerous place, and we moved through it with caution. If you were weak or foolish or reckless or had a death wish, like Hector, you became a good person to stay away from. Self-defence was instinctive, and in the end it was every man for himself and his own family. I didn't think that was the reason I hadn't seen Hector for a while, but I couldn't be sure, and the uncertainty made me feel guilty.

'He thought the sun shone out of your backsides, you lot,' Dot said, 'but we never saw one of his family. His sister, that cow, she made it plain she thought I was a slag. They never accepted me.'

She was right about that and I thought she would have minded less if she'd believed that they were hostile because she was white. But Hector's first wife had been white too, and although they were a bit iffy about her not being a nice girl from home, they were impressed and subdued by the fact that she was well educated and came from a prosperous middle-class background. An Oxford graduate too, as Hector's mother used to say afterwards. Besides, she charmed the socks off the old bag. The funny thing was that Hector's first wife had driven him half out of his mind, while Dot, whom his relatives sussed right away as a bad woman and a common tart, had nursed him tenderly through the worst time of his life.

'I don't mind for myself,' she said. 'It's that poor child. She didn't have no time for me. I was just the old scrubber her dad married. But his precious family — that's the only reason she's over there. She wants to be one of them.'

Her face was cracking behind the make-up and I could see that she was about to burst into tears. For the first time that day I remembered that she was older than Hector, and I wondered what would become of her now. It wasn't my problem I reminded myself. On the other hand it was true that I had intended to take a trip to New York, partly to see my brother, partly to be with Sophie. Freelance work was always up and down, and the way things were I could afford to take time off. I wasn't doing anything anyway.

'What is it you want me to do, Dot?' I asked her.

Thinking back, I kept seeing Dot's eyes, red rimmed, crusted with mascara and brimming with tears. I switched on the light and sat up. The telephone was on a table near by, within easy reach. I picked it up and dialled the number Sophie had given me. Somewhere in Manhattan. On the third ring someone picked it up and a man's voice said, 'Hola.'

He sounded a nice friendly guy. 'Hey,' he said when I didn't answer, 'dígame.' But I couldn't think of anything I wanted to say, so I put the phone down quietly, switched off the light, lay back on the sofa and gazed up into the dark.

Chapter 3

In the morning I rang Rupert. A woman answered and I said who I was. A brief silence and then she told me he was out at work. He'd be home later that evening. I broke the connection and rang Sophie's number. No answer.

I could hear Hadida bustling about, and in a moment she came in with a cup of coffee for me. She was wearing a dark calf-length dress and gold hoops in her ears. Today there wasn't a hint of the casual air she'd had when I first saw her. She looked terrific.

'You look terrific,' I said. 'Where are you going?'

She smiled. 'Administration meeting,' she said, 'I need some time looking at how the OR works, and they've got to clear it, and I need computer time. That sort of thing. You want them to take you seriously you got to look good. In Europe I used to see these important people dressed like shit. But it doesn't work like that here. You don't dress like a bum, especially if you're black.'

I knew what she meant, and I could have added some rules of my own. *Don't be ill, don't get angry, don't be ugly, don't be tired, don't look old.* Instead I nodded as if I were filing away an important bit of information. She asked me what I was going to do and I said I'd just be mooching around.

I didn't mention Sophie or Hector's daughter, because I

didn't want to talk about either of them. So I waited till she'd gone before I rang the London office of the glossy magazine for which Sophie was working. She had decided some time ago to do a collection of photos about women who'd emigrated from the Hispanic Caribbean, and she had various sources paying her for picture stories about different aspects of the same subject. She'd been working on these pictures in New York for a few weeks, but I knew the deadline was more or less due. The picture editor would certainly have heard from her, because she'd need to clear expenses and maybe discuss progress.

Kitty answered on the first ring. She was a mop-topped suicide blonde whose short skirts and hairstyle made her look younger than she'd ever been. I'd done a few stories for her over the last couple of years and she knew about me and Sophie. She'd tell me where she was.

'Sophie?' She sounded surprised 'That's funny. She rang a couple of days ago. You've got the address, haven't you?'

'Telephone doesn't answer.'

'Hmm, I don't know what to suggest.'

'Did she say what she was doing?'

'Yes. She was taking some pictures in the Bronx.'

'That's a big place.'

'I can't remember where. Oh. She mentioned the Bronx Zoo. Yes. She said she was starting off in a West Indian area at some church and walking across to Bronx Zoo. Then she'd be in a road near a university, or perhaps it was the university.'

'Which university?'

'I don't know. Columbia?'

'That's nowhere near the Bronx.'

'Well, I'm sorry. I know she mentioned a university.'

I thought about it. The Bronx. 'Fordham?'

'That's it. Fordham Road. And she mentioned the Grand Central — or was it Grand Concourse?'

'The Grand Concourse.' Now I knew where. 'Gun Hill, Bronx Zoo. Grand Concourse and Fordham Road.'

'That's right.' It was coming back to her. 'She had some people lined up there. Some cafés, I think.'

'Got it. Thanks, Kitty.'

From Gun Hill to Fordham Road was a big semicircle. I intended to go and visit the address in Manhattan, and if she wasn't there I could spend a couple of hours trying to locate her in the Bronx. I knew the way she worked. She'd be wandering around, maybe talking to people, getting a feel of the place. Maybe she'd be looking around the zoo. Needle in a haystack, and it would take up most of my day with no certainty of finding her, but I had nothing else to do for the moment. In any case, I was in no hurry, because now I knew where she might be I wasn't sure that I actually wanted to see her. I could never be sure from time to time how we'd feel about each other, especially when we'd been separated for a while.

I was still torn between reluctance and expectation when I arrived at the building where she was staying. I had got off the E at West 4th Street and wandered around a little before I found the address. Part of the problem was that I didn't recognize it when I saw it. The place belonged to a friend of hers who taught at CUNY, and Sophie had told me it was an apartment block. I'd been expecting something several storeys high. But this block was a soaring tower faced with huge plates of smoked glass, separated from the street by a small plaza.

I walked across the courtyard, craning my neck to see the top, and stopped in front of the two black men, both in uniform, who were sitting just inside the lobby. I told them whom I'd come to see, and one of them picked up a clipboard, looked at it and frowned.

'No one here by that name.'

Jamaican by the sound of him. I told him the apartment number. 'She's a photographer. She'll be carrying cameras. Stuff like that.'

The other man broke in suddenly. Also a Jamaican; his American accent more ingrained but you could still tell. 'Yeah. I know her. Spanish kind of lady? She left early this morning.'

I could feel their curiosity burning holes in my back as I left. I was curious about them too, and in a different time and place we might have stood around talking about who we were and how it was shaking. But outside the Caribbean it's hard to hold on to that sense of ease.

Walking back towards the subway I suddenly found I was hurrying. My mood had shifted and I wasn't noticing much, so it wasn't until I got off the A and on to the overhead line running through the South Bronx that I started looking around me.

Not much had changed since I'd last seen it. Still the same deserted air, a vista of empty houses with boarded-up and broken windows. On the other hand, there seemed to be more people in the streets and more cars intact and moving around down there. More life. But I was so high up, so distant from the ground that it was hard to tell. Besides, I was struggling with the sense that there was something different about the sounds around me, and when I turned from the window and took a good look it struck me that it was the voices. Almost all of the people in the car were from one Caribbean island or the other, and I began amusing myself by trying to guess where each one was from. Two young Jamaican women opposite. No doubt about that. Down the aisle some more Jamaicans. Then a little Dominican family. Then two twelve-year-olds, one dark, the other with a pale skin, curly hair with reddish streaks. Speaking Spanish. Puerto Rican maybe? More likely Cuban.

I was so absorbed in my little game that I nearly missed the station. You can't see the name till you're right on top of it, but I remembered the church. Church of the Immaculate Conception. That gave me a bit of a laugh, thinking about Sophie charging around there snapping, but I knew that by now she would have lost interest in the church and moved on.

I was right, or at least the doors of the church were locked and there was no one in sight. I looked around, getting my bearings. A notice on the nearest lamppost told me that it was reggae nite every night down on White Plains. I turned my back on it and walked down Gun Hill Road towards the zoo.

It was a fine warm day, even under the watery sun. Approximately every half a mile, the look of the place changed dramatically, like crossing a border. Past White Plains Road Caribbean English suddenly gave way to Caribbean Spanish, then after the Montefiore Hospital and down past the Bronx Museum I was in a street so Irish that it could have been Kilburn, every detail precisely similar. Green-painted shamrocks on dirty brown, and outside the Green Isle Pub two drunks weaving sporadically at each other.

At that point I gave up and got on the subway downtown, but I changed my mind again when I saw the sign that said Fordham Road. I got out on the Grand Concourse then walked back and round the corner. *Mandango y comidas criollas.* I looked through the window, past the fried seafood and pastries, and saw her right away. For a moment I wasn't sure because her hair had changed its shade and style. Now it was back to the glossy mane of black curls she'd sported when she arrived in London from Argentina. It was shorter too, and although I was sure that the person I was watching was Sophie, there was also something strange and dislocating about the fact that she looked so completely relaxed and at home. I watched her, thinking about what she was like without me and what sort of person she appeared to her friends. My friends weren't a coherent group. Mostly they were people I'd known for a long while or worked with from time to time, and in any case they were wary of her. Her friends were mostly Latins or women like herself whose work occupied most of their lives, and our relations were amiable but distant.

Her relaxed pose in this place seemed to show that she felt herself to be among friends. She was sitting with her back to me opposite two young men of about twenty. Pale ochre skins, curly brown hair. Two shades lighter and they'd be the same colour as Sophie. They had smooth, pretty looks. Not ghetto smooth, with the gold chains and tailored hair. These looked more like college boys in a movie.

I walked straight in. The waitress, a young light-skinned

woman, came towards me but I waved her away and sat down at the table next to Sophie. The two boys looked at me: no change of expression but danger signals in their eyes. As I settled back in the chair she paused in mid-sentence and looked round as if to check me out, the frown on her face turning to an expression of disbelief. I said nothing, just sat there smiling. Then her face split into a wide grin, and I knew everything was fine.

'Hey,' she said, drawing the word out. She laughed. 'Hey.'

She raised her arms and put them round me, kissed me on the lips, then turned round and shouted something in Spanish at the waitress. It was too fast for me to get a grip on, although I heard *Inglaterra*. The boys grinned and the waitress screeched with laughter and shouted something back. The boys were smiling politely, with a touch of deference, and when my eyes rested on them they got up simultaneously and told Sophie they were leaving. She introduced us, Rodolfo and Cesar, and we shook hands, then they were gone.

'Who are they?' At the back of my mind was the thought that they'd taken off rather abruptly when I came in, but I didn't want to say that to Sophie. No point in stirring things just yet.

'Those boys?' She sounded surprised. 'They're students. Dominicans. I'm photographing their mother.'

The waitress came up and said something to me. She was laughing loudly and Sophie screeched and answered in the same tone. The two of them were practically in hysterics and I wished I could follow what they were saying, but the inflection was different to anything I'd ever heard before.

'What was that?' I said.

'You don't want to know.'

'Yes I do.'

Sophie looked at me, smiling a little. 'I'll tell you later. It's dirty.' She giggled. 'What do you want to do? You could eat here. *Plátanos. Camarones. Bombas.* The sort of food you like.'

'I'm not sure,' I said. 'What are you doing?'

She shrugged. 'I'm about finished today. You can come

home with me if you want. I have *plátanos, camarones*. Everything you like.' She flipped her eyebrows at me, and gave a sexy pout.

'Let's go,' I said.

We went out. I began heading for the subway entrance but she pulled me in the other direction. She was driving a rental, a light grey Honda, and she backed out and slotted smoothly into the traffic along the Grand Concourse.

I told her how I decided to come on impulse and partly because of Hector but mostly because of her. She raised her eyebrows, then gave me a sweet smile when I said that.

It was odd. Somehow it felt as if I'd forgotten what she looked like, or as if I were face to face with a new and different Sophie. In London she'd seemed foreign, maybe Italian, Spanish, something like that. Exotic, but without knowing it was hard to tell what she was. Here in New York she looked not unlike a dozen of the women I'd passed that morning, with the Spanish Caribbean air: high-nosed profile, curly black hair, and a skin dark enough to announce the ubiquitous African blood. Her manner had changed too. Now she was more open. Laughing a lot, and with something a little swaggering about the way she carried herself.

Back at the apartment building the two Jamaican doormen were still on duty. They recognized me quickly enough and the big one gave me a curious stare while his shorter mate grinned slyly at me.

Upstairs the apartment seemed huge, an expanse of carpeted flooring stretching away to end in a bank of glass commanding a wide vista. Wood, concealed lighting and tiles. It looked like luxury to me, but there was something impersonal about it, like being in a huge version of an executive businessman's hotel room.

'Who owns this place?' I asked her.

'Oh. She's just a professor here.'

In the short time she'd been away she'd started to sound American. No, not American exactly. The inflection had that quality I'd been hearing in the Hispanic voices around me. Not strange considering Sophie's background, but it felt like a new thing.

I put my arms round her and she pressed up against me.

'Oh, no,' I stalled. 'First you tell me what that woman said.'

She stared at me, smiling, and she gave a little nod. 'I told her that you had come all the way from England to see what I was doing, and she said, "*Un pelo de la chochada es más fuerte que una soga.*" It's one of the things they say.' The look on her face was half tease, half challenge.

'Ok,' I said. 'What does it mean, then?'

'One hair of the pussy is stronger than a rope.'

'Is that what you think?' I said.

She leaned backwards a little way from me and pushed her hips up against mine. 'Let's find out, *cholo*,' she said.

Chapter 4

The day was over when I set out to see Rupert. I hadn't meant to leave Sophie, but she said she had an appointment to talk to some people and she'd be gone for a couple of hours, so I told her I'd get the visit to Rupert over with and call her later. I was carrying the letter Dot had written for Hector and I intended to give it to Bootsy and wash my hands of the whole thing.

By the time I got down to Queens and out of the subway at Parsons Boulevard it was growing dark. Rupert lived on the other side of St Albans where it butted on to Cambria Heights, and I realized that I'd been travelling now for about an hour and getting there would take at least another thirty minutes. My heart sank. Riding on the hard subway seats was tiring in itself, and everyone around me had a drawn, exhausted look. Even so they were waiting in disciplined lines. Everyone said that the city was descending into chaos, but as far as I could make out all its routine operations were surprisingly orderly. The other strange thing was the fact that, standing at the Parsons bus station, everyone I could see was black. The shades varied: some skins were deep and dark, framing eyes and teeth which flashed a brilliant white; here and there were people with skins lighter than many Europeans I knew; and in between there was an infinite variety of complex blends.

I found myself staring eagerly again. It was a scene that I was accustomed to in the Caribbean, but at this point I was a mere day away from London. My eyes were only now beginning to adjust, and the sight of a crowd made up entirely of black people gave me a peculiar little thrill.

A horn hooted peremptorily at my elbow. I turned sharply and bumped my shoulder against the wing mirror of a van which had prowled up behind me. Its windows were decorated with little square stickers. Green, black and white. The Jamaican flag.

'Francis Lewis,' the driver said, reaching out to readjust the mirror.

People were already pouring through the open door. I scrambled after them just in time to squeeze myself into the last seat and the van took off. Immediately the sound of soul music flooded the vehicle, drowning out all attempts at conversation. The driver's mate sang along in a quiet falsetto, giving the words a Jamaican twist, but no one objected. Most of the passengers were Caribbean, and in any case this van was Jamaican territory. It had started about the beginning of the eighties, when an enterprising Jamaican began running a private service up and down the avenues in south Jamaica; and it became a common occurrence to see these vans with a full load zipping past the half-empty city buses. As if in response the city bus service had improved, making this one of the easiest places in the city to get around, day or night.

The trip didn't take long. Halfway up Francis Lewis Boulevard we were into Hollis and most of the passengers got out. I craned my neck, saw we were crossing Linden Boulevard, and called out to the driver.

Off the main road the streets had a quiet, hushed feel about them. Each house was separated by a neat patch of lawn and a fence. The doors gleamed with coloured glass and numbers picked out in shiny brass. This was an island. On one side of it the neighbourhoods were deteriorating, the streets spawning the usual networks of liquor stores, bars and junkies. On the other side was a clutch of housing schemes. Looking around I wondered how long it would take before the middle-class black people would begin to surrender their difficult defences and move on out.

Rupert's house was painted white. Walking up the drive I found myself comparing it with the sort of house he might have in London, but the picture didn't fit. A building as large as this, with a garden round it, would simply cost too much back there. I was trying to put a price on it when the door opened.

If I hadn't known it was little Bootsy I wouldn't have recognized the man in front of me. He was wearing a white shirt and a tie. Home from work, he must have only just taken off the jacket. When I last saw him he'd been a little waif. Now he was a tall thin man, and I had to look up in order to meet his eyes.

'Boots,' I said.

'Sammy? Is it Sammy?'

He was staring at me as if he'd seen a ghost, and the same expression was probably mirrored on my face. This was the usual reaction whenever I ran into one of the people who'd been part of my childhood, but it took me the same way every time, no matter how often it happened. In my mind the scenes of my childhood played and replayed over and over again in the same frozen time, so that the people I saw there stayed where they were, and the men and women they'd become seemed like strangers impersonating them.

'Big man,' I said.

We shook hands, then he reached out and hugged me, and drew me into the house.

'I heard you were about here from time to time, but I never managed to catch up with you. Glad to see you, man.'

On the inside the look of the place matched the impression I'd had as I approached it. The hallway led immediately into a big front room which stretched along the width of the house. In one corner was a grove of plants climbing up towards the ceiling, and along the walls was a series of large photos of tropical fruits and flowers. They reminded me immediately of the pictures at my brother's apartment, but there the display had been private, with the effect of a secret room. Rupert's house was elegant but stagy, as if the rooms had been designed to tell you that this was a prosperous family with a background in a tropical country.

As we went in a woman got up from the cream-coloured leather sofa, and Rupert told me she was his wife, Carmen. She was short, with straight black hair and a pale skin which gave her a Spanish look, but when she spoke it was with the familiar accent of our country.

'I knew your family,' she said. 'But youall left when I was a little girl.'

Portuguese, or mostly Portuguese, I guessed. Her maiden name would probably be Da Costa or Da Silva, and to judge by her voice and manner she came from our own village or one just like it.

I didn't have to wait long to find out. Her father had been John Perez, a Portuguese who wore gold-rimmed spectacles and walked with a limp, and who owned a grocery in the market square. She'd come over to the States nearly twenty years ago, run into Rupert and married him. The odd thing was that I remembered her distinctly, a little sprite with a black pony-tail and a naughty smile.

'You always wore long white socks,' I said.

She clapped her hands with delight. 'Yes. I used to love those socks.'

Rupert watched her with an indulgent smile. Now our mutual credentials had been established she was eager to talk. Rupert had still been going to college when they met and they had begun their married life in a tiny apartment in Brooklyn, during the worst years, a riot every weekend. Rupert had worked hard. He'd stuck it out with his firm, a group of design consultants, and now he wasn't far from being offered a partnership.

During this I nodded, smiled politely and looked amazed at what I took to be the right moments. This too was familiar. Their story had the monumental banality of an epic, and I'd

31

heard it all before, but they had to go over it again, because their success was final proof that they'd been right to come to the States and go through the trials of an immigrant life, and the difficulties they'd overcome simply demonstrated that they were brighter and stronger and more determined than most.

Eventually Carmen remembered her manners and went off to get me some coffee.

'So what's happening with you?' Rupert asked. 'How they treating you in London?'

I shrugged. 'As you see.' I wasn't going to get dragged into a long account of my life. Start that and we'd be there all night. 'I really came about Hector's daughter. You know what's happening with him?'

He nodded sadly. 'I know. I ring Dot every week.'

There was a touch of something defensive about this, as if he was worried that I might accuse him of neglecting his brother. I took the letter out and gave it to him. He turned it over in his hands. 'It's not Hector's writing.'

'Dot wrote it.'

He stared at it as if he were trying to decipher the words through the envelope.

'Go ahead and read it if you like,' I said.

He got up and walked out of the room. As he did so Carmen came back carrying a tray. She gave him a curious look when he walked straight past her, and she opened her mouth to speak, but then she seemed to change her mind. Instead, she gave me a big hostess smile, came over to where I was sitting and began fussing around with coffee cups and slices of fruit cake. After a little while she sat opposite and gave me the big smile again.

'Rupert was telling you about our troubles with Mary?'

In reply I told her about seeing Hector and about wanting to contact Mary. The smile left her face and her mouth went tight.

'She's a big woman. At least she thinks she's a big woman.'

The phrase had nothing to do with size. The way Carmen

used the word meant adult, and hearing her say it I began to get a sense of what might have gone wrong between her and Mary.

'She's still my niece,' Rupert said. He'd come back just in time to catch the last part of the conversation, and now Carmen looked at him with a trace of resentment.

'I know that,' she said. 'I know that very well, but tell him the truth about how she was. She is your niece. I ain't saying nothing. But I only glad the father wasn't here to see it.'

She glared at Rupert defiantly, and somehow I knew what was coming next. When Mary arrived, they'd thought she would be there for a short holiday, a few weeks maybe. After a while it became obvious that she wasn't going back to England in a hurry, which would have been no problem, if only she'd been a different sort of girl. For a start she had no manners.

'Rude? I thought the English were supposed to be so polite,' Carmen said, 'but like nobody ever taught her anything!'

To make matters worse Mary had no way of making a living. She had no green card or social security number, which would not have been a disaster if she'd been prepared to do the sort of menial job illegal immigrants could get while they were looking for a sponsor and getting themselves a lawyer who could sort out their status.

'This country you can't idle. You have to get up and go. And she was lucky compared to some. Her uncle. He would have done anything to help, but she didn't want. Look him there.'

She pointed to Rupert. Now she'd got going her speech was decorated with the rhetorical flourishes we used in our dialect, and the American inflection I'd first heard in her voice was almost gone.

Mary only wanted to hang out, she went on, and before long all kinds of people were coming to the house, half of them not even West Indians, and nearly all of them people no decent girl should mix with. A couple of times it was crazy Rastafarians, talking shit about Babylon. Another time it was one of those Muslim guys like you see in the subway selling African things. The last straw was when Carmen had come home to find her smoking dope with one of her friends, a boy who said he was a student at CUNY, right there in front of her kids. They'd had a row, and Mary had walked out with the boy, there and then, and she hadn't been back since.

'That was the last time I saw her,' Carmen said. 'Since then she don't come back, even to say cat dog thank you. I don't understand people like that.'

I could have told her. Mary was English and she'd have had no idea how to behave in a Caribbean household as proper as this one. Perhaps if Mary had known Hector's sisters better she would have recognized Carmen's attitudes and been able to get on with her. As it was Carmen would have taken Mary's neglect of the proper forms as deliberate rudeness, while Mary would have seen Carmen's version of parental concern as harsh and oppressive. To make matters worse Mary would have come here looking for adventure, her only knowledge about the country gleaned from English TV and newspapers. From what Dot had said I also suspected that she had come over determined to behave like a real black person, her head full of distorted notions about what that might mean. Hector would have tried as hard as he could to make her understand something about our lives, but there were some reflexes that came with a mother's milk, and it took a long time for someone with a white parent to see that the contradictions they experienced were real things in the world, and couldn't be changed by a simple exercise of the will.

'Is that the last time you heard from her?'

'No,' Rupert told me. 'She called me the next week. At work. She said she had a job looking after an old couple in Manhattan. I took her things up there. I didn't see her but they seemed like OK people.'

'Can I have the address? Hector and Dot would like to know.'

'I called them as soon as I knew Hector was in hospital,' Rupert said quickly. 'But they said she had gone.'

'Was there some trouble?'

'I don't know. They said that she just picked up and went.'

'It doesn't surprise me,' said Carmen.

Her tone was resigned, but there was an undertone of malice in her references to Mary which was getting up my nose. The problem was that I understood. Hector's daughter had been young and inexperienced, her imagination framed by the simple certainties of English liberalism. She'd been brought up in a council house in an English provincial town, and in Carmen and Rupert she would have seen a pair of snobs living in luxury. But that was a view of her life that Carmen would never appreciate. As a teenager she had arrived in New York with nothing and lived among people she had only heard of back in our village: junkies, prostitutes, petty thieves. Over the years she'd learned to defend herself and her family with a grim determination.

Rupert too had lived with the daily terror of falling down and out, in a place where the road to security was a greasy pole and all you could rely on was your capacity to work harder and faster than the next man. Mary's behaviour had opened their doors to the threat of the street life against which they had fought so long and so hard, and neither of them would easily be convinced that she had only been driven by youthful idealism.

'Well, give me the address anyway,' I said.

Rupert got up and went out again, and I braced myself for another instalment of complaint about Mary, but before anything could be said there was the sound of a key in the lock and a moment later two teenagers came in. In a flash Carmen's expression was transformed and she beamed fondly as she introduced them.

'Nita and Ronald. This is your father's friend Sammy. All the way from London.'

They were pretty kids. The girl was about sixteen and had a mass of black curls which climbed down her neck. Her brother, a couple of years younger, was nearly as tall as me, with a stiff pad of hair perched on top of his neatly shaven skull. They shook hands warily, and I asked them a few awkward questions about school. Carmen looked on, smiling proudly.

I wanted desperately to ask them about Mary, but I was sure that Carmen wouldn't like me doing so, and in any case they weren't likely to tell me anything useful in front of her. The conversation flagged and I sensed that Carmen was about to launch into an account of their accomplishments, but Rupert saved us from that by coming back. He held out a piece of paper.

'I wrote down the details,' he said.

The two children seized their chance and left the room quickly. Carmen gave me a quick farewell and went after them. I had the feeling that it was time I went too. I'd asked all the questions I could think of about Mary and after the initial euphoria of our meeting I couldn't find anything else to say to Rupert.

'Glad to see you again,' he said. 'Anytime you're back in town, let me know.'

I said I was glad to see him too, and that I would contact him next time I came to New York, then we shook hands warmly and I left.

I'd only been there a couple of hours, but the streets had a quiet empty feel about them. It was the end of a long day, and I guessed that I still hadn't adjusted to the change in time zones. On the other hand, the lassitude I was feeling had something to do with the fact that I hadn't solved anything by visiting Rupert. I'd intended to bring my involvement to an end by seeing him, but somehow I'd ended up by being dragged further in.

Back in Corona the lights were on in the room facing the street, and I could see figures moving behind the shades. My heart leapt with the thought that my brother had cut his trip short and come back unexpectedly. For some reason nothing else occurred to me, and I hurried to unlock the front door, turning over my opening line in my head.

I tiptoed along the hallway and threw open the door with a

flourish, but as soon as I did so I could have kicked myself, because the man who was sitting on the sofa kissing Hadida was a total stranger to me.

'Ah. Sorry.'

I couldn't think of anything else to say, but before I could close the door and back out, as I intended, she got up, made a face at me, came over and drew me into the room. 'Come on in. You're not interrupting anything.'

Looking at her friend I wasn't so sure about that, but I came on in anyway. In the circumstances I probably wouldn't have been as relaxed as he seemed to be, but he had the sort of cool friendly manner which made it hard to read his mood. His name was Oscar Clayburn, Hadida told me. He worked in the mayor's office, and looking at his dark grey pinstripe I guessed that he was something more than a minor functionary. She'd already told him about me, he said. In any case he knew my brother and he'd heard about my life in London before. As a matter of fact, he'd been over for a conference a few months back, and he would have called me if he hadn't been so pushed for time.

I got the picture. He was a heavy hitter. Had to be, even though he looked like a man just pushing thirty, and he had the sort of handsome features you could imagine looking at you from the pages of a glossy magazine. He'd started university at the same time as Hadida, and they'd shared a graduation party. After that he'd done his MBA and worked his way into the city administration.

'Washington can wait,' he said, giving Hadida a sidelong look and a lift of the eyebrows. They both laughed and I guessed that this was a private joke.

'I've been telling Oscar about your problem. Your friend's daughter.' My face must have shown the irritation I felt when she said that, because she hurried on to reassure me. 'Don't worry. His father comes from home too. He understands.'

'I really do,' Oscar said. 'I'll butt out if you feel like I'm interfering. But I thought maybe I could help. Check the missing persons for you. That kind of thing.'

37

For a moment I wondered why he was so eager to help. Then I remembered. Politics. Aspirants like Oscar began their careers by building their own networks, tying people to them with a chain of small favours and services. Helping me would probably chalk up one more tiny credit in Oscar's little black book. Besides, if his father came from our country, he'd want to help me, like a homeboy would. Suddenly my reserve seemed gauche.

'I've got her last address,' I said.

I showed him the paper Rupert had written on. He looked at it and turned it over thoughtfully. 'Howard Schumann. Seems like I know that name.'

He thought some more.

'There was a Schumann in City Hall. He had a stroke and retired a few years back.'

'Sounds likely,' I said. 'Does it help?'

He shrugged. 'No. I don't think so.' He shrugged again, but I had a feeling that there was something worrying him behind the polite mask.

Soon after this he said that he had an early meeting and had to go. Hadida saw him out to the door and they seemed to stay out there for a long time, but that might have been my imagination, or it might have been the fact that, by the time she came back in, I'd drifted off to sleep on the sofa. When I opened my eyes she was busy clearing up, but she must have felt me looking at her, or heard the change in my breathing.

'A woman called you,' she said. 'Sounded English.'

That would be Sophie. To my ears there was no way that she sounded English, but if she was trying to reach me on the telephone she'd be speaking with the sort of inflections she used in England. To an American that would be enough.

'Who is she?'

'A friend.'

Hadida gave me the raised eyebrows. 'White?'

'I don't know what you'd call her over here.'

The raised eyebrows again. Quizzical would be the word, I thought. 'You've got two choices,' she said. 'Black or white. Which one is it?'

'She was brought up in Argentina. Her mother was a dark-skinned Hispanic-looking lady. I've seen the pictures. You'd definitely call her black.'

The photos I'd seen had been taken in a café, and Sophie's mother had been caught in an extravagant pose, wearing a dress with flounces and a tight bosom. She looked beautiful, but Sophie had been reluctant to show me in case I laughed.

'So how come she's in England?'

'Her father was a Scottish engineer. I guess she came looking for her roots.'

She hadn't found them, but that was another story.

'She sounds a lot more white than black,' Hadida said. 'Black folks don't go looking for no roots in Scotland.'

There was a challenging edge to her tone, but I was in no mood to pick it up. Instead, I lay back on the sofa and kicked my shoes off. 'Turn the light off for me, please,' I asked her. 'I can't keep my eyes open any more.'

'Sure,' she said. 'Goodnight.'

She sounded irritated, but I was in no mood to worry about that either. I thought for a moment about ringing Sophie, then I thought about getting up and taking my clothes off, but before I could do anything about it I was fast asleep.

Chapter 5

The telephone woke me from a deep sleep. I had a vague memory of starting up from a dream in which someone monstrous was trying to get in through the window. I always had nightmares, but by now I was living easily with them, and this one hadn't kept me awake.

The voice on the telephone confused me though. It was Hadida's mother, Grace, asking for Bonny, and it took me a couple of beats before I remembered who she was and what she was talking about. But when I did I told her who I was and we had a long chat about my parents and about the old days back home. She lived in Washington now, she said. There was no point in moving to be near Bonny because Bonny wouldn't settle down in one place. As we talked the strangeness of it faded. Her voice had changed, but it still echoed the accent of our country, and in a moment the sound had uncorked a flow of memories. Disgrace, we used to call her, and I remembered her as dashing and sexy. She'd had a boyfriend who was a motorcycle cop, a big square man named Mr Livingston, and one of my first memories was of Grace taking us, the children of the house, to see him riding through a hoop of fire at some kind of military parade. Afterwards we had surrounded him, breathless with awe, tentatively reaching out to touch the hot steel on which he rode.

I kicked things around with Grace a bit more, then I went and got Bonny. After she'd put the phone down I rang Sophie. She sounded brisk and businesslike, preoccupied with her work. I told her I'd be in Manhattan later on, and she said she'd be in the Bronx all day. Why didn't we meet near the Grand Concourse at lunchtime? I said it might be difficult. Take a raincheck. She said OK and she'd ring when she got home. As I put the phone down Bonny came in. An odd switch had happened in my mind since I'd talked to her mother, and now I couldn't think of her as anything but Bonny. She had a cup of coffee in her hand and a sarky smile on her face.

'How's your girlfriend?' she asked.

'OK. How's your mum?'

'Fine. You made her day. She thinks we're kind of, ah, doing something.'

The idea gave me a little shock. I couldn't tell whether it was excitement or surprise. 'We're cousins.'

'That's what I told her.'

She didn't seem too bothered by the idea, but I couldn't tell whether she was just teasing me or whether she had something else in mind. Either way I didn't want to know. As soon as she'd gone out of the room I turned on the TV and pretended to be absorbed in the news. On the screen the world looked the way it usually did. Several murders, three wars, a summit meeting, a budget crisis, a glittering première and a hurricane in the Caribbean. When Bonny stuck her head through the doorway and said goodbye, I picked up the phone and rang the number Rupert had written down.

A woman's voice answered. She sounded old and a bit shaky. I told her I was a friend of Mary's father and I'd come from England to see her.

'She left. It must be months ago.'

I told her I knew that, but that I wanted to talk to her and her husband about Mary. I guessed that she'd feel safe with an English accent, so I poured it on. I told her about Hector's illness and, taking a chance, I said that I wanted to pick up the things she'd left in the apartment.

'She didn't leave much. A few clothes maybe. I was going to throw them out.'

That was enough. I told her I'd be coming over to get them later in the morning, and after a little hesitation she agreed. I put the phone down with the feeling that I'd committed myself somehow.

Next step: I went into the bedroom. It had a woman's smell about it. Perfume and make-up. A book beside the bed. *Faith in Fakes*. One side of the room was a walk-in closet, and I pushed it open with a blend of guilt and pleasure. I was sure that my brother wouldn't mind me wearing his clothes, but there was still a secret delight in the thought that I was taking something of his without his knowledge.

I picked out a suit with a label which said Dior. The label was a fake, because the suits were all copies that he'd bought in a Puerto Rican store in Manhattan. That was what he'd told me anyway, but I couldn't tell the difference and I was willing to bet no one else could.

I dawdled over the business of choosing a shirt, getting shaved, dressed and all the rest of it. It was about another hour before I could get myself out of the apartment and down to the subway. Thinking about it I realized that I had taken such a long time because there was something final about going to see the Schumanns, like setting off on a long journey about whose outcome I was uncertain, and I had the feeling that, once started, I wouldn't be able to turn back.

The address was in the East 50s, so I got out on Lexington and walked till I located the building. It was a massive flat-fronted block with self-consciously old-fashioned trimmings, like two carriage lamps framing the arcade at the entrance. As I approached, the doorman, a black man wearing the uniform of a nineteenth-century footman, was ceremoniously levering an aged white woman into a limousine, and I nipped into the doorway before he could do more than give me a curious look.

The lobby wasn't too grand. Just grand enough to tell you that rich folks lived there. Another attendant, a white man in a suit this time, was sitting behind a desk in the corner. His eyes ran over me with the detailed professional interest of a policeman examining a suspect, but I must have passed muster because he pointed me to the lift as soon as I asked for the Schumanns' apartment.

A middle-aged Jamaican woman opened the door. Mary's replacement, I guessed.

'You are Mr Dean?' She sounded surprised.

'Yes.'

'From London?'

'Yes.'

'OK. They're waiting for you.'

She led the way down the corridor, past several closed doors and into a huge L-shaped room which ended in a set of French windows. Beyond them was a small terrace. Just inside the windows was an old man in a wheelchair playing chess on a computerized board. He had to be Howard Schumann. His wife had just come in from the terrace with a watering can in her hand. She was younger than the old man, about early sixties, and she had brilliant black eyes set in thin even features. You could see that she'd once been a beauty, or at least that was how she carried herself, with a hint of a pose in the way she stooped to put the watering can down.

'Mr Dean. The gentleman from London,' the Jamaican lady said.

Mrs Schumann came across the carpet to meet me and shook my hand firmly. 'Rose Schumann. This is my husband, Howard.'

Howard flicked his eyes at me without speaking. Rose waved me into a chair nearby, and sat down opposite.

'Evie. Bring the package please.' Evie left and Rose fixed me with a look of open curiosity. 'You've come a long way, just to pick up some old dresses.'

'Oh, it wasn't just a question of picking these up. Mary's father asked me to get in touch, and I wondered if you'd be able to tell me anything that would help.'

'Ah. I knew it.' She sounded triumphant. 'Mary wasn't the

usual run of domestic help.' She turned to the old man. 'Did you hear that, Howard?'

'Shit,' the old man said explosively.

'*Howard.*'

'Yeah. Sorry. He just beat me again.'

She smiled indulgently. 'You won yesterday.'

The old man sat back and pulled his cardigan closed over his sunken chest. 'I cheated. You know that.' He grinned and winked at me. The movement transformed his face. He'd looked like an old dodderer when I first walked in, but now I could see he had all his wits about him.

'She left suddenly,' he said. 'Without telling us. If we'd known she was in trouble we'd have helped. We liked her.'

'What kind of trouble are you talking about?'

'I don't know,' he said, 'but she must have been in some kind of trouble to leave us like that. We liked her. Our friends liked her. She had no reason to disappear without telling us.'

'Your friends, are they likely to know anything?'

'No,' Rose said sharply. She sounded offended, and the old man shot her a sideways glance, as if he recognized the note in her voice and was checking. She paused, and Evie came and put a neatly wrapped paper package beside my chair.

'Evie,' Mrs Schumann said, 'get our visitor some tea. The British drink tea.'

'Coffee,' I told Evie. I smiled at Mrs Schumann as politely as I could. 'Please. If you don't mind.' I wasn't going to risk American tea. At its best it would be lemon tea bags. At its worst it would be some horrible herbal mixture.

Rose smiled knowingly at me as if she'd been reading my mind. 'Of course not. Evie, bring him some coffee.' She picked up the thread as soon as Evie went out. 'No. None of our friends would know any more than we do. Why should they?'

'Sorry. Just checking. I suppose I'm looking for anything that might help. For instance, what did she do in her spare time?'

'I'm not sure. She didn't bring her friends here, of course. Sometimes she talked about going to the theatre.'

44

'Off Broadway,' the old man said. 'I tried teaching her chess. She had a good mind, but she didn't have the patience.'

Evie came back with a tray, put it down and poured some coffee. She gave Rose a cup, then she gave me one, then she left the room, without offering Howard anything. They were fine stoneware cups with blue flowers running round the outside, and the old man watched them with the eyes of an addict. I guessed he was on some sort of stringent diet.

'Decaff,' Rose said.

'Of course. How did Mary get in touch with you?'

A pause. She frowned and looked over at Howard.

'A friend of my son knew we were looking for someone,' he said.

'Your son?'

'He probably won't remember,' Rose said quickly. 'He gets a hundred calls like this every day. Find somebody a job. Relatives, friends, voters. He sent us, oh, maybe ten or twelve women. Mary was the best one.'

The old man pushed his chair back and turned it to look out of the window. I followed his eyes. Far down below I saw the red surface of a tennis court with some figures in white knocking balls about. Rose stood up and blocked my view. 'I hope you find her,' she said.

I hadn't noticed her making a signal, but Evie had come back into the room, and now she picked up the parcel and handed it to me.

'Please show Mr Dean out,' Rose said.

'If you think of anything further. Anything at all that might be useful,' I said, 'please call me.'

I scribbled the number on a piece of paper and held it out to Rose but she didn't take it from my hand. Instead she gestured towards the table and I put it there next to a frame which held several photographs. There were a number of people in them, including the Schumanns, but all of them featured a tall distinguished-looking man with grey hair and a black moustache which made him stand out among the other faces. Suddenly I realized that I'd seen three, or four portraits

45

of the same person hanging on the walls. I picked up the frame.

'Your son?'

Her expression went stony, her eyes angry as if this was a piece of information she hadn't wanted me to have. Then she took the frame out of my hand and put it carefully back on the table. 'Yes.' Then she remembered her manners, smiled frostily at me, ducked her head in farewell, turned her back and began pushing the wheelchair through the window on to the terrace. I followed Evie. Halfway down the corridor she looked at me.

'My son is in London,' she said. 'He's in computers.'

For a moment I thought she was going to give me a message. That was how it used to be when I was younger. Meet a West Indian anywhere in the world, and they'd give you a message or a parcel for a relative somewhere else. Most of the time there wouldn't be anything as precise as an address to go with it, just a postal district or a place where the person hung out.

'Computers,' I echoed lamely, but Evie didn't continue. Instead she opened the door and handed me the parcel.

'Can I ask you something?' I said.

Her eyes seemed to focus on me for the first time, as if she was turning over in her mind who I was and what I wanted. She frowned. 'No. I don't think so,' she said.

Back in the elevator I began puzzling over whether I had learned anything worth knowing. The trouble was that I'd begun to feel as if I was looking for a needle in a haystack. This wasn't my city. In London I would have already started piecing together a chain of circumstances; I would have known what a false note sounded like when I heard it; and I would have known how far to push the Schumanns. Here in New York, I didn't even know what questions to ask.

I wasn't even the kind of person who could handle investigation easily. In the past I'd worked with reporters who could read the phone book, check out a list of names in a military directory, talk to a truck driver, make a few guesses, then come up with the location of every nuclear facility in Europe.

46

It was a talent, like a magician's sleight of hand or the ability to solve *The Times'* crossword, which I admired without envy.

Think, I muttered to myself. My emotions were the problem. I needed to forget about who Mary was, to forget about the fact that I was in a strange city, and apply myself to this like a puzzle on a piece of paper. There had been something in the Schumanns' response when I asked about how they'd met Mary. Rose had been a little too quick to tell me that she'd only been a name on the telephone to their son. Maybe that was why I felt they knew more than they were telling, or maybe it was the fact that they'd bothered to see me at all. I had no idea whether people of their sort would normally spend nearly an hour of their time being questioned by a complete stranger about a domestic they'd employed months ago, but I didn't think so. They had to be hiding something, but I hadn't a clue what it was.

The men at the door didn't even glance at me on the way out. I wasn't a resident and I guessed they understood that I wasn't the sort of visitor who would cross their palms with green.

In front of the building I looked around for a bar on the opposite side of the street, but there wasn't one in sight. It was that sort of neighbourhood. Instead I found a coffee shop a couple of buildings down from which I had a clear view of the Schumanns' apartment block. I hurried across, ducked in and sat at a table next to the window.

At the next table was a white-haired man wearing a beige corduroy jacket and a green knitted tie. With him was an old woman in what looked like a Laura Ashley print and a single string of pearls round her neck. I wasn't sure about the language they were using, but it sounded like German. In a moment a young woman in a tight, short black dress came up to my table, and I ordered a coffee and a cake with a German name. It was odd. Everything about the place had an incongruously familiar feel, like a café in Central London, perhaps Marylebone High Street. The effect was comforting. Walking around among these huge buildings about which I knew nothing, I'd begun to feel dwarfed and isolated, but this place gave me the sense that I'd found a temporary refuge. I unfolded the newspaper I'd bought in the subway and began reading half a page of gossip about the mayor's hobbies.

It was well over an hour before anything happened. By then I'd drunk four cups of coffee and started on the advertisements. Evie must have come out of the entrance to the building and walked several paces before I noticed her, because by then she was opposite me and moving fast. I got up and went over to the counter to pay the bill, but when I got out of the coffee shop she had disappeared. I ran to the corner cursing my momentary lapse, but as I dashed round it I saw her immediately. She hadn't gone very far down and she was standing still, looking intently into a shop window. I walked up to her and stopped a few paces away, but she must have sensed me coming because she'd already looked round.

'Hello,' I said. I couldn't think of anything else.

'Lost yourself?' Her face was impassive but her tone was definitely sarcastic.

'I was waiting,' I told her, 'to talk to you.'

She looked at me seriously, frowning. I couldn't tell whether or not she was angry but she certainly wasn't happy to see me. 'I don't know anything,' she said. 'And I don't want to know.'

'All I'm trying to do,' I said, 'is locate this girl, and all I want to know is if you can help at all.'

'You stupid or something?' Everything about her had changed. Upstairs in the apartment she'd been a silent presence, fetching and carrying to order. Now she seemed bigger, her eyes lancing straight at me.

'What?'

'Hiring people without papers is illegal. You scared those old people with your questions. They were only trying to help the girl. They don't want no trouble. You understand?'

I understood. They would have imagined that the whole episode was over and my phone call must have been a shock.

'I don't want to cause any trouble,' I said, 'only I promised

Mary's father I'd try and see her. He's sick. Sick bad. And he wants to see her. You know what that's like. You've got kids.' I was pleading openly and her face relaxed a little.

'Nothing I can tell you,' she said. 'The only thing is that she was studying some kind of course in Brooklyn. Or maybe it was Manhattan. I found a card, and there was a little book in her room with some addresses and phone numbers.'

'Have you got it?'

Her face twisted thoughtfully. 'I don't know. I might have thrown it away. I'll look.'

'What about the son? What's his name? Would he know anything?'

The frown came back, and she looked straight into my eyes, as if she was trying to tell me something without saying it. 'Ben. I don't know. He's a city official, like his father was. But he's different to the old man. If I were you I wouldn't go fooling about with him.'

I wrote down my brother's phone number and gave it to her. 'If you find the addresses, call me. And if you think of anything else.'

She shrugged. 'Sure.'

I watched her walking away. She held herself upright, and her feet came to rest solidly on the pavement with every step, like someone taking possession of every piece of ground she covered. There was something familiar about it, and I didn't have to search for the memory. My mother walked like this, and I pictured myself as a child watching her walking down a street in London: unobtrusive, nobody noticed her, but she had that same solid quality, as if nothing could shift her out of her way.

In that moment I realized that I didn't know Evie's surname. I hadn't even thought about asking her, but by the time the idea occurred to me she had disappeared into the subway entrance, and it was too late.

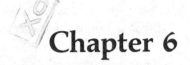

Chapter 6

I walked over to Lexington and called Bonny at the hospital.
I'd been bracing myself for a long explanation, but to my
surprise they put me right through to her as soon as I asked.
She sounded pleased when I said who I was.

'Hey. How you doing?'

I asked her for Oscar's phone number, and the line went
silent.

'You want to see him?'

Her voice had changed. Now she sounded cautious. I told
her that I wanted him to check some details about Mary, and
after she'd fiddled around for a couple of seconds she gave me
the number.

'What are you doing later? You about?'

'I'm not sure,' I said. 'Depends on how things go.'

'OK. But you're invited to a party tonight. If you're in the
mood.'

'Whose party?'

'A friend. She's just got tenure and it's kind of a
celebration.'

She didn't ask about Sophie. I hung up, hunted for some
more change and dialled the number she'd given me. A
woman answered and when I asked for Oscar he came on the
line without any fuss.

'How's it going?'

'Could be better,' I told him. 'I could use a little help, man.'

'Anything.'

I told him I'd seen Howard Schumann and that I wanted to fix an appointment with his son Ben. A long pause.

'Why do you want to see that person?'

For some reason he didn't want to say Ben's name.

'He sent Mary to them. Someone must have sent her to him. If he can tell me who that is they'll probably know where I can find her. Perhaps he's got her address. I don't know. There's no one else to ask.'

'Yeah. But this is a busy guy. Maybe he'll see you. Maybe he won't.'

I was getting fed up with this. 'All he can do is say no.'

'OK. Here's what you do. Call City Hall.' He gave me the number. 'Ask for his office.'

I could have figured that out for myself, I thought. I had imagined Oscar picking up the phone and fixing me an appointment, but it was obvious that he didn't want to be involved.

'Sorry I can't help you more,' he said. 'But he's not, like, someone I know.'

He sounded apologetic. I told him it was fine and that I hoped we would meet again soon. Then I hung up. By now I'd run out of change. I went down the subway entrance, bought the *Daily News* and got some change. Coming back I went past two cops, one black, one white, questioning a black man wearing a torn anorak and a desperate look.

'You know you're going to give it up, asshole,' the black cop said. 'Save us the trouble.'

The man didn't reply. Instead he shuffled his feet and his eyes flickered at me, as if I could tell him the answer. He put me in mind of a trapped animal and I didn't want to see any more, so I turned my head away and hurried back to the phone.

I got nowhere fast. They put me through to Ben's office, but that was the end. The woman who answered asked me

51

who I was and what I wanted. I told her my name and said it was a personal matter.

'Ahuh. Thank you, Mr Dean.'

As she said this there was a buzz and a voice told me to put more money in. I scrambled desperately, but before I could do it the buzz stopped and a loud tone replaced it. Cut off. I dialled the number again and eventually got the same woman. I repeated what I'd said previously and she told me that Mr Schumann never made unscheduled appointments on the telephone. I should write a letter stating my business. Then she thanked me for calling and the line went dead.

A blank wall. I could try harder, push. No problem. But right now I had no idea where or how to push. Perhaps, I thought, this was the clue. If the job's impossible, give it up.

One more thing. Oscar had mentioned checking on missing persons. I dialled his office again. This time a woman answered and told me to leave a number. He'd call me back as soon as he was free. I gave her the number in Corona and hung up feeling foolish.

The subway was crowded and I stood, hanging on to an overhead strap. After a couple of stops, a black man on crutches swung down the centre of the car holding out a tin cup. One of his legs ended in a freshly bandaged stump, and I could hear him coming along the aisle by the sound of the coins rattling against the metal. Opposite me a white man in a neat dark suit stretched out and dropped some coins in without looking up from his paper. No one spoke, and in another moment the one-legged man had disappeared into the next car.

The telephone was ringing as I let myself into my brother's apartment.

'Mr Dean?' A woman's voice.

'This is Sammy,' I said. 'Walter's out of town.'

'That's right. Sam. You're the one that came this morning. This is Evie. I looked up those papers.'

Silently I cursed my luck. I'd been about ready to give up. She said she'd found a card with the name of a college on it, and I wrote it down automatically. CUNY.

'There's an address book and a couple of other things.'

'Can I come and get it?'

She hesitated. 'OK. Tomorrow. I'll finish about one. Meet me at the same place.'

I slammed the phone down with the sense that some unkind fate was on my trail. I'd have to check out what Evie had told me; at least take a look at the address book. I knew now it would be a useless quest. I knew too little about the place, and I hated the thought of another day traipsing around the city asking useless questions. But every time I thought about giving up a picture of Hector lying comatose in the hospital bed flashed through my mind.

'Could have been me,' I muttered aloud. 'Easy. Could have been me.'

Chapter 7

I told Bonny about the telephone call on the way to the party. When I mentioned the name of the college she repeated it thoughtfully.

'A friend of mine works there.'

Another thread in the rope.

'That's a coincidence.'

'Yes and no. There'll be a network of black women academics in every city. Then there's the Caribbean connection. Especially at the open-access colleges.'

We were rolling up towards Union Turnpike and she waved her hand out of the window. The gold earrings she was wearing swung around when she moved, and they made a tiny jangling sound which I could hear above the noise of the engine.

'Look there. On the left. St Johns University. I've got friends there. If we'd gone the other way it would have been Queens College. Any place like that I can find you somebody you can talk to.'

I was beginning to know her, and I could tell she was showing off, but it gave her a vulnerability which made me feel affectionate. Suddenly I began to enjoy myself. It crossed my mind that I hadn't spoken to Sophie, but in the same moment I forgot about it. When I'd called her number there'd been no answer, and in the ordinary way of things I'd have tried again, but this time I hadn't wanted to. Standing in front of the window listening to her phone ringing I'd wanted a release from the frustration and turmoil I felt with her. Thinking about it I frowned and Bonny caught my expression out of the corner of her eye.

'We're almost there.' She made a left turn and we were in a suburban street.

'Will your friend be there?'

She smiled at me. 'Wait and see.'

Something about her manner had changed. Up to the point I got in the car she'd been friendly enough, but there was a distance between us, as if she hadn't decided how to behave. But sometime during the journey she'd become warmer and now there was a flirtatious undertone to the conversation.

She parked by the side of the road and we walked up to the house. It looked almost identical to the one that Rupert lived in, but this time the door was open and we could hear the music as we came into the yard.

The porch was crowded, and Bonny began greeting people as we came up the stairs. I smiled and nodded and shook hands automatically without registering the faces. 'How you doing?' everyone said. I was looking at Bonny. Suddenly I was more aware of her than I had been since the moment that we met. She was wearing a short black dress cut low at the back, and as she moved around I could see the muscles tensing and relaxing under her skin. Several of the women were wearing dresses which showed off their backs in the same way, but Bonny's was most eye-catching.

Someone put a hand on my shoulder from behind and I turned round. It was Oscar, dressed in a light grey suit with a faint chalk stripe. Beautiful. 'Let's talk,' he said.

We threaded our way through to the back yard where a couple of tables covered with food and plates were laid out. The inevitable fried chicken. Potato salad. Steaks. Serious food. The bottles were wine and spirits. No beer in sight.

I told him that I'd had no luck getting through to Ben Schumann and he nodded.

'Ahuh. I talked to a couple of guys at Police Plaza. They're checking it out.'

'What does that mean?'

I wasn't sure why Oscar made me feel irritable, but in any case the oblique and euphemistic style of some informal American speech often confused me. Talking about concrete things, they could be startlingly direct, using precise, graphic images. When it came to more abstract matters their language could become vague and general. Oscar gave me a slightly puzzled look.

'It means I gave them the description, her name, where she was seen last, and I asked them to' – he paused – 'check it out.'

He paused again, looking at me as if to gauge my reaction.

'They'll check the computers. See if it matches up with anything they've got. Your best shot, they come up with nothing. You know?'

He'd left me feeling graceless again. I knew enough to know that, at any given moment, there'd be hundreds of people in the city looking for missing children. If he'd done what he said it had probably taken a lot of effort and persuasion.

'Thanks,' I said, smiling nicely. 'It's a big help.'

He shrugged. 'Por nada.'

'What about Ben Schumann? Every time I mention his name someone warns me to back off. He must know something.'

'I'm not so sure about that,' Oscar said. 'The way it is: a guy calls you. He says, do this favour for someone I know. In the neighbourhood or a relative maybe. OK. You do it. Sometimes you know absolutely nothing about the circumstances or the person. OK. You go into Schumann's office, you say tell me about this. He's going to think, what's this guy trying to do? What's he accusing me of? Hey. I know that's not what you're doing, but you see the problem.'

'I see the problem. But I can explain. All I'd need to know is the name of the person who called him. If I can talk to them maybe I'd get somewhere.'

Oscar laughed as if I'd said something funny. 'Man. That's worse. How's he going to know what you'll be coming down on this guy with? Come on. Trust me. There's nothing to gain. Not in that direction. Nowhere to go.'

If he wanted me to trust him he was pushing too hard, but there didn't seem to be any point in arguing about it.

'How soon,' I said, 'do you think your friends will come up with something from the police computer?'

He shrugged. 'Maybe Monday. Tuesday maybe. Maybe never. I'll hassle them pretty good.'

I couldn't think of anything else to ask him right then, but fortunately Bonny came up, put her arms round his waist and kissed him on the cheek. 'Sorry,' she said. 'I've got to break this up. I want you to meet the lady who's giving this party.'

She grabbed my hand and pulled me back towards the house. Our hostess was in the kitchen standing against the fridge, talking with another couple of women. They were all fortyish, big strapping women, whose exposed flesh made them look even more confident and powerful.

'Bella,' Bonny said, 'this is my cousin Sammy. The one from London.'

Three heads swivelled as one, and I found myself the focus of an intent triple gaze. The woman standing to the right of Bella had what seemed to be the largest and most revealing cleavage in the room, and it was hard not to look.

'Well. Well. Well,' Bella said. 'You are a good-looking family.' She eyed me in a way that was frankly predatory. 'You girls go away,' she said. 'I want to talk to this child. Privately.' She gave her friends a comical look and linked her arm through mine.

'Too late,' Bonny said. 'He's got himself a ladyfriend. She calls him every day. I swear.'

'She's here?' Bella asked.

'Uh-uh,' Bonny replied. 'She ain't.'

'All right then. Goodbye girlfriend,' Bella said.

They all laughed, enjoying themselves hugely. The lady with the cleavage reached across to pat my cheek. 'Oh oh,' she said. 'You're embarrassing the man. He's shy. The men in England are shy. You so bad, you just scare him.'

'Honey,' Bella said. 'If he's straight, he don't take drugs, and he's got a good job, I'll take him. I don't care how scared he gets to be. I'll take care of that.'

She was teasing me, but I had the feeling that underneath the mockery she meant exactly what she said. I smiled back at her, trying to match her manner. The problem was that her friend was more or less right. She had embarrassed me a little. By now I was so accustomed to the tight pallid style of social life in England that it took time to adjust to dealing with women who were so bold and confident.

'You just stop that,' Bonny said. 'This is my cousin and I'm looking after him.' Her friends mugged at each other, and Bella withdrew her arm and stood back ostentatiously. 'He wants to know,' Bonny continued, 'about one of the city colleges.'

Bella's face took on a serious expression, and the atmosphere changed immediately. 'Which one?' she asked.

I told her.

'What do you want to know?'

'I'm trying to get in touch with a friend's daughter. I think she's enrolled on one of the courses there.'

She thought for a moment. 'Jean,' she said. 'She teaches there. I don't know if she's still here. Let's go see.'

Jean was a short, thin, intense and very dark-skinned woman in a flowered caftan-style dress. When she heard what I wanted she seemed to light up. Her eyes fixed seriously on my face, and she began to ask me a series of questions.

'She would not have been on any of the courses I teach,' she said eventually. 'I don't know how you can locate her easily without knowing the department she's in, but it's possible that you can find her through the central computer. If she's in the school she'll be there but that information is confidential. There's no way they'd let you search the records without some kind of authority.'

Another dead end. She must have noticed my disappointment, because she put her hand on my arm and looked up at me with a sympathetic expression.

'That's not the only option,' she said. 'You can come and look. If you're around long enough you may see her.'

'I don't know what she looks like,' I said.

Jean made a pained face. 'That's bad. There's so many people, doing so many different things. I teach developmental skills — that's where you find most of the immigrants and foreign language speakers — but I guess the way you've described her that's not where she'd be anyway. But, you know, we've got a lot of people coming in on their way to other courses, because everyone's got a right. In the city colleges in my department they're mostly black, Hispanic, Asian, Koreans, Chinese. Everything. I've got a seventy-year-old Dominican in one of my classes. He's doing well too. But even the kids who are qualified to go to other schools get steered to the city colleges. It's open access, you see.'

She paused for breath, and at the same time a man in a dark suit danced between us and hugged her emphatically. She struggled half free, her eyes still fixed on me, but I guessed that this was going to be my best opportunity to get away. I thanked her for her help, and asked her if I could come over to the college and take a look around.

'Of course,' she said. 'Call me when you are ready.'

I said I would, and sneaked off while the going was good.

In the back yard the party was swinging into gear. It was a warm humid evening, with occasional gentle gusts of wind bringing hints of the scorching heat that would come in full summer. A few couples were dancing out there, most of the food had gone, and a knot of men standing against the fence were locked in an intense discussion. The talk was about jobs, money, Bill Clinton and, inevitably, the mayor, but I'd only been listening for a short while when Bonny came up and took my hand.

'Come on. Let's dance.'

I looked around for Oscar, but he seemed to have gone.

Inside the house Bonny put her arms round me, and we embraced. Smoochy.

At the back of my mind, I'd been trying to figure out what was going on between me and Bonny and what Oscar's part in her life was, but now I gave up thinking about it. Bonny was taller than Sophie, and her body had a hard, sinewy feel.

'How you doing?' she whispered in my ear.

Her breasts and her hips moved against me. I was doing fine, I told her.

We stayed another couple of hours, and by the time Bonny had said a series of protracted goodbyes, it was well past midnight.

In the car she turned the radio on. The DJ's voice had a soft Caribbean sound. WLIB.

'Is Bella married?' I asked.

She gave me a sly look, eyebrows raised. 'Why? You interested?'

'I might be.' I gave her the sly look back and we grinned at each other.

'She's been married twice. The first one got shot, and she split up with the second one two years ago. He sold the car and left her with some serious debts. Last seen heading west. She's been kind of unlucky with husbands. But that's usual. It's what happens to black men around here. I went to a private school, otherwise my mother would have sent me back home. The survival rate is better in a school like that, but the kids in the street, kids I hung out with, take a look at the men – some are dead, never reached twenty-one, a couple are in prison, some on dope. Black men. They're all in some kind of obstacle race with death and disaster.'

Her voice had taken on an intense and angry note, and she banged sharply on the steering wheel with her hand. 'Shit.' Then she looked round and smiled.

'That's not how it is in England, huh?'

'It's getting that way,' I said, 'but it doesn't compare. Nothing over there is so extreme. This is different.'

She smiled. 'I figured.'

I thought about my son. My last conversation with him had been about drugs. He'd listened to what I had to say with a grin on his face. 'Dad,' he'd said, 'I'm laughing because if I was going to take drugs you're too late. Since I was about twelve people have been offering me Ecstasy and crack. They call it E. Just walking down Camden High Street, man. I'm young and black, so they think I'm a raver. You don't need to warn me. Me and my friend are the only teenagers around here who don't do it. You don't know what goes on, man.'

Remembering what he'd said I wondered how he was doing. In the last year or so he'd grown in confidence and begun to make his own decisions, but the more he did so the more scared I was for him. Now all I could do was keep my fingers crossed. At least he wasn't growing up in this city.

'What about your friend? The kind of black lady.'

I guessed she'd misinterpreted my silence. 'What do you want to know?'

I hadn't intended it but there was an edge to my tone. She picked it up and glanced round at me, her eyebrows raised. 'Nothing,' she said. 'Nothing at all.'

Back in the apartment she stretched out on the sofa. I took my cue from her and went over to the cupboard where my brother kept an exotic collection of booze. I picked out a bottle of bourbon and brought it back to the sofa. When I began to pour it into the glasses she got up without a word, went into the kitchen, and I heard her open the fridge and begin breaking out ice cubes. When she came back we raised our glasses and drank in the same companionable silence.

'What about you,' I said. 'I thought you had something going with Oscar.'

She hesitated before replying. 'Used to. At college. Now we just meet sometimes. He's got as many women as he wants, and more than he needs.'

She smiled and lifted her hands in a helpless gesture. What to do? I wasn't sure whether or not that meant she still cared for Oscar, but I was too busy examining my own reactions to worry about that. I had grown up and begun to shape my ideas about myself among people who were reflexively hostile or suspicious of me. Even now my relationship with Sophie had a screwed-up undertone of frustration and distrust. Being with Bonny was like swimming in clear water, and niggling at the back of my mind was the sense that this was too simple. Too easy.

'So you don't have to worry about Oscar,' I said.

We were looking intently into each other's eyes. Bonny shook her head. A small hesitant motion, but I couldn't read what it meant because I was struggling to breathe. Suddenly I was panting, fighting to draw the air into my lungs.

Bonny stretched her body along the sofa towards me, put her glass down and lay back. 'Come here,' she said.

We kissed and I lay on top of her, one body moving hard against the other, difficult to tell them apart. My hands moved about of their own accord, touching her everywhere. Her skin was soft and smooth, underneath it, taut muscle. When my fingers trailed along her thighs she moaned a little. After a while she pulled her mouth away from mine.

'Hey,' she said. 'Is this incest?'

'Maybe. A little bit. I don't know.'

She freed herself from my grasp and sat up. 'Ah ha. I've read about this. Close relatives meet after a long separation. First thing they do is say hello. Next thing they do is screw. Shit.'

'Come on,' I said. 'We're only cousins. Cousins do this all the time.' I kissed the back of her knee, then moved on up and nibbled her thigh. She pushed at my head with her hand.

'That's what you say. We're not doing this.'

She got up, pulled her dress down over her hips, sat down, and put her arms round me. We kissed again.

'Let's think about it,' she said.

She got up and went away. I waited, but in a few minutes the usual bedtime sounds started. The shower ran, the toilet flushed, and after a while I heard her pull the bedroom door shut. I stripped my clothes off, threw them on the floor, turned the lights off and lay back on the sofa, thinking about her body and how she'd felt. Perhaps, I thought, she was doing me a favour. Going any further would merely have complicated things with Sophie. I would see her during the day and tonight's denial would make me feel strong and virtuous. OK. The last thing I remembered was the faint sound of a police siren, moving fast in the distance, then I must have fallen asleep.

I dreamt that I was walking down a street in the village where I'd been born. It seemed odd to be there, because the last time I'd seen it I had been a child, and at the end of the street I could see all the boys I used to play with. Hector was there, and for a moment my mind struggled with the fact that I knew him to be grown up and lying in a hospital bed in England. Just then someone came up behind me and called my name: 'Sammy.'

I woke up and Bonny was bending over me. Before I could collect myself she climbed on top of me, and stretched out along my body. Her thighs parted and gripped fiercely round my leg. I eased back into the sofa and hugged her tight.

'I've thought about it,' she whispered in my ear. 'Let's do it.'

Chapter 8

Saturday nudged me awake slowly, like a timid Samaritan trying to rouse a drunk in an alleyway. Sometime during the night we had shifted from the sofa to the bed, and when I woke up Bonny was standing beside it offering me a cup of coffee. I thanked her and fell asleep again. The next thing I heard was the accusing sound of the telephone. I lay there waiting for it to stop, and when it did I began drifting away. But just as I was poised on the point of oblivion the ringing started again, and suddenly I was awake. I climbed slowly out of bed and headed for the phone. The ringing stopped.

I looked around for Bonny, and I was just about to call out her name when I remembered that she'd gone to visit her mother in Washington. That was what she'd been telling me about earlier on. The shuttle to Washington. In the bedroom the cup of coffee was lying beside the bed, cold and untouched. I made myself another one, went back to the phone and dialled Sophie's number.

She answered on the first ring. 'I was trying to call you.'

'So was I. Yesterday.'

She said she'd been working late. I told her I'd been seeing some old friends.

'I'm on my way out,' she said. 'I'm doing some pictures at

the market. If you leave now you can come with me. I'll pick you up at the subway.'

I was just about to agree when I remembered that I'd fixed to meet Evie. 'I can't. I'm meeting someone.' I explained.

'OK. OK.' She sounded impatient. 'Meet me in the Bronx. At the bodega.'

I agreed, put the phone down and looked at my watch. Just enough time.

Only just. Evie was standing in front of the store looking impatient. 'I was just going,' she said without preamble.

'Sorry.'

She put her hand in her bag and hesitated. 'I'm giving this to you because you are a friend of the family. If you find that girl, take her back where she came from. Get her out of here. This place is good if you know what you're doing, otherwise it's no place for a young girl.' She stared at me sternly.

'Right,' I said. 'Right.'

She handed me a small package. 'That's all there is.'

'Is there anything more you can tell me? Did they say anything?'

Her mouth tightened and she glared at me. 'I'm not a spy. What they said doesn't matter.'

'OK. Sorry.'

Her expression softened. 'The son, Ben. He came. He got in a childish temper when they told him about you. He questioned me: what I said to you, what you asked me. They're nice people, but he is a rude, conceited boy. Think he's the most important thing in the city. Can't mind his own business.'

I should have guessed. She must have rung me after he'd talked to her. Maybe this was her revenge. Or maybe she felt something was wrong, and she hadn't wanted Ben to have the address book. Just in case.

'What did you tell him?'

'I don't know anything to tell him,' she said energetically.

'I've done all I can for the girl. Leave me out of it after this. Don't call. You understand me?'

I nodded. 'I understand. Thank you.'

Alone again, I walked aimlessly round the next corner. It was too early to meet Sophie, and I didn't know anyone in Manhattan. Besides, I wanted to take a look at the address book. A bar. I went into the next one I came across. Something familiar about it, but for the moment I couldn't pin it down. Realization came gradually as I took in the brand names on the bottles: Glenfiddich, Jameson, Guinness.

'What would you like?' the woman behind the bar said.

She was dark haired with a small firm mouth and delicate pretty features. Her accent was familiar. 'Belfast,' I said.

She grinned at me. 'This is an Irish bar. Where are you from?'

'London.'

She raised her eyebrows and leaned on the bar. 'Oh. I studied in London. Sidcup.'

'Sidcup,' I said scornfully. 'Where the hell is Sidcup?'

She laughed again. 'A bloody snob. Sidcup's just as much a part of London as any of your inner city districts.'

At the back of the bar, where it said 'GENTS', a door opened and a man dressed in a white jacket and a chef's hat emerged. He stood there looking at me with a scowl on his face and then he went back in and slammed the door. The Irish girl pulled back from the bar. 'Try my special,' she advised.

'What is it?'

'All the white drinks. Tequila, vodka, Cointreau and all the rest. It's strong.'

'Let's have it.'

While she mixed the drink I began leafing through the address book. The addresses were mostly in Queens and Brooklyn. I recognized Rupert's, but nothing else. After a while the girl put a tall glass down in front of me and I sipped it. She was right. It was strong stuff for lunchtime. I told her so and she made a superior face at me. Behind her a short red-faced man with brown curly hair and a long white apron emerged from the doorway of the kitchen and stared aggressively at me. The girl turned away and began polishing glasses. I turned away and concentrated on the address book.

The taste of the drink had kicked something loose in my head and I began turning the pages looking for the name Ben. I found it written sideways on the last page. Under it was an address and a number in Manhattan. Bingo. If Mary had Ben's private address in her book it didn't necessarily mean that there had to be a connection, but I was willing to gamble that there was.

There was a promise of action here, and my mood lifted. I waved goodbye to the Belfast girl and headed down the street to the nearest telephone. I punched out Ben's number with my fingers crossed, hoping that, after all this, he would be in.

'Yes,' the voice on the other end of the line said. It sounded cold and aggressive; and I hesitated for a second before answering.

'Who is this?'

He was snapping out the words with a curt impatience which was probably meant to be intimidating, but I gave him back my smoothest inflection and told him who I was.

'What do you want?'

I told him I was trying to locate Mary on her father's behalf, but I'd barely got the words out when he interrupted me angrily.

'You're in deep shit already. You harass my parents or me again and I'll have you arrested. I can do that.'

I believed him.

'Mr Schumann,' I said plaintively. 'Why are you so angry? I'm merely trying to get in touch with my friend's daughter. I don't know what you've been told, but I didn't harass your parents. I called them and they invited me round. That was it.' I was working on the principle that the soft answer turneth away wrath, and there was a brief silence while he adjusted.

'Listen carefully,' he said eventually. 'My parents don't know anything about this girl. They hired her and she left. I don't know anything about her either. Someone called me and gave me her name. I sent her to them. I spoke two words to her when I visited the apartment. Hello and goodbye. When she left I found them another one.'

'Who got in contact with you in the first place?'

'I don't remember. People call me every day with shit like this. OK. Now you know everything I know. I don't expect to hear from you again. I really don't.'

The line went silent, then I heard the tone. I hung up gently. My head was spinning with questions, but I knew now Ben wouldn't answer them easily, and I needed to know more about him and about the situation before I spoke to him again.

Back on the subway I drew a mental map of the problem. Even now I wasn't sure whether I wouldn't just run across Mary if I could only work out where she might be. I hadn't yet turned up anything which would suggest that she was missing or involved in anything dangerous. Ben Schumann's response, though, seemed like more of a warning signal than the standard paranoia I'd picked up everywhere else. He had to know more than he was telling and I had a gut feeling that his agitation about my enquiries meant there was something wrong somewhere. I'd held back the fact that I had found his number in Mary's address book. It might turn out to be useful ammunition, but for the moment, I wasn't sure what to do next.

The Nation of Islam was out in force at Parsons Boulevard. Black trousers, white shirts, maroon braces. They looked distinctively smart; elegant even. I bought a copy of the *Final Call* when one of the boys thrust it at me and he gave me a charming grin. 'Read the truth and spread the word, brother,' he said.

I smiled back and nodded. I didn't know what the word was, but in a time and place where addiction and murder were everyday occurrences in the lives of young black men, the clean-cut style of these boys was downright reassuring.

I walked over to Jamaica Avenue and went into Alvin's shop. The afternoon was drawing to an end, but the place was still crowded with customers. Alvin's entire family seemed to be there, busily moving around, shifting clothes about, selling and shouting at each other. Alvin himself was making a leisurely sale to two young women in short skirts, jeri-curled hair and heaving sculpted sweaters. Alvin's eyes were gleaming and he was showing out with the kind of gallantry we'd learned from our elders and betters back home. He saw me coming, beamed gold at me and waved with a familiar carelessness. It was a gesture I remembered from when we were kids, but it looked odd on this middle-aged man, as if he'd somehow taken over the Alvin I knew and stolen his mannerisms.

'You'll have to wait, boy,' he said loudly. 'I have to deal with these two beautiful ladies.'

One of them had big soft eyes, and she gave me a flash of them from under her eyebrows.

'Take your time, Alvin,' I said.

'You hear that?' Alvin said to the women. 'This is my old schoolfriend. He know. I always take my time.'

The women giggled, but I didn't hear the reply because I moved to the back of the shop and sat down. Watching Alvin operate I felt a sudden and unexpected jolt of nostalgia. This was how I remembered adults behaving during my childhood. The ponderous double entendre, the sexy body language, the sidelong glances were part of a style that the people I knew in England would find incomprehensible or offensive, but to me it was like re-encountering a partly forgotten and instinctive language.

After a couple of minutes Alvin waved the women goodbye and came over. 'What's happening?'

I told him about my visit to the Schumanns and the phone call. He listened with a deepening frown.

'You know what it sounds like to me,' he said. 'Could be the guy was giving her some licks. He don't want it to come out. She was illegal. He is a city official. See how I mean? Or could be something happen and now is cover-up time.'

'So what do I do?'

'Don't ask me, boy. I don't have no experience with this kinda thing.'

I hung about a bit longer, while he told me about some of the other boys we'd known and where they'd ended up. Most of them seemed to be scattered round the States. In a little while I realized that he was sneaking looks at his watch and peering over my shoulder, so I told him I was on my way to the Bronx and went.

When I left Jamaica some of the shops were already closing and by the time I approached the Grand Concourse there was already a Saturday night feel in the air, the streets emptying and quieting down into a murmuring hush as if they were readying themselves for a special piece of theatre. On the way I'd made a detour and dropped into the apartment, partly to change my clothes, partly to see whether Bonny had come back. I wasn't sure why. She wasn't there, but I'd showered, shaved and appropriated a black silk shirt and a light grey suit, whose label said YSL. Closing the door behind me I'd felt good, and coming up the subway stairs into the Grand Concourse I still felt OK.

Sophie was in the place where I'd seen her before, sitting at the same table, but she was with a couple of older men this time. One of them was olive-skinned with a long drooping moustache, the other had deep brown skin and African features. Oddly enough they looked vaguely similar, white-haired, portly, with loose-fitting white shirts, and the general air of once having been pretty smooth articles.

The waitress saw me first and she mimed an expression of surprise, whipping her hand up and down in front of her. '*Ay, novio,*' she called out.

Sophie turned round and as I approached the two men got up, bowed slightly and we shook hands while she introduced us. Fernando, Emiliano. I smiled and bowed back at them. Close up to the sonorities of Latin vowels I was beginning to feel my name was too short and lacking in weight, or perhaps it was the men's formal courtesy which put me a little off balance. The English pride themselves on their politeness but their social manners tend to be curt, and, even at the best of times, a little offhand. Caribbean manners are warmer but it was still something of a strain adjusting to the detail of these rituals.

I sat down eventually and Sophie began telling me about the men. They listened with grave smiles, their eyes intent on what she was saying about them. They were Cubans, she said, both musicians, and they sometimes played at a nearby restaurant where we'd be going later. We were waiting for their singer, a woman whom they'd been supporting for twenty years, ever since they'd arrived from the island. Nowadays they performed less often, but they were still great. Sophie was going to photograph her tonight.

The old men nodded their heads gravely as if to signify that she'd got it all right. The black one, Emiliano, said something in Spanish to his friend and they both looked at Sophie with wide smiles. She turned to me.

'Did you understand?'

'Not really.' I'd been thrown by their accents. By now I was used to the jerky, buzzing sound of Stateside Spanish, but the language these men spoke was softer with longer cadences. Emiliano leaned a little closer.

'I was speaking of her mother. I saw her dance. Many times. She is like her.' He shook his head, still gazing at her. 'In the Caribbean and South America we share one thing in common. *Sangre caliente.*'

'Hot blood?'

'Sparkling.'

We laughed together and the old man reached over, picked up Sophie's hand and kissed it.

The waitress came over and filled up the coffee cups, then she brought us each a small glass of white rum.

'*Bienvenido,*' Fernando said. We drank. 'In Europe,' he said, 'you have visited Spain?'

'Yes. Yes, of course. Beautiful.'

Smiles all round. They too had visited Spain. Two more glasses and Fernando confided that he'd once had a fantasy about playing his guitar in the Gaudi park in Barcelona just as the sun came up. He'd even tried to do it once but the gates had been locked. The sunrise, he said, the sunset; the light, clear and full of colour like the soul of an artist. There was no light like it, except on the island. I replied by telling him about sitting on the beach in the Eastern Caribbean watching for the green flash, and the two men laughed.

'The green flash?' Sophie asked.

'They say this all around the Caribbean,' Emiliano told her. 'At the point when the sun enters the blue sea there is a green flash. One second and it is gone. But I have never seen it.'

We argued amiably about the possibility, then we had a couple more drinks and kicked around a few more memories before they left to start work. When they'd gone Sophie told me they were lovely guys and I agreed, then she asked me how the day had gone and I told her about Schumann. She listened intently.

'Suppose,' she said suddenly, 'all this conspiracy is in your mind, and the girl is fine. She's simply gone to Oregon or the Caribbean for a trip. Get away from everything, including her father. You see?'

I saw. I said it was possible but I had an instinct it wasn't so. She smiled.

'In your version of the world,' she said, 'the next thing to happen will be bad.' She was only half joking. But I knew what she meant.

'Tell me,' I asked her. 'What is there in your experience to make you think differently?'

She leaned back, thought for a long moment and then shrugged. 'We've survived.' She waved her hand around the café, taking in the whole area and the people and the bodega itself. 'We were not meant to. We come from people who were expendable, yet we are here, all of us. We've survived.'

Later on we walked across the Grand Concourse over to Jerome Avenue and on down. She must have been working the area for a while because people kept saying hello and she answered with a polite little smile and an inclination of the head. Usually when I'd seen her working she'd been business-like, even curt, but I'd never seen her in this reserved, almost stately mood. On Jerome, she took my arm as we passed under the shadow of the railway tracks. The cars stopped for the lights here and half a dozen prostitutes in hotpants and short skirts were cruising the drivers. A junkie was staggering down the middle of the strip spouting a stream of rhyming gibberish at them. Sophie grimaced and glanced round at me.

'If you ever need a woman,' she said, 'don't come here.' She pointed ahead to where the Bronx Lebanon towered over the apex of the hill. 'They've just put in a new wing there. Aids. And there's lots of customers.'

She was silent for a moment.

'What makes me angry,' she said, 'is that when people in Manhattan hear I'm working down here, they act as if it's a cross between a leper colony and a wild beast reserve. The ghetto. It's no use telling them that a lot of good people live here because some of them have to and a lot of them want to. We speak Spanish so we're all pushers or prostitutes. You know?'

Her hand was gripping my arm tightly. I smiled. 'You're telling me?' I said.

She looked at me, laughed and relaxed. 'OK. OK. I'm just kind of letting off steam. I called Kitty in London yesterday. She gave me a big pain in the ass.'

I knew what she meant. For Kitty the pictures would be all to do with style, and they would have to confirm the prejudices of her readers, without disturbing them. 'That's the job,' I told Sophie. 'It's their magazine and they can play what games they like with it.'

Her grip on my arm tightened. 'I know that,' she said. 'It's not their power to impose the way they see things on me that I hate. I'm used to living with that. It's the fact that they sound so stupid, and I start thinking, do they think *I'm* as stupid as this.'

On the next avenue we got to the restaurant. From outside it looked like nothing very much. A small neon sign said 'EL MILAGRO.' A couple of bouncers in suits with broad *indio* faces, like Latin versions of Mike Tyson, were checking people at the door, but they waved Sophie in without any questions and I squeezed in alongside her.

It was still early, about ten when I looked at my watch, but the place was crowded and the band was already going: two trumpets, a guitar and a synthesizer. Two couples were dancing; not quite a rumba, but the way they moved was almost like a routine, hips swaying and heels clicking precisely. I recognized Fernando and Emiliano up on the stand, but I had to stare in order to pick them out because all the musicians seemed to be about the same age, stout white-haired men. We sat at a table on the edge of a small dance floor, next to a big party which seemed to consist of one family, Mum, Dad, Granny and a few assorted teenagers. They had an expectant, jolly air, as if this was an outing at which they were determined to enjoy everything.

'The singer's coming on later,' Sophie said. She had to lean close to me and shout into my ear above the music, and I nodded my head in reply. She smiled at me, suddenly warm and relaxed. 'When she gets on I'll be working.' She put her hand on mine. 'You don't mind?'

I signalled that I didn't, and she drew her chair round so that we could hear each other. Our legs touched under the table and I could feel her warm breath on the side of my face when she spoke.

'What sort of place is this?' I asked her.

'Sort of Cuban but everyone comes here. It's licensed. No trouble to speak of.'

I guessed what she meant. All around the city there were clubs, in cellars, apartments, wherever. They'd be unlicensed fire traps, and there'd often be a shooting. A couple of years back a fire had wiped out most of the clientele in a cellar. The clubs were dangerous. A decent man might drop in for a drink or to check out a friend, but he wouldn't take his family.

The food came. Standard Caribbean: shrimps, fried plantains, blackeye peas and pork. We were halfway through the meal when the lights dimmed and the singer bounced on to the stand.

At first I had the impression of a young woman in a sequinned red dress, but as I got a closer look I realized that she was actually on the old side of middle age, sixty perhaps, but her movements and the strength of her voice made that seem impossible.

Sophie stood up and hauled her camera out of her bag and began screwing equipment together. In a minute she was gone, darting about the front of the room, the camera whining and clicking as she moved.

Left to myself I sat and let the sounds drift over me. I was feeling the effect of the drinks I'd had earlier. Alcohol makes me drowsy, and had the chairs been more comfortable I would have fallen asleep. As it was I came near to dozing off several times, and I couldn't concentrate hard enough to understand the words of the songs.

After an hour or so the singer bowed and kissed hands to the audience and Sophie came back. 'Let's go,' she said. 'I've had a long day.'

She'd parked the car on the next corner, and I climbed into the passenger seat with a feeling of relief.

She looked at me as she put the keys in the ignition and grinned. 'OK, you poor old man. You can go to sleep now.' She must have seen me dozing off.

'I had a hard day too,' I said with as much dignity as I could muster.

She turned the ignition on and raced the engine. She chuckled quietly as she steered the car into the traffic and I looked over at her. All of a sudden the tension that had been present between us was gone. She's my friend, I thought.

'What are you giggling about?' I asked her.

She glanced over and gave me a big stage cackle. 'Your day isn't over yet, *muchacho*.'

Chapter 9

Sophie woke me early. 'Sorry,' she said. 'I'd stay, but I've been waiting for weeks to photograph this woman. She's a healer, like in the islands, but they wouldn't let me see her. Today's the first time.'

I shifted around in the bed, trying to focus. 'What?'

'Candles. Chickens. Shango. Ogun. You know about that.'

I sat up. 'What? They do that stuff here?' Now she had my attention.

'Right.'

'And you're taking photos?'

'I don't know. Maybe. Go back to sleep.'

'When are you coming back?'

'I don't know.'

She disappeared, and I lay back. I was accustomed to her vanishing into other people's lives. Usually, I liked the way she came and went, but sometimes it left me feeling strange and disconnected. The funny thing was that if she'd been different we probably wouldn't have stayed together. Neither of us wanted someone around all the time. My own life would have had to change drastically if we'd been a conventional couple, and at the beginning the whole thing seemed perfect. The best of every possible world. But after a while it had begun to go in cycles. We'd drift apart, get interested in other people, and getting back together would take time and effort. It wasn't a way of living that people from a more settled background could handle, but both of us understood the feeling of not belonging anywhere, and both of us felt that the surfaces on which most people lived were ephemeral and treacherous. Anything could happen, and when it did you were better off travelling light.

It was another couple of hours before I could get out of bed and set out for my brother's place. By this time the Sunday church-going crowd were on the way home or just taking a break, and all the way up to Corona on the bus, ladies dressed in white and clutching Bibles or hymn books kept getting on or off, talking in hushed voices.

By the time I got back to my brother's house I was in a serious Sunday mood. I had bought the *Times*, a huge bale of a newspaper, and I was already imagining myself stretched out on the sofa going slowly through each of the sections. I did get to the stretching-out part, but I had only just separated the advertising from the readable bits of the paper when the phone rang.

Evie.

'I found a name,' she said. 'It was written on a poster, as if she couldn't find paper. It had a time under it as well, like they made an appointment. I was just going to throw it away, but then I thought of you.' She paused. 'Well, not you really. That poor girl.'

'What is it?'

'Arnold Jackson.'

'Arnold Jackson? Who's he?'

'I don't know,' she said.

I thanked her, hung up and lay down on the sofa. I was about to pick up the paper again when I had an idea. I got up and went across the room to where I'd dumped the address book and, when I looked in it, there it was. Arnold Jackson, in spindly writing. Under it was a number and address in Brooklyn.

I dialled the number and got a recorded message which told

me that the number I had called was no longer valid. I slammed the receiver down in a temper. Then I sat down again and thought about it. I had intended going through the book and calling some of the numbers, but there was no guarantee that Mary would be known by anyone I reached. A lot of these could be numbers she'd intended to ring for a job or an apartment or people she'd met casually once. But if she'd written down an appointment with this guy somewhere else he must be important. If I couldn't reach him on the phone I'd have to go there.

Perhaps this was where it all started. Looking back, I took the decision casually. Spur of the moment on a Sunday afternoon when I had nothing better to do. But this was the final move that locked me into the chase. If I hadn't gone up to Brooklyn that day I might have given up and gone about my own business. Later on I'd have told Hector that I'd done my best. Instead, I headed out for Brooklyn with a sense of mild curiosity. *Take a look.*

I took the A, then discovered I was on the express to Rockaway and had to come back and find the local. All this seemed to take hours, getting on and off and winding my way through interminable tunnels. When I climbed out at Van Sieclen I felt released, blinking in the late afternoon sunshine and stumbling a little, like a long-term prisoner emerging into an unfamiliar world. Casting around to find my bearings I found myself in Miller Avenue, then I turned myself around and went back towards Atlantic. I'd been here, more than a dozen years before, but now, unlike most of the city, it looked cleaner and brighter than I remembered. Some of the apartment blocks were neat and newly built, and along one of the cross streets three men were working on a boat parked by the side of the house.

In a little while I went past a church. African Methodist. Next to the building a man was mowing the lawn with the deliberate care and concentration of someone performing an important and sacred task. He looked up as I approached. Short, thick, a smile of genial benevolence on his fleshy face. 'Afternoon, brother.'

I nodded and smiled, wondering whether he had spotted me as a stranger. On the opposite side, another church. A storefront this time. Apostolic Evangelist. Next to it a barber shop, with a blackboard advertising its services: 'JERI CURL. HIGH-TOP FADES.' After that yet another church. Christ God in Jesus. Growth industry. The mark of a desperate neighbourhood.

It wasn't the London suburbs, but it wasn't half as dilapidated as you might expect. If I hadn't known I probably wouldn't have guessed that this was the neighbourhood which had the highest yearly total of drug-related murders in the city.

I found the apartment block close by Atlantic Avenue. The place had suddenly changed as I turned the corner. Here, there were men lounging in front of the houses, and cars arriving, double parking for a moment, then zooming off. The building itself was several storeys high, grimy and crumbling. The entrance was a dark alleyway leading to a flight of stairs, which grew darker and darker the further up you went.

As I went in the smell hit me hard enough to make me hold my breath for a few seconds. Concentrate of subway tunnel. The remains of old cooking, garbage, sweat, pee. The smell added to the impression of claustrophobia, and as I reached the top of the stairs I hesitated, trying to picture Mary here.

On the landing above me, something stirred, and when I looked I could see a little group of people, two men and a woman, sitting on the floor. One of the men stood up and glared at me, while the others stayed where they were. No reaction I looked the other way, signalling that I hadn't seen anyone and didn't want to. Then I pushed open the swing door to the first floor. If the apartment's any further up I thought, I'm not going. As luck would have it, number nine was practically in front of me. I braced myself and rang the bell. Nothing. I could hear noises behind the door. Children. I rang again, keeping my finger on it.

'Who is it?'

A woman's voice. I took my finger off the bell. The

apartment had gone silent, and I guessed that someone was looking at me through the spyhole in the door. 'Arnold Jackson,' I shouted.

There was the sound of locks turning. One. Two. Then the door opened a crack and, just above the glint of the chain, part of a woman's face appeared. 'Are you a cop? Can I see some ID?'

'I'm not a policeman,' I said. 'I'm looking for my daughter. He's a friend of hers.'

She thought this over. I'd said my daughter to simplify things, and also to reassure her. Everyone could understand a dad looking for a runaway. 'He moved,' she said. 'But I don't know where he's gone.'

She was definitely from the English-speaking Caribbean, I thought now, but her accent was so overlaid with the American inflection and rhythms that it was hard to be certain which country she belonged to.

'There's no trouble,' I told her. 'I just want to see if he knows about my daughter. If you've got a phone number, that's all I want.'

'I told you, mister,' she started, then something happened to the bit of her face that was visible and her voice changed. 'Is it Mary? The girl from England?'

'Yes,' I said eagerly. 'You know her?'

She frowned, as if the experience had been disagreeable. 'She came here once, but he didn't want her coming here.'

I didn't blame him.

'He left soon after. He didn't say nothing. He didn't tell me where he was going.'

'Are you his mother?'

She frowned again, as if I'd said something offensive. 'No. He's my brother. And I don't know anything.'

'You sure?'

'Yes. I'm sure. You could try CUNY. The college down by the bridge. But I don't know if he's still going there.' Behind her in the apartment there was a screech and her face moved sharply. 'I got to go.'

I thanked her, and she slammed the door abruptly. I left, clattering down the stairs to the sidewalk. Outside on the street, the dark was seeping in, a kind of murky gloom spreading out from the buildings to stain the sky. I turned right, trying to retrace my route from the subway station. I went round one corner, then another, and in a moment I realized that I'd lost my way. I could hear singing, some kind of hymn, but somehow the churches I'd gone past before had disappeared. In the shadows of early evening it was like being in a completely different place. The side streets were quiet, and the absence of traffic made them feel abandoned, so that when, from time to time, a car crept slowly past me, it had a sinister, prowling air. On some of the blocks a little knot of men stood, talking in soft voices. But occasionally someone gave a shout, violent and obscene. 'Muthufucka. That ain't shit. Suck my dick.'

I wasn't apprehensive, although a couple of the stories I'd read in the newspapers about this area passed through my mind; and if I'd been in a different part of the city I might have been more wary. But this segment of Brooklyn had been settled by Caribbeans for two decades. I felt secure, but without thinking about it, my movements had fallen, automatically, into a pattern I'd learned years ago. Second nature. I was walking steadily, not fast, but as if I knew where I was going. Head straight. None of the looking around which might tell people I was a stranger.

I had just found my bearings when the strange thing began to happen. The junction of Jerome and Sutter Avenues had a familiar look, and at once I realized where I was. I had come the wrong way and I'd have to turn around and walk down the next block to get back to Van Sieclen. A few paces later I heard a sort of shuffle behind me, and suddenly it struck me that I'd been hearing it for a while. Another few paces and I was sure. They were wearing sneakers, but one of them walked with a stutter, a sort of hesitation, as if he couldn't quite pick up both feet in the same way.

I couldn't be mistaken, I thought, and the problem was that

I had been wandering around, backwards and forwards through the cross streets. It wasn't likely that anyone would have been following me by accident.

I crossed the road, glancing back as I did so. Two men. There was something oddly familiar about them, but their faces were concealed by the shadows, and they were bigger than I liked. I speeded up, turned the corner and, just as suddenly as I'd noticed them, they were gone. I stopped and looked around, the thought flashing through my mind that they might be silently creeping up on me. Nothing. Behind me only an empty stretch of sidewalk.

'Pathetic,' I muttered. Now they had gone I was downright embarrassed by the way I'd felt only a few seconds before. Paranoia. For a couple of minutes I'd been a boy again, walking home late at night in London, checking every shadow for an ambush, listening for the sound of scurrying feet.

'Pathetic,' I said again, shaking my head and laughing at myself. At that point I drew level with the corner, and someone came out from behind the wall, grabbed the front of my shirt, pulled me off balance, then hit me hard on the back of the neck.

Long afterwards I remembered being hit several times, but that night my first clear recollection was of lying on the sidewalk with hands pulling at me, going through my pockets. Above loomed two figures whom I took to be the two men who'd been following me. I tried to speak, but my first thought was that they might be about to kill me, and I kept quiet, marshalling my strength for a sudden move. If I rolled away fast, I thought, I might be able to get up and run. But even while I was beginning to flex my muscles in preparation, the men straightened up and walked away, and when I raised my aching body and looked around they had gone, disappearing swiftly and smoothly into the night.

I sat up, feeling myself all over and shaking my head clear. Then I stopped abruptly as a bolt of pain lanced through me. There was a lump at the back of my head and every part of my body hurt, but all my limbs seemed to be functioning, still in working order. I levered myself off the sidewalk and clung to the wall to stop myself falling over. I stood there for a little while, thinking furiously while I tried to quiet my nerves, and waited for the strength to come back to my faltering, rubber legs.

They hadn't taken much. There wasn't much to take, except for a ten-dollar bill, my little notebook and a couple of old letters I'd forgotten to remove from the pockets of my jacket. I smiled, thinking about the thieves' annoyance and puzzlement as they read through a letter reminding me that my NUJ subscription was overdue. Then I stopped smiling, because in that moment I got a flash which told me exactly where I had seen at least one of them before. He'd been the one who stood up as I climbed the stairs to Arnold's sister's place.

That put a whole new complexion on things. It was possible that they were just a couple of junkies who had followed me from the building, but junkies wouldn't have taken my letters and my notebook. On top of that I'd somehow picked up an impression of what they were like, and I was certain that their clothes and the way they carried themselves had nothing in common with the doped-out bums or rapacious kids who might have robbed a casual passer-by. Besides, I knew that I didn't look like someone who you'd mug casually. In this neighbourhood I'd be a former athlete, or an undercover cop maybe. Such people were usually safe, and that wasn't vanity. It was part of the knowledge I'd gained over the years about how things were.

I walked slowly out to the avenue which ran down the end of the block. On the right was a small shop. Behind the counter were a couple of Indians who could have been the brothers of the man who ran the shop on the corner of the street where I lived in London.

'Where's the nearest police station?' Perhaps it was his familiar look that made me use the English phrase, and I amended it immediately. 'The precinct house. The nearest one.'

He frowned as if he hadn't understood me. 'Precinct?'

'Yeah,' I said, raising my voice. 'Muthafuckas stole every-thing I got. Credit cards and shit.'

That should get through to him, I thought. But his face showed no concern at all. On the other hand he came out from behind the counter and directed me to Sutter Avenue, and told me to keep straight on once I got there.

It was a little further than I thought, and I kept looking round to check that the same men weren't on my trail, but I got there in one piece and in less than ten minutes. In the lobby was a big banner which said 'WELCOME', and when I walked in I was greeted by a receptionist, a tall pretty girl with a light brown skin and a vivacious smile. Lucia Hernandez, the badge pinned to her bosom said, and her forehead creased with concern while she listened to my story. Halfway through she stopped me. 'You must see the sergeant on duty,' she said.

The bosom heaved. She sighed importantly, smiled at me, wiggled her way out of the chair, and going over to the barrier behind her lifted it and waved me through.

'Sergeant Richards,' she called out, and pointed at me. The sergeant turned around and there was a slight battle in his face at the sight of me. He looked a nice young man, though, white, short brown hair, a thin intelligent face, and he gave me a polite smile. I'd expected some grizzled veteran down here in the precinct with the city's highest murder rate, and this youthful college boy in a uniform was something of a shock. I braced myself and began telling him what had happened. He took notes, looking at me with a sympathetic expression, and at the end he asked me if I wanted to make a complaint.

'If it doesn't mean waiting all night,' I said.

'All right, sir,' he said, still polite. He lifted the phone and spoke rapidly. Then he called out to Lucia. 'Please. Take this gentleman upstairs to robbery. Detective Boon. He'll explain the procedure to you.'

I followed Lucia's tight bottom and long legs up the stairs, but the mention of a complaint had started me thinking that maybe this wasn't such a good idea after all. The plan was to talk to a policeman, and under cover of telling them my story, find out whether they knew anything about Arnold. He was a local boy after all, but now I was wondering whether I'd bitten off more than I could chew.

'Are you a police officer?' I asked Lucia.

'Me?' She sounded surprised. 'No. But one day I hope to be.'

We came out into the first-floor corridor. The building looked like an institutional building anywhere. Concrete floors with some kind of tough matting covering them. Walls in a heavy-duty green and cream colour. A disinfectant smell.

Halfway down the corridor, a policeman, gun still swinging on his belt, approached and spoke to Lucia in Spanish. 'Who is he?'

Both sets of eyes flickered at me, to see whether I understood, but I kept my face straight.

'Some tourist,' Lucia replied, also in Spanish. 'I think he came up here to make a buy and they beat him and took his money. Now he's complaining.'

The policeman nodded straight-faced and muttered something about *sus cabales*. It was a while before I remembered it was the phrase for being off your head. By that time Lucia was pushing open the door marked 'ROBBERY'. She waved me in and Detective Boon got up and pointed to the chair opposite his desk. Like the sergeant he was younger than I'd have expected, in his twenties. A boy with a light brown skin, curly black hair, and a big black gun strapped to his waist. I avoided looking at it.

'Siddown, sir.'

All these characters seemed to have gone to some kind of charm school. I sat down and looked around. The room was a large open-plan office in the same colours as the corridor with notices up against the walls, but it was more or less empty except for a couple of men in shirtsleeves in one corner. I'd been expecting hustle and bustle, people in handcuffs, the way it was on TV.

'It's a slow day,' the detective said. He seemed to be apologizing.

For the third time I went through the recital. Boon nodded and scribbled while I talked. When I came to the end I saved him the trouble of asking. 'I didn't come here to buy drugs. I came to look for a guy who's a friend of a friend's daughter. He's named Arnold Jackson.' I told him about Hector, then gave him the address of the building. 'I don't want to make a complaint,' I said, 'because I can't identify the men. It happened too suddenly, and I don't have the time to hang about going to court and all the rest of it. They didn't get anything much, anyway. But you can help me by telling me if you know something about this kid Arnold Jackson.'

Boon closed his notebook and looked at me, without the charm this time. 'You don't want to make a complaint?'

I nodded. 'That's right. And I couldn't identify them anyway.'

'OK, Mr Dean. Take the first stairs on your right. That's the way out.'

'What about Arnold Jackson?' I asked him.

He gave me that straight look again. 'You want to report a missing person?'

'No. I don't know if he's missing.'

He sighed, frowned, looked around the room, then looked back at me. 'This is too weird, Mr Dean, and I'm too busy. If it helps you I've never heard of Arnold Jackson.'

He turned his chair away from me, opened a file on his desk and began looking at it. I hesitated for a moment, but he settled further into the chair and waved his open palm towards the door. I looked around. The two detectives in the corner were also hard at work at their desks, and no one was taking any notice.

'Well, thanks anyway,' I said.

Chapter 10

Bonny wasn't back in the apartment yet and the place had a quiet, empty feel about it. That was a relief. I'd found myself up yet another blind alley, taken a beating there, and I didn't want to talk about it. At least I would be alone for a while. I got out an open bottle of bourbon, kicked my shoes off, lay back on the sofa and switched on the TV. Then I remembered Sophie.

Her voice on the phone sounded tired and sleepy. I asked her about her day and she said she'd been to a few places, met a few people, taken a lot of photographs. She hadn't got back home till late in the evening, dozed off right away and I had woken her up. As soon as she put the phone down she was going to bed. Then she asked me about my day and I told her about the bashing.

'Are you all right?' Her voice was urgent and concerned.

'I'm OK,' I said. 'Bruised, battered, but OK.'

'Go lie down. I'm coming over.'

At first the thought pleased me. The worry in her voice had been swift and genuine. Then I thought about Bonny coming back. 'No. Don't do that. It's been a long day, and you'll have a long way to come.'

'Half an hour,' she said. 'Go lie down.'

'I'll be asleep by then.'

'Doesn't matter. Go on.'

She put the phone down before I could work out any more excuses. I looked at my watch. Eleven. Bonny probably wouldn't be back, and I could relax. I lay back on the sofa, and just then I heard the key turning in the lock of the outside door. A few seconds later Bonny came in, closely followed by Oscar. They seemed in high spirits and she flung her jacket carelessly at one of the armchairs while Oscar spun round and threw himself into the other.

'I didn't expect you so soon,' I said. I wasn't pleased to see Oscar, especially since Sophie was likely to arrive soon. I was now hoping that, if they had to meet, the two women would take to each other. But I had a feeling that Oscar's presence would complicate matters and make it an awkward occasion.

'I made it back early,' Bonny told me. Then she stopped and peered at me. 'What happened?' She came close, put out her hand and held my chin so she could turn my face around and take a good look. 'Wow,' she said.

Oscar peered over her shoulder. 'Wow.'

'It's not that bad, is it?'

In fact I felt a kind of tightness about the face, but there was no real pain, unless I moved suddenly.

'Go take a look in the mirror. No. No. Stay there. Don't move.'

I stayed where I was, and she disappeared in the direction of the bathroom. Oscar bent over me, his face creased up into a mask of concern. 'Hey. You're looking pretty good there, man.'

Bonny came back with a mirror, a bottle and some cotton wool. She began tilting my head and feeling it, gasping aloud when she found the lump on the back of my neck. Seeing my reflection looking back at me, I wasn't surprised. One eye had puffed up, the swelling almost closing it, and my lips were swollen and lopsided. I didn't have time to look at the minor bruises because after a moment Bonny took the mirror away and told me to lie back. Then she began dabbing at my face with the antiseptic.

'OK. What happened?'

I told her.

'Jesus. Place getting more like Bosnia every day. It's the dope.'

'I don't think so,' I told her. 'I think someone's pissed off with me asking questions about Mary, or about this kid Arnold Jackson.'

There was a moment of silence while they thought about this one.

'How come?' Oscar asked. His tone was carefully neutral.

'I don't know.'

Bonny stood up briskly. 'I'll take you in tomorrow and get a doctor to look at you,' she said. 'I don't like those lumps on your head.'

I couldn't resist the cue. 'I don't like them either.'

Oscar stood up. 'You should get some sleep. I'll take off.'

'OK. But don't hurry on my account. I'm not going to bed yet. I've got a friend coming.'

That got their attention, and I told them Sophie was on her way. I had a feeling that I ought to let Bonny know about that before Oscar left. If she was expecting a replay of the previous night's proceedings things would be even more awkward if Sophie turned up unexpectedly.

'Hmm hmm,' Oscar said in a cute voice. 'I think I'll just take off anyway.'

'Oh no you don't,' Bonny told him. 'I want you to stay and meet the beautiful Sof-eye-yah.' She stretched her arms out, did a shimmy and pouted at him. 'Maybe you'll like her.'

Her tone of voice made that sound an unlikely prospect. Oscar rolled his eyes at me.

'Shit,' Bonny said. She looked at her watch. 'It's nearly midnight. I'm going to make some coffee.' She walked off down to the kitchen where we could hear her banging about.

'Maybe I should go,' Oscar said.

'No way,' I told him. Now I'd got a taste of Bonny's reaction I wanted him to stay. In any case I wanted to tell him about Schumann. I picked up the address book from the table where I'd put it and showed him the entry which gave Schumann's address and telephone number. Then I told him about our conversation.

When I'd finished he sat back and looked at me without speaking, then he clenched his teeth and grimaced. 'Look,' he said. 'I don't know what's going on, but this' – he gestured – 'this thing might be over your head. Schumann has connections. OK? These are guys if I was swimming off St Thomas and I saw them behind me I'd jump out the water and check that I still had all my limbs. You know what I'm saying?'

'You're saying he's corrupt.'

Oscar laughed abruptly as if I'd said something funny. 'This is public service, man. One way or the other everybody's corrupt. What matters is what you're doing and who you're doing it with.'

'So what are you saying?'

'I'm saying this is a good guy to stay away from.' He made a gesture, forefinger extended in warning. Then he must have seen my scepticism. 'Tell you something,' he said. 'The way things work. I worked on a site the year I graduated, while I waited for things to happen. New Federal Building. I worked for the Supervisor. Gofer this, gofer that. One of my jobs was checking out the yard. You know: deliveries, trucks and stuff coming in. So these guys would be driving up from California or Florida, far away, with all this stuff, building materials, machines, everything got hauled in. The foreman of the yard was black. Big guy, built like a truck himself. And he met every truck as it came. Stuck his hand out. Documents. Most of the drivers knew exactly what to do, but sometimes you'd get one guy, he'd say like, what documents? Union book. And he'd hand over the book, and the black guy would look at it, and he'd say, this book ain't right. So if the guy was stupid he'd start arguing maybe, and the foreman would say in a kind of bored voice, turn this fucking rig around and get outta here. And that would be it. But like most of the time they'd catch on or they'd know and there'd be a few bills stuck in the middle of the book. And if it wasn't enough he'd say like, this book still ain't right. You know? He did that every day with every vehicle that came in. A regular industry. This foreman, he's black, but he's connected. Like he sees me standing there watching and he doesn't turn a hair. It doesn't matter and he knows it doesn't matter what I see or what I say. All right. I went up to the supervisor when I was sure what they were doing, and he was like, very efficient, big reputation, cool guy, he's in line to run one of the City Commissioner's offices now. Heavy hitter. And – get this – incorruptible. OK? Listen, I say, what I found out. So I tell him about all this, and he looks at me deadpan bored. And he says, ahuh. Taking care of business, huh? He's a good foreman, he says. Then he changes the subject and that was it.'

'What's the point?'

'The point is, that's how it works.'

The doorbell rang before I could reply, and I got up and went to let Sophie in. She looked at my face and touched it cautiously with one finger. Then she asked me how I felt, her eyes searching my response. I said I was OK and we went in.

Bonny was already handing round coffee and we sat up on the sofa drinking it as if we were visiting relations, which was, I guess, exactly what we were doing. Suddenly Bonny had the air of a hostess, her manner animated and a little patronizing. Sophie in contrast was subdued, her face pale and tense. Tonight she looked different again. Out on the street, moving around the Bronx, I could see Africa in her movements, in the shape of her face, the curl of her hair. Sitting here in the apartment, opposite Bonny and Oscar, she had the exotic look of a white person, her skin flushing red under her tan.

I don't know what Bonny had expected, but I could tell that the way Sophie looked had set her nerves on edge.

My face was the immediate subject, but in a couple of minutes Oscar asked Sophie about her photographs. She talked patiently about it. She'd got some good photos in the city, she said, but she wouldn't be able to tell quite how well it had turned out until she got back to England and saw all the prints as a whole. Oscar told her that after she'd finished she ought to check out some Asian women, and maybe do something with them. Nobody noticed them much, he said, the way they did Latin American women. Sophie nodded politely.

'She's heard this before,' I told him. 'Everyone's always got their own ideas for a new subject.'

'Ah,' Oscar said. 'Big mouth.'

'It's helpful,' Sophie said quickly. 'It sparks off things in my mind.'

I kept my face straight. Normally she hated the way some people would skate over what she was doing and then begin suggesting subjects in which she had no interest.

Bonny was off on another tack. 'You're from Argentina, right?'

Sophie nodded. 'Yes.'

'How come you end up in England? I thought you folks fought a war.' There was a strident and aggressive undertone to her voice I hadn't heard before, and she stared at Sophie without smiling.

Sophie looked back at her calmly and explained, her accent suddenly more pronounced. 'I had to make decisions,' she said. 'I'm British, but sometimes, yes, I want to go back.'

'Hey,' Oscar said. 'That's tough. I've been in Panama. You been in Panama? That's wild.' He began talking about Panama and the politics of reconstruction after the war. Now the poor people in the poorest countries in Latin America, he said, had discovered the market for drugs in the USA, there was nothing that would stop the trade, short of taking them over and offering them a standard of living equal to our own.

'Strange thing,' I said. 'All of us or our parents were born down there, and we live somewhere else. We can travel all over and feel at ease in a lot of places – or maybe we can feel uneasy in a lot of different places – but, anyway, it's not impossible. We're not confined to one country. Sometimes I feel privileged compared to most people, like they're mentally stuck in one place, can't share other people's lives.'

'That's miserable,' Bonny said sullenly. 'That's the two of

you. I know that my parents come from somewhere else but this is where I live. I don't want to drift backwards and forwards. That's a punishment, man. The Flying Dutchman. Wandering the earth for eternity. You crazy?'

'It's late,' Sophie said abruptly. 'I've got to go.'

She sounded calm and friendly but I got the feeling that underneath her polite manner she was seething with rage. She got up and said goodbye. Bonny said it had been nice to meet her. Oscar told her he would like to look at her photographs. If she needed any help, he said, he would be glad to do what he could. He told her where he worked and said, drop in any time. Sophie said all the right things, turned and left. I followed her out, but when we reached the door she didn't hesitate, instead she opened it quickly with a twist of her wrist and stepped straight out, down the steps and on to the sidewalk, heading for her car. I went after her, and caught up with her as she put her key in the lock.

'Hey. I've been beaten up once already today.'

She turned and leaned on the car. She breathed out loudly, then she bowed her head. I put my arm round her shoulders and hugged her. She didn't cuddle up to me, but she didn't move away.

'I hated that,' she said.

'I'm sorry.'

'What for? It was the way I expected. The guy was all right, but your cousin didn't like me at all. Hostile.'

My fault, Sophie. I wondered what to tell her, or whether to tell her anything about Bonny. This wasn't the right time, but a right time might never arrive.

'Get in the car,' Sophie said.

We got in. Maybe, I thought, if we were going to talk, this would be a chance to get everything out into the open.

'I think someone's watching you,' Sophie said. 'Across the road up ahead. Two guys in a car. They were there when I came, over an hour ago. They're still there.'

'I'm the one who's supposed to be paranoiac,' I said. 'If they're watching anyone it could be someone else.'

Sophie gave me a look in which patience and irritation were mingled. Then I remembered. She had lived in Buenos Aires through the disappearances, and when I'd heard her talking with other South American exiles such matters always came up. Disappearances, torture, being followed. It could well be paranoia, but this was something she knew about.

'OK. What makes you think that's what they're doing?'

'A feeling,' she said. She leaned forward and switched the engine on. 'Let's find out.'

We rolled slowly down the road towards the car she'd pointed to. A dark grey Ford. I caught a glimpse of the men in it, both black, but I was looking straight ahead and that was all I could tell as we went past.

She crossed into the next block at the same deliberate speed, and we were halfway along it when she motioned with her head at the driving mirror. 'Take a look.' There were headlights behind us. 'OK,' Sophie said. 'We'll circle round a bit.'

She was calm, a little smile on her lips. For a moment I couldn't believe it but it was obvious that she was enjoying this.

'You're enjoying this,' I said, and she turned to me, frowning with surprise.

'How could I? If these guys are following it's not a joke. Don't say such stupid things.'

I didn't believe her, but I shut up. She looked at me again, still frowning, then she turned her attention back to the road, spun the wheel and speeded up into Flushing Main Road. A little way up she stopped in front of a bar. The Ford slid past and stopped half a block in front of us.

'Go buy something,' she said. 'Cigarettes, anything.'

'Why? We know they're following us.'

'We know, but they don't know yet. If we just go back they'll know that this little trip was just for the purpose of finding out. You know what's going on. If they think you haven't noticed you'll have an advantage.'

I agreed, but I couldn't think what good the advantage

would do me. I didn't even know what game we were playing. But I did what she said.

We drove back in silence, eyes on the rear-view mirror. The car stayed behind us all the way.

'What are you going to do?' Sophie asked me.

'I don't know,' I said. 'Tonight I'm going to sleep, then tomorrow I'll try and find out who they are.'

'How?'

I shrugged. All this had started since I spoke to Ben Schumann. Put it together with Oscar's hints and it had to be something to do with him. But why? If I'd been in London, I'd simply have gone up to the men, asked them, and tried to figure out something from their responses. But I had no idea what would happen if I did. I had to be cautious.

'Let's talk tomorrow,' I told Sophie. 'I'll call you first thing.'

She nodded, leaned over to kiss me on the cheek as I got out, and then took off. I watched her tail lights turn the corner. The Ford stayed where it was. Ahuh.

Back in the apartment Oscar had disappeared while I was out. As I sat down on the sofa, Bonny came out of the bedroom and walked over to me. She was wearing a T-shirt which barely covered the top of her long bare thighs. 'Hi. I thought you weren't coming back,' she said.

Every inch of my body seemed to be aching and if I moved my head suddenly it felt as if it were about to fall off. As I'd sat down on the sofa I'd been absorbed in the problem of the mystery men who were following me. Now I realized that I couldn't get up and if I tried I would probably fall down. I told her about the men outside and she went to the window and looked out.

'You can't see them from here,' I told her. 'Anyway, there's nothing I want to do about it tonight.'

'Come on,' she said. 'Come into the bedroom and I'll rub some stuff on you.'

I knew where that would lead. Sophie crossed my mind, and so did the memory of Bonny's hostility towards her. 'I'm too tired,' I said. 'I'll just lie here and pass out.'

She tugged my shoes off and helped me get out of the rest of my clothes. Then I lay back and she spread a blanket over me and turned the light off. We hadn't talked about Sophie, but I supposed that we would sooner or later. For the moment I couldn't think what I wanted to say, so I put it out of my mind and let the darkness take me.

Chapter 11

Bonny woke me the next morning and asked me if I was feeling better. I said I was. I felt terrible but my headache was gone and I turned down her offer to come into the hospital and get myself checked over. She gave me a glass of orange juice and some aspirin, laid her hand on my forehead, and said she'd ring later to see how I was. Then she left and I went back to sleep.

The phone woke me again when it rang. Sophie. She asked me how I was and I said OK. Then she asked whether the two men in the Ford were still there. I said I didn't know. I hadn't looked. Then she asked me whether I'd thought about who they might be and I told her I thought it was to do with Ben Schumann and whatever reaction I was stirring up by going round asking about Mary.

She was silent for a moment, then: 'I've had an idea.'

'What's that?'

'Are you still trying to find the boy Arnold?'

Here it comes, I thought. 'He's the firmest connection I've got to her so far.'

'How are you going to do that?'

I held on to my patience. She'd probably get to the point sooner or later. 'I think I'll go up to CUNY and ask around. If he's there he'll turn up sooner or later.'

'Suppose he isn't there. If he's in any kind of trouble he won't turn up.'

'Well, I'd ask around. Come on.'

'All right. But suppose no one tells you anything.' She sounded triumphant.

'In that case I won't know what to do,' I said.

'Let me do it.'

I knew she was going to say that.

'I knew you were going to say that,' I told her. 'If we were in London you know it would be no problem, but this could be dangerous, and I don't see how you could find out anything I couldn't.'

'Well, I knew that *you* were going to say *that*. But you're wrong. Once I get permission to take photographs around the place I can talk to anyone. I'm a woman, and I speak Spanish. It's Tribeca, and that's about as safe as anywhere. Which one of us would you bet on?'

She was right. And she could handle herself well in difficult circumstances. The trouble was that I had no idea what was going on and she might end up getting herself hurt and I couldn't live with that. 'Let me think about it,' I said.

'No. Don't think about it. That means you want to say no but you can't think of a good reason. Just say yes. You can't do much today. You should stay in bed.'

'What about your photos? You've got a deadline.'

'I'm about finished. Besides, this might give me another story. If I go there today I can see how it goes.'

I understood her eagerness. We lived in different places, had distinct lives. We shared very little and that was partly what made our relationship work. But whenever there was half a chance to get involved in what I was doing she grabbed it with both hands. Except for sex, or by accident, she'd told me once, those were the only times she felt really close to me, something more than a good friend, and those were the only times she could see into the future, beyond this phase, and see us together.

'OK,' I said. 'But be careful.' I told her about meeting Jean at the party, and suggested she saw her first. Then she said she'd ring me later and hung up. As I put the phone back on the floor I could imagine her bustling round, getting ready, loading the camera, zipping up the bag she carried, and I suddenly wanted to call her back and stop her. She'd lived in places where bodies were thrown into the street like fish on to a beach, and where surveillance by secret enemies was commonplace. It had given her an indifference to danger which I envied, but it also seemed to be leading her to underestimate what might happen in a place like this.

The phone rang again, and as I picked it up I was hoping that it would be Sophie, saying that something else had come up, or she'd changed her mind.

'Mr Dean?'

It was a teenage girl's voice. American, a bit hesitant, as if she wasn't sure what reception she'd get.

'Yeah. Who is it?'

'Nita.'

It took me a moment, then I remembered. This was Rupert and Carmen's daughter. Her voice gave me a strange odd feeling of dislocation, though. When I thought of her mother, I thought of our village and the grocery in the market square. A half-open sack of rice, channa, stacks of flaking saltfish. There was something odd about hearing this American voice coming from the mouth of Mr Perez's granddaughter.

'I couldn't tell you,' she said ''Cause of my mother. If she knew I knew anything about it – boy.'

'Hold on. What do you know?'

'I don't know anything really. But I'm worried about Mary. It's been weeks since I saw her and she didn't tell me she'd be away or anything. You know?'

'No. I don't know. I didn't even know you'd been in touch with Mary.'

'Oh yeah,' she said. 'She's my cousin. She's almost like my sister. But someone should do something.'

'Wait a minute. Slow down, and tell me this from the beginning, Nita. Do you know where she is?'

'No. That's why I'm calling you.' Her voice expressed the sort of weary patience any teenager had to summon up for dealing with an old fool twice her age.

'OK. What are you trying to tell me?'

'Oh. I can't now. I gotta go back to school. I'll call later. No, I'll meet you. I only just found your number. No way I could ask my dad what it was. Where are you staying? I'll come there if it's in Queens.'

'It might be easier on the phone.' I wasn't sure I wanted a tête-à-tête with Rupert's sixteen-year-old daughter.

'I can't call from home. And I do not want to stand in the street doing this.' I could imagine her rolling her eyes.

'All right,' I said. Then I thought about the men in the Ford. 'No. Don't come here. Meet me in Jamaica.' I gave her the address of Alvin's store.

'I know it.'

'Meet me there between four and five.'

The phone went dead abruptly, and I wondered whether she'd heard the time, but there was no way to check and I guessed that she'd go there after school which would be about right.

I lay back and thought about what I had. Up to now I'd had the feeling that at any moment I'd run into Mary or that someone would tell me her new address and I'd be able to go there and tell her about Hector, and then get on with my own business. But now I knew that had been just a dream. Schumann or someone else had men following me. That could only be to do with Mary, and, thinking about it, I was certain that the assault of the previous night was tied in somehow. I'd lived in big cities most of my life, worked amid chaotic circumstances and dangerous characters, but since I'd been a boy in London I'd never been attacked on the street. Moving around safely was part of my stock in trade, a tool of my work as a journalist, and I couldn't believe that the attack on me had been random or casual.

So the fact that I was asking about Mary mattered a lot to someone, and that could only be because she was in some kind of trouble. Nita's phone call confirmed that. For the moment I avoided thinking about what kind of trouble it could be. Things were bad enough.

I must have drifted off again, because when I woke the sun was slanting across the floor. Afternoon. I grabbed at the clock and saw that I had just enough time to get down to Jamaica.

The bus was crowded with the usual assortment of schoolkids going home. Behind me two girls were talking about a classmate with a violent boyfriend.

'The last time, I told her, you have to leave this guy. You have to. And the worst of it is she expects you to keep quiet about it and talk to this creep like he's normal.'

'I don't understand,' the other girl said. 'Why does she do it?'

'Love. That's what she says. She loves him.'

I sneaked a look. Tall, beautiful girls, about seventeen, light brown skins, curly brown hair, so much alike in their style and manner that they could have been sisters, but one of them had a broad freckly face and more African features. For kids just out of school they had a coolness and elegance which would have surprised me, if it wasn't for the fact that I could see variants on the same style all over the bus. They could have been schoolgirls or models or hookers. My own schooldays had been different, and these girls looked nothing like the scruffy articles I saw mooning around at my son's school. They're just kids, I reminded myself. But it was hard to imagine what that meant in this place.

Alvin was standing in a relaxed pose at one of the counters drinking coffee, and he greeted me with a handshake and gave me a cup. 'So wha' go on?' I told him about Nita coming and he raised his eyebrows. 'Be careful,' he said. 'These girl children not like we used to be, you know.'

The remark irritated me, then I remembered Alvin and I had lived in different worlds. Back home girls often became mothers at fourteen or fifteen. In the countryside they got married even younger to men two or three times their age. For some men, a pretty sixteen-year-old would be fair game. But it gave me a shock that Alvin thought I might be up to something with Rupert's schoolgirl daughter.

'Don't talk balls,' I said. 'The child wants to talk to me. I'm a big man, you know. We're too old for that shit.'

He gave me a sceptical look. 'Hmm. All right. You can talk to her behind here.'

He indicated the curtained doorway at the back of the shop. It led, I knew, to a workshop where a couple of his cousins sat sewing. They made up curtains, altered and repaired dresses, the sort of handiwork which was essential in the kind of make-and-mend society we came from. Here in the city such skills were hard to come by. Everything you bought was manufactured at a distance, and it was mostly easier to buy a new thing than to fix one you already had.

'What happened to your face?' Alvin asked.

I was just about to tell him when Nita came in the front of the shop. 'Long story,' I told him. 'Tell you later.'

Nita looked flushed and harassed, as if she had been hurrying. With Carmen modelling her parenting on a strict Caribbean pattern, I guessed that if Nita was late she'd have to account for where she'd been.

I went to meet her, shook hands and led her quickly through the shop, while Alvin made himself ostentatiously busy. I saw his son, Moti, staring, but Alvin, frowning, called him over and sent him to do something.

In the back room one of the cousins was sewing busily under the naked light bulb, but she didn't lift her head when we came in. Over in the corner there was another table, covered with cloth and skeins of wool, and we went over and sat there.

'I got a bit confused on the phone,' I said before she could get started. 'I'd like to know about Mary. From the beginning.'

She licked her lips nervously and settled herself. Close up I could see she was Carmen's daughter. She'd inherited her pale skin, her snapping black eyes, and her pert manner. But Carmen was a short lumpy woman, and only her vivacity made her attractive. This girl had long legs, and sharply drawn well-proportioned features under a mass of curly black hair which seemed to shine and glow even in the gloom of Alvin's storeroom.

'Mary was OK,' she said. 'I'd only seen photographs of her before, but when she came we were like sisters. You know? But you know my mother. She thinks life is still like it was back home.'

Back home. I was willing to bet Nita had never been there. Or if she had it would only have been for a couple of weeks. I wondered what Carmen would have thought if she'd heard the tone of resentment with which Nita pronounced the word mother. Maybe she wouldn't have picked it up. My son flashed through my mind. How would he talk about me?

'Well, when my mother threw her out and she went to live in Manhattan I saw her a few times. I went up there and we went to a few places.'

'What sort of places?'

She shrugged. 'Nowhere special. Restaurants. Tribeca. The Village. She knew some people around there. We just talked.'

It was the nature of the age. Two confused teenagers pouring out their feelings to each other. But I wasn't altogether surprised that Carmen had been worried.

'Then she left that place. The people were nice but they were sort of old. You know. It was like they were driving her crazy. So after a while she got this great apartment in Tribeca. I helped her fix it up.'

'Wait a minute – how did she do that? She didn't have any money, did she?'

Nita's eyes slid away from mine. She looked down, then up again, as if she was deciding how much to tell me. 'This guy she met. He was the old couple's son. He was really nice to her. It was his apartment. He didn't live there,' she added hastily. 'He just let her have it.'

'Have you got the address?'

She gave it to me and I wrote it down. Tribeca again. A few blocks from Chambers Street.

'She's not there,' she said. 'She hasn't been there for weeks. The phone doesn't answer or anything.'

'OK. She might have just gone away for a bit and not told you.'

She was indignant. 'She wouldn't do that. Anyway all her stuff is still in the apartment. Her clothes. Her passport and everything. She wouldn't go and leave them, would she?' She gave me a stricken look, as if she was hoping I'd tell her it was all right after all, but I couldn't.

'How do you know all this?'

'I've got keys. Not all of them. There're two locks, but when I was coming and she wouldn't be gone very long, she left the outside lock open. I had the key so I could get in any time I wanted, even if she wasn't there. She knew what it was like at home, and she knew I might want to get away somewhere by myself sometimes. When she wanted to be private she'd tell me. If she was going to be away or anything she'd have called me.'

There was a self-conscious dignity about the way she related some of this, as if she wanted to impress on me that she was grown up, and these stratagems were only due to the feeble-minded silliness of people like her parents.

'This man. The one who owned the apartment. Did you ever meet him?'

'No. She said she didn't want me to meet him. I don't know why. He came to see her sometimes, I think. But I don't know what he looks like.'

I nodded slowly. If everything she said was right, then Mary had to be in trouble.

'Do you think she's all right?' Nita asked me. She was watching my expression anxiously.

I put on my most reassuring voice. 'I'm sure there's a simple explanation. Something probably came up unexpectedly, and she went off on impulse. Like she might have got a job out of town for a couple of weeks and had to go off in a hurry, something like that. I'm sure it will be OK.'

She probably didn't believe me, but she was in a mood to

clutch at straws. 'I've got to go,' she said. 'But if anything happens, please, please, please call. If you tell my mom or my dad I'll know pretty soon. OK?'

'Can I borrow the key?'

'There's nothing there.'

'Still, it might help if I can take a look, and the way things are you probably shouldn't go there till you hear from Mary.'

She thought this over, then took a key ring from her bag, detached one of them and gave it to me with a slowness that signalled her reluctance. As I put it in my pocket she got up and acknowledged my thanks with a gesture, then she hurried out. I stayed where I was, thinking over what she'd told me.

Alvin came in as soon as she'd gone, his nose twitching for the news. I told him what she'd had to say, then I went over the events of the last few days. When I was finished he leaned back in his chair. 'Bad news, man. This is got to be drugs.'

'It could be anything, Alvin.'

He shook his head as if I was being impossibly naïve. 'In this city, boy, everything is drugs. You know how I mean. Think about it. A foreign girl comes here. A few months later she's set up in a fancy apartment. Come on. What does that sound like to you?'

'I don't know.'

'All right,' Alvin said. 'You say that. What I'm telling you that when you get down to the long and short of it, you'll find it's drugs. And don't say I didn't tell you. I warned you long time. Look at your face. Once you doing something those guys don't like and they know where you live and they can follow all your movements, you dead, boy. Remember that.'

105

Chapter 12

'There's a spot,' I told Sophie. 'You can park there.'

She gave me an impatient look. 'No. We should park out of sight. We need to be careful. Anything might happen.'

I couldn't argue with that and she kept on moving round the corner and down to the next block. Then she parked next to the kerb and we got out. At last. She was wearing black: black jeans, a black sweater, black sneakers, black gloves, and she had an air of suppressed excitement which was unusual for her, but which was beginning to affect me.

'You don't think you're going over the top?' I asked her.

For a moment I thought she was going to say something irritable, then she grinned. 'I don't know what you mean.'

'Calm down,' I said. 'We're not burglars. We've got a key, and we're only going to look and see what's up there. OK?'

She looked past me, frowning. 'What happens if someone comes?'

'We just tell them that we're friends of Mary's.'

She gave me one of her quizzical looks and in the circumstances I could see the problems of that explanation right away.

'OK,' I said. I reached into the back seat and unrolled the package I'd brought with me. In it were two spanners I'd pulled out of a closet in the apartment. They were heavy, about a foot long and shaped like pieces of pipe. I'd felt melodramatic when I got them out, but now, standing in the empty street, it didn't seem such a silly idea after all. I gave one of them to Sophie, and she tucked it down her waistband at the back. 'Does that make you any happier?'

'A lot,' she said. 'And don't sound so superior. You brought them.'

I didn't have a snappy comeback for that one. In fact I wasn't so sure that her instincts were wrong. When I'd asked Nita for the key it had seemed a good idea to get into Mary's apartment and see for myself. Later on I'd sat in my brother's place for a couple of hours waiting for Bonny to get home from work. But round about nine when she hadn't shown up I'd rung Sophie. To my surprise she'd agreed that it was a good idea, and it was only when she insisted on coming along that I began to have second thoughts.

The Ford wasn't in its usual spot, but I didn't want to take any chances on anyone following me to Sophie's building, so I got on the 7 in the subway, changed over to the F a few stops down, then got back over to the E in Manhattan. By then I was sure no one was behind me. To make certain I walked round the block a couple of times before going up to Sophie's apartment.

The address Nita had given me was in a low-rise block. From here you could see the bulk of City Hall not far away and smell the river. The entrance was barred by a pair of big frosted glass doors. Locked.

'Have you got the key?' Sophie asked.

'No. The key I've got is for the apartment upstairs.'

'Oh.' Her disappointment was almost tangible.

'Don't worry,' I told her. 'Watch this.'

I leaned over to the entry-phone grille, rang a bell near the middle and when a man's voice answered I put on my most toffee-nosed English accent. 'Sorry to disturb you, but I'm staying on the floor above and I've forgotten my keys. Would you mind letting me in?'

There was a slight pause. Then: 'Come again?' the man's voice said.

107

I enunciated carefully and loudly. 'Look, I'm a visitor to the city. From London. I'm staying upstairs and I've forgotten my keys. Would you mind pressing the buzzer and letting me in?'

Another slight pause. 'Where'd you say you were from?'

'London, England.'

The buzzer sounded and Sophie pushed the door open and blew me a kiss. 'Magic.'

One of the elevators was standing open and we took it up the floor where the apartment was.

'Suppose,' Sophie whispered as we got out, 'the key doesn't work?'

I shrugged. 'We think again.'

But we didn't have to. The key turned easily in the lock and the door yawned open quietly.

The apartment was in darkness and I had to search around for the lights, but as I was patting the wall next to me I touched the switch by accident and they came on.

We were standing in a sort of lobby area from which three steps led down into a huge living room. It was a lot smaller than a football pitch, but that was the comparison which immediately came to mind. The apartment ran the entire width of the building, and, over to the left, a corridor led to the other rooms. The whole thing was furnished in a weird mixture of period reproduction and post modern artiness.

'Ay yi yi yi yi,' Sophie said. 'Unbelievable.'

She walked across the floor to look at a painting which dominated the wall near us. It was a view of a wagon train winding its way across the prairie. The foreground was full of detail: an abandoned piano; a broken wagon wheel; the faces of the settlers fixed on the far horizon, full of strength and optimism. In the background was a cactus, and the white scattered bones of cattle. On the other side was a line of pictures, all of them showing Supergirl in different stages of flight. The artist had faithfully repeated the comic-book style, but her breasts and buttocks were slightly exaggerated, so that the whole thing had a salacious pornographic feel to it.

Those were the things which grabbed our attention right

away, but the walls were lined with other pieces which had the same expensive look of collectors' items, with the same extreme contrast in taste and style.

Sophie walked down the steps and sat on a love seat covered in red velvet and put her feet up on the chair opposite, which was in the shape of a nude woman sitting with her knees drawn up, all in black leather. 'How did your little girl find herself here?' she said.

I guessed that the question was rhetorical and I didn't answer. Instead I headed for the corridor and the first door I could see. Sophie came behind me, looking around and uttering the occasional gasp of amazement.

The bedroom behind the door was less of a surprise. White carpet, dark Colonial wood furnishings, white satin bed, big enough for five or maybe six at a pinch. In one corner a big TV set and a VCR, with a cabinet of neatly stacked cassettes. I went over to a chest of drawers, but before I could open it Sophie nudged me from behind. I looked round and she held up her gloved hands. 'Fingerprints.'

I laughed at her, but she didn't move, so I stood aside and let her pull it open. Nothing. The same all the way down. The drawers were all empty.

There wasn't much in the walk-in closets either, except for a couple of men's suits, a white satin robe and a small stack of new shirts on a shelf.

The next room along looked like a rich man's study out of a thirties musical. A big desk, three brown leather armchairs, and a huge coloured globe of the world which lit up with tiny lights showing the major capitals. Two walls were covered with bookshelves, the books mostly hardback editions of modern novels. They looked clean and new, entire sets of each author's work standing in line.

Sophie snapped the globe on and off and the sound grated on my nerves. 'Don't do that,' I said. 'Let's get this over with.'

She looked at me, eyebrows raised in surprise. I'd surprised myself. Something about the apartment, the absolute quiet, the wealth and strangeness of the furnishings gave me the eerie sense of being in a deserted museum stocked by someone who was mad as a hatter. I couldn't picture Mary here, and I couldn't imagine why the person who owned it would lend it to her.

The next room gave us a kind of answer. It was the smallest one so far, and it looked like the sort of room you'd find in an ordinary suburban house where an ordinary teenager lived. A few posters: Save the Whales, New Jack City, Malcolm X. A cut-out newspaper photo of Spike Lee. Michael Jackson. A medium-sized divan bed with a multi-coloured quilt. On the dressing table an assortment of bottles and jars. Sophie opened the closet to reveal a row of jeans, sweaters and shirts, a few dresses. Nothing remarkable.

'Who's this?' Sophie said.

She was pointing to a picture of Hector, sitting at a table in his house. Behind him you could see the garden through the glass doors at the back. It had been taken some time ago, before he fell ill, and he had that careless lopsided smile that drew people to him. Next to it, on the table beside the bed, was a big photograph of a pretty girl, who I guessed was Mary, holding hands with a young black man. They were both smiling broadly into the camera, a good-looking couple who gave off an aura of charm and youthful optimism. Looking closer I thought I could see a resemblance to the child I remembered.

'The man in that one is Hector. Her father. I think that's her in the other picture.'

'Ah. So this is her room. She was here.'

I nodded abstractedly and, forgetting about fingerprints, took the photo out of its frame and slipped it into my pocket.

'You know what I think?' Sophie said. 'This is the maid's room. She must have been looking after this place. Then maybe she found another place. Somewhere she liked better.'

I had come to the same conclusion. It made sense. Except for the other things which had been happening, Schumann's reaction, the men following me, Nita's visit. There had to be more to it.

'You know it could all be about something else,' Sophie said. She was reading my mind again. 'This is' — she waved her hand around — 'Aladdin's Cave. Smuggling, taxes, robbery.'

The possibility had crossed my mind, and it had also crossed my mind that if that was the way it was we ought to get out quick. There was nothing to indicate that anyone might turn up, but I was beginning to feel like Jack, waiting in the Giant's cave and listening for the sound of those mighty footsteps.

Sophie had pulled open a couple of drawers and now she called out to me. 'Look at this.'

It was the passport Nita had talked about. It was one of the little red Euro books they'd started issuing a couple of years ago, and the photograph showed the same girl as the one in the big picture with the smiling boy. There was no mistake. I took it out and put it in my pocket next to the picture.

'Let's go,' I said.

'Wait a minute,' she said. She had gone back into her bustling mood. Now she was over at the closet again, handling the clothes. 'You know something,' she said. 'These are expensive dresses. All designer stuff. Any one of these would pay a maid's salary for a month.'

'Let's think about it later,' I told her. 'I want to get out of here.'

I led the way out. Then, in the corridor, a memory which had been niggling away at the back of my mind surfaced, and I turned off into the master bedroom.

'There's nothing here,' Sophie said.

I pointed to the VCR. Most of the tapes had manufactured labels with the names of movies but there were a few at the bottom of the stack which were blank. I pulled out one of them, stuck it in the machine, and turned it on.

It was the picture of Hector that had done it, because when I saw it I'd started to ask myself what he would think about it all, and thinking with a father's fears I'd started figuring out how a girl like Mary would find herself in an apartment like

111

this with some of the priciest dresses I'd ever seen hanging in the closet. After that instinct took over, and drew me to the tapes.

When the machine clicked on and started running, I was expecting what I saw. It was a good clear picture, taken, I imagined, with one of the new Japanese minicams. It hadn't been edited, so it was obvious that this was a home movie. The camera waved around a little then focused on the bed we were sitting on. Mary came into view, sat down on the edge, picked up a book and began to read. 'Go get her, boys,' a voice said.

Three naked, middle-aged white men came into the frame. One of them had grey hair and a dark moustache which gave him a dignified intellectual look, and I recognized him with a spurt of anger. Ben Schumann. Another one had a bald patch with a sandy fringe like a monk's tonsure. The third man was clean shaven with a full head of black hair and hair all over his chest, shoulders and back. Without his clothes he had a shambling apelike appearance. Bizarrely, they were all wearing condoms. Mary put down the book and staged an attempt at flight. Immediately the men grabbed her and wrestled her to the bed. 'Let me go,' she said repeatedly, her Gloucester accent sounding incongruous and exotic in this setting. 'Bitch,' one of the men said over and over, 'fucking bitch.' The screen went black and when the picture came back a couple of seconds later the four of them were on the bed, Mary sandwiched in between two of the men who were thrusting slowly into her, the other kneeling in front to push his penis into her mouth. The sounds of grunting and a muffled moaning filled the room.

'Turn it off,' Sophie said. She was looking at the wall, her face set and hard.

I turned it off.

'Oh shit,' she said. 'Shit, I should have guessed.'

I pressed the 'EJECT', slid the cassette out and put it in my pocket.

'What are you doing?' Sophie asked suspiciously.

I was about to reply when we heard the sound outside. I motioned at Sophie to shut up, and we listened. Everything was silent, but something had changed. It was impossible to tell what it was, but it was as if, while our attention had been absorbed by the video, the house had woken up and was holding its breath.

'Let's go,' I whispered to Sophie. 'Slow and careful, eh?'

We got up and began moving towards the door and we were only a few yards away from it when a black man moved into sight and stood solidly in front of us. As we backed away another black man moved in behind him.

'You an intruder, asshole,' the first man said, grinning. 'You just keep coming.'

I recognized them then, although up to that point I wouldn't have been able to describe them. This was the pair who'd beaten me up in Brooklyn.

'Hello,' I said genially. If I played it stupid I might at least puzzle them for a bit. I turned to Sophie as if this was a sociable occasion and I was about to introduce them. 'These are the men who beat me up last night. They are dangerous.' Then I switched into Spanish and said the next bit as quickly as I could, struggling for the words. 'I'll go back to the window. You get round them and run for the door.'

'Hey,' the man said. 'Cut the gobbledegook, muthafucka. You weird enough already.'

'Yeah,' the other man said. He laughed, a high-pitched cackle. 'Weird muthafucka.'

'OK. OK,' I said. 'But this is Mr Schumann's apartment. You think he wants anything to happen here? Blood all over the place?'

He made a gesture, and suddenly there was a gun in his hand. 'I don't know no Shoo-man,' he said. 'And I don't know who this apartment belong to. I just know you. You unlucky, man. You and this bitch gonna get wasted in the street by two junkies. Stupid as you are walking round the city late at night.'

'Bitch gonna get fucked too,' said the other man. 'Poked and smoked.' He laughed that crazy laugh again.

I held his eyes and began backing away from him. I put my right hand behind me on the spanner in my belt.

'One problem,' I said. 'How you gonna get me downstairs?'

He laughed and came towards me. He held the gun out at arm's length, to within a few inches of my head, and he cocked it, a loud clicking sound which made me flinch. He laughed again. 'Come on asshole,' he said. 'Make my day.'

The man near the door cackled in company with his friend, then he stopped abruptly as Sophie bent at the waist to gain leverage, brought her arm all the way over and whacked him on the side of the head with the steel spanner. It connected with a solid clunk and he cried out once and went down.

'Hijo de la chingada,' she screamed, and even at that moment the words coming from her mouth shocked me a little. I'd never heard her use such language. 'Chinga tu madre,' she shouted.

I'd been ready for something like this and when he heard Sophie scream, and the sound of his friend falling, the man with the gun did what I'd been expecting. He shifted his eyes, his head jerking round like a puppet on a string. I ducked away from the gun, pulled the spanner out of my belt and in the same motion hit him with all my strength on the elbow. The gun flew into the air, he grabbed at his right arm with the other, and I hit him again in the neck. He grunted and bent over, and I had to hit him one more time before he fell to his knees in front of me, as if bowing in prayer.

I brushed past and ran to join Sophie in the corridor, leaping over the prone figure in my way. We dashed for the front door, jostling each other in our haste as we went through it. The elevator was waiting, just as we'd left it, and in a couple of seconds we were running through the ground-floor lobby. It wasn't till then I noticed that Sophie was holding the pistol.

'Stop,' I told her as she pushed open the street door and followed her through. I took the gun out of her hand, pulling it a little, because she had a firm grip on it and wouldn't let go for a moment. I put it in my pocket. 'OK,' I said. 'They aren't following. Not yet. Just walk.'

We walked round the corner. It wasn't Olympic speed, but close. The little rental was still parked there, the sight of its squat shape greeting us like a familiar friend, and Sophie turned on the engine and took off as soon as we'd climbed in.

'Slowly,' I said. 'Slowly. We're in good shape.'

She nodded without speaking, her hands tight on the wheel, but she slowed down, and we drove the few blocks to the university apartments without speaking. When we got there she stopped abruptly, the brakes screeching, and sat without moving, her hands still gripping the wheel; and I looked at her for a while before she turned round.

'Oh my God,' she said. 'I was scared.'

I reached over and hugged her. She was trembling convulsively, but after a few moments she quietened down into the occasional tremor. Then she began to cry, pressing her face against my shoulder.

'Oh my God,' she whispered. 'I could have killed that guy. I was so scared.'

Chapter 13

We didn't talk much until we'd got upstairs and we were sitting down. Sophie poured a straight rum, and sat in the armchair opposite me. It felt as if we'd just come back a long way from some crazy country.

'What do you think?' Sophie said eventually.

'I just hope we crippled the bastards,' I said.

'Probably,' she said absently. 'But what I mean is, we know what she was doing but why? It wasn't like they were raping her or something, it was like a movie. She was sort of acting, I suppose, and they can't have kept her prisoner. She was going out all the time. She could have got away.'

'I don't know.'

'Was she the sort who'd do that for the money?'

'Maybe. I don't know.' Her questions were setting my nerves on edge. I didn't know the answers, and I didn't like thinking about it. She changed tack.

'Why do you think they were trying to kill you?'

Interesting the way she'd left herself out of it. I shrugged. 'Could be they were just trying to frighten us.'

She looked surprised, as if she hadn't thought of that possibility. 'You think so?'

'No. I think they were serious.'

'So what happens now?'

'I don't know.'

She made an impatient noise and it struck me that she was right to react irritably. This last question was something we had to think about.

'All right, apart from being careful about walking round corners, we've got to find out what Schumann's after, or why he's so disturbed, and get him to stop. Otherwise we might not be so lucky next time.'

'It's got to be him?'

'It's got to be,' I said, with more confidence than I felt. 'And there's Mary. She's the key to the whole thing. Find Mary and we'll know what's going on.'

'Yes.' She sat up, drained her glass and poured another one. I stretched out my glass and she leaned over and filled it up. 'I was at the college today. I saw your friend Jean. She's a nice woman. She said she'd ask around about which classes Arnold was taking. Either he'll be there or I can check out his friends. I said I'd be back tomorrow. I mean today. It's today now.' She giggled. I felt a little light-headed myself but I'd been waiting for this bit.

'I don't think you should go again,' I said. 'Not after tonight. It's the same district.'

She made a scornful noise. 'Oh yes. And what should I do? Wait here till they come to kill me? *Cagada*. They don't scare me.'

In this mood there'd be no shifting her. 'OK. OK. Let's talk about it tomorrow morning.'

I looked at the clock. Gone two a.m. I hadn't told Bonny where I'd be and given the events of the last couple of days she might be sitting around worrying about what had happened to me. I went over to where the phone was by the wall, dragged it back to where I was sitting and dialled. Sophie watched me impassively, but she didn't comment.

The ringing seemed to go on for a long time and I was just about to put it down and start again when she answered. Her voice was sleepy and slow. 'Who is it?'

'Sammy.'

'Oh, Sammy. Where are you?'

'It's been kind of hectic. A lot of things happened. Anyway, I'm staying here in Manhattan tonight.'

She'd know that meant Sophie's place. 'OK. Call me tomorrow. I've got something to tell you.'

'What is it?'

'It will keep. Call me tomorrow. About lunchtime?'

'OK.' I put the phone down.

'Like your mother,' she said.

'Oh, my mother never waited around to see where I was at night.' Not true, but I had to come back with something.

Sophie drained her glass. 'I'm going to bed.'

I got up and followed her to the bedroom door, and she pushed it open, but, as we moved through it, instead of turning on the light she turned on me, threw her arms round my neck and pushed me back against the wall, pressing hard with the whole of her body. Her hips ground impatiently into mine, and when I reached down and gripped her circling buttocks in my hands, she jumped up and wrapped her legs around me.

We felt our way through the darkness to her bed, tangled around each other like this, and when I felt my feet touch the base I fell forward on top of her. From then on we were swimming in a glittering black electric current, in which our senses reached out and twisted round each other so that it was hard to tell where she began and I ended. I tore at her at the waist and the zipper on her trousers as she was tearing at mine, and when we had kicked them somewhere into the dark I felt her come apart under me and I felt her wet naked crotch and I slid deep into her without effort.

When it was over we lay with our arms still wrapped around each other, and I must have fallen asleep, because I woke up to feel her pulling away gently. I let her go and she sat up and took off her sweater. Then she lay down again and faced me.

'That was something,' she said. '*Qué estupendo.*' She reached down and held my penis. '*Muy cachondo.*'

I looked away from her. I knew what I was going to say, but I didn't know why I was saying it right then. Examine my head, I thought, that's what it needs. 'I've got something to tell you,' I said.

She let go of me and shifted her weight a little so that we almost stopped touching. 'You did the bad thing with your cousin. OK. I know.' She turned and faced the other way.

'How?'

'I know you. I saw.'

'Sorry. I meant to tell you before.'

'OK. I slept with someone since I came here. I didn't tell you.'

A cold empty feeling started from a spot high in my stomach, then it turned hot and began spreading. I took a deep breath and held it in. 'Who?'

'An old friend. We were at school together. You don't know him.'

'What happened?'

'You know. We went out. It was fun, and it happened.'

'Did you use a condom?'

'Yes. Every time. Of course. I promised you.' She had. And I had promised her. 'Did you?'

'Yes,' I said. 'Of course.'

She sat up. 'Maybe you should have told me some other time. Not right now.'

She gritted her teeth and banged her fist on the pillow as she said the last words. Then she got out of bed and pulled on the long nightshirt she slept in. 'You want some coffee?'

I said I did and she padded out to make it. In a moment I got up and followed her out to the kitchen. I was still drowsy, and I didn't want to be asleep when she came back. In any case I didn't like drinking in bed. Somehow the liquid always seemed to start dripping on to my chest or the bedclothes.

We sat where we'd been sitting before in the living room, moving to the same chairs like actors following a routine. Sophie sat curled up with her head down, avoiding my eyes.

'So what happened with this guy? Where is he now?'

'I told him you were here, and that we would be together. He left.' She shrugged, then she looked straight at me with something hurt about her eyes.

'Did you know he would be here before you came?'

'Yes,' she said. 'I saw his sister, Maria, in London. I telephoned him.'

I nodded. There was nothing more to say. We had learned that when such things happened it was best to avoid prying into motives and circumstances. I sipped my coffee. Sophie hadn't touched hers. 'Drink your coffee,' I said.

'I want to tell you about the colonel,' she said.

I searched my memory for a colonel. She'd never mentioned him, so I guessed that it would be someone with whom she'd once had an escapade, and right now I didn't want to hear it.

'The colonel?'

'My stepfather. Well, he was never married to my mother, but they were together a long time. From the time I was a little girl. He treated me as a daughter, although he was not my father. For a long time I thought he must be, and then I realized that he had another family. Sometimes I think perhaps there were other women, other little girls and boys waiting for him to come once or twice a week. It's a sort of nightmare. But I didn't think that till later. I didn't really know anything about him except that he wore a uniform and brought me presents, until I had grown up and I was at the university. That was when I learned more. Other people were frightened of him, or hated him. The kind man I knew was a killer, someone who ordered torture, disappearances. It was like the ground opened up under me. You understand?'

'What made your mother stay with him?'

She looked at me, smiling. Then she looked away again. 'She loved him. She was admired by a lot of men. But she loved him for all those years.'

'What happened?'

'He was assassinated. He had four children, older than me. They stood in line greeting people. Afterwards they led his widow away, weeping. They walked in a little group and everyone looked at them with respect. Even then I wanted to be one of them. My mother and I, we looked at them that way too, and she didn't cry till we got home.'

She stopped. I watched her, struggling with a feeling of unreality. In all the time I had known her she'd never told me any of this. She felt my eyes on her, looked up at me and hugged the nightshirt tight round her.

'For a long time I slept with men who had been in trouble for politics, tortured or imprisoned. I didn't know I was doing it, you know. Sometimes you don't know what you're doing? A friend told me. It was becoming dangerous.' She picked up her coffee, drank some of it, made a disgusted face, and put it down again. 'All this was a long time ago.'

I wondered what the time was, but the curtains were drawn and we were so many floors away from the street that it was impossible to hear the sounds of the city. Thinking about it, I seemed to have a vague memory that the kitchen clock had been saying five. She'd been telling me something important. The trouble was that I didn't quite know what it all meant. For a moment my mind struggled with various ways of pursuing what she'd been telling me. Then I retreated, as I often did, from confronting Sophie's pain.

'Did I ever tell you 'bout the goat races back home?' I asked her.

'Goat races?'

'Yeah. Racing goats.'

She smiled. 'No.'

'Well, they used to race goats. Right?'

She laughed and shook her head. 'I don't believe this.'

'How you mean you don't believe it? I telling you something and you don't believe?' I was speaking to her in the idiom and the accent I would have used with Alvin or someone else from back home. It made her feel comfortable and relaxed, she'd told me once, because she knew that nowadays this was a way of speaking I only ever used with my family and my oldest friends.

'OK,' she said, grinning, 'I believe.'

'All right,' I told her. 'They have these goat races in a stadium. Bank holidays, national holidays, and people bet on them. Like horses. But of course is the goat jockeys who are the really important part of it.'

'Goat jockeys?' she cried out. 'Goat jockeys? How big are these goats? Sorry.'

I looked at her sternly and she clapped her hand to her mouth, gagging herself. She watched me like this, her eyes creasing up with laughter.

'Don't be so silly. The jockeys don't ride the goats. They put a long leash on them and run behind. They don't have to be small, just fast, because it takes a lot of skill, you know, guiding the goat, making it go on a straight course and racing against other men at the same time. Of course, sometimes the goats wander off and the ropes get tangled, and the goats start butting each other.'

'This is true?' she said.

It was true, although I'd told it like a tall story. 'Of course it's true. The funny thing is the best goat jockey I knew was a little guy named Pepsi. I'd see him out running every morning. He was small and neat, so he could run the bends without trouble.'

'It sounds like the kind of sport they should introduce to the Olympic Games,' she said. 'Bring some poetry to it.'

'You know the rest of the world doesn't have the imagination. You only get things like that on the South American continent.'

She made a wild gesture, waving her arms around. 'Yeah. Fantasy Island.' She shook her head. 'I'll be dead tomorrow. What time is it anyway?'

We climbed back into the bed moving like sleepwalkers. On the way in I had intended to set the alarm clock by the bed, but by the time my head hit the pillow I had forgotten, and in a moment I was asleep.

Chapter 14

We were up early. About twelve. I woke up with that feeling you have when something special has happened, the new day coming in like an anticlimax, calm after the storm. On the other hand, it was as if the experiences of the night had chased away some devils and we were back on an even keel, smiling at each other and making a couple of jokes as we had breakfast and mooched about the place, showering and getting dressed.

It wasn't till I saw her checking her equipment and stuffing things into her bag that I remembered. 'About Arnold,' I said. 'I'm not sure it's such a good idea to go looking.'

'Why?'

'After last night?'

She stopped what she was doing and turned to face me. 'In this bag,' she said, 'I've got a personal alarm which can be heard for a block when it goes off. I've got a can of Mace and I've got a pipe which would probably kill someone if I hit him hard enough. Anyone fucks with me he's in trouble.'

'Good thing I didn't know that last night,' I told her.

'What are you going to do?'

'I'll try and see Schumann later.'

'Be careful.'

When she'd gone I rang Bonny at the hospital.

'How you doing? How was last night?' she said.

It wasn't what she wanted to know, but I gave her a version of what had happened at Schumann's apartment. 'Hey,' she said slowly. 'This is serious. Did you talk to the cops?'

'Are you serious?'

'OK. When you coming back tonight? I want you to touch base with a guy I know.'

'Who's that?'

'Someone who might help.'

She wouldn't tell me any more and eventually I said I'd be back in the evening, before ten at the latest.

The next thing I did was to look up City Hall in the directory and call Ben Schumann's office. I got the same frosty woman, who told me that Mr Schumann couldn't speak to me on the telephone and if I wrote a letter I'd be answered shortly. She didn't seem to remember that she'd said the same thing to me only a few days ago. I broke the connection and thought about dialling Schumann's home before I remembered that I didn't have the number or the address. Bad news. I could go back to Queens and get the address book, but I had no way of telling whether the two heavies would be waiting for me, or what would happen if they were, and I certainly didn't want to find out. On the other hand I had to reach Schumann today. Apart from finding out any more about Mary, my plan was to get him to call his dogs off by threatening him with the video cassette, so I had to get to him before they got to me.

I called Bonny again.

'What's happened?' she asked quickly.

'Nothing.'

I told her the problem. I was hoping that Oscar might have a way of finding out or that perhaps, at a pinch, she'd volunteer to go and get the notebook.

'Melda,' she said immediately.

'Who?'

'Melda. You know. Upstairs. She's on late shift. She'll be home. I'll call her. Where is it?'

I told her, gave her Sophie's number and hung up.

It was nearly another hour before she called back with the address and phone number. I dialled the number and got a recorded message which said that there was no one available to answer my call. I broke the connection before the message ended and called Oscar.

When he answered his voice was hushed and conspiratorial. 'Hey. What's happening, man?'

'You wouldn't believe.'

'You OK?'

'Sure.' I told him what I wanted, and he said he'd check it out and call me back.

After that I could only wait. By now it was early afternoon. Time for the daytime soaps, and when I switched on the TV it swept through a variety of scenes, all of them stocked with good-looking young white men and women with smooth neat features and glossy tumbling hair. I clicked into the ads on one station, and a woman's voice suddenly said, 'I like having as much as I want, the way I like it, whenever I want.'

For a moment my attention was riveted by the incredible assurance of the greed with which the voice addressed the world. On TV, when they showed the ravages of famine from Asia, Africa, and Eastern Europe, you could see nothing but hunger and agony; even the babies made humble, beseeching motions. All they wanted was to survive. But now I was on a different planet, a planet where deprivation meant not having what you wanted when you wanted it.

Another woman with a tight, sculpted body and glossy hair came on the screen. This time it was some kind of insurance, and the actress bared her teeth as if she knew how incredibly perfect they were. Perhaps it was my mood, but something about the sight had an element of fantasy which depressed me. The problem wasn't the way they were using these beautiful bodies and faces as a commodity. That had been happening across the world since people began trading one thing for another, and I could live with it. What got me was the sense that these images represented a sort of parallel universe into which viewers were plunged, however hard they resisted. To most of them, this world of shining hair and teeth would be a lot better than the reality they faced, but at the same time it was a world which could live only in their imagination, unreachable. Perhaps, I thought, if Muslims dreamt of a paradise in which they were surrounded by beautiful houris and cascading fountains, Americans dreamt of a heaven where all the angels had blue eyes, big tits, narrow waists and neat round behinds. 'White man's magic,' I muttered to myself.

Back home our magic came in the shape of powerful spirits and objects which invoked them. Chicken feathers, goats, packages of mysterious things, chanting and drums in the night. Here the magic was the same, but the packaging was different. Its ceremonies were celebrated on the screen in front of me, in which its worshippers could see a reflection of their souls.

The picture of Mary writhing under the bodies of the men in the video crossed my mind. Perhaps the men needed to photograph the scene because the pleasure they were getting from the act hadn't been real until they saw images of themselves in performance.

The telephone buzzed and I started up from the half-sleep I'd been in and grabbed it. Oscar.

'Right,' he said. 'I'm about as sure of this as I can be in the circumstances. This is secretary-to-secretary stuff. He'll be leaving about five, and going home to dress for a function later on. So he'll be at his house between five and seven. About that. And listen. You didn't hear it from me. You didn't hear it from anyone. OK?'

OK. I hung up and looked at my watch. Schumann lived on the East Side, not far from his parents' apartment. If I hurried I could be there in time to intercept him.

I got there in about half an hour. It wasn't quite going-home time, but the avenues were beginning to acquire the depleted look which signalled that business was nearly finished. Schumann's building was halfway along a cross street with an imposing church on the corner, and I dawdled around a bit, looking at it. Then I walked down to the next block and back again.

I was on my third trip when I saw a taxi pull up. Schumann got out and hurried across the sidewalk and under the arcade. I turned and walked the other way to the telephone outside the church. I had written down the number but by now I could remember it easily, and I dialled it without a hitch.

'This is Samson Dean,' I told the answerphone. 'I know you're there, Mr Schumann, because I just saw you come in. I picked up one of those tapes you made at the apartment. If you want it back, it's easy. I'll be downstairs in two minutes. Talk to me now. The alternative is that I take this to someone else, and I don't need to tell you what that would mean. Two minutes.'

I hung up and walked back to the building, passed through the arcade, crossed the red carpet in the lobby and smiled at the attendant. 'I have an appointment with Mr Schumann,' I told him. 'He's expecting me.'

'Your name?'

'Sam Dean.'

He nodded and showed me to the elevator, and in less than a minute I was standing in front of Schumann's door. I rang the bell and it chimed prettily. I stood well back in the wide corridor. I didn't know what to expect. I had seen the man come in alone, but for all I knew he might have an army in there with him. Not that he'd have needed an army. One of the men I'd encountered the night before would have been enough.

When he opened the door, though, it was something of an anticlimax to recognize in the satyr of the tapes a harassed-looking middle-aged bureaucrat. He looked past me along the corridor, right and left, then he stood back.

'Come in.'

I walked in behind him. It was a big apartment with the same kind of layout as his parents'. Just inside the door the walls were lined with what looked like Haitian and Jamaican primitives. I spotted a Kapo, but I didn't get far enough to take a close look at it, because he turned and faced me as soon as we were in the door.

'I don't want to hear any of your shit,' he said pompously. 'The facts are that you broke into an apartment and stole some of my property. If you don't give it back I'll have you arrested.' He pointed a finger at me. 'If this is a shakedown, you've come to the wrong place.'

I had to admire his nerve, but I could tell he was bluffing. 'This isn't a shakedown,' I said gently. 'But the tape is safe, and if you don't tell me what's going on I intend to use it.'

'There's nothing incriminating in it,' he said quickly.

'You're probably right,' I told him. 'But who cares, eh? A couple of copies in the right places and that won't matter. Think about it. Imagine what Al Sharpton could do with a tape like that.'

His jaw dropped, and a look of pure terror crossed his face. 'What do you want?'

The irrational thought that he was pathetic flashed through my mind. Villains had to be harder than this. Stupid, I told myself. In his place I would have been worse. But then I wouldn't have been in his place.

'I want to know about Mary,' I said. 'I want to know what happened, what you did to her, where she is. Is she alive?'

My mind had played with the thought before, but I'd always pushed it away out of sight, and the fact that I'd asked the question, straight out, startled me. But if the idea startled me it shocked Schumann rigid. His face flushed then grew pale.

'Of course she's alive,' he said. 'I spoke to her only a few days ago.'

'You spoke to her? Where is she?'

He shrugged. 'I don't know.'

'What do you mean you don't know, if you spoke to her?' I said. 'Where was she?'

'She telephoned,' he said.

I laughed. The more I heard the crazier it got.

'I don't believe this,' I said. 'You set her up in an apartment. You're having orgies with her. She's disappeared. You've got two guys following me. They beat me up, threaten to kill me, and now you tell me that she's ringing you and chatting on the telephone. Just like that. Come on.'

'None of that was meant to happen,' he said earnestly. 'They exceeded their instructions.'

Close up he looked tired and drawn, as if all this had been too much for him. He'd laid down his briefcase and taken off his jacket, and in his shirtsleeves you could tell he was running to fat. In the video he'd looked like a leering monster. Now the wind and piss had leaked out of him he was just another shagged-out office worker. At the same time he retained a quality that made me cautious, a shifty sense of power that came from making deals and decisions which could shake small worlds. He took his glasses off. 'Look,' he said. 'Come in and sit down. None of this is what it looks like.'

It never was, I thought. I followed him into the big sitting room with its French windows and balconies, which looked out towards a clump of treetops that I figured must be the park. He waved me into a big leather armchair and sat opposite me in its twin.

'Mr Schumann,' I told him. 'I don't care about what you did. I mean I don't want people following me around. I want you to do something about that.'

Pretty mild, but I was feeling my way. He nodded.

'Mary's what's bothering me now,' I said. 'I need to know where she is, what she's been doing and what's happened to her. And the apartment, the video and all that stuff. How come?'

'Let me explain,' he said. 'A friend put me in touch with an agency. It's a sort of unofficial network. They place domestics. My parents had trouble with the last one, she stole and then she left them suddenly one weekend. They had women who only spoke Spanish. My parents are old-fashioned. They couldn't communicate. It's harder than people think. You can't get Americans. We asked for an English-speaking Caribbean, and they sent Mary.'

129

He spread his hands in a gesture which was, I supposed, meant to tell me how hard it all was, employing domestics.

'It was OK for a while. My parents liked her. They're frail, and a man in my position hasn't got the time. I was grateful to her. I helped her enrol in classes, took her to a lawyer and started processing her work permit. She was friendly and charming, unlike . . .' He suddenly thought better of what he was about to say and stopped. He sighed.

'Then things changed. I took her to the apartment you saw. I share it with some friends. It's a place we go to relax.'

I didn't have to ask why things had changed just then. He stopped again, and his gaze shifted to the window. He frowned as if he was wondering how much to tell me.

'She began hassling me about letting her stay in the apartment. She wanted to leave my parents. In the end I said yes.' He ran his hands over his face, got up, poured himself a whisky and came back with the glass in his hand. He didn't offer me one. 'I had to let the others know,' he said. 'And it went on from there. Things happened.'

'I saw.'

He gave me a scornful grimace. 'Don't imagine she was some kind of innocent victim. She got well paid.'

'So why did she leave? If that was the way it was she should have been having a ball.' I believed the bare facts of his narrative, but I couldn't believe the twist he was putting on it.

He shrugged. 'She changed. She got harder. She'd lost her innocence, I suppose. She acquired a boyfriend. I suppose he needed money. I saw them out together, but we decided not to do anything about it, as long as she didn't bring him to the apartment. There were a lot of valuable things there, you see.'

'That was big of you guys,' I said.

He ignored the sarcasm. 'It didn't occur to us that she might steal anything. We'd have noticed, and it would be difficult to get anything much out in one trip. But she stole something. Very valuable. One of my friends hired those men to get it back. They used to work for a security firm we used sometimes. Then you turned up. We thought you might be part of the scam or that you might lead us to her. It was their idea to stir you up. Get things moving. They were fired today. One of them has a broken arm.'

'Good. Just one thing. Why didn't you get the police? If she stole whatever it is. Police Plaza's right on your doorstep. A guy like you must have a few favours to call in. Keep the newspapers out of it.'

He frowned. 'That wasn't an option.'

I changed tack. 'So why did Mary call you?'

'She wants to sell the item back to us.'

'Why doesn't she just sell it? What is it anyway. A painting?'

'No. It doesn't matter what it is. She couldn't sell it on the open market.'

I sat back, considering. I could have guessed some of what he'd told me. But now I knew the rest of it I wasn't much further forward. On the other hand, I distrusted a good half of what he'd said, but I suspected I wouldn't get any more.

'If she calls you again,' I said, 'can you tell her I'm trying to get in touch with her? A friend of her father's. She'll remember.'

He leaned forward. 'I may not get the chance,' he said. 'And if I told her that she might think it was a trap. But if you do find her you could let me know, or persuade her to give it back. You could name your price.'

I looked at him straight-faced. If I found Mary I would certainly try to persuade her that stealing, ransom, and living on the run wasn't worth it. Why would this asshole think I needed paying to do that? But I already knew the answer to that one.

'I'll see what I can do,' I said, and I got up.

'What about the video?' he said.

'I think I'll keep that,' I told him. 'When this is over I'll get rid of it. As long as nothing happens to me, you're OK. And you can tell that to your buddies.'

'How do we know you won't' – he gestured – 'do something with it?'

I glared at him, letting my anger show. 'That's my best friend's daughter. He's lying in a hospital bed dying and thinking about her. You think I'd show that to anybody else just like that? Who the fuck do you think I am?'

He didn't reply but he watched me carefully, as if he was facing an unpredictable animal.

I grinned at him. 'And if you don't believe me,' I said. 'You'll just have to take my word for it, hope for the best and sweat it out. That's how most people live.'

I turned and walked to the door. Then I looked back. He hadn't moved, and he was still sitting bolt upright, his eyes following me with that same wary look.

I reached out for the handle and smiled at him one last time. 'I'm off then,' I told him. 'Ta, ta.'

Chapter 15

I called Sophie's number from the phone on the corner. No
answer, but I wasn't worried. It was about half six and she still
had enough light to be working. I wasn't completely reassured
by Schumann's claim that the two 'security' men had been
fired, because even if it were true they could still go in for
some freelance revenge, but I had the feeling that unless we
ran across them it was unlikely.

I dived into the subway and rode out to Queens, absorbed
by the problems that my conversation with Schumann had
raised. What had Mary stolen which couldn't be sold else-
where? If not a painting, then perhaps it was some special
piece, Aztec jewellery, a relic, something smuggled in, or
stolen, which would be why Schumann hadn't called in the
police in the first place. A great golden bird with jewels for
eyes flashed through my mind and I laughed out loud. Pure
fantasy.

All this had held my attention so firmly that the trip
seemed to have taken up very little time, and before I knew it
I was in Corona walking towards my brother's apartment. I
wasn't whistling and carefree, but during the last few days I
had begun to feel as if I was walking through a maze, and my
talk with Schumann had at least lifted a corner of the veil. I
didn't feel like a target any more, and the job in front of me

had narrowed itself to a straightforward question of finding Mary and making sure she was alive and well. That just shows you, I thought, smiling, the last few days had been so bad that I had begun to think of that complicated task as simple.

The windows of the house came into sight and I began feeling for the keys, pleased with myself because I hadn't lost them or left them lying around in Sophie's place. Then I almost stopped in my tracks, my heart pounding with surprise and shock. I'd walked past a black Buick Regal without noticing anything unusual about it. But now as I stood in the doorway I could see that there was a solitary white man sitting in the driver's seat, his eyes following me. Straight black hair, brown eyes. A neat white collar. When he saw me staring, he looked away. For a moment I told myself it was coincidence, but that was unbelievable. This was a street exclusive to blacks and Hispanics. There were a few white people in the neighbourhood, but I was willing to bet he wasn't one of them, and the odds were against a white man of his appearance having any business which required him to park here for any length of time. I debated going up to the car and asking him what he was doing there, but as soon as the thought came into my head I knew it was a bad idea. In any case I wanted to get inside now and get to the telephone.

I called Schumann and he picked up almost immediately.

'What is it?' he asked irritably. 'I'm on my way out.'

'Yeah. Maybe you are,' I said nastily. 'But I need to know what's going on. There's a car parked outside my house with a white man sat in it watching me.'

'It's nothing to do with me. Those security people I hired are history. Either they're doing it for their own reasons or it's somebody else.'

'Was one of them white?'

'No. No. The people we hired were black. For obvious reasons.'

I put the phone down, thinking furiously. Either Schumann was lying or these were completely different people. Or both. There was a credible logic there when I thought about it. I

134

was certain that no one had been following me when I went to meet Sophie. The men who had beaten me up and confronted us in the apartment could have been waiting at both places, while this bunch simply sat in front of my brother's house and watched me. But if they weren't connected with Schumann I couldn't begin to guess who they were. Therefore he must be lying. Or maybe not.

Bonny opened the door and came in. 'What happened?'

I told her about the apartment, the fight and my conversation with Schumann.

She listened, frowning and intent. 'Oh boy,' she said. 'Big trouble. Who is that motherfucker?'

She used the word awkwardly, and I was a little startled because so far I'd not heard her using this kind of street language. But she'd said it with a venom that showed she was disturbed and worried.

I shrugged.

'OK,' she said viciously. 'Let's find out. Come on.'

The phone rang before I could ask her where we were going and I picked it up. It was Oscar. 'How ya doing? How was the man?'

When he spoke to me now, I noticed, his tone was different, as if he'd decided that I was to be taken seriously.

'OK. Come over later. I'll tell you.'

Bonny took the phone out of my hand. 'Oscar. We'll be at La Rêve.' She slammed it down, and pulled at my hand. 'Let's go.'

The Buick pulled out after us. There were now two men in it. I saw Bonny noting the headlights behind us, but she didn't comment.

'Where are we going?'

She gave me a quick glance and smiled. 'You shouldn't be so easy. Don't even know where you going.'

'Only because it's you.'

'A friend of mine named Claude. He's a Jamaican guy owns some of the buses.' These were the vans which competed with the bus services up and down the district. 'His mom used to work with my mother, so I've known him years.'

135

'What's the relevance?'

'You need protection, and Claude knows about that stuff.'

'How come?'

She pondered. 'It's how he got where he is. This is the Wild West. Anyone can start anything. After that it's a question of fighting to survive. We have everything we need, and a lot of things we don't even want. The only way to get up there' — she made a gesture skywards — 'is step on somebody else's toes. Start something new and it's king of the castle. We went to the same school. Claude was lucky.'

She reconsidered what she'd said, pursing her lips.

'No. He was very smart and he was lucky. He came late. He was about fifteen and he got his diploma, ignored the whole college thing. He had good SATs, but he dropped out or his mother couldn't afford to keep him on. I don't know. Then he studied business part time. I used to see him around, but it looked like he was into the street. Then I heard he was working as a car salesman. Next thing I know he's set up his own business, working on his first million.' She paused. 'The thing was he came because of his mother. He had nowhere else to go, but he hated it here. He was full of these Rastafarian ideas without being one. At that time I was only fourteen, and I still had the stupid idea that you could change everything by self-improvement, getting out of the ghetto culture, and proving your worth. He used to laugh at me. He said the establishment culture was a trap designed to keep things the same. You couldn't win, and the only way to beat the system was to pretend it wasn't there.' She paused again. 'I used to think he was a dumb Jamaican. Now I know better.'

We rolled down into Jamaica Avenue, turned a corner and pulled up in front of a used-car lot. The Buick went past and as it reached the next corner, its tail lights glowed and blinked. Bonny ignored it. We got out, walked past the row of shiny cars and into the shopfront next to the lot.

There was a Jamaican flag, green, gold and black, painted neatly on the front, and three Jamaican men were standing next to it the way they would have been in London or

Birmingham. Past the door we were in the sales area, men in suits scurrying back and forth. Bonny waved casually at one of them, and I followed her through the back entry. A short flight of stairs, then she paused, knocked at the door at the top, and pushed it open.

We were in a big room which ran the depth of the shop and overlooked the street and the car yard. At the back a man and a woman were answering telephones and talking into the microphones on the table in front of them. At the front of the room between the windows an enormous Jamaican flag was stretched along the wall. Above it was the picture of Marcus Garvey in his plumed hat, under it two desks. At one of them a woman sat working at a terminal. Opposite her a man in his thirties dressed in a dark blue suit and a white shirt open at the collar was leaning back in the big easy chair, his feet up on the desk, telephone pressed to his ear. When he saw us he waved. The woman opposite him got up, smoothing her skirt down over her thighs, moved a couple of chairs into position for us on the other side of Claude's desk, and went back to her terminal without speaking.

Claude put the phone down, came round the desk, hugged Bonny and shook hands with me. He was wearing a gold chain on one wrist, a big solid gold watch on the other, and several rings on his fingers. His skull was shaved clean, close to the scalp, giving him an air of bullet-headed vigour and authority.

'So, Mistress Bonny,' he said. 'I don't see you. High degree and thing.'

Bonny laughed, hugged him again and we sat down. He asked her how her mother was and she asked him the same question and they kicked around a few reminiscences before he turned to me.

'How London, bro?'

I shrugged and spread my hands. 'It deh you know. The same as here only less.'

I meant the same as far as we were concerned, but he knew that. He had family in Stoke Newington, he told me, and I told him I knew the place. I'd only been away a few days, but it was already hard to picture Stoke Newington, and all I could call to mind was the stretch of railings along Clissold Park.

'So wha' go on?' he asked eventually.

Bonny looked at me, and I gave Claude the edited highlights of the last few days. He listened carefully, an abstracted smile on his face, nodding a little.

'I can't help you too much with the girl,' he said when I'd finished. 'These kids do crazy things. This is Babylon, you know what I'm saying?'

I nodded.

'But this guy who is following you. That's another matter.'

There was something familiar and reassuring about the way he switched back and forth between the dialect and standard English. We all did it, and it made me feel I'd known him a long time, like Bonny. The other thing was his readiness to help. No questions. I'd noticed that about Oscar too. Bonny had vouched for me, and that was enough. This was the defensive network my brother talked about sometimes. The African-Americans liked to think it was a black thing, he said, but they'd lost it in the grim struggles of the northern slums, and then TV had taught them that human worth could be measured by possessions, and that happiness was an escape capsule. The Caribbeans still pulled together because that was part of the immigrant heritage. But it only worked for some people, sometimes, and one day we too would come to believe that the highest goal we could aspire to was a bigger car.

Claude twisted round and picked up the phone. 'Let's check on it.' He relayed my description of the Buick to someone on the other end. Then he stood up. 'We're going to La Rêve. I would take you in the Merc, but he might lose you. You follow me. We want him with us. Keep the guy entertained.'

We went down through the office in a little procession which made me feel like part of Claude's entourage.

It felt the same as we drove to the restaurant. We followed

Claude, the Buick followed us, and we rolled down the avenue for a few blocks before we turned off.

The restaurant was a small square building which looked like an office block except for the flashing neon sign outside, 'LA RÊVE'. Claude's big black car stopped in front, he got out and it moved off again. He stayed on the pavement and waved us to a parking slot lower down the street. As we manoeuvred the Buick went past, and we could see its rear lights begin flashing as the driver looked for a place to stop.

Claude had found a tie somewhere, a hand-painted job with a hibiscus climbing down the front of it. He grinned at us. 'Under control,' he said. 'Don't worry 'bout that guy no more. Let's go eat.'

Inside, the head waiter greeted us with a professional effusiveness: 'Bon soir, Monsieur Claude.' He led us to a big circular table near the centre of the room, and stayed while a couple of waiters fussed with our chairs and handed us the menus.

Looking round it was easy to tell that the waiters were Haitians. That is to say, they looked a lot like Jamaicans but with a kind of prissy smoothness to their style and movements. It was harder to tell about the customers. Mostly English-speaking Caribbeans, that was easy enough. Customarily reserved with Spanish speakers from the same part of the world, they seemed to find no problems about bridging the gap with Haitians.

The food was Caribbean. I ordered soft-shelled crabs, and I asked Bonny if she remembered seeing them back home, where we'd looked on them as a sort of aquatic vermin, ignoring them in favour of the big blue-backed crabs with the red legs. She hadn't, but we kicked the topic around, while Claude listened with an indulgent smile.

From upstairs we could hear a jazz piano tinkling and Claude saw me noticing the sound.

'They're good,' he said. 'More jazz around here than you get anywhere else. They all used to live here: Armstrong, Count Basie. Fools don't know that. They still running about Harlem looking for the action.'

Bonny waved and Oscar came over and sat down.

Quickly I gave him a summary of events and he took it all in frowning, but without comment. While I talked, Claude looked at him unwaveringly, something speculative about his expression.

'How come,' he said to Oscar abruptly, 'your man don't make some changes? Do something for us? Everytime something happen he kissing ass. How come he don't kiss our ass? Election night I was over there in Rochester pulling voters out. Up and down. Nowadays black kids get killed he's talking peace. Policemen carrying Uzis. Shit.'

The subject of the mayor had to come up, I thought.

'Hey. Wait a minute,' Oscar said. 'You want an answer or you want to write a column in the *Amsterdam News*? Make a speech in the subway.'

'OK.' Claude smiled. 'You tell me.'

Oscar began talking. Money, connections, contracts. I'd heard this before, and so had everyone at the table, but the subject and its fine detail fascinated them, the talk passing through a landscape with sharply delineated features: Al Sharpton, Yusuf Hawkins, Giuliani, Bensonhurst, D'Amato, Gotti, Riker's Island, Jesse, Crown Heights. The names and places changed, but the big question stayed the same. How come we're losing out all the time?

Claude, bored by Oscar's defence of the mayor, shifted ground and told an Arjune story. Arjune was, in a manner of speaking, one of us, an Indian from Guyana, who had lived in a street not far from where we were sitting. He'd decided to testify against the crack dealers in his street, then had to go into a witness-protection programme after the cop guarding his house was shot. Since then he'd become a public figure, cropping up in various parts of the country denouncing police harassment and telling his story over and over again. He'd been a minor nuisance to the local hoodlums, and by an irony which tickled the neighbourhood wits, he'd become a bigger problem to the law-enforcement system than he'd ever been to the crack dealers. They'd had to move him several times, setting his family up in new locations, and each time Arjune had blown his cover by going to the newspapers or getting himself arrested.

'It's a new kind of public relations,' Claude said. 'The man get on the news more often in hiding than he ever did when he was walking around.'

'What's wrong with a man having a conscience?' Oscar said.

'Conscience?' Claude laughed so hard that he spilled a little wine on the white tablecloth. Immediately a waiter was at his elbow dabbing at the wet patch. Claude waved him away.

'Oui. Oui. Fâche pas.'

There were unpredictable depths to Claude, I thought. When I first saw him he'd been speaking a Jamaican dialect with a Jamaican accent; when he talked about the politics of the city he'd sounded like an African-American, up from the South a generation ago; now French with a Haitian accent. I wondered whether he spoke Spanish too.

'Conscience?' he said. 'That ain't no conscience. That's a game. Where I come from, it's Spanishtown. When I was a kid we used to live next street up from Hangman Prison.'

That was where the Jamaicans put the prisoners who were due to hang. Every night there was a gathering of youths around the prison gates, talking, playing games and passing messages in and out. I wondered whether the others had got the reference, but I supposed that it didn't matter.

'Tough place. I didn't know it then. That's the funny thing. The violence in JA didn't used to be about coke the way it is now. It used to be about politics, but it was the same. Kids, younger than me, used to get a gun, go out and shoot someone. You know why? For a few dollars. You know what it's like when the choices are like that. Black and white. You shoot or you die. Conscience, shit. You know what everybody's ambition was? Real desperate. Goal in life: to get out. Go foreign. When I left I thought I was out. Desperation behind me. Then I saw the same thing here. Life or death, babe. Mostly when you black you have to run the race unless you very lucky. Jump the fences. Survive, lose or win. Strong enough, desperate enough, you come out the other side, look up in the white man's face and say, fuck you, nothing he can do about it. Some suckers think there's some kind of short cut. Climb on the other assholes' backs, jump up over the wall and you're free. But that's the worst way to lose. They got you by the balls then, cause there ain't nowhere to go. All you can do is run around on TV telling them how you saved the world dumping on your own people.'

Oscar shrugged and Claude looked at his watch.

'Showtime,' he said.

Out on the pavement Claude was all business. 'My man Omar here will drive you, Sammy.'

A tall dreadlocked Jamaican had appeared at his elbow. Claude turned to Bonny.

'They'll take your car. No sense confusing the mens dem.'

'Who am I going with?' Bonny asked.

Claude sniggered. Oscar rolled his eyes at me.

'You ain't,' Claude said. 'You're going home with Oscar.'

'You're an asshole,' Bonny said, exasperated.

'Ain't it the truth?'

She handed the keys to Omar, and kissed me on the cheek. 'Take care.' She looked at Claude. 'This is my cousin. You know what I'm saying?'

'Sure,' Claude said. 'He's safer than the President. Go. Go.' He made shooing motions with his hands, mightily amused by her indignation.

'Where're we going?' I asked Claude when she'd stalked off with Oscar.

'Greenacres, the mall in Rosedale. Long time since I been there. Nice place.'

'What are we going to do? I only want to know who the guy is.'

'That's it,' Claude said. 'We're gonna find out. OK?'

I had a feeling it wasn't OK, but now I'd started this I was

142

in Claude's hands. Omar pulled out sedately, and grinned into the mirror when the Buick showed up a block later. He didn't speed up and we rolled towards Rosedale at the same deliberate pace.

I recognized it by the big red neon sign on Alexander's store, but the rest of the shopping centre was wrapped in gloom. Deserted. The mall formed two sides of a rectangle facing the car park and Alexander's on the other side. We drove along, right to the end of the plaza in the middle. Omar stopped and switched off the lights and, after a while, the Buick crept through the entrance, hesitated, and stopped. Its lights went out and Omar picked up the portable phone and pressed a button.

'All set.'

He put the phone down, reached under his jacket, took out a pistol, worked the action, put it back again, switched on the engine and the lights, and began reversing at speed towards the other car.

The driver in the Buick was quick. He started moving immediately we went into reverse, and he'd completed half a turn before another two cars came up the ramp, headlights blazing and blocked his exit. By the time Omar backed up to it, the Buick was at a standstill. In front of the windscreen another two dreads were posed in a shooting stance, holding pistols pointed straight through the glass.

The two men in the front seat were sitting quietly, their hands up by their heads. They didn't look very worried, more as if this was a routine transaction, like being stopped by the police. Both of them were white, with straight dark hair brushed back.

Claude's car had stopped behind the other two, and now he got out, walked up to the driver's window, rapped on it, and made winding motions with his hand. In a moment it slid down.

'What's this shit?' the driver said, glaring.

'I wanna see your driver's licence,' Claude said in a peremptory voice. He snapped his fingers and after a short hesitation the driver handed it over. Claude leafed through it.

'How come you following my man here, Sal? And doing it so bad,' he said conversationally.

'How come?' Sal reached out and twitched the book from Claude's hand. 'They tell us follow the guy, we follow him.'

'Yes,' Claude said, his tone harder. 'But I asked you how come?'

Sal looked at the two men standing in his headlights, then he looked round at his companion who shrugged.

'He's looking for his kid, his girlfriend, whatever. Right? We're looking for her too.'

'Why?'

'She's a fucking thief,' the other man said suddenly. 'Stole the man's property.'

'What man?' I said.

The two looked at me, but no one answered. Then the driver looked at Claude again.

'You finished?' he said. 'Because if you don't get those fucking monkeys outta my way I'm gonna lose my patience.'

Claude straightened up. 'OK,' he said. 'But one thing. Remember you in Jamaica. You ain't in Howard Beach or Bensonhurst. You know what I'm saying?'

The driver gave a quiet snort of laughter. 'Yeah,' he said. 'Big fucking deal.' The window started to slide up.

'Wait a minute,' I said, but by the time I got it out the window had closed and Sal had started the engine.

'Just a minute, Claude,' I said, but he shook his head, stepped back and waved the dreads out of the way.

The Buick backed up and went round us, the two men staring straight ahead as if we weren't there.

'I wanted to ask them what she stole and who owned it,' I told Claude.

'They wouldn't have told you,' he said. 'Those guys were professionals. If I'd known maybe I wouldn't have messed with them. You've got all you're going to get there. Think about it.'

He turned, leaving me standing there, and went back to his car. As he reached the door he fluttered his hand in farewell

144

and Omar started back to Bonny's car walking fast. I followed him, and by the time we got to it, the plaza was once again silent and deserted.

Chapter 16

'It's got to be a scam,' Oscar said.

'How do you mean?'

I had an inkling, but I wanted to get it clear. When I'd described what happened to Bonny and Oscar, their faces had gone thoughtful and sober. Oscar, in particular, had seemed worried, agitated even.

'I didn't want to talk about this,' he said, 'because it's only a rumour I picked up. There's all kinds of bullshit going around all the time. But the word is that Schumann is being investigated. Something about contracts.'

'Who's investigating him?'

'There's no answer to that. I can't guess. There'll be several agencies conducting investigations in several different areas right now. Links to organized crime. That's big. Corporate investments. BCCI. Contracts. You know who's doing the investigation you usually know what it is. Federal is my guess. But in between the state monitoring agencies, the cops, the DA, the regulatory agencies, and the federal authorities, you don't know who the hell is doing what most of the time.'

'So what are you trying to say?'

'These guys tonight were organized crime. If Claude said they were professionals, that's what he was saying. Right?'

I nodded my agreement.

'OK. So what do they care about some bullshit art object? If they stole or smuggled something so valuable they'd worry about losing it, they would never ever keep it in an apartment they don't control, no security, a couple of amateurs can just walk in, with some hippy dippy kid they don't know living in it. Could be Ben and his buddies have some weird thing going with paintings and stuff but not together with the mob. Too upfront. No. Whatever the kids stole it's something else and if the mob are interested it's something incriminating, not art, something that can be used against them. If Ben's involved, it's some kind of scam that uses his position or his inside knowledge.'

'Sounds reasonable,' I said. I was convinced.

'Reasonable?' Oscar said. 'It's outstanding.'

In a short while he said he was going and Bonny said she was going to bed and I called Sophie. In the last few hours I'd forgotten about her and what she was doing. She answered on the first ring.

'I called you. But there was no answer. I was kind of worried.'

'I saw the man,' I told her. I was being guarded because it had suddenly occurred to me that someone could easily be tapping the telephone. 'It's OK, but better if we don't talk about it now, on the telephone. I'll come over early in the morning.'

There was a short silence.

'OK. Make it as early as you can.'

Bonny came in as soon as I put down the phone. She sat down, looking at me purposefully. She'd been talking for what seemed like a long time out by the door with Oscar, and I had a hunch that there was something she wanted to tell me.

'Today was bad. Sounded bad,' she amended.

'Yeah. I suppose.'

She was staring straight at me. 'I know you're not a kid,' she said, 'and you've got a lot of experience in London. But you were brought up there and you know the place. It's more peaceful too. Over there the cops don't carry guns and stuff. This is a different ball game.'

'I know,' I said.

'But you don't understand,' she said. 'Checking out a friend's daughter is one thing, but she's not an innocent girlchild, not according to what you told me. You're in over your head. The way it is right now, you can get yourself killed and you don't even know why.'

'I know,' I said.

'Don't just say "I know",' she told me. 'Just drop it before they blow you away.'

'I can't,' I said. '*You* don't understand. I'm doing what Hector would do if he was here. Alvin too. Whatever he says. When we were kids back home none of us ever imagined what would happen to us, where we would be now and how it would turn out. When I left home I was ten, eleven, a baby, it was going to the moon. When you got on the boat to go to England or wherever none of us knew what would happen, whether we would ever come back. When you left it was like dying, everything familiar disappearing in one go, just like that. Everything you were going to see from then on was cold and dark and strange. The dark side of the moon. And most of our lives we've been walking through the dark, putting one foot in front of the other. Maybe that's not what it's really like but that's how it feels, and nobody but us knows what that means. When I think about it my real self is still there, tied up with those guys. Right now I can see Hector and me in short pants and singlet playing marbles in the yard, and at the same time I can see Hector trapped in a hospital somewhere in England, and all I can think is that he needs me, and if I walked away from that I wouldn't be the same person any more. To you it's the old days, or part of your background or something to do with your mother or black history or some exotic romantic bullshit. Back home, back home, y'all say as if you know what you're talking about. To me it's the foundation of my life. I don't understand it, because I'm not that kid any more and I'll probably never go there again, but it's what I am. *I owe this.*'

I hadn't intended to say any of that and I wasn't sure I

knew exactly what it meant. Bonny was looking at me as if she'd never seen me before.

'Who do you owe it to?' she said.

'I don't know. Me.'

She looked away, grimacing, as if there was a lot more to say but she didn't know how to go about it. 'What about Sophie?' she said. 'She's not one of us.'

'She's one of me,' I said. 'I decide that. You keep coming with all these hints. You think I didn't notice the shade of her skin? I'm loyal to my friends and my memories and want progress for the race. That's how we were brought up, you know that. That don't change. But there's no reason, whether it's psychological or sociological or mystical or whatever, that's gonna make me join that exclusion shit. You can think what you like about me, but no gang is going to tell me how to feel and who to like. The heavens can fall, but that's how I am and how I'm going to be.'

I don't know what I was expecting her to say. I thought she might get angry, or begin telling me how screwed up I was, or go over the familiar accusations of racial betrayal. Instead she looked away from me and got up.

'I'm tired,' she said. 'I'm going to bed.'

By this time it was quiet again. It was past two in the morning. I lay back thinking about what I had told her. Most people thought that they did whatever they did because it would have desirable consequences of one kind or the other. But no matter how smart you were or how hard you tried you could never make reliable predictions about what would happen as a result of this or that action. Even when you knew exactly what would happen in the short term there were always other secondary consequences that you couldn't control. Fools and politicians pretended to be masters of destiny, but in the end all you could do was listen to your instincts and act according to what they were telling you. My instincts were telling me that Mary was in big trouble and that she needed somebody who cared about her.

I rolled off the sofa and looked at my watch. It would be a

little past eight in London, and my son would be getting ready for school. I picked the phone up and dialled the number. It rang for a while and I was just about to put it down when he answered.

'Dad. I was just going out the door. How are you? I dreamt about you last night.'

'What?'

'I can't remember. It's funny though, dreaming about you and you ringing up this morning.'

'No, it's not. It happens in our family all the time. Every time I rang my mum she used to say, "I was thinking about you".'

'I'm in a hurry, Dad.'

'OK. How are you?'

'All right. There's a test today.'

I told him I was fine too, then I said goodbye and put the phone down. Then I remembered that I hadn't asked him what the test would be about. For a moment my mind was there with him, riding through the spring morning on the way to school. Then I came back to where I was, sitting on the floor, my hand still resting on the telephone. I had my own tests coming up, I thought, and I had no idea what they were or whether I would pass or fail.

The door opened slowly, and Bonny came in, her long bare legs silhouetted against the dim light in the passage. She closed the door behind her and walked across the room, climbed over me and lay on the sofa. Her hand cupped my face, her fingers scraping through the stubble on my chin. I turned and stroked her flat belly, moving my hand lightly over the crisp patch of hair. She sighed and made a movement and my fingers were sliding in the wet silk between her legs. Her hand gripped my neck, pulling me up and over her, and we ended clutching together on the narrow sofa, her legs wrapped tight around me, my penis slithering against her as she pushed against me.

'This is just tonight, OK?' she whispered. 'Tomorrow we'll talk. Tonight, let's just do it.'

150

Chapter 17

Sophie was already up, dressed in a pair of shorts and a T-shirt and making tea, when I arrived. I told her what had happened the day before while we were drinking it, and when I got to the bit where Schumann told me about Mary, she frowned and twisted her lips scornfully.

'*Canalla*. Pig. He's lying.'

I looked at her, a little surprised that she was so angry on Mary's behalf. It hadn't occurred to me that she might feel passionate about defending a girl she didn't know and had never even seen.

'I don't know,' I said. 'There's a bunch of lies somewhere in there, but I'm not certain what they are.'

I told her about Claude and the two men in the Buick.

'And no one told you what she stole?'

'No. Oscar reckoned that the mob might be tied up in some kind of art object scam with Schumann, but they'd never keep those things in an unguarded apartment where Mary could come and go as she did. He thinks it's got to be something incriminating that she got hold of somehow.'

'That makes sense. If it was valuable she or her boyfriend could sell it or pawn it.'

'Maybe,' I said. 'But whatever it is I can't think of anything to do except keep on trying to find Arnold Jackson.'

She smiled triumphantly, and leaned forward with a business-like air. 'OK. They told me which classes he was taking. I spoke to the instructors, but no one has seen him for weeks.'

The look on her face told me she had more, and I waited.

'Then I talked to a girl who knew one of his friends and she said she would bring this friend to meet me today.'

'What time?'

'Towards lunchtime.'

'I'm coming.'

'If you're there you might frighten them off.'

We argued about this for a little while, and eventually decided that if Arnold's friends agreed to talk to me she would bring them to a restaurant near the college in a couple of hours.

She left soon after, eager to get started. I mooched around a little; watched a game show on TV; watched another. Then I went out and began walking down towards the college.

It was a fine bright day, and I dawdled along Broadway. The grandiose arch of City Hall towered above me like a cliff, the solidity of the grey bird-streaked façade giving it the look of a grim imperial boast. But nowadays its air of civic triumph felt like a bluff, and perhaps it had always been that way. Further on the bridge, a clump of spindling threads and columns, signed the way over the river to Brooklyn.

The garden next to the college buildings was filling up with office workers, munching the sandwiches and salads they'd bought from the delis and lunch counters which crowd the area. I sat there for a while listening to the voices around me. I had a lazy tired feeling which I suppose was the aftermath of the day before, and I was so drowsy that I almost missed seeing Sophie going past with a tall black boy wearing jeans, a basketball sweater and a high-top fade which made him loom even taller above her.

I got up to follow, then I realized that I knew where they were going and I guessed it would make sense to give her a little time to settle him down and soften him up. So I walked the other way over to the basketball court in front of the college buildings and watched the young men knocking the ball about for a while, before I turned round and went after them along Chambers Street.

The place was a Caribbean restaurant. There was a blackboard leaning on the front outside it advertising a familiar mixture of dishes, blackeye peas and rice, saltfish, okra. Under the menu it said that bona fide students could have ten per cent off the bill if they spent more than six dollars. Inside there was a little bar near the door, and beyond it a room jammed full of tables, half of them occupied. Sophie and the boy were sitting at the back, already eating, and I went right over and sat down. Neither of them looked surprised, so I guessed she'd already told him about me and that I was joining them. She introduced us deadpan, not giving me any sign or hint about how things were going.

'Truman Powell,' I said. 'Like Colin Powell?'

He nodded. I suspected that he'd heard this before.

'You Jamaican too?'

His eyebrows rose a little, but he didn't give any other sign of what he thought. 'My parents.'

At my elbow, the waitress, a short black dumpy woman, her hair in a turban: 'You eating too?'

I ordered shrimps and pumpkin. I told Sophie it had been one of my favourite things as a child, and she made the right noises, but the boy didn't react. Instead his eyes rested on his plate and swivelled round the restaurant from time to time, never once meeting mine.

I shrugged at Sophie. It was obvious that small talk wasn't going to get me anywhere, so I plunged right in.

'I'm trying to find Arnold, and I hear he's a friend of yours.'

'That's right.'

'So can you help me?'

'No. I don't know where he is. I told her.' He nodded at Sophie.

'So why did you come?'

He looked up and grinned for the first time. 'Offer I couldn't refuse. I like coming here.'

I tried another approach. 'You know Mary Cummings?'

'Yeah. I saw her a couple of times with Arnold. I don't exactly know her.'

'Has she been about lately?'

He considered the question. 'No.'

I didn't give up right away. I told him I had nothing against Arnold, and that I only wanted to locate Mary. I told him about Mary's father and how she would want to know, but none of it seemed to make any difference.

'I wish I could help you,' he said eventually, 'but I ain't seen him for a couple weeks and I don't know where he is. He might have just took off, you know. Things getting too much, maybe. I don't know.'

'If you should see him,' I said. 'Give him this message. I'm a friend of Mary's father and I want to know where she is.'

I took my notebook out and wrote a note on it. Truman watched me quizzically. 'I don't know when I'll see him again,' he said.

'Just in case,' I said. 'Please do me this favour.'

He shrugged. Sophie gave me an envelope out of her equipment bag, and I sealed it, then I scribbled my name and telephone number on the outside and handed it to him. He glanced at it and tucked it into the pocket of his jeans.

'I got a class,' he said. 'Gotta go.' He got up, smiled at Sophie, rapped on the table and walked away.

'Shit,' I muttered. I'd been hoping for more.

'Sorry,' Sophie said. She gave me a rueful look.

'What for? Not your fault. You did good.'

'Perhaps,' she said, 'he really doesn't know anything.'

I shrugged. 'It's hard to believe that Arnold didn't say anything to any of his friends or that they don't have any suggestions about where he might be if he suddenly dropped out. If these kids hang out together they'll know almost everything about each other's movements and moods. He would probably have seen it coming.'

'That doesn't mean,' Sophie said, 'he knows how to find him.'

'You're right. But I've got a teenage boy, remember? I've got this feeling he's hiding something. Pretty sure.'

'So what are you going to do?'

'Let's find a phone.'

She took me back down the road to the college. The building we went to was a tower with sliding glass doors, inside which stood a black security guard holding a walkie talkie, but when Sophie spoke to him, he grinned and waved us in. She flipped her fingers at him and led the way, walking confidently, to the first floor. There was a library there, stretching across the width of the tower, and, in the lobby, a bank of pay phones.

I picked one up, got the operator, asked for Claude's office number and when she told me, I fed some quarters into the machine and dialled. When Claude came on the line he sounded cool and relaxed. All's right with the world. I thanked him for what he'd done the night before and he dismissed it airily.

'Hey. No problem. It was fun.'

'Good,' I said. "Cause I have to ask you another favour.'

The line went silent for a few seconds. I could hear him breathing heavily. Out of the corner of my eye I saw Sophie disappearing into the library.

'That's different,' he said slowly. 'What happened last night was one thing. We ran across those guys. Could have been anything. But I got enough doing here. You know what I'm saying? I go looking for those guys it's serious shit.'

'It's nothing to do with them,' I told him, crossing my fingers. 'Nothing at all. But it's something I can't do, and I need your help.'

I told him about Truman Powell and my gut feeling that the boy knew more than he was telling. It wasn't the only connection I had to Mary, I said, but it was the only one that didn't involve messing with a set of bad men. I had given him a note and I wanted someone to follow him and see whether he tried to deliver it.

I could hear him breathing on the line while he thought it over.

155

'OK,' he said suddenly. 'But you have to promise to do something for me.'

'Anything.'

'Wait till you hear.'

'OK.'

'I got a boy in England. He was born back home but the mother got hooked up with some guy and took him there. I know where they are. Luton. It's just by London there.'

'I know,' I said.

'All right. I write to them and she don't answer, all I got is a picture. I want you to go see the boy. He's fifteen, sixteen. Convince him to come and see me, or telephone, anything, you understand?'

I could guess the details. Almost everyone from Claude's background would have a child somewhere in the world. Somehow as they got older it crept up on them, this urge to be the parent they had never been.

'How am I going to do that?'

'I don't know,' Claude said. 'If I knew I'd have done it already. But you promise or no deal.'

I wondered what made him so sure I'd keep my promise.

'I trust you,' he said, as if he'd been reading my mind down the phone. 'And if you don't do it Bonny will be on your ass.'

'OK,' I said. 'I promise.'

'I'll send one of the boys. He's a baby face. Looks like some kind of student. No problem. But all he's going to do is follow this kid and see wha' go on. Anything else he's out.'

I told him that Truman's classes would probably be over soon and that his man would have to arrive in time to pick him up before he left. Then I told him where we'd be waiting.

'Forty minutes.'

I put the phone down and went into the library to find Sophie. It was a light airy space with a glass wall facing out on to the river, and a number of sculptures and paintings dotted about. In Britain, I thought, its equivalent would have been gloomy and bursting at the seams. Sophie was standing at the side of the room, gazing out at the river. I started walking over to her, and stopped in front of a chain saw with its blade sheathed in a pink knitted cover. Sophie turned and when I saw her looking I mimed a chain saw maniac. She giggled, someone said sshh, and we hustled out of the library feeling like a pair of naughty kids.

For a moment we forgot about Mary and Arnold and all the rest and took a fast walk down to the fast food stalls in the alleyway next to City Hall and bought a couple of chicken rotis. Then we came back to the garden and sat on a bench eating them and feeding bits to the pigeons and the seagulls.

Too good to last. We'd barely finished when a young man wearing dreadlocks, jeans and a baseball shirt came across the pavement, scattering the birds. He had a friendly open face and a big grin.

'Mr Sammy?'

'Yeah. You from Claude?'

'That's me. Books. Booker.'

I introduced Sophie and he shook hands politely, his eyes sweeping her from head to foot.

'I'll go and wait by the steps,' she said. 'Just in case.'

She picked up her bag, kissed me and went off to sit on the steps in front of the college. Through the railings we could just see her gazing intently at the boys playing on the basketball court.

'Nice thing,' Books said.

I stared at him, letting the silence grow, long enough to remind him that I was an older man and to tell him that I didn't like what he'd said. In a couple of beats his eyes fell and he shrugged. It probably wouldn't have worked, I thought, if he hadn't been a Caribbean kid fairly close to his roots and brought up to show respect to his elders.

'OK,' I said. 'She's nice, but she ain't no thing.'

'All right.' He grinned at me. 'I got it. Wha' go on? He said do what you said.'

I showed him the picture of Arnold and Mary, and told him he was to follow Truman till he saw them.

'How long?'

'How long is a piece of string? I guess after midnight if he's home and in bed you might as well leave.'

He nodded, grinning. I hoped he was going to do the business, but I guessed that if Claude had sent him he was going to be capable, and that he'd do exactly what he was told.

We shook hands, then I moved to another bench. It would defeat the object if Truman saw us together. I settled myself for a long wait, but it was barely a quarter of an hour before Truman came down the steps with some other kids, all of them holding books and talking animatedly. I looked at Booker to draw his attention but he was already watching closely, frowning with concentration.

Sophie got up and laid her hand on Truman's arm, and he moved away from her a little nervously. His friends walked on, then looked back and somebody said something which he ignored. Sophie handed him a card, and he shrugged and put it in his pocket. Then he too walked on while Sophie came towards the gardens.

Booker had already gone. Impressive. One moment he'd been sitting forward looking at the steps, next moment he'd disappeared, and when I looked round for him he was nowhere to be seen.

Sophie sat down next to me and touched my hand. 'OK?'

'Let's hope so.' I said.

Chapter 18

I'd been expecting something different, of course, perhaps someone with wild hair and piercing eyes. Instead, this was a small neat woman with her hair in a tight bun, wearing a flowered dress with sneakers on her feet. Sophie had told me she was a fortune teller, but she also conducted ceremonies – 'kind of a magic lady'.

We'd come from Chambers Street on the subway and swung off the Grand Concourse into a side street. The old lady's apartment was on the ground floor of a huge sprawling block and it was just as much of a surprise as she was. Big and light, the walls were covered with paintings, portraits of saints with the faces of South American Indians, a couple of them black men dressed in white robes. Along the sides, the tops and the bottoms of the paintings were crudely drawn figures of birds and other animals, sometimes people, walking and talking, ignoring the figure posed in the middle. In the big living room looking out on the street was a shrine of some kind: a big picture of the Virgin Mary, flanked by a smaller one of Jesus and some other saints whom I didn't recognize, with candles flickering in front of them. All the faces had the broad Andean look and eyes which were black and liquid.

We hadn't wanted to go back to Sophie's apartment for a while, because later on we'd be stuck there waiting for Claude to call, and Sophie had suggested going to see Sor Maria in the Bronx. On the way she told me a little more. Sor Maria healed people and it was rumoured that she could cast spells or make charms which would ward off bad luck.

'You don't believe in that stuff, do you?' I asked her incredulously.

She shrugged. 'It's part of what makes the culture too. It's hard not to believe a little bit.' She laughed. 'You've been in England too long.'

Maybe she was right. Thinking back I could remember one of my grandmother's friends who was a see-far lady, a bony black woman who could scare you with a look.

'Right,' I said. 'I was brought up with all that, but that don't mean I take it seriously.'

She'd made a face at me and we'd laughed, but looking at Sor Maria's flat, black eyes I was beginning to get the uneasy feeling that there might have been better ways to spend a couple of hours. She shook my hand, repeated my name and laughed heartily.

'This is not what you expect, eh? You think I crazy old lady, smoke cigar, jump up and down shaking shac shac.'

I smiled feebly, because that was exactly what I'd been thinking.

She nudged Sophie and said something in Spanish that I didn't catch. Sophie looked away and bit her lip, suppressing a laugh. The old lady cackled.

'You want to know the future?' she said.

I didn't think I did, but now I was here I had to play along. 'Yes.'

'Tell us what you see,' Sophie said.

The old lady took my hand and, holding it firmly, led me over to a straightbacked wooden chair in front of the shrine. She sat opposite me on its twin and, still holding my hand, began looking at my face, cupping my chin in her hand and turning it round. After a bit of this she smiled merrily and began looking at my hands, turning them over and over and stroking my fingers lightly with hers. Her face was serious now, and she began muttering under her breath. I couldn't make out the words. They weren't Spanish or any other language I could recognize. Now she was holding my hands tightly, squeezing them painfully, with a strength I wouldn't have guessed that she possessed. Suddenly she let go, and turning to the shrine began addressing it conversationally, pausing and starting again, as if she was listening to its replies. I glanced at Sophie but her eyes were concentrated on the old lady. The candles flickered, and for a moment, there was something eerie, almost menacing about the painted faces. There were so many of them, all gazing blankly, but somehow communicating with Sor Maria. Now she was breathing deeply, her eyes fixed, the air whistling loudly through her clenched teeth. There was a sort of vibration in the room, a sense that something was about to happen. She began humming quietly, and something strange began happening in my head. I felt dizzy, disorientated, as if time had slowed down. The room began to dim around me. I shook my head to clear it, and all of a sudden, she stopped, sat still for a few seconds and looked up at me, smiling again.

'You searching for a child. She is alive.'

Startled, I looked over at Sophie, wanting to ask whether she'd told her. But she gave me no sign.

'You will find the one you're looking for,' the old lady went on. 'But this is very bad. Much sadness.'

'What do you mean bad?' I asked.

She shrugged.

'Much sadness.' She hesitated. 'You believe in the justice of men. But there is no justice in the world. Only the power of the saints. There is a traitor. Men will kill. Watch out for snakes in the desert.'

Then she grinned at me roguishly.

'Eat plenty. Plenty strength for women. Many women.'

She moved away from me and pulled Sophie by the arm out into the corridor, and I heard her talking in a low voice. Then she came back, went to a chest in the corner and took out a necklace of black beads with a little clump of feathers woven into it. She held it out to me.

'Wear this,' she said. 'It will protect you.'

The beads had a warm supple feel, but I felt embarrassed about putting them on, so I stuck them in my pocket.

We travelled back to the apartment without saying much to each other. Sophie seemed cheerful, but when she thought I wasn't looking her expression was abstracted, a little anxious, and I determined to get out of her what the old lady had said.

'What did she say?' I asked her.

She shrugged. 'The usual things. Many children. You're a good man, but softhearted. Danger.'

'Danger? How?'

She shrugged again. 'She didn't say. She doesn't give you names and addresses. Dates. Well, I've seen her do that, but not usually.'

'Did you tell her about looking for Mary?'

'No.'

I felt an irrational surge of hope. Perhaps the old lady had seen something after all.

'I don't like the sound of the danger bit,' I said.

When we got back it was already night, and I rang Claude, hoping that he'd still be in his office. He was.

'Any news?' I asked him.

'Yeah. Your man's gone home, and Books is waiting to see what happens.'

When I put the phone down Sophie said she had some captions and lists to write and she disappeared into the bedroom. I had the feeling that it wasn't simply that she had work to do. She'd been with me all day, and for even longer she'd been occupied with my concerns, now she wanted to be alone. I understood, and I didn't mind, but it was as if she'd withdrawn, and, once again, I sensed that she was absent, a long way distant. I rang Bonny, told her what was going on, and said I was going to wait at Sophie's place for a call. Then I settled down to watch TV.

I woke up hours later, not quite sure where I was. I'd had one of my recurring nightmares, in which I was chased and bitten by dogs, and when I tried to stand, I crumpled up in agony from the cramp in my right leg. When I'd finished hopping about and cursing the pain, I took a look in the bedroom. Sophie was in bed, sound asleep, breathing quietly. I thought about joining her for a second, but I guessed that if she hadn't woken me, it was because she still wanted to be on her own, so I tiptoed back to the TV.

The phone rang before I'd sat down. Claude. There was a triumphant sound to his voice.

'OK. We got your man. Place in Brooklyn. He went in. Booker got the apartment number. Then he went to a bar with another guy, and Books got close enough to check. It's the guy in the photograph. Arnold Jackson. Right?'

'He's sure?'

'Please. Yeah, he's sure.'

'Are they still in the bar?'

'No. Arnold went back to the house, and Books stayed with him. I wanna tell him come on back.'

'OK. Give me the address.'

He gave it to me and I wrote it down.

'So you going on out there tonight?'

'Not tonight,' I said. 'In the morning.'

'Right. Smart move. Likely you'd get your head blowed off, interfering with people's business this time of night.' He paused. 'Something funny. Books had an impression – he couldn't get close enough to be sure – but he had the impression that they were meeting another guy. A white man. Just an impression. Yeah? But be careful. If these assholes are playing games you could be in deep shit. You know what I'm saying?'

I didn't know whether I did, but I didn't propose to find out till the next morning. I'd been lucky locating Arnold's friend because I'd met Jean and she had led me to him. That put me ahead of anyone else who might be looking for the boy. But now I knew where he was, I felt apprehension rather than triumph. If something terrible had happened to Mary I didn't want to know.

Chapter 19

I wasn't up at the crack of dawn. Neither was Sophie. I turned on the TV and watched the news and the morning chat shows without taking very much in. Somehow it was as if I was trying to hold back the day.

When Sophie appeared round about ten, I told her about Claude's phone call, and she listened to me without surprise. 'Do you want to go there now?' she said.

I shook my head firmly. 'I'm going, but I'm going alone,' I said. She opened her mouth to argue, but I cut her off. 'Mary knows me, and it's going to be easier to talk to her or even to get her to stand still long enough to talk, if I'm alone.'

'Suppose there's some trouble?'

'There won't be.'

She gave me a sceptical look, but it was obvious that she couldn't think of any better arguments so she left it alone. That was a relief, because I wasn't half as confident as I sounded. On the other hand, as it turned out, I was worrying about the wrong things, because the next step was easier than I would have dared to hope.

Less than a couple of hours later I was in Brooklyn, not far from the spot where I'd been beaten up by Schumann's thugs. This time I'd taken the bus down from Queens, missed the right stop and begun walking back towards Utica Avenue.

Around here the streets had the familiar feel of the Caribbean. The Montego Bay. Sandy Creek Bar. Plantain. Ice Fish. Sapodilla. The Mango Grove.

Along the avenue a line of middle-aged men standing. Before I got close I'd assumed that they were the usual group of bums you'd see in front of the foodstores and markets in a district like this, but as soon as I heard their voices I realized that they were Trinidadians, and that they weren't juiced up or doped out of their minds. All they were doing was standing there, talking to each other, as they would have done back home, where every market square or public place would be a forum for successive waves of people, gossiping, arguing and just hanging around. This was yet another Caribbean thing about which I'd almost forgotten. But I remembered enough to smile and nod as I went by. 'Right,' someone said, and I flipped my hand at him, wondering for a moment whether I knew the guy.

The next corner was the one I wanted, and it was guarded by the bulk of a huge church building, red brick faced with white, and a newish fresh paint look about the façade. In front of it a huge sign in white letters on a black background announced, 'God Is Love'. Beyond it a terrace of three-storeyed houses, constructed, I thought, for a community that had been more prosperous and settled than the people who lived here now. Next to the church a uniformed policeman was sitting on a wall, wiping the inside of his hat with a handkerchief. He looked up, saw me watching him and gave me a blank stare. I let my eyes flicker away and carried on walking past the houses. About a hundred yards on the road curved and just beyond the bend a low-rise block of apartments reared up on the right. This was it.

The entrance was barred by a door with thick glass panels, through which I could see a row of mailboxes. Locked. I looked at the row of bells and tried to guess the odds against Arnold and Mary answering – or letting me in if they did. I decided not to risk it. I looked at my watch. Half past twelve. People would be out to work, but there was a chance that someone might come along and let me in. A woman shopping or a shift worker maybe. I waited about twenty minutes, but no one came, and by then my patience had begun to run out.

I walked back to the avenue, found a shop and bought some writing paper and envelopes. On the sidewalk I wrote Mary a note. In it I told her who I was, and that her father was sick and had given me a message for her. Then I wrote her name and the apartment number on the envelope.

Back at the apartment block I buzzed the lowest bell, and almost immediately a voice spoke out of the grille by the door.

'Yeah. What?'

'Delivery,' I said.

There was no answer, but almost immediately I heard the sound of footsteps. The man was a little taller than me, going bald, with a dirty grey fringe round a gleaming brown scalp, and his check shirt flapped open to show a dirty white singlet underneath. He took a good look at me through the glass and I held up the letter. In a moment he opened the door a fraction and stuck out his hand.

'You Cummin's?'

He hesitated. 'What's in it?'

'Come on,' I said. 'You ain't Miz Cummin's.'

'I look like Miz Cummin's? What number?'

I told him.

'Shit,' he pointed behind him. Up the stairs. 'That's four floors up.'

'Oh. Shit. I gotta climb up there,' I said. I pushed at the door and he backed off, letting it swing open. I followed him as he turned to go back down the hallway.

'Where's the elevator?' I called out.

'Don't work.'

He disappeared, leaving a cackle hanging in the air behind him like the Cheshire cat's grin. I braced myself and began climbing the stairs. He'd got it wrong. It was five floors up, and by the time I reached it I was grateful that it wasn't any higher.

I rang the bell and waited. Nothing happened. I rang again

several times. Listening to the silence I wondered if they were there, but if they weren't where would they have gone? Eventually I took the envelope out and pushed it under the door. Then I listened again. Nothing. I stood poised, trying to imagine myself as a cat waiting outside a mousehole, but the way I felt it was a difficult illusion to maintain. I weighed the other letter Dot had given me, from Hector to Mary, in my hand, and wondered whether to push it under the door as well. But I had promised to give it to Mary personally. I had to see her, and I had to find out for definite whether she was in the apartment. I would have to wait some more. It could take two hours, three hours, maybe all evening, before anyone came in or out. It didn't matter, I thought, I had nothing more important to do.

It was about twenty minutes or so before I heard a rustle behind the door. I pressed my ear to it, and thought I heard voices. I rang again and when nothing happened, I scribbled, 'Mary, please talk to me, Uncle Sammy' on a piece of paper, and slipped that under the door.

Nothing happened for a minute and I was just reaching out to ring again when I heard the sound of a chain rattling and locks turning and before I could adjust to the fact that it was happening Mary was standing in front of me. She was wearing a pair of tight, faded jeans and a sweater, and she'd grown into a tall, pretty girl with something of her mother's bold, cheeky look about the eyes and mouth, but the little girl I knew hadn't quite disappeared and even without the photo I think I'd have known her.

'Hello, Mary,' I said. It was all I could think of.

'Hello,' she said right back.

'Can I come in?'

She was frowning and she looked behind her. 'How did you know I was here?'

'I didn't. I was looking for your friend Arnold.'

She frowned, thinking about it, then she gave a little sigh of impatience, and her face took on the blank, snooty expression of a busy person having to deal with a tramp at the door.

'You said there was a message.'

In the first moment I saw her I'd felt an enormous surge of relief, which was rapidly beginning to be replaced by irritation. I'd gone to all this trouble, I thought, to find this little girl who used to climb up on my knee, and now she was giving me this bullshit.

I took a deep breath. 'I saw your father and Dot before I left. He wanted me to talk to you. They've been writing and telephoning and trying to get you for months. They're worried.'

'Oh yeah?' She sounded matter of fact, don't care.

'Hector's in hospital. It's serious. Really serious. I don't care what you think about him. Every child has problems with their parents. But he's your father. If you want to know about him I'll tell you. If you don't give a shit I'll go back and tell him.'

A calculated gamble. I had no intention of going away. She bit the inside of her lower lip and screwed her face up a little. It was one of Hector's gestures.

'Come in,' she said.

She backed away and led me into a short corridor with a few doors leading off it. She opened one on the right and we went into a living room which looked as if someone was camping out there. Sofa, TV, a round dining table, a few cushions, not much else. Some clothes were draped over the sofa, and a pair of sneakers, obviously too large for Mary's feet, stood posing on the table.

Moving quickly ahead of me, she picked up the sneakers and put them on the floor, then she swept some newspapers off the sofa so that we could sit down. At that moment Dot flashed through my mind. Hector always accused her of being horribly houseproud, a sign, he used to say, of how deeply her class had internalized the prescriptions which kept them in their place. But Dot always used to ignore the jibe, because he was usually pissed stupid by the time he started talking like that.

'You've been living here?' I asked her.

Mary scowled, as if I'd said something wounding, and her face took on a sullen cast. 'It belongs to a friend.'

I wondered where the friend was, but I decided not to ask, at least not yet.

'How's my dad?'

I told her what I knew, and she listened, screwing up her face a little and chewing on her lip.

'He's desperate to see you,' I told her eventually.

She looked down at the letter and turned it over and over in her hands as if she could read it through the envelope. In the periphery of my attention I thought I heard a sound like something clicking against the door, and when I listened I heard it again.

'If money's a problem,' I said. 'I can get you a ticket.'

'I don't know,' she said. Her voice was quiet and worried, her aggressiveness and cynicism gone for the moment. She made a tiny tear in the corner of the letter.

'Read it if you want,' I said. 'I'll wait.'

She nodded, already ripping it open. Then she got up and moved away from me towards the window, reading as she went. I was looking at her back, but I could tell that it was a short letter, only one page. She'd probably got to the end of it by the time she reached the window, but instead of turning round she stood there reading it over and over again.

All of a sudden the letter fell to the floor, and Mary's whole body began shaking. She bent at the waist, held on to the window sill, and began sobbing loudly. At first I thought she was trying to say something, but I could only distinguish one word. 'Dad, dad,' she was saying, over and over again. I got up to go to her, but as I did so the door banged open and a tall boy, about twenty, rushed into the room. Light brown skin, yellowish-green eyes, and he was giving me a murderous glare.

'Leave her alone,' he said. 'Muthafucka. Leave her alone. Get outta here.'

I stayed where I was, and he went over and grappled her in his arms.

'What'd he do? What'd he say?' he asked her, but she merely shook her head and carried on bawling. He half freed

169

himself from her grip and faced me. 'I told you to get outta here.'

'Take it easy,' I said. 'I'm a friend of the family. I've known her since she was this high. I just came to help.'

He looked round uncertainly, and Mary, her face pressed against his shoulder, said something in a voice that was too quiet for me to hear. He put his arms round her again and they hugged each other some more. Then she broke away abruptly and walked quickly out of the room, her face buried in her hands. For a moment Arnold looked as if he was going to follow her, then he changed his mind, bent down, picked up the letter, and read it through carefully, frowning and clicking his fingers as he did so.

'I guess you're Arnold,' I said. 'I'm Sam Dean. I'm an old friend of her father.'

He looked at me and nodded. 'You said that.'

He turned and gazed out of the window. I sat and looked at his back. Neither of us spoke. I wasn't sure how long this went on, because something odd had happened to my sense of time since seeing Sor Maria. I knew the minutes were ticking away, but somehow I couldn't feel what that meant.

It seemed only a short time, though, before Mary came back. She wasn't crying any more, but her eyes had a damp sheen to them which told me that the tears weren't far away. Arnold made a move towards her, but she ignored him and sat next to me.

'I can't go right now,' she said. 'I think I lost my passport anyway.'

I took it out of my pocket and handed it to her. She took it, handling it gingerly, as if it was a strange object which might explode in her face.

'Where did you get it?' she asked me.

I was certain that she already knew, but I told her anyway. As I spoke she looked down at the scuffed carpet and hugged herself. Arnold made a sound across the room, but when I looked, he had merely drawn up a chair and sat down at the table, his elbows resting on it, his hands covering his face.

170

'I don't know what's going on,' I said. 'But if you told me I might be able to help.'

'There's nothing going on,' she said. Her voice wavered a little as she said it and she still wouldn't raise her head to look at me. 'Thanks a lot for bringing me the letter. But I don't need your help. I'm all right.'

'Mary, love,' I said. 'You're talking to me. Don't try and kid me. There's nothing right about all this.'

'I don't know what you're talking about.' Her voice was stronger and she sat up and looked straight at me. Up to now her accent had been muffled, difficult to distinguish, because she'd begun to speak with an American intonation, broadening her vowels and softening her consonants. But now her voice was pure Gloucester.

'What's the point?' I said. 'I didn't specially want to be involved in all this, but all I had to do was start asking about you and all this stuff began coming down on me. Ben Schumann, for a start. Then some serious gangsters were following me. I saw Nita as well. She told me about the apartment. I went there. I don't know what you thought you were doing.'

That last bit slipped out, because I was trying not to sound as if I was making judgments. I didn't say I'd seen the videos, but she must have guessed that I had, because she glared at me.

'It's none of your fucking business,' she said.

'Yeah,' Arnold said in the background. 'That's right. Ain't none of your fucking business.'

I looked round and saw him glaring at me too. I was losing it, but I couldn't think of anything to do except keep ploughing on.

'OK. It's none of my business, and I don't know what kind of scam you two have got in mind, but I can tell you one thing. Ben Schumann don't intend to pay you anything, and even if he did I don't think it's up to him. Whatever it was you stole, it's not his. Somebody else is after it, and these are bad people. You're sitting on a bomb. Look, I'm a stranger here and I found you in a couple of days. How long do you think it's going to take them?'

That shook her.

'What people are you talking about?'

I told her about the men who had been following me and the confrontation at the shopping mall. That got their attention. I didn't bother telling them about the two men we'd run into in Tribeca. I didn't need to. When I repeated the dialogue between Claude and the two men I heard Arnold breathe out explosively.

'Oh shit. Shit. Damn,' he said.

Mary's reaction was quieter, but even more dramatic. At first she tried to hide her panic, clenching her teeth together and squeezing her fists against her face. But in a moment she lost control, and slowly at first, then more and more quickly, she began to shake, her head moving in small jerks, her knees pressed together, her hands clutching them tight to try and suppress the movement. She looked over at Arnold, a look of terrified appeal on her face, and he got up immediately, came past me, and sat next to her. She leaned against him, and he put his arm round her shoulders, hugging her tight. All their defiance had gone, and now they just looked like two scared kids clinging to each other.

'You need help,' I said, 'and I'm the only one here. Tell me about it, please.'

Chapter 20

'I'll tell you what's happened,' she said. 'But my dad mustn't know.'

It was on the tip of my tongue to say that he wouldn't understand whatever I told him, but I nodded solemnly. 'I won't tell him anything,' I said.

'Nor Dot.'

'No. I wouldn't say anything to Dot either.'

She looked relieved, as if that had taken a load off her mind. That was funny, I thought. She was involved in blackmail, hiding out, chased by gangsters, and one of her big worries was her dad finding out.

'All right. What do you want to know?'

'Start at the beginning. Since you went to the Schumanns'.'

'I don't know. There's not much to tell about them. They were all right. But it was kind of a waste of time. It was just that I needed somewhere to stay after that old bat made me get out my uncle's house.'

The old bat must have been Carmen.

'How did you get hooked up with Ben?' I asked her.

She looked away, and for a moment I thought I'd been too eager. Perhaps I should have let her work up to that in her own time.

Arnold stood up.

'Arnie?' Mary said in a questioning tone.

'Be back later,' he said.

He squeezed her shoulder reassuringly, and walked off without saying anything to me. Mary gazed after him with a worried frown, and as his footsteps sounded in the hallway she got up and dashed out. I could hear their voices arguing, but she had closed the door behind her and I couldn't hear what they were saying. In a couple of minutes I heard the front door slam. She came back in and sat down, her eyes lowered, her fingers picking at each other, the set of her body signalling dejection and distress.

'Everything OK?' I asked her.

Stupid question, but that didn't seem to worry her, because she nodded her head and screwed up her mouth in a forlorn attempt at a smile.

'You were telling me about Ben,' I said.

'Who?'

'Ben Schumann.'

A long pause, in which she picked agitatedly at her fingers.

'He helped me. At first. I didn't know what to do. I mean, the old dears were all right, but I didn't want to be their domestic skivvy for the rest of my life. I didn't have much choice, though. You can't work without a proper visa and a national insurance number and all that.'

'Why didn't you just go back home?'

'You're joking, aren't you? There's nothing to do. No jobs. The only thing was going to college, and I thought I'd rather do that here. That's why I came. Ben reckoned he could get me some work in a design studio when my papers were sorted out. One of his friends was a lawyer, a really big lawyer. He was advising me about how to fill in the forms and all that. He reckoned it wouldn't take long.'

She stopped again, picking at her fingers and staring at the floor. I sneaked a quick glance at my watch. It had taken nearly two hours to get this far. I prompted her: 'So why didn't you just stay with the Schumanns till you got things sorted?'

'I would have,' she said moodily. 'But then I went to the college to find out about enrolling and I met Arnold. I needed the space, you know. To live my own life. So I moved out.'

She stopped again, and I wondered whether she was thinking about how her life had become her own, but she went on before I could say anything.

'Ben had this apartment. He said I could stay in it for a while.'

'Did the parents know?'

'No.' She hesitated. 'I don't think anyone knows about it. It's like he shares it with these other guys.'

'Who are they?'

'I don't know.' She paused. 'One of them is the lawyer I told you about. Another one is a doctor. The other one, I think he works with Ben or something. They collect pictures and things. They keep them there, and they have meetings, and do deals.'

'What kind of deals?'

'I don't know.'

'Didn't you hear anything?'

'No. I had to go out when they were meeting people. It was only a couple of times.'

'So what did you steal from them?'

She looked up resentfully. 'I didn't steal anything.'

'You must have taken something.'

She got up and paced over to the window, but she didn't look out, instead she turned and paced back to the sofa, touched it, tapped it with her fingers as if she was testing it for dry rot, looked around, turned her back to me, and stood still.

'They owe me money,' she said harshly. 'I was supposed to be looking after the place. They had plenty of money. But they just kept messing me about.'

'Wait a minute,' I said. 'What are you telling me? They didn't pay you so you just nicked their stuff and shoved off?'

She whirled on me angrily. She was gripping the arm of the sofa and I could almost feel her body vibrating through it.

'You don't know what you're talking about,' she shouted. She wrapped her arms round herself and turned her back on me again. 'Why don't you just go?' she said. 'It's bloody pointless, this.'

I could have given her an argument about that, but I guessed softly softly was the best way to go. 'Can I go to the loo?'

She made an impatient sound, then signalled assent with a shrug of the shoulders, and I got up and went out. It was a small flat, so I didn't bother to ask where the loo was. In any case, I thought, looking for it would give me the perfect excuse to open a few doors.

The place was a mess. Whatever Mary had learned over here, housekeeping wasn't on the list. In the bedroom there was a mattress on the floor topped off by a tangle of blankets. Around it there were clothes piled on the floor and a couple of suitcases propped against the wall. I would have loved to go in and take a closer look, but it struck me that if she caught me doing that it would all be over, so I turned away and tried the next door. This was the kitchen. A sink full of dirty dishes. Patches of grease caked on the dull grey linoleum. Behind me, on the opposite side, was the bathroom. It looked oddly stark and clean, but just before I began peeing into the bowl I had the impression that there was something glinting there. By the time I made the connection it was too late to stop, so I did the business, worked the flush and then peered in. Somehow the action of the water had washed the needles back into view, and they lay there in the shape of an X. I pressed the handle again, and they disappeared.

Back in the living room Mary was sitting down with her chin propped over the back of the sofa, away from me. The childishness of her pose made a touching contrast with everything I knew now, and for a moment, I felt the guilt of a bully.

'Drugs, is it, Mary? Drugs, is it?'

'Never touched them,' she said, without changing her position.

'So it's Arnold. All this is for Arnold. Arnold is a junkie. Right?'

'I don't know what you're on about,' she said. 'Why don't you just tell my dad you couldn't find me. I'll sort it out myself. I don't need all this hassle.'

My self-control went, surprising me just as much as it must have done her.

'You're full of shit,' I shouted, bending over and pounding my fist on the back of the sofa. She flinched, throwing up her hand to protect the side of her face. The gesture shocked me and brought back a quick jolt of the guilt. I knelt in front of her and took her hand in both of mine. She didn't resist, but her hand was cold, and I could feel it trembling in quick fluttering spasms like an exhausted bird.

'Listen to me,' I said. 'Your dad's my friend. We were born about the same time back home. He's like my brother. If you were my kid I wouldn't want him to walk away. I can't leave you like this. I don't care what it is. We'll sort it out. I promise you.'

I was half expecting another show of defiance, but instead she gave a convulsive gasp and nodded quickly.

'All right,' I said. 'I saw the videos. Was it something to do with that?'

She shook her head vigorously, pulled her hand away, crossed her arms in front of her, and sat forward again. I got up and sat on the sofa, not touching her.

'What was that about? Why did you do it? Did they force you to do it?'

She sighed impatiently.

'Arnold was in trouble,' she said suddenly. 'He owed some people money. You don't know what it's like. They were going to kill him. We needed a couple of grand. I asked Ben. At first he said no, then he rang up later and said there was a way I could earn it.'

I thought about it. A doctor, a lawyer and two civil servants.

'Did Arnold know about this?'

She shrugged her shoulders without answering.

'They didn't pay you?'

'The first time they did. Afterwards they kept coming back. It wasn't so bad at first, but then I didn't want to do it any more. They wouldn't stop, and they wouldn't give me enough money. It was just enough to keep Arnold going, but not enough to get out. I was like a slave. The last time I went mad and screamed at them. They beat me up. I had to get out.'

She was speaking quietly, but the sound of her voice was high and wavering, and she seemed close to hysteria.

'Why didn't you go to someone? The police?'

She laughed angrily.

'Oh yeah. I go to the police and tell them I've got a junkie boyfriend and I've been getting money off these respectable pillar-of-society guys so he can pay off his debts and score. My word against theirs. A lot of help that would be. Anyway I'd overstayed. I'd been working. I'd have been the one in trouble. Can't you understand that?'

I nodded. I wasn't sure how bad it would have been, but I understood her reluctance to go to any official agency. Illegals had to keep their heads down at any cost.

'OK. So you took whatever it was to get your own back?'

'Yes.'

'What was it?'

'I'm not sure. It's a briefcase full of papers.'

'Papers?'

This was crazy. I'd expected diamonds, at least.

'He kept it in the safe. He said it was his insurance. We thought it was money from bribes or something. I knew the combination. He used to open the safe in front of me.'

'Why would he do that?'

She sighed and clicked her tongue. 'It was like I wasn't there.' She shrugged. 'I was in a hurry. The briefcase was locked. Arnold said we could open it later. We didn't want to hang about. One of them could have turned up any time. They didn't leave me alone much.'

The rest of the story was easy. They'd opened it when they arrived at the apartment, which belonged to a friend of Arnold's. After they'd got over the disappointment at the contents of the case, they'd looked at the papers and decided that Ben had locked them in the safe because they were valuable and that he would most certainly pay to get them back. They hadn't known how much to ask, but in the end, they'd worked out that fifty thousand was reasonable, and Ben would never miss it.

I listened to the story with a growing sense of horror. It was hard to believe that Mary could have been so naïve, and that both she and Arnold could have been so dim about the realities they were facing. Even worse was the fact that I didn't know what to do next.

'Can I see the papers?'

She got up, went out, and came back in a few seconds with a red leather case with a shiny combination lock. She put it on the sofa between us, fiddled with the combination and opened it.

'How do you know the combination?'

'It was in the safe.'

I turned it round towards me, but at that moment my mind wasn't on it. There was a question I wanted to ask Mary and now I had the briefcase in my hands it was as good a time as any.

'How did all this happen?'

'All what?'

'I can understand you coming here,' I said, 'and why it was difficult just to go back. But I didn't think there was anything so bad about where you came from. Hector's got his ways but I always thought he tried his best. You're smart and good-looking. So getting mixed up with Arnold and the videos, all that stuff, I don't understand.'

'You mean how is it your best friend's daughter turned out like this?' Her voice was angry and sarcastic and she was glaring at me again.

'That's not what I mean exactly.'

I searched for the words. I knew asking direct questions wasn't the way to go about it, but I couldn't think of anything else. If we were going to work out some way of stopping what they'd started, I'd have to get closer to what drove her. I kept thinking about how I would put it to my son, but I couldn't and I didn't want to imagine my son in this fix.

'I mean I can understand you getting friendly with Arnold, but the rest of it . . . You've got more sense. How come you thought it was worth it?'

She looked away from me without answering, and after a little while I gave up and started pulling the case towards my end of the sofa.

'Nobody gives a shit,' she said suddenly. 'What do you know about my life?'

I wasn't sure what I would have said, but she didn't give me the chance. The words shot out as if impelled by a manic urge.

'I grew up outside of everything. We didn't belong any- where. Nobody wanted me. What do they call us? Half-breed. Half-caste. I had some cousins I went to stay with once. They took me to the beach and then they left me there while they went off to play with some other kids. All day I was sitting there. They never even spoke to me. I couldn't tell my dad even. He thought they were being nice to me. When I came back he asked me if I had a nice time. And the blacks. They hate you for being what you are. They call you different names but at best they think you're weird 'cause you're not like them, like you don't know or give a toss about back home or the mystical mystery of true blackness. All that shit. You're fucked. Screwed up. Brainwashed. Trying to be white. Come out with anything real they say you're crazy. What do you know? Arnold accepted me. Right? He's my friend, and I don't care what you think. I don't care what I did. I'll do anything to help him. What do you know anyway? What do you know?'

I'd asked for it, and now I didn't know what to do with it. Playing daddy was harder than it looked.

'It's not all like that,' I said.

The moment I said it I felt like biting my tongue, because those same words had been said to me all too often, and in similar circumstances; and true as they were I knew they were also meaningless. I had been fearing another outburst, but Mary merely made a contemptuous sound and turned away. Relieved, I pushed the briefcase wide open and began digging into it.

The papers were clipped together in a sheaf with a black leather notebook resting on top of them. They looked like a collection of minutes, receipts, invoices, shipping certificates. At first glance I couldn't make head nor tail of them, so I opened the notebook. There was a date at the top of each page, then lines of writing and figures. I couldn't understand that either. I looked at Mary. 'Do you know what it is?'

'No.'

I went back to the papers, with the idea of trying to match the receipts against the dates in the notebook, but when I picked them up a photograph fell off the end of the file. A snap in clear black and white, which showed a small group of men going into a restaurant. Three of them were white, but the one in the middle was black. All of them were dressed in expensive suits, but if it had been a contest the black man would probably have had the edge. There was something strange about him, though. Oddly familiar but definitely peculiar. I looked at the picture trying to work out what it was.

'You know this guy?' I asked Mary.

She shook her head, then she frowned. 'Yes.' She pointed to the shortest white man in the group. 'Him. Leo. He's a lawyer.'

'A lawyer? You mean one of the guys at the apartment?'

She didn't answer, but as soon as she'd said it I recognized his face from the video. The doorbell rang, cutting suddenly through the atmosphere in the room. Mary leapt up, spilling the briefcase and its contents off the sofa and all over the floor. The doorbell rang again.

'Is it Arnold?' I whispered.

She shook her head. 'No. He's got a key.' She was whispering too.

'Maybe it's the super.'

I was hoping it was, but the next moment the bell rang again, and a voice outside shouted: 'Open up. Police.'

Mary put her head in her hands, wailed aloud and fell back on the sofa. I pulled her hands away and put my face close to hers.

'Is there another way out?'

'No. No. Except the window.'

We were five floors up.

'OK,' I said. 'Open it. You don't know what they want. I don't think Ben will have called the police. Probably Arnold got nicked, and he wants you to bail him out or some damn thing. Maybe they're evacuating the building.'

A thought struck me.

'Have you got any drugs in the house? Or Arnold? Is he holding?'

She shook her head vigorously. 'No. That's why he's gone out.' She put her hand back in front of her face. Behind it her features were screwed up, her teeth bared in a rictus of emotion. 'Oh shit,' she said repeatedly. 'Oh shit.'

I pulled her hand away and held her chin so she had to look at me. 'Listen to me. It's nothing to do with you. Open the door or they'll probably break it down. Go on. They don't have anything on you. Even if they've nicked Arnold, they'll only be coming to search the place. Think about it. You're OK. Just open the door and find out what the problem is. I'm here. You'll be all right.'

She took a deep breath. I'd got through to her, more or less. She was still frightened, but the panic had receded. She stood, hesitated, and I gave her a little push. The bell rang yet again and the cop's voice shouted: 'Open up. Police.'

'Ask them to show you their ID,' I said. 'Go on.'

As she went through the door I gathered the papers up and stuffed as many pages as I could into the inside pockets of my jacket. I tucked the rest into the waistband of my trousers under my shirt. The notebook went into my back pocket. About a quarter of it stuck out, but if I kept my jacket straight it wouldn't show. That task finished, I picked up a couple of newspapers and magazines from the floor, shoved them into the case, closed it, and threw it behind the sofa.

182

I did all this without bothering to work out precisely why. At the back of my mind was a confused idea that if Mary was arrested it would be a good thing to keep possession of the papers, because it might be the only lever I'd have. In any case, I had already determined to sneak some of the pages out and show them to Oscar.

I had just finished when Mary came back in, followed by the two men, and my expression must have showed them what I felt, because they both smiled broadly at the same time. They'd both recognized me, I could tell, but there was nothing friendly about the way they were looking at me. I'd last seen them at the Greenacres mall but now they were standing up I could see that these were big, muscular guys. Dark brown hair, light brown eyes. Their colouring, along with their size and shape, made them look alike. Tweedledum and Tweedledee, except they weren't short and fat and funny. Their suits didn't bulge, but something about the way they carried themselves and the flat staring look of their eyes told me that they were accustomed to being on the dishing-out side of any violence that was going.

'You're not policemen,' I said. It must have been the shock, because I knew how stupid that sounded even before I said it.

'Smart boy,' the one nearest to me said. Now I was close up I could see that he had pock marks on his face. 'You're right. We're not the poeleece.'

He said the word in a drawling accent which I imagined was meant to lampoon black speech. I guessed that he hadn't noticed the way I spoke, and I guessed also that he probably wouldn't. The colour was enough for him. Or maybe I was doing him an injustice. Perhaps he had noticed, and this was his way of making fun of my English accent. Either way I decided to give him a break and ignore the sarcasm.

'What do you want?'

He glanced at his partner, the sarky grin still pasted on his face. 'What do we want?' He sniggered. 'This ain't Jamaica, boy. You way out of your ground. You know what I'm saying?'

That drawling lampoon again. This time I could feel it beginning to irritate me.

'What's going on?' Mary said. 'Who are they?' She'd recovered from the state she'd been in before she opened the door, and now she seemed more angry than frightened.

'We're collectors,' the pockmarked one said. 'We collect bags. Where is it, bitch?'

'Piss off,' Mary said.

He shuffled his feet and, before I could stop him, he reached out and slapped her across the face with the back of his hand. The action was so sudden that it was over before I could react, and the thwack of the blow was still echoing in the room as I moved towards him. It was a reflex fuelled more by rage than good sense, but I'd given him too much time already. As I set myself to hit out at him, he stepped back, and in the same motion his hand swept up, a gun in it, pointed straight at my head. I stopped and stood still. The world stood still. The only movement in the room was the vibrations set off by the sound of Mary sobbing.

'Come on, asshole,' he muttered between his teeth. 'Come on.'

Behind his outstretched arm, his eyes were fixed on mine with such an extraordinary intensity that I had the weird impression I was facing three bottomless holes, and I could read death in each and every one.

Cautiously I inched backwards, the gun barrel shifting and following every movement I made. Somewhere off to the side of the room I could hear the other man sniggering, but I couldn't drag my eyes away to look.

'All right,' I said, my gaze still fixed to the deadly glitter of those eyes, 'all right. What you're looking for is behind the sofa.'

On the periphery of my vision I saw the other man walk round behind the sofa and pick up the briefcase. He held it up and shook it. 'OK,' he said. His first words.

The man in front of me lowered the gun slowly and reluctantly. He blinked twice, then he smiled. 'OK,' he said to me. 'That's reasonable.'

I said nothing. I couldn't trust myself to speak.

'Hey,' the man with the briefcase said. 'It's locked.'

Pockmark levelled his eyes at me again. 'Open it.'

'We can't,' I said quickly. 'They don't know the combination and they didn't want to damage it. It might be one of those security things. You know? Mess with it and it sprays you with shit or sets off an alarm. They didn't want to risk it and they didn't want to know what was in it.'

That last bit seemed to convince him. He shifted his gaze, glanced at the other man and nodded. 'OK. We're going down to the car. We're going to get in it and drive away. You and that' — he pointed to Mary — 'will get in the back. If you fuck around I'll shoot you. You understand?'

I didn't reply. My mind was busy working out our chances.

'Say you understand.'

'I understand,' I said.

'OK.'

At that point I determined that it would be better to be shot than get into their car. The end of this was that we would die anyway. But I would have to make my move in the street where the possibilities were more open.

I didn't see it, but Pockmark must have made some kind of signal, because the other man walked over to the door and went out. I went over to Mary and sat next to her on the sofa. She had been crying steadily since she'd been hit, and when I put my arm round her she buried her face in my shoulder as if she wanted to shut out what was happening.

'Don't worry,' I told her quietly. 'It'll be all right. Don't worry.'

I don't suppose she believed me. I didn't believe it myself.

'Where are we going?' I asked.

The man looked at me briefly. 'Shut the fuck up.'

Another minute went by like this, then he looked at his watch. 'Let's go.'

We went down the stairs in a curious little procession. I led the way, supporting Mary, while he walked behind us, just out of reach, the gun dangling from his hand. As we passed each flight my thoughts grew more and more desperate; as we came in sight of the ground floor I took a good grip on Mary, bringing my head close to hers, and whispered: 'Faint when we get near the door.'

I couldn't tell whether she heard me or understood. Pockmark noticed something though, because he grunted behind me again: 'Shut the fuck up.'

If Mary hadn't understood me, I thought, I would trip her up in front of the door and take it from there, but as we came down into the hallway and moved towards the entrance, her steps grew more and more faltering and a couple of paces from the door she gave a loud groan and collapsed. It was a beautiful performance. If I hadn't set it up myself I'd have been down there patting her cheeks. Instead I stood back and gave the gunman my most helpless look. 'She's fainted.'

His expression simply grew more impassive. 'Pick her up.'

I bent down laboriously, gearing myself up mentally. Mary would be heavier than the weights I normally worked out with at home, but I was accustomed to doing fast lifts and the principle was the same. I wrestled with her a little, pretending that she weighed a ton, then I got a good hold, took a deep breath, and straightened my knees quickly, so that her body came up in the air while I was doing a quarter-turn which hammered her feet directly at his head.

I hadn't expected much help from Mary, and I was reckoning on swinging a dead weight round. If it didn't work, I thought while I was picking her up, we'd be full of holes. But I'd misjudged her, and in the event she did me proud. As I reached the top of the lift, she came alive, shifting her weight and kicking out with both feet. The move caught him by surprise, and he was still standing there with the sneer on his face when both Mary's feet slammed into the point of his nose.

He reeled backwards, colliding with the wall and falling to the floor with a shout of muffled agony. I dropped Mary and shouted at her to run. I'd have gone after her, but there was still the gun to reckon with, and as I scrambled away from

Mary I had a blurred view of him beginning to sit up and take aim. I took a quick step and leapt at him before the gun came level. From somewhere outside my body I could see myself jumping feet first. The pictures clicked past, projecting themselves through my mind frame by frame. Dirty tiles, black and white; the man's pale bumpy face grimacing with effort; a close-up of his hand moving and the gun pointing. I heard the booming roar of it, then I hit him in the chest with both feet. The gun flew through the railings and down the basement stairs, and I ended up sprawling on the floor in the corridor. I swung round, levered myself painfully to my knees and got up at about the same time as Pockmark. We faced other in the dim light. Behind him I saw with relief that the hallway was empty.

Then I noticed that he'd produced a knife from somewhere. He was giving me the dead stare again, but this time it was different. I'd faced knives before. I knew about this and I watched his eyes, staring back intently, waiting for the action that would probably begin with a slight contraction in the muscles of his face.

Behind me there was a sudden movement, and a door banged open.

'You muthafuckas better stop doing what you doing,' a voice shouted. 'The police is coming.' The door banged shut again, and behind it I could hear the super's voice yelling again: 'The police is coming!'

For a moment the man didn't react. But then the tension was broken by a clatter of footsteps on the stairs. He glanced upwards, looked back at me, straightened up, folded the knife, put it in his pocket, pointed a threatening finger, turned and walked quickly out of the front door.

Chapter 21

I leaned against the stairs breathing deep, pulling the reluctant air into my lungs, but I'd only taken a couple of heaves when the pure relief I felt was succeeded by a swift flood of terror. Mary. I ran for the door propelled by a rush of adrenalin. I fumbled and wrenched it open just in time to see the man I'd been fighting slam the driver's door of the Buick and switch on the engine. But what made my heart skip a beat was the sight of Mary in the back of the car. The other man had his arm round her neck, and from a distance it might have seemed like an affectionate embrace, but I could see from her agonized grimace that he was choking her into submission. The car was already moving by the time I was across the kerb and as I grabbed the handle it took off with a jerk which threw me on to the sidewalk.

I lay there, almost crying from rage and the frustration of it. In any case I felt weak and exhausted after the exertions of the last few minutes. It would have been easier just to lie there, but after a few seconds I pushed myself upright. As I did so, a couple of drunks weaved their way across the road. One of them was bald, his brown scalp neatly bisected by a scabby wound which ran the length of his head. The other, in ironic counterpoint, had a hairstyle which sprang into the air in the electrified hedgehog style favoured by Don King.

'Way to go, brother,' the bald one said. 'Kick some ass.' He cackled.

'Got some change, my man?' his hairy friend said in a low and urgent tone.

I ignored them and limped away as rapidly as I could. I wasn't sure that the super really had called the police, and I guessed that even if he had it would take a while, in this neighbourhood, before they arrived. The thought crossed my mind that as a law-abiding citizen I should be going directly to the police, but I rejected it immediately. In London I would have known where to go and whom to trust, and even there I would have thought twice. In this city my instinct was to keep away from the cops. Even if I could find policemen whose integrity was guaranteed, I thought, I still wasn't confident that they could do anything useful to find Mary, and I would have to tell them the whole story, which could make things worse. The police would be my last resort, but now I had the contents of the briefcase in my pockets I had some cards to play.

I stopped at the telephones on the corner and dialled City Hall. Eventually I got through to Schumann's office and they started giving me the rigmarole about writing him a letter.

'Listen to me,' I said in the most authoritative British accent I could muster. 'This is very important and very urgent. Mr Schumann will want to hear this. Tell him that Sam Dean rang. That is Sam Dean from London. Tell him I've been in touch with Mary. I have the papers we talked about and I must speak to him. Tell him I'll call back in five minutes.'

If my guess was right she'd be accustomed to enigmatic calls from foreigners. Sure enough the impatience in her voice vanished when she heard the message and she said she'd tell him right away. I put the phone down and walked a few blocks to the subway. Outside it I phoned City Hall again. This time I got through to Ben.

'You've got it?' he asked eagerly.

'Yes,' I told him, 'but there's a problem.'

'How much?'

I kept my temper with difficulty. 'It's not money.'

I told him that Mary had been snatched and I was willing to hand over the papers if they would let her go unharmed.

'I can't do that,' he said angrily. 'It's nothing to do with me.'

'I'm making it something to do with you,' I said, 'and don't give me no bullshit about not knowing who they are. Either you do or they've got a crystal ball. I don't know whether they're your partners or competitors, and at this moment I don't care. Just get to them and tell them the deal, and if they hurt her at all it's off. You hear me?'

I was shouting. At the edge of my self-control.

'You do it or these papers are going to the *Daily News* and the *Times*. It's in good time for tomorrow's headlines. I'm giving you two hours. Then I'm going to call you at your apartment and you'll tell me it's a deal. You got it?'

There was a long pause before he said yes, and as soon as he got the word out I slammed the phone down. Then I picked it up again and called Claude. I wasn't sure what I was expecting, but I had the feeling that Claude was the only person I knew who could help.

'Yeah. Englishman,' he said when he heard my voice. 'What happen?'

I told him.

'Are you sure it's the same guys?' he asked when I'd finished.

'We were eyeball to eyeball the whole afternoon,' I said. 'Course I'm sure.'

'All right, calm down. I'll see what I can find out. Call me later.'

'What are you going to do?'

'I'll ask people I know who know people who might know something. But one thing. Don't go back to Corona.'

I put the phone down and thought about it. He was right. My brother's apartment was the one place where they could find me easily. I didn't think they would have tracked me to where Sophie lived, but I wasn't going to make any assumptions. The first thing was to warn Bonny. I called the hospital and felt a tingle of relief when she answered.

'Hiya. I wondered what happened to you.'

Her voice was cool. There was some kind of undercurrent running, but I ignored it and told her about finding Mary and what had happened.

'Oh shit,' she said. 'Oh my God. What are you going to do? Did you go to the cops?'

'No.' I told her why.

'You sure about this?' She sounded dubious.

'Of course I'm not sure. But I'm going to go with my instinct.'

'OK,' she said. 'But remember, it's not your ass.'

'Not right now, but it might be soon enough,' I told her, 'and come to think of it, you should get someone to go back with you tonight, and maybe you should go and stay somewhere for a couple of days.'

There was a long silence while she thought it over.

'All right,' she said eventually. 'I'll get Oscar, if he'll come, pick up some things and swing by his apartment. Have you got the number?'

I couldn't remember and she gave it to me. I wrote it down and told her I'd call her later.

I called Sophie's apartment next. No answer. I put the phone down wondering what to do. I had another hour before I called Ben again. I glanced down the avenue. I hadn't seen any police cars or even heard a siren since I got to the phones, but I felt naked and defenceless standing there. I couldn't even think of anywhere to go where I'd feel safe, apart from Alvin's shop, and I didn't want to turn up there, just in case. In that moment I had a sense of being cut adrift, a solitary speck in an ocean of the unknown. But underneath it all there was a fugitive gleam of delight. Free at last.

The papers stuffed into my waistband were beginning to fall out, and I went into the nearest shop, bought the newspapers and got a plastic carrier bag with them. In the subway tunnel I pulled everything out and stuck them all in the bag. Then I went down to the platform and took the A to Chambers Street. I wanted to go back to the restaurant where we'd met Truman, and it was close enough to Sophie's apartment to get there in a hurry when she got back.

It was about six when I got there, and the place was nearly empty. Too late for lunch, too early for dinner. A couple of black men in suits were sitting at the bar, talking in low voices. I took a good look at them but they had the preoccupied air of commuters putting a few down before getting on the train. I sat in the darkest corner I could find, and when the waitress came I ordered beer and the first thing I saw on the menu.

So far so good. I hadn't eaten all day but when the food came I had difficulty touching it. The events of the day had left me in a state of jangling anxiety and whenever I heard a loud noise or glimpsed a sudden movement I had to will myself not to jump out of my skin. I read the *News* slowly. The front page was an account of a shooting in Brooklyn. Three dead. No wonder the police had taken their time turning up – that is, if the super had bothered to call.

After half an hour of this I walked over to the phone on the wall near me, rang Sophie's number again. I was just about to slam it down when she answered. Her voice sounded annoyingly carefree and cheerful.

'Hey. I just got in. Did you see him?'

I dragged my mind back to the morning, when I'd last seen her and had been setting out to try and find Arnold.

'Yes. But I can't talk now. I'll call you again in a few minutes.'

'Why don't you just come? Where are you?'

'I'll call you.'

I put the phone down. She would probably be irritated by the mysterious way I'd behaved, but I didn't want to tell her everything standing where I might be overheard by the waiters or anyone else. Probably paranoia, except that now I thought I had good reason to be worried.

I paid the bill and headed for the phones on the corner. From here I could see the squat bulk of City Hall.

'What's going on?' Sophie said immediately. 'Where are you?'

192

I told her.

'Are you coming or what?'

I outlined the events of the day quickly.

'Oh boy. What are you going to do?'

'I don't know. I've got to find somewhere to go.'

'You can stay here. It's safe here.'

'I don't want you involved.'

'Aiee. I am involved.'

'OK. But I'd rather be somewhere else. Just in case.'

'All right. All right. I've got an idea. There's a place we can go.'

'What's this "we"?'

'You always argue. Meet me in the Bronx. At that place you saw me. About half an hour.'

'Soon as I can.'

I put the phone down smiling. I didn't want her hurt, but I couldn't deny my relief at the thought that she was there. I wanted to stay out of sight while I worked out how to get to Ben or whoever had Mary, but I knew for certain that Sophie had been in tougher, more dangerous spots. She'd know what to do, I thought.

I looked around. I was beginning to feel uneasy about standing out in the open for too long. Besides I needed to be in a place where I could take Ben's papers out and look at them. I didn't know what good it would do me, but I needed to know what this was all about.

I dozed off on the way to Fordham Road, and by the time I climbed out on to the Grand Concourse I felt bleary eyed and exhausted. Sophie was waiting in a corner of the restaurant. Black jeans, black sweater, black leather jacket. Her face pale and tight, eyes glittering and restless. I guessed that this was her way of looking unobtrusive. The man with her was pretty eye catching too, in his way. He was light skinned with a thick moustache and curly brown hair, about my height, but the size of his chest and shoulders made him look shorter. He looked up as I approached, then Sophie said something to him and the stare he'd begun working on relaxed into something warmer. It wasn't exactly a smile, but at least he'd stopped looking like an angry pit bull.

'This is Bastiano Bustamente,' Sophie said. 'Connie's husband.'

She nodded over at the waitress, and this time Bastiano smiled openly. We shook hands.

'How you doing?'

'OK.'

'He doesn't speak too much English,' Sophie said. 'But he'll stick around with us for a while.'

'I'm not sure I need a bodyguard,' I told Sophie.

'Think of him as a status symbol,' she said. She turned to Bastiano and translated, and he laughed, leaning over in the chair and making his massive shoulders heave. Connie came across the room, laid a hand on his back, smiled at me and said something to Sophie. Her dialect accent fooled me again, but Sophie translated immediately.

'She says that he is also an Englishman and he's your brother, because his grandfather was born in Jamaica.'

Smiles all round. Connie put both hands on her husband's shoulders, squeezed as hard as she could, then clasped them in front of her, rolling her eyes and shivering dramatically. Bastiano lolled in his chair, smiling a little, like a man accustomed to this kind of admiration. I looked over at Sophie, trying to signal my impatience.

'I have to make a call now,' I told her.

'OK. We're going.'

Sophie led the way to the back of the restaurant with Bastiano walking a couple of steps behind me, and we went out into a dark alleyway, then round the next corner into a small apartment block. On the second floor Bastiano brought out a set of keys, opened three locks and thrust the door open with a flourish. Sophie took them, and kissed him on the cheek, then he crushed my hand in his, turned and crunched his way down the stairs.

We went into a tiny hallway lined with mirrors, through a beaded curtain and into a living room crammed with plush armchairs.

'*Culo*,' a voice said and I whirled round, bumping into Sophie and nearly knocking her over. She held on to me, laughing.

'It's only a parrot,' she said.

Somehow I'd missed the bird until it spoke up. It was a small green parrot, perched in a cage near the window, shifting its feet and turning its head away as if it was trying to pretend we weren't there. The telephone sat on a table near it. I picked it up, winked at the parrot, sat down and dialled Ben's number.

He answered on the first ring and when I said hello he started talking quickly. 'I've located the item you wanted,' he said.

'Is she all right?' I asked.

'Give me a number,' he said. 'I'll call you back.'

I almost gave him the number, then I thought better of it. 'I'm in a bar,' I said. 'I can't talk here.'

'OK,' he said. 'Call me back in fifteen minutes on this number.' He gave it to me and I wrote it down.

'Was that him?' Sophie asked when I hung up.

'Yes. He wants me to call him back.'

'Maybe he thinks they're tapping his phone.'

I looked around. 'Whose apartment is this?'

She shrugged. 'A cousin of Bastiano. He's away for a while. We're safe here.'

'*Pelotas*,' the parrot said clearly.

'Don't believe him,' Sophie said. She sat next to me and put her arm round my shoulders and I lay back against her. 'Was it bad?'

I told her the details, trying to make it sound funny, but she didn't laugh.

'You've got the papers,' she said. 'If they're so important, they won't hurt her while you've got those.'

I wasn't so sure, but there was no point in arguing.

She lifted the carrier bag, which I'd been holding all the time, and shook its contents out on to the floor. The photograph fell out right side up and she picked it up and studied it with a frown on her face.

'This man is familiar.'

'He's one of the men in the video we saw.'

She shook her head. 'Not him. The African.'

I left her to it and rang the number Ben had given me.

'They'll exchange her,' he said, 'for the papers you've got. But we have to talk. To arrange things. Where can I meet you?'

I thought about it. I wanted to make sure that he wasn't bringing a posse with him. That meant seeing him before he could see me.

'The Bronx,' I said.

This patch of the city was Caribbean and Spanish, which would, I thought, give me a slight edge.

'Are you crazy?' he said. He sounded angry. To a white man like him, this was the jungle.

'Take it or leave it,' I said. I gave him the directions. 'When you get there, park and wait. I'll contact you.'

I put the phone down. Something Sophie said had hit me while I was talking to Ben. She was still gazing at the photo.

'You said African. Why?'

She looked surprised. 'He's African, I think. Not American.'

It hadn't occurred to me, but now she'd said it I could see it clearly. Most black people outside Africa descend from a racial mixture of one kind or the other. Europeans, Indians, Chinese, all of them have at one point or the other stuck their fingers in the New World's black gene pool. Even in the odd place where that didn't happen the people were mixtures of various tribes and races from Africa itself. In any case, after two hundred years or more, finding a pure-bred descendant of the Yorubas or the Ibos would be miracle. But the man in the photograph had a classic West African face and build, and once I saw that I knew who he was.

'He's a government minister, Sierra Leone? Somewhere like that. They locked him up sometime last year when there was a coup.'

'That's right,' Sophie said excitedly. 'I saw him once at the airport in London.'

We stared at the photo, trying to remember the name.

'Why is his photograph here? What was he doing?'

I was beginning to get an inkling, but I couldn't put it into words right then. 'That's one of the things I'll ask Ben,' I told her.

'*Chinga tu madre,*' the parrot said.

Chapter 22

Even though I denied being hungry Sophie insisted on going out to the restaurant for some food, and when I was alone with the parrot I picked up the phone and called Claude. No answer. I tried Bonny next. Still no answer. I went back to the papers which were still lying spread out on the floor.

I'd been thinking about how to make sense of them and I decided the first thing to do was to divide them into categories. Most of them seemed to be minutes, with a date and a short row of initials at the top, under what I took to be the company name. Medwise. Then there were what looked like invoices and receipts, all of them stamped with the logo of another company, Westwaste Fla.

In a while I had four little piles of paper, and I started going through the minutes. I guessed the initials BS stood for Ben Schumann, but there was nothing else I could recognize. Most of it seemed to be a record of dealings with various companies, cryptic in the way of company minutes, and it struck me almost immediately that I'd have to know a great deal more about the business they were describing before I could work out why they were so important. There were no references to Africa or any Africans. I began going through the receipts and invoices and gradually a pattern started to emerge. I kept coming across the word landfill and it was now obvious that the deals were about waste and waste disposal. I went back to the minutes and began checking off the names of the companies, a picture forming in my mind. This was a company which collected waste from various sources and shipped it to various parts of the country. So far so good, but no closer to understanding the importance of these papers.

I was just gearing myself up to have another go at working it out when I heard the key in the lock and Sophie came in. She began doling the food out of the cardboard containers without a word. The usual stuff: rice, pork, beans.

She'd brought a ripe banana for the parrot and when she stuck it through the bars the bird pecked suspiciously, drawing its head back and making sudden darts at the fruit.

'Even if you didn't know,' I told Sophie. 'Everything about that bird would tell you it was an immigrant.'

She rolled her eyes, picked a piece of fried plantain off my plate, chewed a bit and mimicked the parrot's voice. 'Pelotas.'

I gave up. She wasn't in the mood for philosophical speculation, so I told her what I'd gleaned so far from the papers.

'Waste disposal,' she said. 'That sounds about right. Drugs or waste disposal. That's where the money is.'

'That's simple enough, but where's the connection between all these people and why are they so anxious to get these papers back?'

She shrugged. 'I'm no good at puzzles.'

I wasn't either, and neither of us knew enough about the context in which all this was happening to make educated guesses.

'Oscar could probably figure all this out.'

'So show it to him.'

I picked up the phone and dialled again. Still no answer.

'Don't worry,' Sophie said, 'it's only nine. They could be anywhere.'

I nodded. I wasn't worrying about them. I was worrying about myself.

'Is Bastiano coming?'

'Yes. He'll be here in a minute.'

'Listen,' I said. 'You sure he doesn't mind?'

She smiled. 'It's nothing. This is his back yard, and he's kind of macho. He'd do it just because I'm a friend of Connie and I asked. To refuse would be inhospitable. And we might think he was too nervous or something. It's just a question of asking in the right way.'

The doorbell rang and she gave me a cocky gesture. 'That's him.' She went to the door and came back with Bastiano. He made the room look smaller, until he sat down. I didn't trust my Spanish so I told Sophie to translate. Leaving out the stuff I thought he didn't need to know, I told him I had an appointment with a man I didn't trust, and I needed to check that he was alone and unarmed. Then I told him what I wanted him to do. He listened carefully, nodding seriously, but with no surprise, as if all this was all in a day's work. After I'd finished he thought a bit.

'OK,' he said. 'No problem.'

I told him I was grateful for his help, and he shook his head with an embarrassed little smile.

'Is OK,' he said again.

'The parrot,' Sophie asked. 'What is its name?'

He looked relieved at the change of subject. 'Colón.'

Sophie saw him out of the door, and when she came back I was already immersed in reading through the minutes. Behind me she muttered something, but I took no notice.

'The name of the lawyer was Leo,' I said. 'I bet one of these initials is his. LF. Leo F.'

She didn't answer, and in a moment the beaded curtain rattled as she went through it. The parrot squawked and I looked round but all I could see was the curtain swaying. 'Shut up,' I told it.

I began looking through the minutes again for names, but all they used was initials. The thought struck me that the names of the people in the photo probably matched the initials. That was something else Ben would know. The parrot squawked again and the curtain rattled, but before I could turn around I felt something cold pressing against the side of my

200

face, and I knew right away it was a gun. My heart skipped a beat, and I turned my head slowly to see Sophie standing above me, holding the gun at arm's length an inch away from my face. Above it her eyes were cold and narrowed, her lips pressed tightly together. My first thought was that this must be the gun we'd taken from the two men in the Tribeca apartment. My second thought was that she looked terrific without her clothes.

'You shouldn't play with guns,' I said. 'I thought you'd thrown that away.'

A thought struck me.

'Jesus. It's not loaded, is it?'

Her expression didn't change. 'You want to find out?'

I shook my head, playing up to her.

Still looking straight at me over the gun barrel, she gripped my chin in her left hand and tilted my face up towards hers. '¿Concha o plomo?' she said.

The words sounded familiar, but I translated them automatically before I remembered. This was a version of the formula that Colombian gangsters were said to use when they confronted public officials with a bribe. A gun to the temple and a single phrase: '¿Plata o plomo?' Silver or lead? I smiled to show I'd got the joke but Sophie's expression didn't change. '¿Qué?' Her features writhed with anger.

'¿Concha o plomo?' she shouted.

Her hand tightened round my chin, the fingers digging into the line of my jaw. Her gaze was stony and implacable, but her breathing quickened, and a couple of inches away from my face I could sense the slow, swelling movement of her body. I put on my air of resignation and raised my hands in a gesture of surrender.

'Concha,' I told her.

Chapter 23

By the time we got off the sofa and started putting our clothes on, it was close to the hour I'd fixed for meeting Ben. I knew that this time I wouldn't be able to stop Sophie coming with me, so I didn't argue. Instead I picked up the gun from the floor, and asked her for the bullets. I wasn't going to take any argument about that, but she gave them to me without comment and watched in silence as I shoved the clip in.

Up on the Grand Concourse the night was holding its breath. The roadway was still crowded with cars rushing by, but on the sidewalk there were only a few people walking around. At the bridge over the cross street which ran up the hill to the hospital we stopped and leaned on the wall. I'd said midnight and we were a couple of minutes early. Ben was supposed to park about a hundred yards along the street below us and wait. That way we could check that he wasn't being followed. I couldn't see Bastiano but I knew that he was somewhere down there.

A couple of minutes later a car cruised under the bridge, moving only a little faster than walking pace. It stopped by the corner of the next avenue and I could see the indicators blinking. Nothing happened for a moment, then two men and a woman came off a patch of waste ground nearby and peered in the windows. Neither of the men was Bastiano and I had an instant of panic before he loomed up behind them. He said something and they moved away slowly, with the slinking gait of street dogs. Bastiano knocked on the window. The junkies must have scared Ben stiff because even though Bastiano must have been telling him I was waiting, it took a minute of argument before the door of the car opened and Ben stepped out, looking around cautiously, with the air of a rabbit ready to bolt back into his hole at the most distant sound of alarm.

In a little while they turned away from the car and came towards us. Ben had the same wary manner, and from time to time he'd glance back and take a good look at Bastiano walking a couple of paces behind him, but I had the suspicion that he wasn't reassured by the sight.

Under the archway made by the concrete pillars below me, there was a staircase leading up to the Grand Concourse. We were on the sidewalk on the right and I had asked Bastiano to follow Ben up the stairs to the left and tell him to keep walking until I contacted him. My plan was to follow him up the street until I was absolutely sure that he hadn't brought help with him.

Sophie squeezed my arm and said, 'Good luck,' in my ear. I saved my breath and trotted quickly away past the steps towards a doorway I'd picked out earlier. I got there just in time to see Ben emerging on to the sidewalk. He looked around, and began walking rapidly past my vantage point. I gave him what I thought was a safe distance and followed on behind. We walked a block and a bit, and I could see he was becoming more and more uneasy. There weren't too many people moving about on foot, but the fact was that Ben, with his white face and his Burberry and his wing-tipped shoes, stood out like a sore thumb. As we walked I saw a couple of guys looking back, wondering whether or not to hit on him, and as we came into the second block, a black woman in blue sequinned hot pants trailed out of a doorway and made him an aggressive offer. He shooed her away and she shouted something abusive. I looked back. Bastiano and Sophie were tracking me half a block behind, and they hadn't seen anything or they would have signalled me. It was time to catch up with Ben before things got out of hand.

I ran across the road, feeling like a kid dodging the traffic, and closed up behind him calling his name quietly. He turned round fast and jumpy, and I slowed down and stopped, my heart beginning to pump dangerously with the exertion.

'You're insane,' he said, before I could speak. 'Do you know where we are?'

'The Grand Concourse,' I told him. 'That's what it said on my map. You wanna see?'

'No. I want to go back to the car.'

'Hey, you miss a lot driving through here with the doors locked,' I told him.

He didn't answer. We both knew the reason I'd picked this spot, and we both knew that I was jerking him around. Up here he wasn't boss. Instead he was just another scared middle-aged man, seeing faces and hearing voices he normally airbrushed out of his consciousness, out on his own, waiting for the moment when the animals would come and get him. He scowled at me, then turned and began walking back the way he'd come. I guessed he felt better now he knew I wasn't setting him up, but at the moment when I caught up with him he hadn't been sure, and I'd got a nasty little jolt of pleasure looking at his pale sweating face and shaking hands.

We were back at the car in a couple of minutes. On the way he shook his head when I spoke to him, and I would have pressed him further, but when we got to the bridge we saw that the junkies who'd been hanging around before were now gathered round the driver's side fiddling with the lock. Ben rushed down the stairs. I ran behind him, surprised at the speed he could turn on when he felt like it. His nervousness seemed to have gone, but I wondered what he thought he was going to do about facing down three junkies at half past midnight in this neighbourhood. The same thought must have occurred to him, because as he came close to them, he slowed up and stopped, looking round at me.

'Let me do this,' I said.

I walked past him. The man who was fiddling with the door didn't move, but the other one who had found a brick somewhere, was just lifting his arm to smash it into the window.

'Ay. *Coño*,' I called out.

It was the worst insult I could call to mind, but there was no point in being anything less than high handed with these bums. I knew that. I also knew that Bastiano was somewhere around, and on top of that there was a gun in my pocket. In any case they'd expect anyone serious around here to treat them like something you scraped off your shoes. Any trace of uncertainty and I'd probably have to wind up shooting one of them. I took a good grip on the gun in my jacket pocket as they turned to stare at me.

'*Vete a la mierda*,' I told them as I moved closer in.

They went reluctantly. I could tell they were thinking about their chances, but there were two of us, and they had no idea who I was. Cursing them in Spanish helped.

'Get in the car,' I told Ben. He got in. I opened the passenger door and held my hand out.

'Keys,' I said. 'We'll talk here and I don't want any surprises.'

He hesitated for a moment, then gave them to me, and I got in. I could feel the adrenalin buzzing through me. If I'd planned a way of getting him at a disadvantage it couldn't have gone better.

'Have you got it?' he asked.

'Not on me. But you didn't bring Mary either, did you?'

'She's safe,' he came back at me.

'How do I know that?'

'You'll have to take my word for it.'

'She'd better be,' I said. 'Or all bets are off.'

'Wait a minute,' he said. 'You don't understand anything about what's going on here. They'll let her go. But they don't care one way or the other. Right now I'm the only thing keeping the two of you alive.'

He might have been trying to scare me but I wasn't sure. On general principles, though, I decided he was bluffing.

'If that was true we'd be dead,' I said, 'and I don't know if I believe in "them". All this could be just you.'

He looked at me and shook his head, as if he was dealing with an idiot. 'Have you looked at those papers?'

'No,' I lied.

'The point is that they're not important. The people I'm talking about don't even know what's in them. All they know is that I had them and now I don't have them any more. That's why they want them so badly, and that is why I don't want them to get their hands on them.'

This time I really couldn't believe what I was hearing.

'Oh no,' I said. 'I don't give a toss what's going on between you guys. If the papers are the price for Mary, they're getting them.'

'You don't understand,' he said again. 'Once they do get them I can't help you.'

'You call what you've been doing help?'

He shrugged. 'I don't want anything to happen to Mary. Whatever she's done.'

That was rich, I thought. Self-righteous son of a bitch.

'You understand what I'm saying?' he went on. 'With the papers I can protect you. Without them you can forget it.'

Now there was a note of helpless intensity about his voice which convinced me.

'If I believed you,' I said, 'where does that leave me and Mary?'

'Give them the papers.'

'What are you talking about? I thought you said not to.'

He smiled. Suddenly I had the sense that I'd misjudged him, or rather I'd let what I knew about him lead me into assumptions about the aspects of him I didn't know. Talking about this he wasn't coming on like a weakling. Instead I had the clear and uncomfortable feeling that I was facing a powerful and subtle mind.

'The photograph is the important part. They don't know

the photo exists. Not yet. You give them the papers and you give me the photo.'

'Why would I do that?'

'Because you don't know what to do with it. Even if you knew what it meant.'

'Who are they? The people in the photo.'

'You don't want to know. You don't need to know. All you need to do is take the photograph out of the package. You don't even have to give it to me yet. Just keep it away from them. We can make whatever deal you want later.'

'I don't want to make any deals,' I told him. 'I just want to get Mary out of this and back home. Let's talk about that.'

'OK. They want you to bring the papers. Hand them over to me, and they'll let her go.'

'I'll have to see her first.'

He shrugged. 'Sure.'

'I choose the place.'

'Where?'

I'd already decided about that. 'Ring me half an hour before and I'll tell you where.'

He laughed. 'Forget it.'

'OK,' I said. I put my hand on the door and began pushing it open.

'Wait a minute,' he said. 'Is that it?'

'Yes,' I told him. 'I may be mad but I'm not stupid.'

He stared at me for a moment, then he gave a sigh of resignation. 'I'll talk to them.'

'When?'

'Tomorrow night.'

'You mean tonight.'

'That's what I mean. I'll talk to them and make the arrangements.'

'So I'll call you in the afternoon and check out the details.'

He nodded. I began opening the door.

'Don't do anything stupid,' he said. 'These are serious people.'

'I'm serious too.'

He put his hand on my arm. His face was lit by the pale gleams of light bouncing through the windscreen from the street lamps, and I could see him giving me a worried frown. 'Let me tell you something,' he said. 'When I said stupid I was thinking that there are things you don't know. If you try to use the papers – say, for instance, you copy them and send them to a reporter or the police . . .'

These were exactly the thoughts running my mind but I shook my head. All innocence.

'. . . You do that,' he continued, 'and what they do is get the stuff giftwrapped, then they'll kill you and the girl just for pissing them off. Am I getting through to you?'

I couldn't be sure what I believed any more, but I nodded at him.

'You'll give me the photograph?'

I nodded again.

'Where is it?'

I shook my head. 'You'll get it when I've got Mary.'

'I need something more definite.'

'What's definite? I'm not going to tell you where we'll be. I'm not going to meet you again. All I can do is deliver the photograph to you within a few hours after we get away. Best I can do.'

'OK,' he said eventually. Then he gave me what I took to be his hardest stare. 'If you're jerking me around everything starts again.'

I didn't bother to reply. Instead I tossed him the keys, got out of the car, slammed the door, and walked away without looking back.

Chapter 24

By the time we got back to the restaurant it was quiet and empty, but Connie didn't seem to be making any moves to close. Instead, she called us over to the bar, set out four small glasses and began pouring rum. Sophie launched into an animated account of how things had gone. She started off in Spanish, and she translated from time to time, because after the first sentence or so I'd got lost in Connie and Bastiano's dialect again. I couldn't remember how much or how little I'd told Sophie to let them know about what was going on, but in any case she seemed to have told them everything, and after a while the conversation turned into a discussion about what sort of scam Ben was running. Connie was convinced that he was the middle man for some big noise in City Hall. She argued her point loudly, making rapid, jerky gestures, and sticking out her index finger at the end of every sentence.

I listened without quite taking in what she was saying, because looking at her was something of a distraction. She was wearing a short tight black dress. I was certain that I'd seen her in it before, but there was something different about her and after a while I realized it was that she wasn't wearing an apron. Somehow it changed her appearance. Or perhaps what had changed was the way I was seeing her.

'Politicians,' she addressed me directly. 'They are only criminals who have not yet been discovered.'

I glanced over at Bastiano. He was leaning sideways on his elbow, watching her with a little smile, and I had the feeling that she was performing for him. Her hair was tied back behind her neck, and now she reached back, unfastened the clasp, and shook her head. Her black eyes gleamed at us through the tangle of hair around her face, and then she turned to the mirror behind the bar and began smoothing it back.

'What time do you close?' I asked her.

She shrugged. 'If there are more customers I stay open. If not maybe soon.'

'Another hour? I want to meet a friend here.'

'No problem.'

I went over to the payphone on the wall at the end of the bar and called Oscar's number. This time he answered.

'Hey. How ya doing?'

I told him I was OK and asked after Bonny.

'She's here. You want to talk to her?'

'Yes. But I want to ask you something.'

'Ask.'

'Can you come and see me tonight? Some things have happened and I want you to look at some papers before tomorrow. I want to know what it all means. Maybe you can figure it out.'

He was silent for a moment. 'Shall I bring Bonny?'

'Yes. I'll talk to her then.' I directed him to the restaurant. 'I don't expect anyone's watching you, but try and check whether you're being followed.'

I put down the phone before he could ask me any questions, and went back to the bar, where Connie was still telling Sophie about how corrupt the politicians were in this part of the world.

'England,' Bastiano said in English as I sat down. 'Is good?'

He had a soft, thin voice, incongruous for such a big man, and I had to strain to hear what he was saying. I wasn't sure I had him right. 'What?'

210

'He's asking you about England,' Sophie said.

I shrugged. 'I'd rather be in the Caribbean,' I said flippantly, then I saw Sophie frowning, and I realized that Bastiano was asking for a serious answer. He wasn't the type who made conversation, and in any case he'd find flippancy of that kind patronizing. Where he came from men talked seriously to each other, and when it was time for comedy the signals would be obvious.

'I mean something more than the weather, the sunshine and the warmth,' I said quickly. They all looked at me expectantly. What the hell did I mean? 'You get used to the weather,' I said. 'Occasionally when I'm in the tropics I miss the hint of dampness in the air. When it rains sometimes, it's like a mist, a thin drizzle or tiny drops carried in the wind, like standing by the sea when there's a strong breeze.'

Bastiano nodded slowly, turning the image over. 'You like to live there?'

'Sometimes.'

'Sometimes why not?' Connie broke in. 'The people? Cold. Like the weather. No?' She giggled. 'Especially the women.'

Sophie was watching me, an ironical smile twisting her lips.

'Not exactly cold,' I said. 'It's just that they have rules for everything, and they believe that what they think or do must be right. If you break the rules you are a foreigner or mad or a criminal.'

'Same thing here,' Bastiano said. 'But you have also' — he snapped his fingers — '*la lucha de clases*. But is the same. Rich and poor. The queen and the prince in their palace, the poor negroes in the barrio.'

I thought for a moment about going into an explanation of how that worked in England, but I didn't have all night so I nodded. 'Something like that.'

Best change the subject.

'And you. Why did you leave the republic?'

He laughed for the first time, as if I'd said something funny. 'In the republic no jobs, except the army, the police. The small people, *¿qué nos tiene reservado el destino?* Here we have the

211

bodega. I do some business.' He spread his hands. 'We can survive.'

I didn't ask what business he did because I had the suspicion it wouldn't be tactful.

'Hey, Sammy,' Connie said. 'I want to be *periodista* like you.'

Without waiting for a reply she turned away, went down to the end of the bar and fiddled with something under it. The sound of music came blasting out. Trumpets, congas and a man singing. Ismael Miranda. Connie danced out from behind the bar and held out her hand to Sophie, who got up and began dancing with her. They moved easily, back and forth, hips switching and grinding, breasts jiggling, shadowing each other's movements precisely, dipping and turning, as if they'd been dancing together all their lives. I'd never seen Sophie doing this before and, watching her, I had the feeling that she was really a stranger to me. The bottle tapped on the counter, and when I looked around Bastiano tilted it and filled our glasses. He winked at me and we clinked them together.

By now the rum was going down easily. It was like entering a bubble in time where everything else had stopped. Listening to the music, watching the women's buttocks pumping, and grinning at Bastiano, I was happy and relaxed for the first time since I'd arrived in the city. The dancing seemed to have been going on only a few minutes, but it must have been longer, because when the door opened and Oscar and Bonny came in it was well past one o'clock, and there wasn't much left in the bottle.

I could tell they felt as if they were in enemy territory by the way they moved. In recent years the Spanish-speaking Caribbeans had been finding common ground with the blacks in city politics, but most of the black people I knew resented the Hispanic insistence on their cultural difference − superiority, some said − and they felt even worse about the way blacks from the Spanish-speaking cultures hung on to their separate identity. So there were times when these individual encounters could be touchy, but I wasn't sure what to do about that, and in any case I'd had too many glasses of the straw-coloured spirit to care.

I waved them over. The music stopped and Connie came round behind the bar while Sophie said hello and introduced them to the other couple. As he shook hands Bastiano's face had suddenly turned impassive and when he said hello, his voice had become even softer and less audible.

'A drink?' Connie asked. 'You want, like, whisky or something?'

Her accent was now more pronounced than it had been earlier in the evening. Oscar looked at the bottle on the bar.

'That looks pretty good,' he said.

Behind him Bonny sighed and raised her eyebrows at me.

'No,' I told him. It was late already and the last thing I wanted to do was sit and watch them all being cool to each other. 'There's some stuff I want to show you. Let's go now.'

Chapter 25

The parrot greeted us without imagination: *'Culo. Culo.'*

'What the hell is that?'

This was the first thing Bonny had said since she'd arrived. My guess was that she felt edgy and uncertain about the situation. It wouldn't take much to provoke her into blowing up, which was another reason I'd been anxious to get them out of the restaurant and back here to the apartment.

'It's a parrot,' Sophie said. 'His name is Colón.'

'Co – what?'

'Co-lón,' Sophie said carefully.

Bonny raised her eyebrows, shrugged and sat down with a touch of petulance. I ignored her. I didn't know how to change her mood, and I had a hunch that if I tried I'd be giving Bonny the excuse she wanted for starting an argument.

'These are the papers I got from Ben's briefcase,' I told Oscar. 'Perhaps you can work out what they mean.'

He grabbed them eagerly and I had the feeling that his interest wasn't merely to do with curiosity or sympathy for the situation I was in. Both of them, Oscar and Bonny, had a streak of civic ownership that didn't exist in their London counterparts. This was their town, their attitude said, and they wanted to know what was going on in it.

They sat side by side on the sofa, Oscar passing the papers

to Bonny as he read through them. Sophie went off to make coffee without being asked, and I went and fed the parrot some slices of mango I'd found in the refrigerator. As I did so my mouth watered. I hadn't touched a mango since I was a little boy, gorging myself on the fruit which fell off the trees in the yard during the early hours of the morning. These anaemic slices didn't bear comparison, but Colón must have been enjoying them because he ate with a savage but precise rapidity, plunging his beak repeatedly into the soft flesh, his bright, blank, golden eye twinkling sideways at me.

'Yep. Yep. Yep. Yep. Yep,' Oscar said. 'I've got it.'

He was smiling and happy now that he knew. Beside him Bonny was still staring at the photograph, frowning.

'Tell me.'

'These are records of meetings of a company. They have a licence for disposing of hazardous waste. Dioxin, hypodermics, body parts, stuff like that. They pick it up here and truck it south. There're a couple of companies down there who dispose of the material in landfill sites, and they deal with them regularly.'

'I guessed all that,' I said. 'What I want to know is why they're so excited about these records.'

Oscar creased up his forehead and twisted his mouth. His face went cute when he did that. 'I'm not sure. There're several possibilities. I'd say they almost certainly own the landfill companies. They could be dumping illegally. With all this environmental shit going down maybe Westwaste is under pressure. What happens is you get local groups kicking the state into action over some site and then it takes on a federal dimension. I haven't heard anything lately but that stuff's going on all the time. I'd have to find out if there's anything big in the pipeline.' He paused, frowning. 'These records show that Schumann's involved. If there's a serious investigation he's looking at a few problems.'

'Exactly,' I said. 'That's it exactly. I can see Schumann's got trouble here, but I don't see why he'd keep these minutes and why he'd think about them as an insurance policy. Or why his connections would kill for them. And who the hell is this African in the photo?'

'I can tell you that,' Bonny said slowly. 'I think I know.'

She was holding the photo, twisting it around and looking at it from various angles. I waited, looking at her expectantly. Oscar and Sophie were staring at her in the same way, but she took her time, turning the photo round and round, refusing to be hurried. Eventually I couldn't take it any more.

'Well, tell us for God's sake.'

'This is George Barre. He is or he was a minister in one of those West African countries. There was some scandal or a revolution. Civil war maybe. I don't know. I don't think he is any more.'

I waited, while she continued staring at the photo, still twisting it around.

'Is that all? How do you know?'

'A friend of mine works at the UN. I went to a party there with her a while back and he was there. I danced with him. They had about six bands playing from all over the world. Every kind of food you can think of. Great party.'

'Doesn't help much. I didn't know his name but I knew roughly who he was already.'

'That's good. But you missed the point.' She giggled unexpectedly. 'Your problem is you don't know shit about this town. If you did you'd have recognized Frank Marinaro.' She pointed to one of the white men in the photo. Oscar reached out and grabbed the picture. He stared at it for a moment.

'Yep. That's Frank.'

The name was familiar but just then I couldn't remember why.

'He's on bail right now,' Oscar said. 'But it's going to be the biggest trial ever.'

Now I remembered. Marinaro was one of the kings of organized crime, a godfather of godfathers. The police had turned one of his most trusted lieutenants, they were about to try him on several counts of fraud and murder, and everyone knew that the attorney general was busy collecting charges against him.

216

'I remember now,' I said. 'But what's he got to do with George Barre? That must be it. Ben Schumann wants the photograph so it must be something about the connection between them. It's got to be about whatever happened to Barre over there. Was it a coup or what?'

'My friend told me,' Bonny said irritably, 'but I wasn't paying much attention, you know. Like I wasn't interested.'

'Call her,' I said.

'Are you kidding? It's past two in the morning. She won't even talk to me. And I don't have her number here. It's in my book, which is at the hospital. OK? You can talk to her in the morning. Best I can do.'

Her mouth was set in a stubborn line, and I knew that she wouldn't give me any more than she already had. A wave of depression swept over me. I'd been looking to Oscar and Bonny to provide the answers which would give me some kind of edge, a lever to tilt the situation my way, but nothing they'd told me seemed helpful.

'Time to go,' Oscar said.

'Not yet,' I told him. 'Give me a minute.' Quickly, I described the arrangement I'd made with Ben Schumann. 'What do you think will happen?'

His face screwed up, and there was nothing cute about it now. He just looked unhappy. 'Don't go,' he said.

'Why?'

He considered the question, looking away from me. 'I don't know what's going on here, but this is the way they work. Make a date somewhere quiet. Blow you away. Goodbye, sucker. Then they don't have to worry about who you are or what you know or what you'll do.'

'What else *can* I do? They've still got Mary and this is my only move.'

'Try the cops. It's their job.'

'What happens then? Your best guess.'

By now he was really looking miserable. He screwed his face up a little more without answering.

'Come on,' I urged him.

'Maybe they dump her somewhere. Maybe not. But she won't be alive.'

'OK.'

He looked at me. 'She could be dead already.'

'I'll take that chance,' I said.

Chapter 26

I sat in the armchair and unfolded the *Times*, but just as I was about to relax the Dobermans bounded out of nowhere and surrounded me. I lowered the paper and tried to climb up on the arm of the chair, but every time I moved one of the dogs seized my hand between his jaws and pulled me back. Eventually I sat still, but that seemed like a signal for them to close right in. I could see the leader staring at my throat with a frightening speculation in his gaze and I began bracing myself for the instant when he would make his move. Our eyes met for a long moment, and as my rage and terror mounted to its peak I gave a mighty shout and woke up.

I looked around, certain that the noise must have woken Sophie, but she was still asleep, breathing calmly against the pillow. Beyond her the sky loomed grey and ugly over the roof of the building opposite.

I rolled out of bed and looked at my watch. Not yet nine. I was probably just in time. Bonny had given me her friend's name and telephone number, together with careful instructions to ring her early, before she left for work at the UN, because it would be hard to reach her once she'd got there.

I got to the telephone as quickly as I could, dialled, and heaved a sigh of relief when a woman's voice answered.

'Can I speak with Yvonne Alexander please?'

'Who's this?'

I told her who I was.

'You're Hadida's cousin?'

'Yes. That's right.'

I'd got so accustomed to calling Bonny by the name the family used that it was a slight shock to remember that other people knew her as Hadida.

'You're the one from England?'

'Yes.'

'I thought I caught the accent.'

You're the one with the accent, I thought. Years of living in New York had almost erased it, so that she sounded almost American, but not quite.

'Yeah. Did Hadida tell you what I wanted to ask you about?'

'Not really. She just called and said I'd hear from you. What do you want to know?'

'I want to know about George Barre.'

The line went silent.

'Hello?'

'I'm still here.' She hesitated. 'I have to go in now. You want to meet up later when I have a break?'

I suppressed my irritation. I didn't want to leave the apartment but I had the feeling that she wouldn't tell me anything on the telephone. I told her I would meet her and she told me to be at the Grand Central Terminal by half past eleven. I broke the connection and rang Claude. When I got through to him he sounded relaxed and amused. As usual.

'Englishman. You still walking around?'

'Yeah. I need your help again.'

I could hear him sighing loudly.

'I dunno man. I got a business to run.'

'Claude,' I said, 'I know that, and I wouldn't ask you if I had a choice, but this is business too. If this thing works out you could have a straight line into City Hall.'

He was silent for a moment. Then he laughed. 'Bullshit. But all right. I like your style. What d'you want?'

I told him quickly and put the phone down.

'What are we doing today?'

I turned round. Sophie was wearing a man's shirt. For a moment I thought that it was mine, then I realized that I'd never seen it before. It was a size smaller than anything I could wear, and it just covered the fork of her thighs. When she saw my reaction she made a face at me and posed, one hand on her hip. Seeing her like that took me back to the previous night. I'd got into bed and gone to sleep as soon as my head hit the pillow. For a moment I found myself wishing that I could go back about twelve hours.

'I've got to go and see this woman at the UN. In about a couple of hours. I'd better go on my own. Anyway, best if you stay here in case the phone rings. I expect I'll be back soon, but just in case.'

'And if anyone calls? What am I supposed to say?'

'What do you think? Tell them to call back.'

She took it without any apparent suspicion and went off to make coffee. I didn't want her with me when I went to get Mary, and I was trying to put some distance between us, but I wasn't sure that I could make it work. The trouble was that while she didn't know quite what was in my mind, I knew that she could sense when I was holding back. She had the kind of curiosity and self-belief which would make her want to be involved and I expected an explosion when I finally told her that I was going to do it alone. Better if it came just before I went. I needed to think and dealing with her temper all day would be too distracting. Just having her around was distracting enough. We'd started clicking again, firing on all cylinders, and I could hardly keep my hands off her. It was one of those times which made up for the periods when we were uneasy and tense with each other. But somehow it always seemed to happen like this, when we were busy with something else, having to squeeze time out of the day to be together.

I fed Colón and used up some time trying to teach him a few English words before I left, but he refused to pay attention or say anything at all. That was the least of my problems, but

221

even so it was the one that occupied me all the way down to 42nd Street. Still thinking about the parrot, I walked past the Trump Tower and arrived at the terminal at almost exactly the right moment. I hadn't been sure how to recognize Yvonne, but I needn't have worried because she was wearing a small nameplate. In any case, it was one of those occasions where something happens. A stare, the eyes meet, then a hesitant smile.

'Samson?'

'And you're Yvonne.'

She looked down. 'I forgot to take this off,' she said, unpinning the nameplate. In fact, now I had a chance to look at her close up, I could tell that she wasn't American, and that she had only been living there for a short time. North American bodies always took up more space than they had to, as if the world owed them a little extra. But Yvonne's movements had a diffidence which marked her out; her skin was a deep rich shade, as if she'd been in the sun a lot; and her body had the fined-down slenderness and thin light bones of someone born poor in a tropical country. That had to be about right. Bonny had told me that her friend worked in the diplomatic service of a Caribbean country, and this spell at the UN was a hotly disputed government posting.

We walked down Park Avenue talking about Bonny. They'd done a course in international relations in Washington together and Yvonne asked me questions about her which I couldn't answer, as if she assumed we were much closer relatives than we actually were. I tried my best to keep up my end of the chat, but after a while I had to tell her that I hadn't seen Bonny for some time and I didn't know too much about what had been happening with her. She gave me a peculiar look.

'How come?'

I shrugged. I didn't know the answer to that myself. I could have told her that our family was now split between two continents and I was stuck in Britain, isolated from its main current, but I guessed that someone whose life, like many Caribbeans, moved comfortably between two countries, would find that answer strange and, perhaps, insincere.

222

The question skimming through my mind was why she hadn't asked me to meet her in the UN building. Then it struck me that she was operating with what must have been an habitual political caution. She didn't know my business, except for my interest in George Barre, and she wasn't taking any chances on being seen with me.

We went into a café on the first cross street we came to. It consisted of little more than a long counter, with a few tables next to the windows. It wasn't crowded, but there were people coming and going all the time.

'What about George Barre?' she said as soon as we sat down. She'd lowered her voice under the buzz of the attendants' talk.

'I don't know,' I told her. 'You know I'm a reporter, and I'm writing something about waste disposal.' That was my story. Nearly true. 'The name came up and I couldn't work out how and why he was involved.'

'Involved? Who's he involved with?' Her thin intelligent face pecked towards me, her eyes curious and questing.

'Wait a minute,' I said, 'what's going on exactly? I really just wanted to know who he is and what he would have been doing when he was here last.'

Suddenly, she laughed. She leaned back, shook her head from side to side, miming distress for my predicament, then leaned forward again. 'Listen,' she said. 'It's a good thing it's me you're asking, because George Barre is a bad name to throw around in this district.'

'How come?'

'They're still looking for him. What he did was loot the store and run.'

'I didn't think that was such a big deal in West Africa.'

She frowned at me, and I could see that what I'd said was close to annoying her. 'That's the myth they hand out for political reasons. You have to take it, but I hate to hear a black man say that.'

'Just kidding,' I said.

She didn't look convinced.

'For every Third World politician who puts his hand in the cookie jar, you'll find a network of crooks running businesses, public bodies and government departments in the industrialized countries, so don't believe that shit. The only difference is that these people have the power to define what is moral and what is not, and they can cover up for themselves, then get up on a platform and condemn Third World politicians.'

'OK, OK,' I said, 'I agree with you. So what's so bad about George Barre?'

She sighed and looked away from me. I suppressed the temptation to nudge her and waited.

'What he did wasn't ordinary,' she said eventually. She tapped her fingers on the table and corrected herself. 'Well, it's not exceptional exactly, but he was unlucky.'

She paused, thinking about it, but this time I couldn't suppress my impatience any longer.

'What are we talking about?' I asked her.

'The Koussou scandal.'

'Koussou? Where is that?'

She raised a pair of astonished eyebrows at me, and I felt a flash of embarrassment. She would have expected this kind of ignorance from a white man, her expression said plainly, but not from me.

'It all came out about a year ago,' she said. 'It was in the Upper Volta region. In West Africa,' she added, sarcastically.

'I know that,' I told her, and she smiled.

'OK. I'll begin at the beginning. At first it was just a disaster. It was a small busy town at the centre of a fairly prosperous region. It had a cement factory, they processed leather, cotton, exported groundnuts, that kind of thing. You understand?'

I nodded.

'OK. A couple of years ago a mysterious disease hit the region. They didn't have a name for it, so they called it the falling-over sickness. At first it was just isolated cases. The local authorities thought it might be some kind of mutation of a local strain, mosquitoes, sleeping sickness, whatever. But

224

when it got worse, and dozens of people began coming into Koussou with it, they figured it was a new kind of plague, and nobody was specially stirred up about it.'

'A new kind of plague, and nobody noticed?'

She sighed, took a look out of the window as if she was searching for something, and looked back at me.

'They noticed all right, but it happens all the time. There are outbreaks of diseases people thought were extinct; there are new things coming through with a couple of tourists in a jeep; sometimes a hundred people go down with a batch of poisoned grain or bad cooking oil. You don't hear about all this every time it happens, and on top of that you've got one kind of plague or the other moving around the continent all the time. On the side everybody's watching out for AIDS. This is Africa. Think about what's been happening in the Horn over the last couple of years. It takes a real disaster to get the alarm bells ringing.'

'So I take it they had one.'

'A few hundred people died in about a fortnight. That started the whole machine. World Health. Médecins Sans Frontières. Suddenly it was serious, but by then they'd found out what it was.'

Flash, and the TV pictures came back to me. I closed my eyes and saw the long line of twisted bodies, neatly laid out like trophies, and a black man, his eyes rolling in his head, his features working and his feet wandering around in a weird dance as he fell into a dusty rut in the road. Dance of death. The funny thing was that what I remembered most strongly was the face of the white reporter, her features set in a tastefully pained expression.

'A chemical dump,' I muttered.

Yvonne's mouth stretched in a grimace of anger. 'It was worse than that. It was supposed to be a landfill, apparently. Barre had granted a licence to a company managed by his brother-in-law. But then it turned out that he owned it. They'd simply dumped a few thousand barrels and containers leaking poison in the bush. By the time the dust settled George was gone.'

'Is he alive?'

She gave me a sudden animated smile, like a teacher tickled by a good question from a slow pupil.

'That's the interesting bit. There were rumours that the buck didn't stop with George. In normal circumstances he'd have had to share the goodies with someone else or a lot of other people. No one who knows the country believes that it could have happened without the knowledge of the President. According to one version he had to disappear quietly in case he talked too much. If they ever find him a lot of big people will be deep in it.'

As if reminded of her initial wariness by what she'd just said, she looked around quickly. 'I've got to go,' she said.

'Just one thing. How does this connect with people in this country?'

She gave me the teacher look again. But this time it was the expression she kept in reserve for the stupid questions. 'The chemicals came from here. Dioxins, medical waste. The sort of stuff that is strictly controlled in this country and can't be exported except under stringent conditions. They traced it to a dealer in Florida. He'd done arms deals with Barre before. This time it was waste.'

'What happened to him?'

'What do you think? By the time they got back down the line to the Florida company he'd disappeared.'

'That was it?'

She reacted irritably to the question. 'What more do you want? There's an investigation still going on here, I believe. One of their Federal agencies, but as far as anyone else is concerned it's history.' She paused, pushed her coffee cup away from her, and gathered up her bag. 'Why are you asking? Do you know something about him?'

'No, no,' I said hurriedly. 'It's just that I came across the name.'

She smiled sceptically. 'OK. It's not my business and I don't really want to know. But let me warn you: be careful. These people don't play games.' She stood up, then hesitated. 'If you find out anything you can tell me, let me know.'

226

I told her I would, and thanked her. She nodded and walked away. As I paid the bill I could see her back moving slowly through the eddying crowds along the avenue. When she said goodbye she'd been looking at me, but her look had reminded me of Sophie's magic lady; abstract, her eyes seeing past me, and her expression had been a little anxious, as if whatever it was she saw in my future worried her.

Chapter 27

There was still no word from anyone when I got back to the apartment. I told Sophie what I'd learned from Yvonne, but she took it without excitement. The trouble was that none of it took us any closer to finding out why the documents were important, or why the picture mattered so much. Obviously it linked Barre with Marinaro, but there could have been any number of reasons for them being together. Perhaps someone smarter or more knowledgeable could have figured it all out, but until they came along I was stuck.

Sophie wasn't much help either. Halfway through my ruminations she'd announced that she had to write up some notes about the work she'd done, and she'd gone off into the bedroom. Left to myself I switched on the TV, and let the afternoon soaps flood over me. I was sure that I hadn't seen the characters or setting before, but there was still something excruciatingly familiar about the progress of the drama. As I watched a young man with a heavy tan and long blond hair rushed into a bar and took a swing at another boy. Same height, same features, slightly darker hair. Then the scene changed to show a blonde woman, chest heaving and eyes tearful, confronting a man in a suit. By this time my eyelids were drooping, but I wasn't aware of going to sleep, and when something woke me I simply opened my eyes and stared at the screen as if that was what I'd been doing all along. A couple of hours must have gone by because it was news time. Nearly the end of the afternoon and I hadn't yet telephoned. In front of me a team of ambulance men were hustling a loaded stretcher into their vehicle. I reached out and turned it off without waiting to hear what the story was, and scrambled for the phone. Schumann answered almost immediately.

He told me that I had a deal. He named a time and said I was to come alone.

'You come alone yourself,' I said in reply. 'Just you and Mary.'

'That's not how it works. There's no way I can guarantee being alone. So you have to remember about the photograph.'

'The photograph?' I repeated stupidly. In my anxiety about Mary I'd literally forgotten what he'd said about the photograph.

'Yes. While you've got the photograph you're safe.'

I thought for a moment. I hated the idea, but I had the sense that trying to bargain with Schumann wouldn't do any good. In any case they could send whoever they liked whatever he promised me on the phone.

'OK,' I said eventually. 'Come to the Bronx. Same place as before.'

'No. There's a better place.'

He named a mall on the far side of Whitestone Bridge. I knew it vaguely, and after a moment I could visualize it. A huge dark half-empty plaza, mostly car park, set in the middle of a few blocks of warehouses and offices which stretched along the river. At night, once the supermarket was closed, it would be deserted. If they were setting me up I'd be all alone.

'No way,' I told him. 'I don't even know where it is.'

A brief silence. I could hear him breathing heavily on the line.

'Use a fucking map,' he said. All of a sudden his manner had changed. His voice sounded shriller, as if he were on the verge of losing control. The dry bureaucrat had disappeared, leaving in his place someone rougher and nastier. 'And don't jerk me around. It's not negotiable. If you don't show up you'll be responsible for what happens next, and it won't be good. I can promise you that. Who do you think you're dealing with? This is New York. Take it or leave it.'

He went off the line abruptly. I dialled his number again, the tone buzzing sharply in my ears, but all I got was the engaged tone. I put the phone down and sat with my arms folded, my eyes closed, trying to calm my racing brain. After a while it seemed to work, and I had begun thinking about what to do, when Sophie came through the door.

'Bollera. Boludo,' Colón screeched.

She gave him a look of mock anger, and waggled her finger. 'You've got me wrong anyway, carajo,' she said. She put her hands on her hips and shook her breasts at him, but the parrot simply looked away contemptuously.

'What's happening?' she asked me. 'I heard you on the phone.'

I told her. As I talked she watched me intently, her forehead creasing and her lips pressed tightly together. When I'd finished there was a short pause while she thought it over.

'I'll go and get Bastiano,' she said eventually. 'And we'll take the gun. For sure.'

'No,' I said quickly. 'Not Bastiano. They said come alone. It's too much of a risk.'

'We can go there now and wait.'

'No,' I told her again. 'They chose this place because you can see all round it from one spot. There is one entrance and one exit. When the market is closed there won't be anyone there, and if there's someone hanging about they'll know right away.'

'It's too dangerous.'

'I've got no choice,' I said. 'I'll be careful, and I'll take the gun.'

She raised her eyebrows without losing the worried look. 'You know how to use it?'

I thought about saying yes, but then thought better of it and told her the truth.

230

She sighed audibly. 'I'll show you.'

'After I make a phone call.'

The call was to Claude.

'I still want the car like I said, but things have changed. I can't take anyone with me. It's too risky.' I told him the conditions Schumann had dictated. When I started on the layout of the mall, he cut in.

'I know it already,' he said. 'We could follow you in, but there's only one route in there, and if they spot us it's your British booty, man. You know what I'm saying?'

'Don't worry,' I said with an assurance I didn't feel. 'There's no way that Schumann would want to be around if anything bad was going down. If I don't see him I'm out of there. But I think it'll be OK. All I need is the loan of a car.'

He grunted doubtfully, then he said the car was no problem and I could pick it up later in Flushing. I told him that was fine and put the phone down. When I turned round Sophie was sitting on the sofa with the gun in her hand.

'This is a nine millimetre Beretta,' she said. 'The US army use it to shoot people with.' She slid the magazine into it and shoved it home with an easy slap of her hand. 'Now it's ready to shoot.' She fiddled with a lever and it slid out again. 'Take it and point it at the wall.'

I'd seen it before, but now I found myself concentrating. It was dull black, the grip chased with a criss-cross pattern. My hand went to it with an eagerness which surprised me, and as I touched it I felt a charge which made me stand up straight. Handling it when we took it away from Schumann's errand boys hadn't felt like this. Maybe, I thought, it was to do with the fact that I might soon be firing it.

'I've fired a rifle,' I said. On that occasion I'd missed the target. Embarrassing. In any case being on the shooting range had felt like shooting plastic ducks at a fairground, a game, without a hint of the emotional charge I was feeling now.

'This is different.'

Her voice was stern, like a schoolmistress talking to a cheeky pupil. I shut up and pointed.

'Higher,' she said. 'Stretch your arm out till you can sight with the little bump. Now squeeze it,' she said. 'Imagine that you are crushing a soft fruit in your hand until something gives.'

I stretched, sighted, crushed and squeezed, and the trigger clicked.

'OK.'

'Is that it?'

'What more do you want? Maybe you won't hit anything you aim at, but if you have to aim it no one will laugh.'

'How do you know so much about it?'

I'd always wondered whether she'd been more involved with the activists of her youth than she let on, and she must have guessed what I was thinking because the look she gave me had a sardonic edge.

'The colonel was a gun freak. So was my mother. It was a passion they shared.'

I waited for her to say more but she didn't. Instead she turned away and began teasing the parrot, fluttering her fingers against the cage.

Chapter 28

It was gone ten o'clock by the time I left the apartment and took the local along Lexington to 42nd Street. I'd spent most of the evening talking to Sophie about Hector, and that had led to our swapping memories about what it had been like arriving in England. She had always found it difficult to understand my feelings about London. She could have been just as happy, she said, in Madrid or Paris or Lisbon. Maybe Barcelona above all the others. We didn't talk about New York. It was as if we'd both decided, just for the moment, to blot the present reality out of our minds.

Halfway through the conversation I had a macabre idea. We should, I thought, have been making love, because if I was killed, it would have been my last chance to do it. A vivid image of myself, stiff and cold, sliding slowly into the mud and murk of the East River, kept popping into my mind. I pushed the picture away, but it came back again and again.

Towards the end of the evening Sophie fell silent, staring at me seriously. Suddenly she slid across the sofa and put her arms round me. 'Don't go,' she said.

That was the alternative kicking around in the back of my mind. But then it was too late. There was no conceivable strategy which would get me out of it without precipitating a disaster, and at the least, Mary had a chance this way. I tried not to think of my own chances.

Earlier on in the evening I had been calm and sleepy, as if I'd swallowed a sleeping pill, a kind of languorous torpor holding me in chains. Now, as the train clattered closer and closer to whatever was going to happen, my entire body seemed to have speeded up, the breathing fast and shallow, my fingers twitching involuntarily. I laced them together and began taking deep breaths, trying to blank everything out of my mind. Harder than I hoped. The Beretta dragged at my pocket, and every time someone went through the subway car and looked at me I felt like putting my hand over it to hide the bulge. Before I'd left I had debated putting it in the briefcase I'd found in Bastiano's apartment, but then I'd decided to keep it separate from Schumann's documents. Eventually I clasped the briefcase under my arm, so that it covered my pockets. But that made my two uncomfortable secrets into a single lump at the side of my body, like a hideous deformity which I was certain that anyone who saw me could spot in a flash. When I got out to change platforms for the 7 to Flushing I almost bumped into a tall subway cop, and my heart skipped a beat. Suppose he'd touched me and felt the gun? My imagination ran riot again, feeding me pictures of myself standing braced against the wall. 'Assume the position.' Did they really say that? I wondered.

I still had plenty of time left when the train pulled in at Flushing Main Street, but I jumped out of my seat and strode along the platform at a rapid clip. Two stocky black women were dawdling ahead of me, and as I swerved to rush past the one on the outside I banged into the shopping bag she was carrying. I was a few paces on before I realized what had happened and I forced myself to look back. They were dressed in white. Nurses. And they were giving me a combined glare of righteous disapproval.

'Sorry,' I muttered. 'Sorry.'

They didn't acknowledge the apology, turning away instead to look at each other, eyebrows raised. I moved on quickly, but the incident had been like a dash of cold water in the face, clearing my head and bringing me back to the reality of my surroundings. I forced myself to slow down and walk calmly through the barrier. As I did so something clicked in my brain, and I realized that I had no memory of the last half-hour. I'd been looking for the lights of Shea Stadium, but I couldn't remember whether or not I had seen them. My mind was a blank, but it wasn't a restful feeling. I shook my head, clutching at the details as they came back.

There'd been a couple of white teenagers opposite me, talking animatedly. The boy had a short haircut which gave him the look of a soldier, and the girl had been clinging to his arm and rubbing herself against it. Occasionally they brought their faces closer together and, as if drawn by some force, their lips would touch briefly. I remembered thinking how lucky they were not to be facing some nameless terror. How fortunate they were, I'd thought, simply to be on the way home.

Main Street was quiet, the shops closed and shuttered. I went past Alexander's and saw the maroon Oldsmobile on the other side of the road opposite Modell's. Books sat at the wheel, coolly ignoring the display of sneakers in the window. As he saw me coming he opened the door and got out.

'Hey. Peace. Love.' He touched his fist to mine in the approved style, then handed me the keys. 'Claude says call him when you finish.'

'If I can,' I told him, and he spread his hands wide in a *¿quién sabe?* gesture. For a moment I wished harder than I could remember wishing for anything that he was coming with me, then I choked off that train of thought, got into the driver's seat, dug the gun out of my pocket and put it in the glove compartment, then pushed the lever into 'Drive' and set off. A few yards up I checked the rear-view mirror, and saw him crossing the sidewalk to peer into the shop window.

The bridge wasn't far away. I drove straight on to where the signs indicated the Bronx, got on to the Expressway and in a few minutes I was going past the airport. The local streets had been practically empty, and by now, approaching

235

midnight, even the highway traffic was sparse. Ahead of me the lighted strip of tarmac seemed like a long arrow pointing into the dark.

The bridge was a blaze of light against the night sky, but I turned off before it and crept cautiously through the narrow approach roads to the mall. The entrance curved round into the plaza which was the car park. At this time of night it was more or less empty, apart from a couple of delivery vans in front of the supermarket, with the only illumination coming from the neon signs in front of the shops and a row of lights along the pavement. The effect was to stain the centre of the huge square in shadows which deceived the eye and made the whole space seem even darker than it actually was.

About a hundred yards to my left a pair of headlights went on, then off and on again. The car was parked at the far end of the square, and somehow I'd missed it. I hesitated, straining to see whether I could make out Schumann, and the lights blinked again, impatiently. I made a slow left turn, drove a few yards and stopped. The two sets of headlamps made a bright alleyway of light down the middle of the mall, but I couldn't make out what was happening at the other end.

Suddenly the other car began moving, quite slowly at first, then speeding towards me like a runaway train. I scrambled back into the car, closed the door and fumbled with the wheel. But if the other driver had been trying to smash head on into the Olds he'd have succeeded, because he had got within a few yards before I'd reacted. He veered off to the right of me and pulled up with a squeal of brakes, only a few yards away.

Now I could see. It was the Buick. In the front were the two men who'd snatched Mary. The driver was laughing, as if he knew he had me scared stiff. A vagrant memory traced through my mind. This was the one Claude had called Sal. Behind Sal, Schumann looked out at me with an intense serious glare. On the other side Mary was lolling against the window. She looked drugged, or perhaps extremely exhausted. I couldn't tell which. I pressed the switch which wound the window down but the Buick had only stopped for as long as it took me to see the passengers. A couple of beats and it took off, made a wide slow circle round me, then stopped again in the same spot. The driver's window came down.

'Get out the car,' he called.

I hesitated, trying to work out whether I ought to get out the Beretta and hold it in my hand or leave it where it was. While I was turning this over in my mind, Sal reached down, and came back up with a gun in his hand. The thing had a barrel which looked twice as long as the Beretta's. Sal was still smiling, and the set of his body looked almost casual, but his relaxed air was as frightening as anything else would have been.

'Get out the fucking car,' he said.

I got out.

'Leave the door open. Turn round and put your hands on the roof.'

I did as he said, my back crawling with a fearful expectation, and I heard the doors on the Buick opening and slamming shut. In a moment the pockmarked one walked past me, round the car, and leaned in the passenger window. He picked up the briefcase, and looked around incuriously.

'Give it to me,' Schumann said behind me.

Pockmark straightened up and slid the briefcase across the roof of the car. Schumann grabbed it, and opened it with impatient fingers. He pawed through the contents quickly, then looked up. 'This is it. OK.'

Sal turned round and said something to Mary. I couldn't hear what it was, but she took no notice. Pockmark had walked back to the Buick's passenger side by this time, and now he opened her door and pulled her out by the arm. Her feet stumbled and dragged on the ground, but he pulled her round the car and shoved her towards me.

She stood swaying and drooping a yard away from me, and I lowered my hands, went towards her, put my arms round her, and began taking her round to the passenger seat. Suddenly I heard Schumann shout something, but it seemed to take a little while before I could understand what the words meant.

'Go on, do it.'

My heart leapt, then seemed to stop. I was trying to move faster than I ever had in my life, but my body seemed to be slowing down, and my hand was still reaching for the handle of the door when I heard a gun go off, and I whirled round just in time to see Schumann slumping over the bonnet of the Olds. As I watched he rolled over and over and hit the ground. He didn't make a sound.

Time stood still. I don't know what messages my brain was sending to my body, but nothing was happening. I didn't move, my eyes fixed in horror on the sight of Schumann's extended hand trailing over the figurehead on the bonnet. It seemed to last a very long time, but I must have been standing like that for less than a second, when some sound drew my attention, and I turned round to see Pockmark staring straight at me, his teeth bared in a grin which wasn't a grin, and his hand resting on top of the car, pointing a gun which looked like the twin brother of Sal's.

'I hate doing a bitch that's given me hours of pleasure,' he said. 'But doing you is gonna to be fun, asshole.'

It was one of those moments when thoughts rush across your brain, speedy and intense like falling stars across a clear night sky. I had some idea of facing up the bullet, then of ducking away as his finger tightened on the trigger, then I thought about Sophie waiting, and I wished I'd known, because I would have told her how much I would regret parting from her, then I sensed rather than felt the Olds moving. In the same instant a cluster of explanations hit me, like a bubble bursting inside my head. Perhaps he'd kicked the car, or perhaps I'd left the handbrake off, or perhaps this was a precursor of death, the air parting, the substantial material of the world beginning to quiver, the angel's wing brushing me with a sign of the unreality of things. All this was running through my head, and I took it as part of the craziness when the gun in Pockmark's hand wavered, his eyes slid away from mine, and he began turning his head. At this point the lid of the boot sprang open with a soft crash, and in the periphery of my vision, a black man in a long coat leapt from behind the car. There were locks whirling like mad snakes in a circle around his head as he dived for the ground and, almost simultaneously, there was a long stuttering roar of automatic fire. Blood spurted from the holes which suddenly appeared in a diagonal row across Pockmark's body. He staggered backwards, his arms flailing, the gun in his hand flying up into the air, then coming down on the roof of the car, before sliding off at my feet. His body, carried on by the weight of its own momentum, stumbled back against the Buick, reeled along the bonnet and dropped in front of it, as if in a conscious imitation of Schumann's posture.

Sal had been moving even before the body hit the ground. He gunned the motor and took off in a racing start, the air burning in a cloud of bluish smoke behind his exhaust. Pockmark's body was pushed along for a little while in front of the car, jerking and flopping, the arms tossing about as if he were performing a comic stunt. Then the Buick took the obstacle in its stride. It tilted sideways and the wheels went over him with a double bump. Meanwhile the locksman had stood up and, running after the car, started shooting from the hip, pouring a continuous stream of bullets through the back window. Sal never paused. The Buick charged straight across the car park, mounted the pavement, turned over and came to rest halfway through the plate-glass window of one of the office buildings.

The Jamaican turned and came running back towards us. 'Jump in,' he shouted. 'Jump in.'

I bundled Mary into the back of the Olds while the dread got behind the wheel. He was moving before I'd closed the door and the car flew out through the exit. Behind us there was a whooshing roar as the Buick exploded into flames.

'Where you going?' the dread said.

I forced my brain to start working again. This was as like a dream as anything that had ever happened to me.

'Claude sent you?'

'Yeah. Claude. Where you going?'

'The Bronx. Where were you?'

'In the trunk.'

'How'd you get out?'

'Press a little ting. The trunk open. Claude said don't come out unless trouble happen. But I hear the shot, you know. Me say trouble.'

I glanced back at Mary. She was half crouched, half lying in the back seat, her hands covering her face as if trying to blot out what was happening to her.

'Mary,' I said gently. 'You all right? Everything's OK now.'

She gave no sign that she'd heard and I touched her shoulder. She was trembling violently.

'You all right?' I repeated.

This time she gave a tiny nod of her head. My instinct was to go back there and cuddle her, but I didn't want to ask the dread to stop, and the headrests made the seats too high to scramble over, so I simply stroked her arm, then found her wrist and held it.

'Bronx,' our rescuer said.

He was a man of few words all right. I began giving him directions, looking at him as I did so. His face was serious, the lips firmly set, but he didn't look tense or nervous or at all worried about the fact that he'd just blown two men away. For a moment I thought about asking him what he felt, then I changed my mind. I couldn't think what words to use, and in any case I didn't really want to know. I never found out his name. I was too shell-shocked to ask and when I thought about doing so, it was too late.

He dropped us off near Bastiano's apartment and drove away before I could say anything, spinning the wheels in his hurry to take off. In the street Mary was slumping against me, lighter, it seemed, than she had the day before. When I heard the footsteps behind us, I turned quickly, getting ready to let her drop in case I needed to use my hands, but, to my relief, it was only Bastiano, padding up to us with a big grin on his face. Without a word he took Mary from me, lifted her in his arms and walked quickly towards the entrance to the building.

Suddenly I was so tired that my body ached and I could hardly move, but I put one foot in front of the other and followed him in slowly.

Chapter 29

On the television screen, Cary Grant, scooting about in black and white, gave that highpitched hoot which used to be his trademark. Sophie ignored him.

'I was waiting up here,' she said, 'in case the telephone rang. I was going to give it another half-hour. I made poor Bastiano wait in the street in case something happened.'

The guy was a prince.

'I'm glad you weren't there,' I told her. 'And it's a good thing you didn't show up.'

She gave a murmur which I took to be agreement, but from the stubborn look on her face she still didn't feel good about having been left out. I'd been back for a couple of hours, but we hadn't gone to bed. Mary was asleep in the bedroom, and we were lying pressed up against each other on the narrow sofa. I had telephoned Claude shortly after returning, and told him I was back.

'Hey. Got ya,' he said. 'Call you back.' Then he hung up.

I guessed that he'd heard by now what had happened, but he hadn't rung back.

'What are you going to do?' Sophie asked me.

'We're going back tomorrow. We'll just go to the airport and buy a couple of tickets.'

'Suppose that's what they're waiting for you to do?'

I shrugged. I didn't know the answer to that, and I was too exhausted to think about it. 'I'll talk to Claude when he rings. Anyway I don't want to do anything till Mary wakes up and we can talk to her.'

She murmured her assent but we both knew we'd have to think carefully about what we did next. The whole business had never been any less than serious, but the night's events had changed everything. Up till then the dangers had seemed remote, and controllable, part of a world which had nothing to do with me. In the back of my mind I'd had an image of myself as clever and fast moving, too smart to be trapped into the sordid reality of the violence which stalked the city. Now the only image in my mind was Ben Schumann collapsing, his blood puddling down the front of the car. This could happen to me, I thought, and it could happen at any moment. I shuddered and Sophie tightened her grip round me, as if sheltering me from harm. The idea was ridiculous enough to make me laugh, but it came out as a kind of moan.

'What about the police?' she asked.

'What about them?'

That night my first prayer had been to stay alive. My second had been that the police wouldn't stop us on the way back.

'She was kidnapped and raped, Sammy.'

'Raped?' The word crashed around inside my head. 'How do you know? Did she tell you?'

'No. She went to sleep right off, but I undressed her. I saw her body.'

'The guys who did it are dead. Anyway, what do we tell the police?'

We were both thinking about the answer to that one when I fell asleep. The dream which followed was a mish mash of practically everything that had happened to me over the previous twenty-four hours. I had been running desperately along a narrow highway stretched over a deep canyon, when suddenly I found myself blasting off an Uzi at a huge, twisted police car driven by Ben Schumann. The car wouldn't stop coming, but someone kept distracting me by poking at my ribs with a Beretta. I tried to brush the Beretta aside, but it kept on poking at me, and I opened my eyes to see Sophie standing over me.

'That parrot eats a heap of bananas,' I said.

Sophie didn't bat an eyelid. She knew, from experience, that when I woke up suddenly I was apt to say something which didn't make sense.

'It's on TV,' she said urgently.

There was something peculiar about seeing the mall in daylight, a crowd of spectators clustering round the twisted pile of metal jammed into the scorched bricks of one of the buildings. The woman on the screen said that Ben Schumann, a City official, had been shot dead. Two other men, as yet unidentified, had also been found dead at the scene. There had been no witnesses and as yet the police had no clues as to why Schumann had been killed or what he had been doing at the deserted parking lot. That was all. Sophie pressed the remote control and another station came up on the screen, a man this time, with more or less the same story. When it came to an end I let my breath out slowly in a sigh of relief. I hadn't been conscious of it, but at the back of my mind I'd been waiting for some mention of my name or perhaps the sight of my picture on the screen. Common sense told me that such a thing would have been impossible, but the unconscious has its own rules, and for a split second the terror I felt had nothing whatsoever to do with common sense.

Sophie nodded her head and gestured at me. She'd been reading my mind the way she did sometimes. 'They don't know anything,' she said. 'No witnesses.'

I nodded back at her, but out of sight I crossed my fingers.

Soon after this Claude rang the doorbell. He'd telephoned first, of course. Which was just as well, because the buzzer sounding without a prior warning would have thrown me into a state of panic. He was parked, he'd said, on the corner, and I'd given him the number of the apartment. As I hung up I heard the bedroom door slam and Mary's footsteps going down the corridor. I looked at Sophie inquiringly, but she shrugged, which I took to be an indication that we should leave the girl alone for a while. I told her Claude was coming up and she began touring the room, straightening the furniture and folding the blankets we'd used during the night. By the time we heard him at the door the look of the place had improved. It still wasn't an advertisement for gracious living, but it looked a lot better than the bottom of Colón's cage.

At seven in the morning Claude was dressed in an elegant grey suit, with black pearl cufflinks, a tie with black and white checks, and grey shoes; and the first thing he did was to shake Sophie's hand and tell her that I hadn't said how beautiful she was. Corny as hell, but he gave it a gravity which made it seem gracious and charming. Sophie was charmed, I could tell. For a moment I'd imagined that, wearing the jeans and T-shirt she'd had on the night before, she would be a little embarrassed. On the other hand, Sophie was nothing if not confident about her looks, and this was a style of speech she was not only used to, but even half expected from a man like Claude.

His next question was about Mary. The apartment was small and noisy enough for all of us to hear the shower running and Mary splashing about, but Claude went through the rigmarole of polite enquiry without batting an eyelid. It was a side of him I hadn't seen before, but then it struck me that this was a social display, company manners, as much for Sophie's benefit as anything else.

'Did you get the car back?' I asked him abruptly. My nerves couldn't take the prospect of his launching into an hour of small talk.

His eyes flicked at Sophie.

'She knows everything,' I said. 'If I'd been much longer she would have been riding to the rescue.'

Claude's eyebrows went up in surprise. He'd been in the USA a long time, but he was still Caribbean enough to be a little shocked at the idea of involving a woman in men's business.

'I got it back,' he said. 'Don't worry about it. Everything is cool.'

I knew better than to ask about the dread who'd saved my skin. In the circumstances Claude wouldn't want to admit his existence or the fact that he'd been there, an attitude which I shared.

'We're going home today,' I told him.

He raised his eyebrows again, frowned, and screwed up his mouth. It was quite a performance.

'I thought you might say that,' he said. 'That is why I came. I feel you should think it over.'

I'd wondered why he'd come all the way over at that hour, but he'd been so painfully polite that I had found it difficult to ask. In any case I had the suspicion that he was regretting having been lured into so much involvement with my problems. But he wasn't a man who could simply walk away. This was his turf, and what had happened would affect him in one way or another. He would be here to try and limit the damage.

'Nothing to think about,' I said. 'This shit is dangerous. I could have been killed last night.'

Saying it made me go weak inside for the first time. Up till then it was as if I'd taken a tranquillizer, so that I could watch all the things happening round me without the extremes of feeling or reaction. Now, all of a sudden, I was standing in the car park watching a fine spray of blood flying from Pockmark's neck, my ears ringing from the explosive clatter of the dreadlock's gun. I sat down abruptly.

'I'll get you some coffee,' Sophie said without prompting.

Claude sat next to me. He propped his chin on his hand and watched me like a spectator in the front row of a serious fight.

'Think about it,' he said. 'Those people don't care about the documents. They're burned anyway. What they wanted was to get you and the girl and Ben out in the open so they could pop you quietly. You understand?'

I nodded. The effort made me tired.

'So next time they'll pop you. Or the time after that. It's not like you get out of town and it's all over. Believe this. This ain't like some bunch of Colombian peasants knocking each other off, you move to the next village they lose interest. If they want to they'll do you wherever you are.'

'But I don't know anything,' I told him. 'I can't connect anything to anybody. I think they must have wanted Ben. He knew where the bodies were buried. I think we were just pain-in-the-ass innocent bystanders. If we leave now, get well out of the way, they'll know we don't want to be involved.'

Claude smiled as if I'd said something amusing. 'You hope.'

Suddenly I was awake. It was as if I'd been dozing for the last few hours and some unusual noise had called me back into focus. I sat up. 'What the hell is the alternative?'

'Make a deal,' Claude said.

It was my turn to laugh. 'Who with, and what have I got to bargain with?'

'Who is easy. Those guys were connected. A phone call is all I need. The other thing.' He paused. 'You got the girl and you got the photo that Schumann wanted. Sometimes you don't need to know why a thing works, as long as it works. They were hot to find her and they were going to smoke her. Maybe it wasn't just about the papers or the photo. There's got to be a reason.'

'What reason?'

'Why'n't you ask the girl?'

As if on cue Sophie came into the room, followed by Mary. Seeing her made me realize that I'd hardly looked at her the night before. This morning she looked fragile, her dark brown ringlets clustered in a glistening cloud around her head, the bruises on her face standing out starkly against the light beige of her skin. They gave her an air of exhausted beauty, like an hibiscus drooping on the stem. The effect was reinforced by the big shapeless man's robe she was wearing which wrapped her round from neck to ankles. She went to the chair furthest from us and sat down immediately, nursing her coffee cup in both hands, her face turned away towards the wall.

'How you doing?' I asked her, and in reply she murmured something I couldn't catch. Claude looked at me with his eyebrows raised again. I ignored him and told her who Claude was, but the only acknowledgement she gave was to move her head slightly without looking round.

For a moment I hesitated, uncertain whether to press her or whether to leave it alone for a while. Claude grunted. 'I don't have time for this,' he muttered.

It was at this point that Sophie intervened. She'd been leaning on the wall near the door, and now she crossed over to Mary, knelt beside her and put her arm round her waist.

'They have to talk to you,' she said. 'Decisions must be made. It's important.'

A little while passed before Mary responded. Then she shifted her body slightly so that she almost faced us. Sophie looked at me and nodded, but stayed where she was. Without waiting I launched into a recital of the options. We could go back that afternoon, I told her, but I had no idea how dangerous it would be, and I had no idea either, whether in a few days, or months, someone would come looking for her. If we were to do the right thing I needed to know whether there was anything she hadn't so far told me.

'It might be just as important,' I said, 'if those guys who grabbed you thought you knew something, even if you don't. Did you get the feeling that they were asking you about anything in particular?'

We waited expectantly. Talking to Mary this morning had the same perverse feel as talking to Colón. You had to launch your thoughts at them, then hang about hoping that something had connected. This time we saw her mouth move in a grimace before we heard her speak.

'Nothing,' she said. 'I don't know anything.'

'Doesn't matter,' I said. 'The question is whether they think you know anything.'

'I don't know,' she said. 'They kept asking me about some man. They showed me a photograph. They kept asking me where he was. I told them I'd never seen him.'

A vague idea crept obscurely into the back of my mind. It was something to do with photographs, but when I tried to pin it down, it disappeared.

'What man? Who was he?'

'I'd never seen him before.'

I took out the photograph of George Barre and showed it to her. She sat up and looked at it carefully.

'Yes. It's a different photo, but it's the same man.'

She was looking at it as if she'd never seen it before, even though we'd looked at it together when I first saw her in the apartment in Brooklyn.

'It's George Barre,' I told Claude. He nodded and then spoke past me, to Mary.

'Was this guy, Schumann, there when they asked you?'

She shook her head.

'No. He only showed up last night.'

'I don't understand,' Sophie said. 'If they already had a photo of this guy, why did he want you to keep that one?'

That was easy.

'Because it's the other man in the photo that's important, or maybe the fact that they're together.'

She reached over, took the photo from Mary and began studying it intently.

'Deep shit,' Claude said suddenly. 'Deep, deep shit. If they're still looking for Barre, it means he's still around somewhere, and they're wasting every sucker who can tie him up with Marinaro. Schumann must have thought he was safe because he had the photo. But maybe they don't care about that. He had to go. You two were just innocent bystanders.'

The words triggered a glow of relief. If we had merely been innocent bystanders we were home free. I nodded in agreement, but even as I did so I was remembering what Schumann had shouted just before Pockmark shot him: 'Go on, do it.' Schumann had known that Mary and I were to be killed, and if that was true, it was part of a prearranged plan.

I told Claude and he thought it over, his expression lugubrious. Eventually he looked up, frowned as if he'd decided on something, and addressed Mary directly.

'Listen, girl,' he said. 'This is your life. What do you know that makes them want to smoke you?'

The question seemed to galvanize Mary. She'd slumped down and turned away from us again, but now she sat up, glared at Claude with her eyes wide and staring. 'I don't know,' she shouted. 'I told you, I don't know.'

'Wait a minute,' Sophie said, standing up and giving Claude a pretty good glare herself. 'Wait a minute. It's probably Schumann. He must have thought that she'd seen or heard something. Something she didn't know was important. Right?'

She had to be right.

'Did anyone come to the flat,' I asked Mary, 'apart from those guys in the video? Like business?'

'Yeah, sure,' she said, in something like her normal tone of voice. 'But I didn't even see them. I had to keep out of the way whenever he had a meeting or something like that.'

It was logical. Schumann would make sure that Mary didn't know anything worth knowing about his scams. I shrugged, then I realized that Sophie was looking at me with her eyebrows raised, one of her private signals. She was trying to tell me something, and, in a flash, I knew what it was.

'That was business,' I said. 'But did he bring anyone specially' — I chose the words carefully — 'to, kind of, party with you?'

Mary's lips pressed together as if they would refuse to open. Her eyes stayed on me, but her expression went blank.

'Listen to me,' I told her. 'I don't care what you did. I just want to work out what happened.'

She took a deep breath. 'He brought a couple of guys around, but I don't even remember them. I didn't look at them too much.'

The idea about the photographs started flickering at the back of my mind again.

'Were any of them black?'

'Yes.'

'African?'

Coming from Britain she would know the difference.

'Yes.' Her expression changed to one of puzzlement. 'But he didn't look like the man in the photograph at all. He was kind of Arabic-looking with curly grey hair, and a narrow nose. Not like this guy.' She paused again, her voice faltering. 'He said he'd been in hospital. He was going away on a trip and never coming back to New York.'

'Plastic surgery,' Claude said. 'On the nose, and maybe a wig. He'd look different. Probably she was the only person except for Schumann who knew what he looked like. That was the guy's protection. He knew where Barre was and what he looked like.'

'He was wrong,' I said.

Claude laughed grimly.

'A lot of people make that mistake,' he said.

Chapter 30

We got to the outer suburbs round about the middle of the day. Westchester. It was Claude's idea and I guessed that this was one of his hideouts. Not that it was any kind of dump. Anything but. As far as hideouts went it was luxury. We drove in by way of a tree-lined rectangular car park, past a black man in a uniform with a gun at his hip. At the end of the car park was a path which led to the front of the house. On the inside it was furnished with a kind of anonymous tasteful-ness, as if someone from a department store had come in one day and ordered the right things for each room.

'I come here sometimes,' Claude said with an air of bashful pride. 'Nobody else does. You'll be OK.'

My mind went to work on why he needed the place, but too many things were buzzing round in my head and I gave it up. I was still curious, but it seemed tactless to question him about it, and besides, I wasn't sure that he'd tell me anything. Before he left he promised to be back in the evening with a Chinese takeaway, and for the rest of the afternoon I sat around with Sophie watching TV. Mary had gone to bed shortly after we arrived, and we had the illusion of being all alone in the silent house.

Claude had offered to take us somewhere safe and quiet, so we could have a breathing space in which to think about what to do, and I'd accepted gratefully. At that moment my head had been bursting with the effort of trying to focus on how much danger we were in and from where. If I was right, then George Barre was the eventual target of people who could kill as casually as spitting on the sidewalk; and Mary was now the only person alive who could tie the man to a face. The mob didn't know that. What they knew was that Mary had seen Schumann's documents, lived in his apartment, and might know a lot more than they wanted anyone to. In the circumstances, my first instinct, which was to head for the nearest airport, could simply be the most convenient way of committing suicide. Even staying in the same place for another day might be dangerous.

'Let's get out of here now,' Sophie had said, reading my mind again.

Halfway through the afternoon we started talking about what to do. The idea in the back of my mind was to drive to Boston or Washington and hop on a plane there, and we took that out and looked at it. We agreed that it might work. There was no reason, I argued, why anyone would expect us to go that far. We didn't even know whether there was anyone looking for us.

'That's not the point,' Sophie said. 'These guys aren't the FBI or the police. They don't have to do that − stop you leaving the country. All they have to do is find you, and they can do that just as easy in London, or anywhere else.'

'So what do you suggest?' I said impatiently. The question was rhetorical. I didn't think she'd have an answer.

'The best thing,' Sophie said, 'would be to find old George, tell the cops or the FBI or whoever where he is, and then split. Once he's out in the open, there won't be much point in anyone pursuing Mary.'

Straightforward reasoning, like a lance through the brain; and I considered it for a moment until I realized what I was doing. 'You're crazy,' I told her. 'If getting on a plane and going home is dangerous, what do you think prancing about the country looking for George Barre would be like?'

'At least,' she said, 'if we do that the whole thing has a chance of being finished. I can't think of any other way.'

That was the problem. Once she'd said it I couldn't think of any other solution.

'How do we do it? It's a huge country. He could be anywhere. Matter of fact, he could be anywhere in the world.' I think I was hoping to squash the whole thing before it went any further.

'There's got to be a clue somewhere,' she said confidently.

A little later I went up to see Mary. I rapped gently on the bedroom door. Silence. I turned the knob and opened it. The curtains were drawn against the afternoon light and the room was dark and shadowed. The bed was over by the window and I could just see the top of Mary's head poking out from under the mauve bedspread. I called to her softly. I think I was hoping that she wouldn't reply so that I could clear out and leave it till later.

'Yes,' Mary said suddenly.

I asked her how she was, but she didn't reply. This was going to be hard work. I sat down on the floor just inside the door and began giving her the gist of what Sophie and I had been talking about.

'You're the only one who knows what he looks like now,' I said. 'Even if we can get some idea of where he might be, you're the only one who can spot him.'

The lump in the bed stirred, as if she was reacting to what I'd said, but she still didn't reply.

'What do you think?' I asked her. 'Do you want to go home instead?'

I hadn't wanted to ask her that, because if she said yes I'd have to take her, and by now I was convinced that, before we left, we needed to close out the whole episode somehow. The reply was a long time coming, but she spoke at last.

'I don't care.'

My turn to be silent. I didn't know what to say.

The bedclothes stirred again. 'What about my dad?'

'I don't know,' I told her. 'I'm going to call Dot in a minute, see what she says.'

'Is he really bad?'

'Pretty bad.'

Downstairs a door banged and I heard voices. I got up in a hurry and went down. Claude had just come in, accompanied by a tall black man dressed in a navy blue pinstriped suit. Claude was smiling as if he hadn't a care in the world, and, I thought acidly, I didn't suppose he had.

'This is Dr Roland,' he said proudly. 'I ran into him this afternoon and he agreed to come and look at Mary. She's upstairs?'

I shook hands with the doctor. He had deep set black eyes with clear brilliant whites which made you want to keep on looking at them. He said he was pleased to meet me with the suave Frenchified accent and manner of an upper-class Haitian, which, being a doctor, I supposed he had to be. Claude ushered him up the stairs. He wasn't actually bowing, but something about his posture suggested it. I looked over at Sophie and she shrugged, smiling, as if to say that she'd stopped being surprised by anything Claude did. He came back down immediately, looking pleased with himself.

'That is a class doctor,' he told us confidentially. 'I do all his transport.'

That didn't surprise me much, but Roland didn't look the type who could be dragged out for a house call on short notice, and for a moment I was tempted to ask Claude what he had on the doctor. Claude must have guessed what I had in mind, because he was watching me, eyebrows raised ironically, as if daring me to ask.

'What do you think we should do?' I asked him instead. I told him the choices. 'The thing is, I'm desperate enough to go out looking for Barre, but I've got no idea where to start.'

'That's the easiest part,' Claude said. 'I don't know if we'll find anything, but we can check out Schumann's apartment.'

'What about the police?'

'I'm talking about the apartment in Tribeca,' he said. 'I don't think the cops will be there yet.'

*

He turned out to be right about that. We arrived at Schumann's bandit cave just before midnight. Once past the outer door we walked softly up the stairs and along the corridor. The building was silent, with only the vague hum of air conditioning to suggest that there were people behind the blank, solid walls. In front of Schumann's door Claude slipped the keys in the locks casually as if he was on the way into his own house, then eased the door open and reached for the light switch.

'Shit,' he said, standing still.

I pushed past him to see what the matter was, then when I saw the devastation in front of me stopped dead in my turn. All the pictures and sculptures had gone, along with most of the furniture, pieces of paper were scattered around, and, all along the big entrance room and the passages beyond it, the carpets had been taken up and removed, so that our footsteps echoed sharply when we moved.

Claude closed the door carefully and put his finger to his lips for silence. Then we paced slowly through the apartment. All the rooms had been emptied, except for Mary's, which looked much the same as before. Once we'd finished our tour of the place, Claude leaned against the wall and gave me a wry smile. 'Seems like somebody else had the same idea.'

'Maybe so,' I told him. 'Maybe not.'

What had occurred to me almost immediately was that if any of Schumann's partners had read about his murder they would want to clear the place of any incriminating traces, and if I'd thought about it before an empty apartment was exactly what I'd have expected to find. The door hadn't been forced and there was no sign of any damage. Whoever the intruders were they had simply carted off the valuable stuff; and my suspicion that this was the action of Schumann's friends deserting the sinking ship hardened as I told Claude about it.

He shrugged. 'Don't matter who or why, does it? They cleared out everything.'

'Not everything.'

I went back to the room where Schumann's desk had been.

It was gone now, but I'd noticed a scattered pile of papers on the floor, some letters poking out from the heap. I knelt down and began going through them with trembling fingers. If there was a clue it had to be here.

I'd opened more than a dozen before I realized that it was all junk mail. Special offers, gift tokens, magazine subscriptions. All rubbish. Claude had given up by then, and he was leaning against the wall, watching me with an air of weary resignation. I ignored him and continued ploughing through the pile until I'd opened the last useless envelope.

'Told you, man,' Claude said, 'they didn't leave nothing.'

Even then I couldn't stop. Somewhere in my head was the knowledge that failure to find an indication of Barre's whereabouts would leave me no choices. The image of Sophie flashed through my mind, compounding my frustration. We'd left her behind because someone had to stay with Mary, who was sleeping soundly under the influence of Dr Roland's sedatives. Perhaps if she'd been here she'd have known what to do. Spurred on by the thought, I moved out into the corridor, shifting the piles of trash in my way. Claude walked behind me radiating an obvious and irritating patience with my madness. I went back to Mary's room. As I opened the door there was a rustling sound and the Jimi Hendrix poster fell off the wall facing me. It must have been there for a long time because it left behind a pale square of clean wallpaper. Near the bottom of this patch Mary had stuck a brightly coloured postcard. Next to the huge picture of Hendrix its colours had been muted and I hadn't noticed it before. Now it stood out, and I walked over to take a look. The card featured a big picture of a rattlesnake in faithful colour. I prised it off the wall and flipped it over. It wasn't addressed to anyone. There was simply the number of the apartment and the address. In the space where there should have been a message there was only a cartoon drawing of a smiling face, the mouth an upturned line. The postmark said SCOTTSDALE. ARIZ.

'I wonder who she knows in Arizona?' I asked Claude. He shrugged as if the answer didn't interest him very much.

257

I went past him, picked up the phone in one of the outer rooms and called the house in Westchester. Someone picked up the phone without speaking and I guessed it was Sophie.

'Ask Mary,' I told her without preliminaries, 'who she knows in Arizona.'

I waited and Claude watched me, his expression breaking down into mild curiosity.

'Sorry, it took a while to wake her up. She doesn't know anyone in Arizona,' Sophie said when she came back.

'Ask her where she got the postcard in her room. The one with the rattlesnake.'

Another wait. Even longer this time.

'She remembered in the end,' Sophie said. 'Ben gave it to her. She said he got it in the mail one day and when she saw the picture of the snake she asked him about it. He looked angry and told her to mind her own business, then he suddenly laughed and said she could have it. "Stick it up on the wall," he said, "with the other junk." So she did.'

I hung up with a feeling of excitement I couldn't explain. There wasn't a reason for believing it but somehow I had the sense that Ben was the kind of man who would enjoy leaving the secret out in plain sight where no one would guess what it was. I handed the card to Claude.

'This is it,' I told him.

Chapter 31

We got on the redeye at Boston. Walking up the steps to the plane I felt that absurd sense of freedom that comes with the release from being on a small island where practically every aeroplane trip takes you abroad. Not having to show a passport or manhandle a huge suitcase felt like cheating. Irrational. Even better, all this was going on my clapped-out credit card. The mood persisted all night and all the way to LA. Better and better. Halfway through the trip I realized I'd left behind in Westchester the amulet that Sophie's see-far lady had given me, but I shrugged off the quick stab of apprehension I felt then. I was too far away from my roots to let that kind of superstition go any further.

We got off the plane in bright sunlight. I'd been expecting the air to have a smoky quality about it, but if it did I couldn't see it, and there was a car waiting at one of the rentals, just as Claude had said there would be.

I got behind the wheel and began negotiating my way out of the airport. Beside me Sophie was muttering to herself. I glanced round at her.

'Watch your lanes,' she said.

'Never mind my lanes,' I told her. 'What are you talking about?'

'Me? Nothing.'

I looked at her again. Her eyes were gleaming. She was gripping the dashboard tight, and there was a wired quality about her that I hadn't seen for a while. In that moment I figured it out. She'd been muttering the names. Santa Monica. Culver City. Pacific Palisades. For her LA was a magic city, the way London used to be for English-speaking Caribbeans. When we'd talked about it in New York, her eyes had started shining just like this. Everyone she knew in her former life, she'd said, had either been to LA or wanted to go there. I smiled at her.

'You'll have to start translating for me in a minute,' I said.

'The dialect's different to New York. So close to Mexico. I probably won't understand any more than you do.'

The words were grumpy but I could see from her expression that she was excited by the thought. Going to LA, she'd said before we got on the plane, was like coming home. Oddly enough, I felt the same kind of pull when I thought about the city. Unlike New York or Washington, it wasn't one of the places where my relatives and friends had gone to settle, but by now I'd heard and read more about it than any other place I could think of; and stray images of LA bubbled up continually in my memory. Even the names in Sophie's incantation set off a weird train of nostalgia. Long before this, so long ago that it seemed to have happened in another world, I'd shared a house in London with some Californian students, and these names had been part of the ordinary stuff of their daily conversation, reverberating in my head years after we'd split up. Turning right into Jefferson I wondered what had become of them. We'd all been kids then, and if Linda or Barbara walked across the car in front of me I wouldn't know who they were.

I looked round at Mary. She was staring out the window, her chin propped up in her hand, her expression blank. The pose was becoming familiar. She'd hardly said anything for the last twenty-four hours, speaking only when she was spoken to. On the surface this was worrying, but when I thought about it I had to admit that it was also a relief. Thinking about what to do next had been enough of a strain without also having to cope with Mary.

Early that morning, after finding the postcard, I'd rung Oscar and he'd agreed to come over at lunchtime with Claude. I didn't want to tell him on the telephone what I had in mind. I wasn't sure myself. As Claude had commented on the way back to Westchester, the postcard could have been sent by someone's mother. But that didn't sound likely to me, and, in any case, my instincts told me that the card was exactly what I thought it was. At one point during the ride back with Claude it struck me that my instincts were highly convenient, but I suppressed that idea immediately.

Oscar and Claude turned up shortly after twelve. I'd spent the preceding hour discussing what to do with Sophie and Mary. That is, Sophie and I discussed, Mary listened. She had a somnolent, listless air, as if she was still under sedation, and she seemed prepared to go along with whatever we decided. I guessed she was still in shock and I followed Sophie's lead, talking to her normally and ignoring the fact that she only replied in monosyllables.

Oscar was bursting with curiosity, and something else. There was an odd expression on his face which I realized, after a while, was a kind of sympathy, like someone visiting a man who was very sick, and I guessed that, from his point of view, my life wasn't worth much. I came straight to the point.

'Can you find out which law-enforcement agency is interested in Barre, and talk to them?'

He hesitated, but only for a moment. 'Yes. I guess I can. But where're you going with this?'

I told him quickly about the postcard. 'I think Barre is in Arizona and we're going there. If we can find him we'll need to let the right people know where he is.'

The look on Oscar's face now was frankly sceptical. 'He could have sent that card and then moved on,' he said.

'Why would he? Why send a postcard at all, and if he was going to, why not send it from Las Vegas or the Everglades or somewhere interesting? This place isn't anywhere I've ever heard of. Have you?'

Oscar shrugged.

'Think about it,' I said. 'He's not like an ordinary tourist sending postcards. This is a message which says I've arrived somewhere and everything is cool. If we'd found it in someone's house with another couple of postcards I wouldn't think anything of it, but it was the only personal thing in the place apart from Mary's stuff. Who else would send a postcard there? For what reason? That has to be it.'

Sophie was smiling at me, and both Oscar and Claude looked impressed. By the looks of it I'd convinced them, which was more than I could say for myself.

'All right,' Oscar said. 'What do you want from me?'

'If we can locate him,' I said, 'I don't fancy approaching the local cops and telling them the story. What we need is some agency which can get on his back, arrest him or something and leak the news back to whoever is looking for him. That way Mary's off the hook. She's not a witness or anything. All she knows is what he looks like.'

Oscar nodded. 'I'll give it to someone close to the mayor. He can talk to the FBI.' He grinned suddenly. 'If it works I'll owe you one.'

I could imagine. Pulling off the discovery and arrest of George Barre would be a considerable feather in Oscar's cap.

'I'll have to tell them about you though,' he said.

I shrugged. 'Tell them I came over to investigate the story and stumbled on his whereabouts. Invent anything you like. Just keep Mary out of it.'

After Oscar left things moved fast. Something had clicked when I saw the postcard, and the intervening period had only increased my eagerness to get to Arizona. Claude suggested a roundabout route. From Westchester we could drive to Boston and get on a plane from Logan to LA. If anyone was trying to trace us, he said, it would make it impossible for them to work out where we were going, even if they managed to pick us up. He laughed, clicked his fingers and picked up the phone. Suddenly, his mood had changed. Ten minutes earlier he'd been radiating the ponderous gloom of an undertaker, now he was fizzing with a mischievous glee. By the time Oscar phoned from City Hall everything we needed had been arranged. According to Claude.

'I talked to that man,' Oscar said cautiously. 'They want to see you.'

'No.' I had no intention of getting involved with a bunch of officials. Or worse.

'OK,' Oscar must have anticipated my reply, because he didn't sound surprised. 'When you see this person call me immediately and let me know how things stand.'

'Will they do the business?'

'Yes. Sure they will. If it's what you say it is, they will.'

'I'll call Claude,' I said. 'He'll get in touch.'

We'd discussed this during the afternoon. If a group of people in City Hall knew what Oscar was up to, phoning him with Barre's whereabouts might be the equivalent of broadcasting the news.

Driving through the LA traffic I turned the conversation over in my mind. The odd thing was that the mere act of travelling from one coast to another seemed to have removed me from the terrors and anxieties of the last few days, and now I felt free. As I turned into the lane which led to the Santa Monica Freeway I gave a whoop of delight. Somewhere inside me an irresponsible little imp was dancing.

Chapter 32

The sun was playing hide and seek behind the palm trees by the time we arrived in Phoenix. Scottsdale was only a small town, Claude had announced. Back in the sixties it had been a one-horse desert settlement. But since then it had become a suburb of the larger city next to it. Phoenix was big and we would be less likely to attract attention staying there. I took his word for it. The hotel he'd booked us into had the tastefully anonymous feel of an international businessman's hotel, the sort of atmosphere I could imagine being replicated in a thousand places all over the world. Piped music in the lift, a carpeted hush in the corridors. On the other hand, the rooms were twice the size of their equivalents in England.

We sat on the balcony of our suite, which overlooked a courtyard with a swimming pool at its centre. Sophie called room service and perched herself next to Mary. Down below us a paunchy middle-aged man, his skin tanned to the colour of brown leather, got out of the pool, took off a red rubber cap and began towelling his arms.

'What do we do now?' Sophie asked me.

I'd been wondering about that myself. The truth was that I had no idea whatsoever. In normal circumstances I'd have begun by looking in the phone book, but it was a safe bet that George Barre wouldn't be using his own name, and for the moment I couldn't think of any way of locating him, short of organizing a line-up of the local citizens and marching Mary past them.

'We'd better think of something,' Sophie said darkly. 'We'll be broke in a few days.'

'Not tonight,' I told her. 'Tonight we're going to eat, watch a movie on the telly and go to sleep.'

The movie was a recent one. Half a dozen actors died in the first couple of minutes, but I never saw what happened next, because after that I was asleep, the sound of gunfire punctuating my uneasy dreams.

We came back to the subject the next morning. This time we were sitting in the restaurant downstairs. I ran through the possibilities. 'We haven't got a photograph of what he looks like now, so we can't show it to people. We don't know what name he's going under, so we can't ask about him or check him up in any local records. We can ask about a black man who's moved in during the last year or so, but there must be hundreds.'

Sophie shrugged. 'Not necessarily. I didn't see many black people around when we came in.'

'Why don't we just go out and look around?' I said. I looked at Mary. 'What do you think?'

She looked surprised to be asked. 'Yes,' she replied cautiously.

I looked at her again, suddenly conscious that I'd hardly spoken to her over the last day. Her eyes skittered away from mine, but now she was sitting up straight and looking around her.

In the car I tossed the map back to Mary. 'We'll wander into Scottsdale,' I said. 'Give us a shout if we get lost.'

In fact I didn't care very much whether we got lost or not. Until we worked out a starting point for tracking down Barre, one place was as good as another. Besides I was beginning to enjoy the feel of being somewhere completely new.

We drove down the freeway which bisected the town, and came off it about seventy blocks downtown. For the next hour we drove around idly looking for a district with a concentration of black people. I had asked the receptionist at the hotel that morning, and she'd looked puzzled and then amused. 'I don't know,' she'd said, 'maybe downtown.'

A disappointment. By the standards of New York or LA, there were hardly any black people here at all. Not walking round the streets anyway.

'OK,' Sophie said, after a couple of hours of this, 'if there's a ghetto here, it's a barrio for Mexicans or Indians. Anyway I don't think we're going to see this guy just hanging out in some ghetto bar.'

I pulled over and stopped on the dusty red shoulder of the road.

'Indian School Road,' Mary said.

'What?'

'This road is called Indian School Road. We're almost in Scottsdale.'

Around us mountains loomed. Close by the road a huge twisted rock thrust upwards towards the sky. My eyes kept being drawn to it. I'd lived in a city for most of my life, and the countryside I'd known as a boy had been flat and green, bursting with water and bristling with plants and trees. This dry landscape was alien, threatening and exciting at the same time. The day before we'd started seeing Navajos. Seeing the first one I'd felt a weird thrill, a combination of familiarity and strangeness, both of them imposed by the images I'd been digesting over a lifetime of Hollywood movies. This was their land, as natural a setting as the city streets were to African-Americans. Yet another image ingrained by the movies, I thought.

'Land,' I said aloud. 'He'd have to go to a real-estate agent, wouldn't he?'

Sophie thought about it for a moment. 'Unless he rented somewhere through a lawyer or whatever.'

A spoke in my wheel of logic.

'I want to try it anyway,' I said. 'Let's go back to the hotel and start ringing them.'

266

'Any chance of something to eat?' Mary asked.

Sophie nodded vigorously. 'Let's go look for some Mexican food,' she said. 'It's bound to be pretty good. Right?' She clicked her fingers. 'If there was an African restaurant here we could try that and see if he'd been there.'

I laughed. 'We couldn't even find a soul-food joint this morning.'

I stopped short.

'Wait a minute,' I said. 'Barre isn't American. He's a French-African. He probably went to university in Paris or Lyons or somewhere like that. French Africans are real big on French culture. What's the first thing he'd look for?'

'A bidet?' Sophie suggested. She was laughing at me again.

'No, stupid. A French restaurant.'

Sophie slapped her hand on the dashboard. 'Yes.'

We rode on up Indian School Road and turned into the nearest gas station. The two men behind the counter in the office looked like brothers. Long black hair, hard impassive brown faces, and sharp black eyes.

'Is there a French restaurant in this town?' I asked the younger one.

'¿Qué?'

I looked round at Sophie and she moved up beside me. 'Buenos días.'

'Buenas días, señora.'

She continued in Spanish, but I missed most of what she was saying because I'd been listening for the choppy, more staccato delivery of the accent she used in New York, and now her voice had a formal, lilting sound, the words flowing in a rapid and musical stream. The younger man smiled and nodded, came out from the counter and led us to the door. As I moved back to the car he pointed down the road, giving Sophie the directions. Driving away I felt them watching us with those impassive black eyes, and I wondered for a moment who they thought we were.

'Where's the restaurant?' I asked Sophie.

'I don't know,' she said.

'What was all that about then?'

'I asked him for the Chamber of Commerce. I didn't think there was much point asking him about French restaurants.'

'You're right,' I told her. 'But it's not nice to show off.'

She grinned at me, then looked back at Mary and winked.

'Big head,' I muttered.

We passed the next ten minutes kicking around amiable insults. The mood in the car had lifted. We'd made our first contact, asked a question, got an answer and actually found out something. It was like a good omen.

The Chamber of Commerce was in the middle of a huge park, flanked by the library and the museum. Huge rambling buildings of stucco and dark glass. Coming at the end of a journey through a vista of cacti and red rock, the massive white walls and sloping green lawns had a surreal feel, like mysterious structures on an alien planet.

I parked opposite the Indian trading post. Over the street in front of the trading post's windows half a dozen Navajos were playing the sort of string and wind instruments I'd heard South American Indians playing. A jaunty, reedy sound which made you want to tap your feet and caper around. I left Sophie and Mary sitting in the car, gazing at the band, walked across the pavement, and went on up the pathway into the Chamber of Commerce.

The receptionist was a middle-aged blonde with sparkling blue eyes and a nameplate which said BOBBI. She looked like she'd once been a cheerleader, and still had the mannerisms to prove it.

I told her I was a reporter from London, England, writing an article about Scottsdale, and showed her my union card, and asked her whether she could tell me where the nearest French restaurant was and the name of the manager. Strictly speaking I was going over the top here, but I had a sense that the Chamber might come in useful and I wanted them to be cooperative and willing. I was counting on the reaction of curiosity and pleasure I usually got from white Americans when they realized that the black person in front of them was speaking with a real English accent and was a bona fide foreign visitor from Europe, for God's sake. So cute. In the same circumstances they might treat an African-American with a well-rehearsed suspicion.

Bobbi squirmed a little, blushed, cocked her head to one side, and studied my union card carefully. It was actually a useless piece of paper, but it looked official and had the word press above my photo. She took that in, then looked up and gave me a full blast of the blue eyes. Obvious, but she really did have charm, and suddenly I could see exactly how attractive she had been twenty years ago. She smiled, as if reading my thoughts, and turned round to call out to the woman behind the other desk in the room.

'Hey. Sandy.'

Except for the fact that Sandy was dark haired, she was in all other respects exactly similar to her colleague. She was already looking, and now she got up and came over.

'This guy's a reporter from London, England, and he's writing about Scottsdale.'

'Hey,' Sandy said.

'Yeah,' Bobbi went on, 'and he wants to know where the nearest French restaurant is.'

'Be helpful to know the name of the manager, too,' I said.

'Love that accent,' Sandy said.

I stood around smiling and trying to look like someone who'd known Robert Morley, while they conferred excitedly. I must have been, I thought, the most exotic thing to walk in here for a long while, and the sheer oddity of it made me want to giggle. I wondered what Sophie would say about that idea, and for a moment I saw the scene as a cartoon image drawn in stark thin lines, a picture of myself standing in front of two women who looked like Hollywood extras, Navajos tootling away outside, framed against a Western background of cactus and rock, a cartoon bubble coming out of my head: EXOTIC.

It only took Bobbi and Sandy a couple of minutes and a quick phone call to solve the problem. The biggest French restaurant was on Lincoln Drive, and it was run by a Marcel Duval. A stranger in town who was looking for French food would certainly go there, at least once. I thanked them with every polite flourish I could think of, and although I was tempted, stopped short of kissing their hands. Then I signed their visitors' book, and split.

When I got out to the street Sophie and Mary were on the other side of it, browsing at the trading store windows, and it took a couple of minutes to get them back in the car.

'I was thinking of buying something,' Sophie said reproachfully.

'Keep thinking. Maybe we'll get back later.'

At the time I thought I was lying shamelessly, because I hadn't any intention of going back there if I could help it, which just goes to show I'd forgotten that anything could happen.

The restaurant was a peculiar compromise. It was a low two-storeyed building, with a broad veranda running round the ground floor. There were rows of tables lining the veranda. Between them flitted the waiters, dressed in white shirts, black trousers and waistcoats, and white aprons. Inside the building the restaurant became a hugely inflated version of a little bistro. Concealed lighting, candles, round tables, each one with a crystal vase of flowers. It would have looked exactly like my idea of a French restaurant, except for being too big. The bar, for instance, was shaped like an elongated O, and stretched the length of the room, and was flanked by a row of drinkers, mostly men.

We sat at a table next to the bar, and once we were settled I looked up at the men sitting nearby. A couple of them were still ogling Sophie covertly, and when I stared, they looked away. The thought crossed my mind that this region wasn't far away from states like Georgia and Alabama. The Deep South.

'Oh boy,' I said to Sophie. 'You look so damn white. They'll be lynching me before the day's over.'

She gave me a puzzled look, then she grinned. 'Oh no I

270

don't,' she said. 'They'll see what they want to see. Three black people, and one of them looks almost white. That's how it goes. At the worst they'll think I'm some kind of Mexican. If I was blonde it might be different. What they're looking at is my beautiful legs.'

I told her she was probably right, and she nodded complacently. 'Course I am.' She rubbed her hands together, pleased with herself. 'Margaritas,' she said. 'I'm thirsty.'

We ordered soft-shelled crabs with the booze. Like the building, the menu was a weird amalgam of the South-West and Europe, with a touch of Louisiana thrown in for good measure. The small print on the menu featured both salsa and New Orleans hot sauce. When our order came, the plates were huge, holding what seemed like inexhaustible portions of food.

We'd worked our way through a few Margaritas, a bottle of California wine and about half the meal, when the waiter came over and asked whether we were enjoying it. He was a tall fair-haired boy with a deep tan, and I guessed he'd probably have been more at home doing something out of doors. Roping horses maybe.

'It's very nice,' I told him. 'But I'd like to see Mr Duval. Is he here today?'

His grin disappeared. 'Is there a problem?'

'No. No,' I reassured him. 'I'm a friend of a friend. Is he here?'

'I think he's in his office. I'll tell him.'

I smiled broadly at him, and he took off. Duval arrived in a minute. He was dressed in a light cream-coloured suit, open at the neck. A short, dark-haired bull of a man, thick chest and shoulders, thick neck, his eyes black and suspicious. He could have been French, but there was nothing about his voice to suggest it. His accent sounded, if anything, more Southern than anything I'd heard in the last couple of days. Louisiana, I guessed. I gave him my spiel about writing an article about the town and showed him my ID. He gave it a quick glance, sat down, and ordered a glass of wine. His eyes swept over

Sophie, then Mary and came back to Sophie. Today she was wearing a white top which left her shoulders bare, and a short black skirt which clung to her behind and showed off her long thighs. As we walked into the restaurant the cowboys at the bar had turned to look, and Duval must have noticed too, because his beady black eyes kept flicking to the edge of the table where Sophie had pushed back her chair and was crossing and recrossing her legs in a flagrantly strategic fashion. She caught his eye and smiled sweetly at him. I cleared my throat to attract his attention.

'This really is a beautiful restaurant,' I told him.

He grinned and nodded. No flattery was too much, I thought.

'Right,' he said. 'We're working on it.'

I put my notebook on the table, started taking ostentatious notes, and Duval took charge. I'd intended to ask him a few questions about the restaurant and the menu, but he surprised me by launching into what was practically a prepared speech. I'd been worried about whether I could sustain the role without showing my boredom, but Duval was enthusiastic enough for both of us. The décor, the mixture of styles on the menu, where he got the crabs. It went on and on. He'd stopped looking at Mary, because she'd clearly lost interest a few minutes after he sat down, and seemed sunk in her own thoughts, continually looking around the room and fidgeting, but Sophie, on the other hand, mimed a convincing fascination. Not that she needed to. Duval loved the sound of his own voice. After he'd treated us to a longish discourse on the differences between the different kinds of French cooking in North America, Sophie nudged me.

'Ask Monsieur Duval about your friend,' she said. She gave him one of her sweetest smiles. He smiled back, his eyes sweeping over her again as if checking her good points.

'Oh yes,' I said quickly. 'Someone I met a while back moved here recently. He was the one who told me about the restaurant. Raved about it. He's an African. Maybe you've met him. He said that this was the nearest French restaurant.'

Duval frowned. 'An African?'

'Yes. From a French-speaking African country. He speaks fluent French. I think he studied in Paris.'

Duval's face lit up. 'Yes. I think I know. What's his name?'

'Damn it,' I said. 'Do you know I've been trying to think of it for the last hour. I know it nearly as well as my own, but can I remember?'

'Maurice?' Duval prompted. He gave it the French pronunciation, the way the Canadians and Americans do. Mowreece.

'That's it,' I said.

Chapter 33

One step forward, one step back. The name of Duval's African was Maurice Rolaire. But he had no idea where he lived. It was somewhere nearby, he knew, because Monsieur Rolaire would drop in late at night sometimes on his way home.

We parted with a lot of bowing and smiling. Duval asked me to send him a copy of the article, shook me and Mary by the hand, then kissed the tips of Sophie's fingers, looking soulfully all the while into her eyes.

'Not bad,' she said, once we were back in the car. 'At least we know his name.'

She'd taken her camera out of the boot and was loading it with film, a sure sign that she was feeling good.

'If it is him,' I said gloomily.

'Stop complaining,' she said. 'Now we know his name you can try the Chamber of Commerce again. Can't you? I knew we'd be going back.' She turned and held the camera out to Mary. 'You want to try?'

Mary hesitated, then took it. I could only catch glimpses of her in the rear-view mirror, but I had the impression that she smiled.

'OK, you bossy bag,' I said. 'Let's go back to the flaming trading post.'

Sophie grinned triumphantly. She'd known that I would

stop at the Navajo store if she insisted, but the pleasure she got from the sense that she had somehow manoeuvred a small victory over me was touching and somehow sexy. If Mary hadn't been sitting in the back, I think I might have pulled over somewhere, kissed her, and put my hand between her long legs. Maybe I would have skipped the kissing bit. During the last few days everything had been too hectic and we'd both been too tired to do more than cuddle briefly. Now I was overcome by a wave of lust. As if reading my thoughts she gripped my knee and gave it a light squeeze.

I parked in more or less the same spot as before and went on into the Chamber's office. Bobbi was typing busily, but when she saw me come in she stopped and greeted me with a fluttering enthusiasm, which in different circumstances would have made my day.

I told her I'd found the restaurant, that it was wonderful to find such a great place in this small town, that I was very impressed by what I'd seen, and that I would be visiting the museum of art very soon. Then I asked her about Maurice Rolaire. I gave her the description we'd got from Mary.

'I don't know,' she said, frowning thoughtfully. Then she made a reassuring face and picked up the phone. In a little while another middle-aged woman emerged from one of the doors off the reception area. This one was older, wearing a pleated skirt, gold-rimmed glasses and a fluffy iron-grey hairdo.

'Miz Hodge,' Bobbi announced.

'Welcome to Arizona,' she said, shaking my hand.

I smiled, trying for diffident charm. It was the effect these women were beginning to have on me. I couldn't work out what it might be like to live here, but if their friendliness was only an act, it was a good one. I described Maurice Rolaire again, and told her he was an old friend. She reacted immediately.

'What a coincidence,' she said. 'He came in a few months ago, checking out some local investments. I've seen him a couple of times since then. Do you want to call him?'

'You have his number?'

She grimaced. 'I shouldn't give it to you,' she said. 'But since you're only here for a day I guess he'll want to hear from you.'

She went over to Bobbi's desk, bent over the terminal on it, and clicked a couple of keys. 'Here it is.'

Over her shoulder I read the address. Two, Mesquite Crescent. Ms Hodge wrote the telephone number down and gave it to me.

'Have a nice stay,' she said. Behind her Bobbi smiled, raised her eyebrows and gave me a little nod.

Outside in the street Mary and Sophie were nowhere in sight. I crossed the road to the Navajo store. Inside, it had the same dark, cool feel that I remembered from the store in the village where I'd been born. Glass cases full of ornaments were distributed in rows through the room. The walls dripped with leather and lengths of cloth. Sophie and Mary were standing under a big Western saddle on the far wall, trying on silver necklaces and holding up earrings for each other's inspection. Mary seemed to have recovered almost completely, I thought, except for the fact that she hardly spoke. I wondered how she would react to seeing Barre again, but then I put the question out of my head. Sufficient unto the day.

Waiting for them to buy whatever it was they were buying, I kicked around the problem of what to do next. There was no point in ringing Claude until we were sure that Rolaire was the same man Mary had seen in New York. This was assuming that he was Barre. We couldn't very well walk up to the door and ask him. But we had to work out some way of seeing him without being seen.

When Sophie got back in the car she was wearing her new necklace, silver, with bright black stones worked into it, and she kept stretching her neck to see it in the rear-view mirror. She looked over at me, her eyes mischievous. 'I've got something for you.'

'What? Let's have it then.'

'Oh no,' she said. 'You have to wait.'

I ignored her, looked back at Mary and gave her the address. 'Can you find it on the map?'

'What are we going to do?' she asked. There was a tremor in her voice.

I leaned forward, switched off the engine, and turned round to face her. 'I want to check the address and see what it looks like. Then we can talk about a way of seeing him without his seeing you, so you can tell us whether it's the same man. You won't have to do anything else.'

She nodded, but there was still the shadow of a doubt about her expression. I ran through the things I could say to give her some reassurance, then dismissed the thought. She seemed to be managing well enough without it.

Mesquite Crescent, according to the map, was in Paradise Valley, still inside the town limits, but halfway up the lower slopes of the mountain ahead of us. Mary took us along Lincoln Drive which was fringed with resort hotels and private clubs, high white walls, and broad driveways lined with palm trees.

'I can smell money,' Sophie said.

She grabbed her throat and pretended to gag. Around us the mountain loomed, bearded with mauve and dusty green bushes, its curves highlighted with dots of yellow and pale pink desert flowers. As the road began to climb, we turned off into a brick lane which ran alongside a long white wall. 'Country club', the plaque on the wall read. On the other side, the houses were separated from the road by an acre or more of railed garden. Occasionally we caught the blue glimmer of a swimming pool. With the windows wide open, all we could hear now was the twittering of birdsong.

'This guy isn't broke,' Sophie told us.

The next turning off Hummingbird Lane was Mesquite Crescent. Number two was a letter box and a long drive which curved away behind the stretch of scrub which hid the house. We sat opposite, looking.

'What do we do?' Sophie asked. 'Wait?'

'Might be a long wait,' I told her. 'And if we sit here long enough the cops might come around and ask us to explain ourselves. It looks like that sort of neighbourhood. What we

277

need is some way of getting him to come out of there so we can see him.'

'Right,' she said, her expression registering the fact that she'd heard this before. 'So what do we do while we're thinking about that?'

'Wait.'

We waited. Above us the mountain began to feel like a giant presence brooding over the drowsing valley. As our ears grew more attuned to the absence of traffic noises and human voices, the piercing whistles of the birds grew into a chaotic chorus. I looked at my watch. We'd been sitting there for close on ten minutes, but it seemed more like an hour. Above us the sun's ghastly red eye rolled towards the top of the whiskered ridge. I looked at my watch again. Sunset started early out here and we only had an hour or so of full daylight left. For a moment I considered walking up the drive to take a look at the house, but then I remembered that this was the USA, cowboy country, and intruders on private land could find themselves in more trouble than they could handle. Like full of holes. The natives seemed extremely hospitable, but I didn't fancy testing their goodwill to its limits. Even nice ladies around here, I thought, like the bunch at the Chamber of Commerce, probably had nice little guns tucked away into their handbags. The image of Ms Hodge, legs apart, crouched in a firing stance, crossed my mind, and I wondered whether she would have telephoned Rolaire to tell him about me, and as I imagined her picking up the phone I got the answer.

'Telephone him,' I said aloud.

Sophie sniggered. 'What? And tell him that we're here?'

'We can be more subtle than that,' I told her. 'Suppose Mary rings him and says that she was passing through and saw him, by accident, in the restaurant. He doesn't know how much she knows. She could have merely recognized him, asked his name and called him. On the other hand, she could be blackmailing him. She asks him to meet her in the same restaurant in a few minutes. There is no way he can refuse. He'll have to turn up and we'll get a good look at him as he comes out.'

'Suppose he's not Barre?'

'Then he won't go.'

'Suppose he leaves before she gets back from the telephone?'

I raised my eyebrows at her.

'Oh. You want me to do it.'

'That's right,' I said.

I dropped her off in the centre of town with strict instructions to wait ten minutes so that we could get into position. Then I drove along Lincoln as fast as I dared. It took slightly longer than ten minutes, but back in Mesquite Crescent nothing had changed. We hadn't passed any cars coming up the lane, and I was certain that there wouldn't have been time for Sophie to finish making the call. I parked in the same place as before, got in the back with Mary and told her we were going to pretend to be kissing if and when we heard Rolaire's car. She could look over my shoulder straight at him. She nodded soberly, and sat back. I watched the driveway and listened to the birds kicking up a racket.

We didn't have long to wait. First the birds went quiet, then we heard the sound of an engine revving. I pulled Mary towards me. She came reluctantly in the first moment, then she gathered herself together and gave me a loose hug, her face burrowing into my shoulder. I swivelled my eyes towards the mirror and listened to the engine roaring and the splash of gravel as a big black Cadillac slid out of the mouth of the drive. He was going too quickly for me to make out the driver, but Mary must have had a clear sight of him, because she stiffened against me and dug deeper into my shoulder. In a second the car had gone past and round the corner of the lane. I pulled away from Mary and looked at her.

'Was it him?'

'Yes. It was him.'

'Are you sure?'

'Yes. Of course I'm sure. It was him.'

Chapter 34

We picked up Sophie at the mall where we'd dropped her off, and drove back towards the hotel. By now the streets were jammed with cars and trucks. On the cross streets leading on to the freeway we crawled, like part of a listless metal snake, slowly dragging its way along the valley floor.

'Where do all these people go?' Sophie said.

Given the size of the city and the volume of traffic, the sidewalks seemed practically deserted. Sophie had been commenting on it all day. In comparison the streets at the centre of Manhattan were a seething mass of pedestrians.

'It's the size of it,' Mary said suddenly. I almost did a double take. After all this time it was startling to hear her speak without being pushed, and in a way, I'd almost forgotten that she was sitting there in the back.

'Everything's bigger than it needs to be,' she went on. 'I reckon when they measured out the proportions they took the length of the cars rather than the human body as the basis for the scale.'

'Gee,' Sophie said. 'You're so smart.'

The way she looked back at Mary and said this didn't sound sarcastic, but I chipped in, just in case.

'Gets it from her father. He was usually at the top of the class.'

I'd said it without thinking, and when I remembered I took a look in the mirror to see what Mary's reaction was, but she was gazing out of the window, her profile unreadable.

Back at the hotel a woman in a tiny black bikini was churning up and down the length of the pool with strong, lazy strokes. Her black hair floated straight out behind the beautiful long body, and every time she made a turn it clustered in a cloud round her face. Another leathery-skinned old man was sitting on the edge of the pool, dangling his feet in the water and watching her. I picked up the phone and rang Claude without taking my eyes off them. A woman answered. Claude was out, she told me coolly. If this was Sammy I was supposed to give her my number. Claude would call back. I gave her the number and put the phone down. Down below in the courtyard the black-haired goddess got out of the pool, wrapped her head in a yellow towel, held out her hand to the old geezer, then walked beside him along the curving path to another wing of the hotel. I watched them disappear out of sight, then sat down beside Mary and Sophie on the sofa.

An attractive couple with light tans, shiny hair and brilliant smiles were reading the local news. Three traffic accidents, a fatal stabbing and the random drive-by shooting of a pregnant woman. After this they grinned at each other, and brought on the weather man. The telephone rang. It was Claude. Only a couple of days and already his voice sounded strange and distant. I gave him the address and he said he'd talk to our man right away, and call me back. There was no more I could do, he said. The best thing was to stay away from Barre, go back to LA and get a plane out in the morning. Or maybe go see the Grand Canyon. Anything. Just get the hell out of there and let the experts do what they do. I told him that was exactly what I had in mind, and hung up feeling relieved, deflated and dizzy, all at the same time.

The news segued into an interminable movie about Stalin. Sometime during the second half we called room service, and after the meal we began talking about what to do next. In fact, it didn't take very long to work it out. I hadn't been thinking about going home till then, but as soon as I knew that I could I wanted nothing so much as to get on a plane and find myself heading back to London.

I wasn't sure that Sophie felt the same.

'Seems a waste,' she said, 'simply rushing back to London right now.'

'You can stay if you want,' I told her, 'but I'm taking Mary back. I think I ought to.'

Sophie nodded. 'I'll come back with you anyway,' she said. 'The job is finished, and I suppose they'll be expecting me.'

'You do want to go back, don't you?' I asked Mary.

'I don't know,' she said slowly. 'I don't know if I want to stay in England any more, but I don't know what else to do.'

'Your dad needs you,' I said.

She didn't reply. Instead she got up suddenly, said she was going to bed, wished us goodnight and walked into her room, closing the door behind her.

'Do you think I should talk to her?' I asked Sophie.

'No. Let her work it out for herself.'

Suddenly the door opened again and Mary was standing there. She hadn't turned the lights on and, framed in the darkness of the doorway, it was hard to see her. 'Is it over?' she asked abruptly.

I nodded emphatically. 'Yes.'

She didn't reply. Instead, she moved backwards, disappearing into the gloom, and the door closed. Sophie turned her head and looked at me.

'Well, is it?'

'I don't know,' I told her. 'But let's just act like it is.'

Another movie. This time the accents were British, and the actors were dressed in Edwardian costumes. In a moment I realized that all the faces were familiar ones from the TV chat shows I'd seen in London. There was something dislocating about seeing them here in Phoenix, like going into a bar downtown and running into a man you'd last seen halfway across the world.

'I hate this,' I told Sophie. 'I get the feeling that thirty years from now I'll be sitting in a hotel room in Timbuktu, and I'll turn the TV on and there'll be the latest movie from Britain and they'll all be dressed in flowered hats and lifting tea cups, and all over the world they'll be looking at it and thinking that's what it means to be British, and it will all be the same bloody lies.'

'Every country pushes myths about itself,' she said. 'Cowboys and Indians.'

'At least that myth starts with some kind of truth. Look outside. It is a hard country. This place is like an oasis in the desert. If they left it alone, that swimming pool would evaporate and the building would fall down and the wind would blow the air conditioning away. And there was a struggle here over territory that's still going on. What do you think those Navajos are doing out there? The winners get to make the movies and tell the story their way, but America's all up there on the screen if you look hard enough. This crap we're watching doesn't say anything about the country I live in. It's a masturbation fantasy for these prats.'

Sophie didn't smile. She usually liked it when I ranted about something, but now she was frowning as if I'd irritated her. I had the suspicion that, at this moment, she didn't want to think about her life in England, or about who she was, or about how she would feel when she got back.

'Everybody knows that,' she said. 'And no one gives a shit except you. Let's go to bed. I'm dropping.'

I hesitated. Claude still hadn't called back. But by now I was being overwhelmed by the effects of the long journey and the time switches. My body felt listless and enervated, while my mind was alternating between racing speed and total shutdown.

'Let's act like it's all over,' Sophie's voice said from across the room.

I woke up at about two in the morning. I'd tottered over and crawled in beside Sophie, but a couple of minutes later our exhaustion seemed to disappear and it was at least another hour before we separated and went to sleep.

Sophie was still unconscious, one pale brown arm hanging over the edge of the bed. I looked at the clock and counted the time. I must have been asleep for four hours or so but then I never normally slept for more than five or six hours at a time, and now I was awake it seemed impossible to get back to sleep. Somehow, during the night my mind had continued working on the fact that Claude hadn't rung.

I got up, mooched over to the window, and looked down at the floodlit swimming pool. Suppose, I thought, that Oscar had never got the message, or that if he'd got it, it would take him hours, even days of horse trading to persuade someone to do something about it. The moment I woke up I'd realized that the plan which had seemed so simple and logical up to that moment was actually a shaky and desperate strategy, with less than an even chance of success. Perhaps Barre had taken fright after Sophie's call and was now packing up, lock stock and barrel, to disappear again. Suddenly I felt a flash of pure rage at my lack of foresight. I'd been dancing the night away when there were so many things that could have gone wrong, and even if they hadn't yet, all my efforts could still be in vain. The idea that had been crawling about in my mind emerged and took a firm and alarming shape. And I couldn't put it out of my head.

A few minutes later I was wheeling the car out of the hotel car park. In my head was a picture of Barre piling his belongings into the Cadillac and driving away. That would be the predictable reaction to Sophie's phone call, I thought, and for some reason or other, I hadn't imagined it would happen or planned what to do about it. There was nothing to do now, except go out there and take a look.

The freeway wasn't crowded, the way it had been earlier, but even at two in the morning it wasn't empty either. It wasn't until I turned off for Scottsdale that the traffic disappeared. Mine was the only car on the road now. Through the centre of town the buildings were mostly dark, the street lamps and the spotlights which outlined the front of the hotels deepening the sense that the world was asleep. In Paradise

Valley, the thick, soft darkness seemed to descend, as if the lights had been switched off. In the lane which led to Mesquite Crescent, the headlights made a ragged circle which lit up an alleyway in front of me. Halfway up, a small furry animal scurried out of the light and I slowed down.

Opposite Barre's driveway I stopped, then backed the car the way I'd come, round the corner and on to the grass verge, then opened the door and got out. I did this as quickly and firmly as I could, because by now I was wishing that I'd stayed safe and warm in the hotel. As soon as I'd opened the door I'd begun shivering. I'd forgotten the one thing that everyone knows about the desert, that it was hot during the day and cold at night, and I was only wearing a shirt and a thin jacket. After a few minutes, though, the cold seemed to stop biting so fiercely, and actually it was no worse than an average spring day in England.

I jogged round the corner and back up the lane. Once the lights were off the blackness had cleared and now I could see by the light of the stars. In the gloom, the white letter box stood out like a beacon. I turned in and began feeling my way cautiously up the drive. In a little while I stumbled across a rock and I bent down and picked it up, balancing the reassuring weight in my hand.

Around the curve in the drive the tangle of bushes ended to be replaced by a wide lawn. The drive continued in a long semi-circle which ended in front of a house two storeys high, with a colonnaded porch running all the way round it, and gleaming white against the dark bulk of the mountain. Somehow, though, the building wasn't quite large enough to sustain the grandeur of the white columns, and it had the air of a dwelling which had set out to look like a Hollywood version of a Southern mansion, then changed its mind.

I stood behind a bush at the edge of the lawn and focused on the house. There were lights on both floors. I hugged myself and blew on my hands. In the cover of the bushes it seemed a little warmer, and I began making bargains with myself about how long I would stay. I would leave in half an hour or as soon as the lights went out, I offered myself. After I was sure he was there I'd go back to the car and wait. Half an hour came and went. I hugged myself, jogged up and down on the spot, and almost missed the sight of a shadow crossing behind the window upstairs. I stopped and concentrated. The shadow came back and stayed in view behind the window for several seconds. There was someone there. At this hour of the night, it had to be Barre. I grinned, ridiculously happy at the thought that I could now go back to the car and sit down.

In the same instant I heard the sound of an engine and the crunching of gravel as a car turned into the drive. I ducked back into the bushes as the headlights came into view and illuminated the lawn and the front of the house. There was something eerie about its presence there at this time of night, and the hair stirred on the back of my neck as it swept slowly round and stopped in front of the entrance. The roof light went on and two men got out, and the car moved off round the driveway. I hardly noticed it go, because I was concentrating on the two visitors who were now banging on the door. There had been something oddly familiar about them, but it wasn't until the door opened and I saw the taller one in the light that I recognized Claude.

I shrank back behind the bushes as the light flooded across the lawn. My brain was whirling. I'd spoken to him only a few hours ago. It couldn't have been possible for him to be here so soon. Unless he'd already been in LA or somewhere nearby. Why didn't he tell me then? And what did it mean? Had Oscar got the message? The logical thing would have been to go over there and ask Claude what was going on, but something restrained me. Perhaps it was the time of night, the isolation or the mysterious way he'd appeared. Even now I couldn't quite believe my eyes. I thought furiously. Could Claude have been involved somehow before I came along? But before I met him he hadn't known about my existence, and he'd saved my life at the mall. I was sure of that. There had to be a simple explanation.

The door closed and the dark came back, but I still didn't move. Claude had warned me to stay away, and he hadn't called me back. Whatever he was up to, it was obvious that he didn't want me around. What I should do, I decided, was get to a phone and call Sophie. It was a decision I should have made earlier, because, as I turned to go, there was a sound behind me.

'Don't move,' a voice said clearly. 'Freeze.'

I froze, and a hand began patting me all over. In a moment it went away.

'A'right,' the voice said. 'Walk up ahead of me to the house.'

Chapter 35

'I told you to stay away from here,' Claude said. He was looking at me with an expression in which concern and exasperation were mingled. 'Don't you ever take good advice?'

'I took your advice before,' I replied, 'and look what you got me into.'

Claude laughed. 'This is business,' he said, 'not personal.' He laughed again. 'I helped you, man. Otherwise those guys would have whacked you long time.'

I shrugged. No doubt he was right, but I hated giving him the satisfaction. We were sitting around the big reception room on the ground floor of the house. It was furnished with a series of big comfortable chairs and sofas, covered in what looked like Navajo patterns. Zigzag streaks and dots. In front of us a curving staircase led to the upper floor. We hadn't been introduced, but I guessed that my companion was George Barre. Next to him was a big Navajo man with a broad brown face and long black hair, who I took to be Barre's bodyguard or something. Barre himself had the narrow hooked nose, straight hair and thin lips Mary had described. His skin was lighter, too, than in the photograph I'd seen, and I certainly wouldn't have recognized him. I must have been staring because Claude grinned and winked at me.

'Yeah. It's him.'

'George Barre?'

Barre gave me a polite inclination of the head, not quite a bow, but we could have been at a social gathering or a business meeting, except that both George and the Navajo had their arms behind them, strands of wire looped round their wrists, the ends neatly twisted together.

The two dreads who had come with Claude were standing behind us, both of them holding what looked like Uzis slung over their shoulders. They weren't pointing them, but even so, no one was making any sudden moves. The one who had marched me in was actually the dread who had shot Sal and his sidekick at the mall, and from the moment I recognized him I'd had a cold feeling in the back of my neck at the thought that he was standing behind me.

'How did you get here so fast?' I asked Claude.

'We flew into Phoenix yesterday. I had a feeling about this.'

'And how did you know I was here?'

'This isn't your game,' Claude said. 'You left the car sitting out there in a neighbourhood where everybody's got acres of yard and ten garages. That's why I sent Bigger to check out who was hanging around. I guessed it might be you.'

'How long have you been stringing me along? Did you know where he was all the time?'

He shook his head emphatically. Shocked. 'No. I wasn't stringing you along at all, man. I've been with you all the way. No. What it is, is that this deal is too good to miss.'

He leaned forward confidentially, his eyes gleaming. His whole manner suggested that he expected me to share his pleasure at a shrewd stroke of business.

'After you left I talked to some people, covering my butt, you know. Turned out all it is is there's some guys in Vegas who want to talk to him. I take him there and you're off the hook for good. I guarantee you that.'

'What are you getting out of it?'

He grinned. 'I'll make a few new friends,' he said.

'We can still make a deal,' Barre said. His accent was

obvious when he spoke, a French voice with West African undertones.

'Sorry,' Claude told him. 'I wish I could do it, but it wouldn't help.'

'You don't understand,' Barre said. 'They need me because of the money. I'll make a deal anyhow, I can tell you that. But this way we can keep the money. There's a lot of money. We can share it.'

It struck me that he was whistling in the dark about the deal he could make. And the intensity of his gaze seemed to betray his real terror. Claude stared at him.

'How much?'

'Millions. No one can get near it without me. That's why they need me.'

He was bending forward, looking into Claude's eyes with a fierce intensity, his posture an urgent appeal. Claude gazed back at him, caught in an almost identical pose. Looking at them, I wondered whether what Barre was saying was true, and I guessed that Claude was thinking the same thing.

A few silent seconds went by, then Claude relaxed and smiled, a little wistfully, I thought.

'No. The answer's still no. Can't take the risk. Money's not the issue. After I hand you over a lot of doors will open. I can make more than you've got. Without the hassle.'

He looked at me.

'Where's your ladies?'

'Asleep at the hotel,' I said. 'They don't know I'm here. They don't have anything to do with this.'

'Call them.'

'What for?'

'I want them here,' he said.

'No.'

He stared into my eyes, and for a moment I thought he was going to lose his temper. Instead he heaved a big sigh. 'Nobody's gonna get hurt,' he said. 'What I'm going to do is leave you guys here with Bigger until tomorrow afternoon. By then I should be in Vegas and my business will be concluded. After that you can do what you like, tell who you like. I don't care. I just want you all quiet till then. So I want them here with you, sitting on that sofa, nice and quiet till Bigger lets you go.'

I almost believed him, but I still didn't want to make it easy.

'No.'

He heaved the big sigh again, got up, and went to the phone. We all followed him with our eyes, but nobody else moved. Having Bigger holding an Uzi behind you was a powerful inducement to self-discipline.

'OK,' he said. 'I'll do it.'

'Claude,' I told him. 'If either of them gets hurt I'll get you.' I glared at him, trying to focus all the rage I felt, but if he was intimidated, he didn't show it. Instead he smiled at me.

'I told you, nobody's going to get hurt.'

He dialled the hotel and asked for my room number. Eventually Sophie answered. He told her it was Claude speaking, that he'd flown up with the FBI on a private jet, and that it was all over. I was talking to the FBI men, he went on, and I wanted Mary to come over and identify Barre. He was sending a car.

He put the phone down. 'Alphonse,' he said. 'Go get those ladies and act nice. You hear me?'

Alphonse nodded and went out. Bigger stayed where he was.

'She won't believe that bullshit,' I said. 'She's probably calling the cops right now.'

But I was whistling in the dark.

'Let's wait and see,' Claude told me.

We waited. While we waited Claude wandered around the house. We could hear him walking from room to room, whistling and opening doors, like a prospective buyer checking out the property.

'What did you do to get all this money?' I asked Barre.

He fixed his eyes on me for the first time, as if he was trying to decide whether I was a possible ally, and weighing up how useful I could be.

'I was only a cog in the machine,' he told me earnestly. 'I had to do what I was told.'

I'd heard that before.

'Yes,' I said, 'but what was it exactly you did?'

'I arranged the licenses for the import of some material. It was supposed to be safely buried. That was what my officials told me.'

'Didn't you check up? You must have known it was illegal.'

He gave me a gentle smile. It told me how naïve my questions were. 'This wasn't my job.'

Claude came back. 'I'm going to lock your man here in the closet over there,' he told Barre, pointing across the hallway.

'Let him go,' Barre said. 'He won't talk to anyone. He'll simply disappear.'

'Yeah. Like Tonto. Forget it.' He addressed the Navajo man. 'Listen, brother. We're going to lock you in the closet. I want you to stay there. When we're going we'll tell you. You ain't got no job no more so stay cool. You come out before we're gone we gonna shoot you. I don't want to do that so stay cool. You understand?'

The Navajo's flat black eyes stayed fixed on Claude's, but he didn't reply. Claude motioned him upwards and he got up.

'All right,' Claude said. 'You don't talk. Just nod your head if you understand. I want to know that you understand.'

The man nodded.

Claude gave a grunt of satisfaction. 'Lock him up,' he said to Bigger.

Bigger took the Navajo across the foot of the stairs to the closet in the hall, sat him down in it, knelt down, wired his feet together, stood up and locked the door.

A short while after this we heard the sound of a car coming up the drive. Out of the corner of my eye I saw Bigger drifting backwards so that he couldn't be seen from the door. The headlights swept across the windows and then came the sound of the car doors slamming and footsteps on the porch. All this time several desperate plans were running through my head, but all of them seemed likely to get me shot, so I stayed where I was.

292

Sophie came in the door first, saw me and started across the floor, then slowed down and stopped. 'What's going on?' she asked. 'Where's the cops?'

Mary had come in behind her and she must have guessed it all immediately, because she turned and tried to get out of the door. Then she screamed as Alphonse, who was coming in behind her, grabbed her round the neck and began dragging her in.

Sophie turned round and, moving towards them, shouted: 'Let her go. Leave her alone.' But now she was facing in the other direction she saw Bigger as he raised the Uzi to waist level and gestured with it. She stopped.

'Claude,' I shouted.

'All right, ladies,' Claude said, stepping forward and making calming gestures. 'Quiet down. Let her go, Alphonse. Loose her.'

Alphonse let go of Mary, moved back, closed the door and stood with his back to it.

'Sit down,' Claude said to Sophie and Mary. 'We're all tired. Late at night. Be cool. Sammy is going to explain everything. Sit down.'

He made to take Sophie's arm, but she twisted away from him, came over and sat next to me. Mary followed her and sat on the other side.

'I have to go now,' Claude said. 'I wish I could stay and talk, you know, but business . . .' He smiled broadly. 'Sammy will explain everything. Nobody's going to get hurt. All I want is for you to stay here until tomorrow. I'm leaving Bigger to keep you company. He won't hurt you unless you piss him off. It should take me till about nine or ten, maybe longer, to get to Vegas and do my business. Bigger will let you go about twelve. Just don't mess with him.'

'You won't get away with this, Claude,' I told him, then I wished I'd kept my mouth shut, because he smiled with genuine amusement.

'What you going to do? Tell the cops? We'll be long gone by the time they get here. Out of their jurisdiction. Oscar might cause me some trouble, but by the time anyone gets round to asking me questions I'll be up to here with alibis. It'll sound like a misunderstanding, and if things get really bad I've got good lawyers. What have you got? You can't even prove who this guy is, especially if he ain't around. My advice, you know, is that this whole thing could cause you more trouble than it will ever cause me. Think about it.'

He smiled kindly at me, and pulled Barre to his feet. Then Alphonse unclipped his wrists and they put a coat on him. Barre didn't resist, moving between them like a sleepwalker as they ushered him into the hallway. As Claude went out of the door he turned and waved, the same kindly smile on his face. Then he was gone, followed by Alphonse, and we listened in silence to the sound of the car pulling away.

Chapter 36

I knew that I couldn't be blamed. In the circumstances Claude might have fooled anyone. But I knew also that I'd missed something important about him. Perhaps if I hadn't met him through Bonny I'd have been more suspicious. In the abstract I knew and understood that anybody at all in the country could be involved in the workings of organized crime, but somewhere in my mind I'd been thinking about Claude as one of the homeboys from way back; and the funny part of it was that, when I thought about what he was doing, I felt a sense of loss that was something to do with my innocent memories of childhood.

Beside me Sophie wriggled and worked her hands round against the wire. When I looked I could see a red band all around her wrists where she'd rubbed them raw. As soon as Claude left, Bigger had tied our hands with wire, snipping the ends off neatly with a pair of pliers. He'd sat across the room and called us over one by one, and even if I'd wanted to jump him, the memory of his speed and ferocity would have stopped me.

'We have to do something soon,' Sophie whispered while he was working on Mary's hands.

I guessed she meant that if we didn't it would be too late to stop Claude. I nodded.

'If I can get close enough I'll mace him.'

'No,' I whispered back, 'it's too dangerous.'

Mary was hobbling back towards us now, and Bigger waved Sophie over. As she came back I saw her swivelling on her heels, her waist switching as she walked back across the room.

'Don't do that,' I whispered when she sat down.

'Do what,' she whispered back.

'You know what I mean,' I told her. 'This guy isn't stupid.'

'Maybe not. But stupid's nothing to do with it.'

I saw Bigger watching us, but it was clear that he wasn't concerned about what we were saying. Not while he was sitting across the room with a gun in his hand. Sophie saw him watching too, and she crossed and uncrossed her legs, then squirmed uselessly in her seat. In the next few minutes she didn't stop heaving, fidgeting and fiddling with her wrists. I followed the direction of Bigger's gaze and saw that the short dress she was wearing had ridden practically all the way up her thighs.

'What are you playing at?' I hissed at her.

'Don't interfere,' she hissed back. 'I know what I'm doing. I'll get him to take me to the bathroom. When I come out attract his attention.'

'No.'

'What are you saying?' Bigger demanded.

'I'm saying that I have to go to the bedroom. I mean the bathroom.'

'Which one?' Bigger was giving her a nasty grin.

'I don't mind,' she said, 'except that if I don't get to go to the bathroom I'm going to go all over the floor, and in a while it's gonna get pretty disgusting.'

She regarded him cheekily and he chuckled.

'A'right,' he said. 'Everybody up.'

'I need my bag,' Sophie said.

'Why?'

'You know anything about women?'

Bigger sucked his teeth, but he picked up the bag, opened it and scrabbled through it. For a moment I thought he'd missed the can of mace, then he held it up in front of Sophie's face. 'Wha' this?'

'Mace,' Sophie said. 'I forgot it was in the bag. I don't need it. You keep it.'

She looked him straight in the eyes and he glared back. My guess was that Bigger had never encountered a woman like Sophie before and he had no idea what to make of her. The risk, though, was that if she continued provoking him, he'd probably end up by hitting her or jumping on her. A few seconds went by, then he looked at me and shook his head slightly.

'Boy,' he said. 'Your woman looking for trouble. If you can't control her I gon' do it.'

Sophie sneered at him, but he simply tossed the can aside, gestured with the gun, and we set off in single file. The bathroom was upstairs. There might have been several for all I ever knew, but the one Bigger had in mind was on the landing overlooking the lobby. At the top of the stairs he made us lie on our stomachs, while he opened the door and looked around. Then he came back.

'Go on,' he said.

Sophie writhed and squirmed, making it look even more difficult than it was, until she'd levered herself into a sitting position. Bigger watched her, his grin coming and going. I couldn't stop Sophie now, if I ever could have, but her tactics were terrifying me. If this didn't work, I thought, we'd be in for a bad time over the next couple of hours.

'I can't even get up,' she said.

Bigger reached out and hauled her to her feet. But at the bathroom door she turned and held out her hands behind. In his turn he stretched out his arm and put the bag in them.

'I can't do it like this,' she said. 'Come on.'

He stared at her for a moment, then took the pliers out of his pocket and snipped at her wrists.

'Thank you,' Sophie said, and went into the bathroom and closed the door shut. Bigger grabbed the handle and pushed it open again.

'Hey,' Sophie said. 'I can't do it while you're watching me. I'll leave it open just a bit so that I can't see you looking at me. OK?'

He nodded, and she went on in.

I shifted about, keeping my movements minimal so as not to worry Bigger, but he took no notice of what I was doing. By this time, I suspected, he was so preoccupied with Sophie that he wasn't much interested in anything else.

We listened to water running and then the lavatory flushed and Sophie started to make splashing noises. By then I'd worked out that a quick roll would bring Bigger's legs into kicking distance.

'Mr Bigger,' Sophie called. 'I'm coming out now.'

I screamed, trying to lose control and let the memory take over. Many years before this, I'd had a job in the canteen of a hospital which was home to a number of chronic epileptics; and I'd seen the same fits over and over again every day. Now I started jerking and arching my body, my face contorted into a screaming rictus. Anything near a good imitation would look terrifying.

Bigger had turned and automatically pointed the gun at me. When he saw that what I was doing didn't look like a threat, he lowered it and came a step closer, peering at me with a puzzled frown on his face. At the same time Sophie emerged from the bathroom. She was stark naked, carrying her clothes and her bag in a bundle in front of her, her face creased up in an expression of amazement and concern. Bigger glanced round at her, then did a double take as she came up to his shoulder and peered past him at me.

I felt a weird sympathy for him. Caught halfway between me flopping about, screaming my head off, and Sophie's naked flesh moving against him, Bigger froze. At that moment Sophie brought one hand out from under the bundle, and sprayed something in his face. Automatically Bigger threw his arms up to protect his eyes, and as he did so Sophie lashed out at him with the bag. She must have put something solid in it, because it connected with a clunking sound and Bigger's gun flew over the banisters down into the lobby below. By this time I'd wriggled my way into position and I kicked out with both feet, catching him just behind the knees. Already dazed, he went over with a crash. Sophie was running now, hurdling me and Mary on her way down the stairs.

'Move,' I shouted at Mary, and pushed at her with my feet. She moved, bumping across the floor on her bottom towards the stairs. I followed, straining frantically, every nerve tensed for the sound of Bigger coming up behind me. But we had bumped our way down half a dozen steps before I actually heard him.

'Blood,' he said. 'Blood.'

I risked a look back and saw him standing by the railings, clawing at his eyes.

'Bigger,' Sophie shouted from down below him. 'Don't move.'

She was standing in the lobby, the gun cradled against her taut breasts and pointing straight at him. She looked magnificent, like something out of a comic book fantasy, and I closed my eyes and opened them again to see if she was still there. Then I looked back at Bigger. He was blinking his eyes rapidly, his face running wet with tears, and I wasn't sure that he could actually see her yet, but when he heard her voice, he reacted to its command, put his hands on the banister and stood still.

Chapter 37

I was full of apprehension and confusion about what would happen when we caught up with Claude, but underneath it all I could feel a thrill of pure pleasure, beating like a regular and relentless pulse.

'I thought you'd had it when he threw the mace away,' I told Sophie. 'Jeez. You don't half take some chances.'

She grinned happily at me. 'Not really. When I was growing up the house used to be full of guys like that. Soldiers mostly. They're big and tough, but easily confused. That's how you beat them.'

In other circumstances I might have tried to prick the bubble of Sophie's complacency a little, but right then I was close to adoring her. We were all in the grip of a dangerous euphoria. Sophie had already told us a couple of times how she'd looked round the bathroom for a weapon, then picked on the can of lavatory cleaner. For good measure she'd packed her bag with the heaviest bottles within reach. Cologne, shampoo, deodorant, they'd all been in there, jumbled up together. A couple of them had broken when she hit Bigger, and the car now reeked of bath-time perfumes.

By now we were an hour out of Phoenix, roaring up the long slow climb on Seventeen to Flagstaff. There were other routes to Vegas, but Claude didn't know the region any better than I did, and I couldn't believe that he'd have risked one of the secondary routes through this rocky desert at night. In any case, there was hardly any traffic at this hour. The highway, I had told Sophie, would be the quickest way to Vegas. Claude was only about half an hour ahead of us, and we might well catch up with him before we'd gone a hundred miles. When I thought about it later, it was one of the most reckless, dangerous decisions I'd ever made.

On sober consideration, there must have been a dozen possible alternatives to setting out after Claude. Perhaps the most sensible thing would have been to call Oscar and let the authorities, whoever they were, sort out the mess. But from the moment I'd recognized Claude standing on Barre's porch, the stakes had altered. He had known I was an innocent abroad and he'd manipulated me expertly into finding Barre for him. At the house that night, when he'd told me his plans, I'd known from the confidence of his mood and the ease of his manner that he was probably right in thinking that he'd be untouchable whatever information I could give to Oscar or the cops or the FBI or to the President of the USA himself.

There was a kind of horror attached to that knowledge. Not because I believed in any fairy tales about crime and punishment. I didn't. In my experience, once you'd got past the mad actions of the insane, crime was the label that people with the most power slapped on the kind of exploitation they couldn't control; and I knew that I could switch on my TV at any time and watch a daily parade of men whose hands were stained with the blood of innocents, mouthing every conceivable sort of pious platitude. What I felt about Claude was nothing to do with saving the world from one more shift in the big wheel of organized crime. It was far more personal.

From the time I met Claude I'd taken it for granted that he was one of us, a kid just like one of the kids from the village where I'd almost grown up, and which, despite everything, lived on as a kind of idyll in my memory. The fact that he'd been deceiving me went together with the destruction for which Barre had been responsible; and all of it was like a blow against everything that had made us.

Somewhere inside me I had still been clinging to the illusion that we had crossed the oceans simply to be free of fear and hunger, and that, after all, we could remain different, something like we had been at the beginning. But after this it would be impossible to think about my life or about the childhood which bound us together with the same belief or the same trust. Perhaps I should have listened more carefully when he talked in the restaurant about the police informant Arjune. Now all I wanted was to confront Claude, perhaps to tell him that he was betraying himself as much as he had betrayed me.

Back at the house, after we'd brought Bigger downstairs, I'd been thinking about getting Barre's Navajo bodyguard to back us up by reporting his kidnapping to the police. But that plan never got off the ground, because once I'd unclipped the wire from round the bodyguard's hands and feet, he'd stepped out of the closet and stood in the hallway for a few seconds blinking in the light and rubbing his wrists. Then he walked to the door without a word, opened it and left. I called out after him, but when I followed him on to the porch and looked around he'd gone.

In any case his disappearance had made up my mind for me. Calling the police wasn't a real option. We didn't have any independent evidence about Barre's identity, and the odds were that, even if they believed our story and took us seriously, Claude would probably be back in New York before they did anything about it.

Sophie seemed to have come to the same conclusion, or at least she didn't argue about what I wanted to do. We found the keys to Barre's car on a table in the hall, and we found the car itself parked round the back of the house. I drove it round the front, where Mary and Sophie got in, and we took off, the Cadillac swinging wildly round the bends in the driveway until I got used to the console. It seemed huge, and I'd expected the cornering to be ponderous, but the steering was light and precise. Driving it was a delight, and if we hadn't been pursuing Claude I'd have been enjoying myself. Enjoying myself more, that is. I was accustomed to driving cars which strained and shuddered at speeds like seventy. In contrast the car we'd rented in LA had zipped along with a refreshing alacrity, and the Cadillac was even faster and smoother. We'd got close to a hundred on some of the straight stretches. But the big car rode so smoothly that it was impossible to tell how fast we were going except by looking at the speedometer, and the speed at which I was going scared me so much that I'd given up doing that, because I'd never in my life driven a car so fast.

In front of me the headlights cut a lane of clear white light, with a continuous cloud of small insects streaming back at me through it, like motes in a beam of sunlight. Caught in the light a huge sign told me that the next gas station would be another fifty-six miles away, and there was something surrealistic about its presence here in the middle of nowhere. The road had begun to climb more and more perceptibly, and from time to time the lights swept across walls of sheer red rock, as we bored through a mountain pass. The landscape was invisible beyond the range of the lights, but somehow I could feel it stretching out to infinity in every direction, reducing us to a restless speck crawling over its immensity.

'How's Mary?' I called out. I couldn't see in the mirror, and at the speed I was going I didn't dare turn my head to look at her.

'If I had that gun,' she said with a venom which surprised me. 'I'd have killed him.'

'He saved our lives,' I replied. 'I'd feel bad if anything happened to him.'

We'd left Bigger sitting on the sofa, his wrists and ankles wired together. I supposed that he'd free himself sometime during the day and find his way back to New York.

'I don't care,' Mary said, 'he'd have killed us just as easy if he'd been told.'

I knew that was true, but there was something more to

303

Mary's bitter tone. I couldn't imagine the terror she'd been through, but underneath the blank stare I'd grown accustomed to in the last few days she must have been boiling with rage. I began framing some words in reply, but Sophie was frowning at me, so I left it alone.

We had just come through another passage between the rusty cliffs and suddenly we were moving along the top of a rise from which we could see the glimmer of the horizon several miles away.

'Look. There.'

Sophie pointed. Way down below us, about two kilometres or so ahead, the lights of another car were crawling, a firefly spark in the darkness. Sophie bent over picked up the automatic and slammed the magazine in, and slung it over her shoulder.

'I want to talk to the guy,' I told her. 'Not start shooting.'

'Is it them?' Mary leaned forward to see, her breath raising the hairs on the back of my neck.

'I don't know,' I said irritably. But I pressed down on the accelerator, and let the car pick up another notch.

I didn't know how long it took to get to the other car. Time seemed to be suspended, but eventually the headlights hit the rear window of the maroon Buick in front of us. There were two people in the back seat and I recognized the clump of dreadlocks on the silhouette in the driver's seat. There was nothing coming the other way, and I pulled out and went past. I saw Claude looking out of the window nearest us, but I wasn't sure that he'd recognized me. I must have been the last person he was expecting to see.

Once past the Buick I pulled in and began slowing down, flashing the warning lights behind. But I must have been wrong about Claude not recognizing me, because as our speed dropped the Buick pulled out suddenly and flashed past us. I stepped on the accelerator again and the Cadillac caught up inexorably, as if tied to the bumper in front by a piece of elastic. I pulled out again, flicking the headlights, but as we came level with Claude, Sophie ducked and shouted: 'Get down.'

I stayed where I was, my reflexes stabbing down on the brake instead, and the Buick shot away from me.

'He had a gun,' Sophie said. She sounded shocked. As I moved up towards the Buick again, she unslung the automatic and pressed the switch to open the window. The sudden rush of air and the sound of the engines howling suddenly hit me.

'Don't shoot,' I shouted at Sophie.

I slammed the switch and the window went up again.

'I was going to aim at the tyres,' she said crossly.

I glanced round. We'd roared our way through the valley and we were going round a long curving stretch. To one side the road dropped away steeply. On the other a sheer wall reared above us.

'Bad place,' I told Sophie.

She didn't answer but she took a look round herself, then put the gun down. I stayed on the Buick's tail all the way round the bend. Through the rear window I could see Claude looking back at me, then speaking to the driver. In a little while the road levelled off and the headlights picked out a traffic sign. I only caught one word — RUNAWAY — but I guessed there would be a turn-off soon with a lane for runaway trucks coming off the long steep incline of the mountain.

'Hold on,' I told Sophie. 'I'm going to try and squeeze him over. Shoot in the air. That should keep his head down. But if he leans out, shout.'

'Yep,' she said. She wound the window down with an eager preoccupied air and aimed the gun out.

'Point it upwards,' I shouted at her above the noise. 'In the air, and don't shoot till I tell you.'

She nodded impatiently, wound the strap round her arm and shifted her aim.

We must have been half a mile from the turn-off and I pulled out and eased the long nose of the Caddy over until it banged against the rear wheel of the Buick. I'd been braced for the shock, but even so the sudden resistance of the wheel nearly tore it from my grip. At the wheel of the Buick,

Alphonse shifted over until he was half on the shoulder of the road, and I speeded up again until the bonnet was level with his rear. I could see the turn-off now, and I stepped down on the accelerator and screamed at Sophie: 'Shoot!'

I came past Claude and swung into him as Sophie loosed off a burst. We barely touched because the Buick seemed to flinch away from us and, as I anticipated, Alphonse followed the white line to the right and found himself plunging up a steep incline by the side of the road. I'd braked and dropped back as he swung over, but even so I had to swerve dangerously to follow him up the side road. It would end in a cul de sac, I knew, and in a moment Alphonse would have to brake and stop at the top of the hill.

Suddenly the Buick began to lose speed, plunging and swerving from side to side. Coming up behind I could see two figures through the rear window struggling in silhouette, and I guessed immediately that Barre must have seized his chance while Claude and Alphonse were distracted and made a grab for the gun.

We were never certain what happened next. Afterwards Sophie maintained that the gun had gone off and that Alphonse had been hit. I didn't hear it, or get a clear sight of what was going on, because I had braked to keep a distance between us, and begun looking round at the road in case they came back down unexpectedly and I had to reverse. When I looked at the Buick again it had made a sudden spurt towards the top of the hill and was sliding fast off the edge of the road.

'Claude,' I shouted for no reason at all. 'Claude.'

Something gripped me by the heart and it seemed to stop. I gasped for breath, slammed the switch and the windows went down. For a second or two, we heard nothing, only the massive, brooding silence of the waiting mountain. Then we heard the car growling and tearing its way downhill. Then there was an almighty crash of glass and metal. Then the boom of an explosion. Then there was a flash of light, and after that a tongue of flame which shot up into the sky, and then died down again into a steady glow.

Chapter 38

Standing in Paddington Station I noted the dampness in the air. I'd expected that, and after the hot, dry desert climate it felt good. Mary had been staying with a friend nearby and we'd arranged to meet on the station forecourt. She was late, and I spent the time trying to work out what it was that felt so peculiar. It was all of ten minutes before I got it. All the women seemed to be dressed in black, like a scurrying mob of widows, rushing off to someone's funeral, and it struck me that, after only a couple of days, I wasn't yet acclimatized to the look of the place, because my brain kept on registering the drab uniformity of the clothes rather than picking out individual features.

Mary got there just before the train left, and we ran for it. We didn't say much on the way, partly because I couldn't think what to say to her, and partly because I simply didn't want to talk. At one point in the journey I asked her whether she wanted some tea, and she'd replied in the same polite tone that she didn't. The incongruity of it all made me laugh. If the big wheel had turned a shade faster or a touch slower we might both have been lying dead somewhere.

The thought sobered me up, because it took me straight back to the desert road where we'd sat listening to the sound of the Buick going down the slope. After they'd gone over the hill, I had got out of the car and run to the side of the road. I could see flames leaping down below, and I'd begun scrambling down. But after I'd gone twenty yards or so I came to a sheer drop. I stumbled along the edge, clinging to the bushes which sprang out of the rock, looking for a place where I could climb down, but after a few minutes I realized that, even if there was such a place, I was as likely as not to break my neck on the way down. I stood there for several more minutes straining my eyes to see whether there was any movement near the wreck. But there was nothing, and in a while I'd gone back up. We decided to call the cops from the next gas station and report the accident, but a few miles up the road we'd heard the sound of a helicopter flying at speed straight towards the spot we'd just come from. Another few miles later two patrol cars came racing by in the opposite direction. All the way into Vegas I'd been half expecting to hear the sirens and see flashing lights looming up in the mirror, but nothing had happened and when we arrived halfway through the morning, we'd parked the car at a meter outside a casino, then gone straight to the airport.

Sitting next to Mary watching the muddy green fields speed past and remembering that night, I found myself once again choking down the sorrow and anger I'd experienced then. Claude, Barre and Alphonse had died, at least partly because of me. I had told myself that Barre would probably have run them off the road even if we hadn't been chasing them; that, in any case, once he got to Vegas he would have been killed for the doublecross that he'd pulled, just as Ben had been; and that Claude had been a bad man who knew what he was doing and had been shaping up to ruin thousands of lives one way or the other. None of it changed what I felt, and I knew that for a long time to come, I would wake up in the night thinking about how I could have handled it differently.

The idea haunting me was that, in only slightly different circumstances, I might have been exactly the sort of man that Claude had turned out to be. I loved power and money too, and my morality was my own, guaranteed only by my own peculiar gut instinct for what was right and wrong. Perhaps if my life had gone in a different direction I would have been a more ruthless and effective villain. I doubted it, but nowadays I had no way of telling. In a roundabout way what I was feeling had started with Hector. His illness had undermined my security, twinning me with death and decay, imposing on me the sense that I was part of a dying generation. Claude had merely completed the job.

As we climbed the stairs of the hospital I glanced over at Mary. Her features were set in the sullen scowl she had worn when I first saw her in New York, and for a moment I wondered whether bringing her here had been the best move I could have made. I didn't have time to worry about it though, because Dot was waiting for us at the reception desk, and when she saw Mary she hurried up to her and gave her a big squeeze. It had only been a few weeks since we'd talked in practically the same spot, but it was strange to see that she hadn't changed at all, as if I'd woken up from years in a coma to find everything still the same.

'I'm really glad you came,' Dot said breathlessly. 'It'll mean everything to your dad. He's better today. You've come at just the right time.'

She hurried us along the corridor and into the lift, then through a doorway to Hector's room. It was as I remembered it, the same twilight illumination, the same sense of animation suspended. Hector was lying on his back with his eyes open, and when Dot spoke to him they moved, vaguely at first, then with a firmer purpose.

'Hector,' Dot said. 'Hector. Look who's here.'

Mary brushed past her, knelt down by the side of the bed and took his hand. The feeble eyes rolled towards her.

'Mary,' he whispered. 'Mary.'

Mary began to cry, great silent heaves, her face pressed against the side of the bed. Hector had managed to turn his head slightly, and now he watched without expression, his hand still lying slack and nerveless in hers.

'I'd better go,' I told Dot.

'No,' she said. 'Not yet. Say hello to Hector first.'

I went to edge of the bed and looked into Hector's wasted face. The eyes came up and fixed on me. The lips moved, but I couldn't make out the sound. Dot rushed forward, elbowing me out of the way, and bent over him.

'What was that, love?'

The lips moved again, and this time the words came out, slow and hesitant, but distinct enough for me to recognize.

'Sammy,' Hector said. 'You bastard. Where you been all this time?'

'New York,' I said. 'I saw Alvin. He said hello.'

'Alvin?' Hector repeated in a wondering tone. 'Alvin?' Suddenly the muscles of his face seemed to fall back into place and he smiled with all his old recklessness and gaiety. 'Alvin? How is he?'

'OK.' I told him. 'He was glad to hear from you,' I lied.

Hector smiled again, then his eyes closed, and his face went vacant.

Dot pulled me by the arm and we backed away from the bed and went out into the corridor.

'What's happening?' I asked her. 'He looks a bit better.'

'Well, he's not,' she said. 'I'm hoping she'll cheer him up. But he hasn't got long.'

Her eyes filled with tears and she took out a handkerchief, wiped her eyes and blew her nose.

'Oh God, Sammy,' she said. 'He could be a bit of a swine, but he was such a nice man.'

I patted her arm without answering. I couldn't think of anything to say. Oscar and Bonnie popped into my head. I had called him from London and told him a version of what had happened. He'd sounded puzzled and a little angry, but I'd told him I'd write to him and explain everything. I wondered whether he'd understand all the things I wanted to say. I suspected that he'd understand nothing about my feelings for the man dying in the hospital room, or for the fat white woman now crying on my shoulder. She pushed away from me and blew her nose again.

'Is she going back with you?'

'I don't think so,' I said. 'She probably needs you and him for the moment. She's had a bad time.'

'I'd better go back in,' she said.

I had the feeling that she didn't want to hear about what had happened to Mary. So I said goodbye, let her go, and walked away down the corridor. I wanted to go with her and embrace Hector again. At the same time I knew that the moment I went back in that room I would want to leave. In my mind was the curious feeling that I was deserting a wounded comrade. Running away.

I had nearly reached the lift when I heard the footsteps clattering behind me. I turned and saw Mary hurrying towards me.

'I wanted to thank you,' she said in a rush. 'I don't know what I'd have done.'

'It wasn't anything, love,' I said. 'Besides, whatever I did was for Hector. And Dot. Give her a chance.'

She nodded. Her face was streaked with tears. She had the tragic and woebegone look of a child who'd fallen over in the playground, and I had the feeling that whatever happened, her problems weren't over.

'Will you be all right?'

'I suppose so,' she said. 'I don't know what to do now.'

The way she said it made me feel that she was asking for my advice, or protection or something, but the truth was, I wanted to tell her, that she'd already had what I had to give. The ties which bound me to Hector wouldn't stretch any further. My love for him was part of the past. It was part of Mary's past too, but that was all it was.

'Look after yourself,' I said.

She smiled tearfully. 'Thanks.'

I reached out, hugged her briefly and kissed her on both cheeks. She smiled again, turned round, and walked down the corridor back to her father's room. I stood watching her, waiting for I don't know what, but she merely pushed the door open and went in without looking back.